Duncan looked around the crashed chopper, saw a couple of water bottles and tossed them out. They would need them if they were going to hike ten miles while evading these fanatics. The sound of incoming fire came from outside, and he leaped out of the helicopter. Black smoke from the damaged engines rose into the sky. Might as well light up flares, he thought as he limbered his carbine and dove for cover.

He landed beside Beau, pointing his carbine over a lip of sand. Across a paved road less than five hundred feet away, a line of at least a hundred Algerian rebels charged their position. A gust of wind blew sand into his face. If he survived this, he was never, ever going to another beach for the rest of his life. He blinked the sand away from his eyes, took aim, and pulled the trigger . . .

**Don't miss
the previous novels in this epic
combat series . . .**

## *The Sixth Fleet*

### *Seawolf*

### *Tomcat*

# THE
# SIXTH FLEET
## COBRA

# DAVID E. MEADOWS

**B**

BERKLEY BOOKS, NEW YORK

This is a work of fiction. Names, characters, places, and incidents either are the product of the author's imagination or are used fictitiously, and any resemblance to actual persons, living or dead, business establishments, events, or locales is entirely coincidental.

THE SIXTH FLEET: COBRA

A Berkley Book / published by arrangement with the author

PRINTING HISTORY
Berkley edition / August 2002

Copyright © 2002 by David E. Meadows.

All rights reserved.
This books, or parts thereof, may not be reproduced in any form without permission.
For information address: The Berkley Publishing Group,
a division of Penguin Putnam Inc.,
375 Hudson Street, New York, New York 10014.

Visit our website at
www.penguinputnam.com

ISBN: 0-425-18518-4

BERKLEY®
Berkley Books are published by The Berkley Publishing Group,
a division of Penguin Putnam Inc.,
375 Hudson Street, New York, New York 10014.
BERKLEY and the "B" design
are trademarks belonging to Penguin Putnam Inc.

PRINTED IN THE UNITED STATES OF AMERICA

10  9  8  7  6  5  4  3  2  1

*To the men and women of Naval Security Group Command*

# *Acknowledgments*

This is the final book of The Sixth Fleet series. To answer some common questions that have arisen from this series, first let me say that there really is a United States Sixth Fleet. It is located in the Mediterranean. While the Mediterranean is a beautiful sea, its shores are crowded with volatile areas such as Crete, the Balkans, the Middle East, and North Africa. The United States Sixth Fleet has been involved in every crisis in this region since World War II, and today, it still sails this volatile sea protecting the interests of the United States and its allies.

To answer another important question, all of The Sixth Fleet books were written prior to September 11th. Only this book has been tweaked to reflect some of the geopolitical and military changes caused by those horrific and evil attacks against America. The genesis for what would become The Sixth Fleet came to me during a plane trip across the Mediterranean in 1998. At the time, talk about withdrawing the U.S. Navy from the naval base in Rota, Spain, and moving the Navy headquarters from London to Naples were on-going while Islamic radicalism was spreading across the Middle East. Below me, spread out across the sea was a United States carrier battle group in all its strength and majesty. In this tinderbox area, this ability to project American power abroad was instrumental in containing so many different volatile situations, ranging from Crete to the Middle East to North Africa from erupting and spreading across the globe.

There are two people who deserve a lot of credit for this series. My wife, Felicity, for convincing me that I should write what I know about; and Mr. Tom Colgan, executive editor at The Berkley Publishing Group, who had confidence in my writing and developed the idea for the four-book series titled The Sixth Fleet.

It would be impossible to thank everyone who helped to contribute to the series by providing comments and technical advice. To the multitude of fans who sent E-mails, left comments in the guestbook at www.geocities.com/igor1610, and wrote reviews, my thanks; your encouragement was appreciated. To Frank Reifsnyder, Sharon Reinke, Art Horn, David Reidel, Samantha Mandor, Angela Webster, Karen Gardner, Kelly Nickell, and Nicole Balenger, my special thanks; every author needs a cheering section and I had that in the enthusiasm and encouragement from Nancy Coffey, my agent.

I have two authors I would like to thank for their encouragement and support. Mr. Stephen Coonts, a fellow Navy veteran and bestselling author of ten novels, which include *Flight of the Intruder*, and his most recent, *Saucer*, and Mr. Joe Buff, known for his undersea war novels such as *Deep Sound Channel* and *Thunder in the Deep*.

# ONE

⚓

**THE STEEL DOORS BURST OPEN TO THE OPERATIONS ROOM**
in the command post. Armed Libyan soldiers, wearing camouflage uniforms, rushed into the spaces, dispersing throughout
the blue-lighted area. Their AK-47 automatic weapons waved
threateningly back and forth as they ran through the room.

"Not here!" shouted one of the soldiers.

"Nor here!" a soldier crouching in a corner, hidden by the
shadows of the blue-lightened space shouted, his voice echoing
from the other side.

The gray-clad Libyan soldiers manning the computer consoles watched, expressions changing from confusion to anxiety
to fear.

The tall, lean sergeant, standing in the middle of the open
steel doors, took one step backward into the hallway. He turned
right and saluted someone out of sight of those at the consoles
and said, "Neither of them appear to be here, sir."

A mumbled reply could barely be heard by the console operator nearest the doors. The voice sounded familiar. The operator's dark eyebrows bunched as he concentrated on the voice.

"Yes, sir," the sergeant replied. He stepped back into the operations room and shouted, "Corporal, search the back rooms!"

A slender black Arab saluted, touched two of the armed soldiers near him, and the three ran around the back row of computer consoles and through the door leading to the briefing theater. They came out a few seconds later.

The corporal looked at the sergeant and shook his head. The sergeant pointed to the galley doors at the far end of the room, partially hidden behind the raised platform chair that overlooked the two rows of computers. The three soldiers ran to the other side and slammed the swinging doors out of the way as they burst into the kitchen.

The sound of metal pots and pans banging together intermingled with breaking china.

"I said, see if they're here, not tear the place down!"

The corporal led the three out of the kitchen. "All clear, Sergeant!" Behind them, three cooks emerged slowly, standing close together, wiping their hands on stained aprons and watching as the armed soldiers surrounded the operators.

The sergeant turned his head toward the hallway.

"I heard, Sergeant," the voice said.

The operator placed the voice, a smile spreading across his lips as he mumbled a prayer to Allah.

A moment later, Colonel Alqahiray strolled through the door. The fear of those at the computer consoles changed gradually to smiles of relief. The hero was back. The soldiers at the consoles stood. A nervous clap by the operator turned into a torrent of standing cheers and applause. The newspapers were wrong. Alqahiray's wounds must have been less serious than believed. That was obvious! Otherwise, how could the man be here? Most recalled how, attacked and wounded in the briefing theater off to the right of the operations room, the colonel had personally shot his assailant—his own cousin! It was truly a miracle. Allah blessed Alqahiray.

Alqahiray nodded and waved at the loyal soldiers manning the consoles as he moved past. His head turned quickly from side to side as he tried to watch everyone at once.

Sergeant Adib shadowed three feet behind the colonel, his sharp eyes tracking everyone and searching everywhere. Any one of these operators could be an assassin. The soldiers' enthusiasm over the return of Alqahiray caused most to miss the sergeant's finger tightening on the trigger of the AK-47. The tall figure standing quietly in the shadows saw the slight movement but remained silent.

Those nearest reached out to touch the hero colonel, the founding father of their new nation. Alqahiray nervously avoided their hands by touching them slightly with his before sweeping past. A dull throbbing pain from the shoulder wound reminded him how close he came to death here four weeks ago. Death did not bother him as it would others. This earthly existence was only temporal anyway. Something to enjoy while alive. What mattered was to complete his mission before he died. Alqahiray's eyes, hidden in deep recesses of abnormally sunken eye sockets and overarching, heavy eyebrows, searched the compartment, looking for Colonel Walid, the traitor, the turncoat, the son of camel dung. The comments he overheard from these worshipers told how they believed he had killed his own cousin, a lie that might serve him well. His cousin had died trying to protect him. Walid had twisted the story to hide how the traitors kidnapped and held him prisoner in his own home. Thanks to Allah, his cousin had foreseen something like this and had made arrangements. Twenty-four hours earlier, when gunfire and explosions rocked his house, he had hidden under a table, thinking Walid had returned to kill him. Now it was his turn, and he would not make the same mistake Walid had. Walid would soon be dead. This time, Alqahiray would leave no one alive who threatened his power. For Major Samir—the one who shot him—his death would be a slow one. *Allah, allow me to honor Islam with the blood of traitors.*

Seconds later, after avoiding most of those in the enthusiastic crowd, he made it through the two rows of computer consoles to where the raised platform in back offered an opportunity to stand and survey the operations room.

He ignored the circle of men surrounding the platform, pulled an Old Navy cigarette from his shirt pocket, and lit it, grimacing slightly from the gunshot wound in the shoulder. The strong, bluish smoke wafted up, slowly sucked away by the ventilation filters overhead. *Your day will come, Walid.* He touched the bandage around his shoulder. Since his freedom this morning from the guarded confinement at his home on the outskirts of Tripoli, he had been salivating at the thought of this moment. This moment when he strolled into his headquarters and resumed the reins of the great jihad against America. He closed his eyes for a few seconds, relishing the prospect of personally pulling the trigger to send Walid into Allah's arms.

Opening his eyes, he saw everyone watching him, waiting for his words.

He smiled. "My fellow warriors, my comrades in arms, my loyal patriots. I apologize for my absence, but I am back. Please return to your consoles. I want each department leader to brief me on his situation. Until then, we must push forward with the Jihad Wahid until we are finished." Jihad Wahid—Holy War One—the overall plan to unite the entire North African coast into one nation stretching from Morocco on the Atlantic to Egypt along the Red Sea. For, whatever had happened, the genesis of a radical Islamic nation was proving fruitful, even if attempts to stop it still existed. What the world needed was an example of the avenging arm of the new Al-Qaida, which he would lead. He had the weapon to do it: a weapon of such magnitude that it would cause the nations of the world to show respect for the new nation. Then the Republic of Barbary and North Africa would leave the rest of the world alone until—

Alqahiray looked down at the electronic warfare officer. "Ahsan, where is Colonel Walid and my intelligence officer, Major Samir?" he asked softly.

The officer snapped to attention at his console, his boots clicking together as he stomped down on the rubber matting, and saluted. "Colonel Alqahiray, welcome back. We are honored you have returned. Sir, Colonel Walid departed several hours ago with Colonel Samir and many others. They left in such a hurry, they failed to say where they were going."

"Did you say *Colonel* Samir?"

"Yes, sir. He is a colonel now, thanks to you, sir."

*Well, he can die as a colonel as well as a major,* thought Alqahiray. The traitors had to be nearby, and they would find them. To seal him off in his house after shooting him and tell the people he was dying. They broadcast false words attributed to him to stir the people's patriotism. *No, Walid and Samir, your deaths will be slow and painful. Your deaths will be a lesson to this new nation I have formed and that I will lead. Plus, the work you did to make me look omnipotent will be put to good use. For that, you only have yourselves to blame.*

"Thank you, Captain!" Alqahiray shouted, causing the young man to jump and start to sit down. "No, don't sit down," he said, calmer, motioning the captain to come nearer. He must control his temper. "I need an aide. You are it. Moreover, we can't have a captain for an aide; you are now a major. Ahsan, what is your full name?"

"Ahsan Hammad Maloof, Colonel!"

It pleased Alqahiray to see the smile spread across the young man's face. It further pleased him when he saw moisture in the young man's eyes. Then he recalled that Walid smiled the same way with moist eyes when Alqahiray pulled him from the ranks and made him a member of their inner circle. He would not make the same mistake with this young officer. This soldier would die for him, and that was what he wanted: unquestionable loyalty. Someone he could shove in front of him, if needed.

The captain—now major—saluted again. Alqahiray reached forward and shook Ahsan's hand briefly. Applause roared across the closed room again and would have continued for several minutes if Alqahiray hadn't held up his hands to stop it. Alqahiray was no fool. Promotions such as this reminded those around him of his power. It would encourage others to remain loyal as they fought for his benevolent attention, and it would strike just the right chord with those who risked their own lives to free his. He silently congratulated himself on his ability to manipulate those around him. He was damn good. So good, that it even amazed him. Every human being begged for recognition of work well done. Alqahiray believed it was his job to ensure awards were recognized in such a way so as to seal loyalty to him.

The new major beamed as he waited for Alqahiray to say something. "Well, Major Maloof—*Ahsan.* See what the cooks can whip up for Sergeant Adib, his men, and me. It has been a long morning, and we have yet to eat. I have missed my strong cups of tea with my croissants."

"*Aiwa, ya* Colonel," the new Major Maloof, standing at ramrod attention, replied, whipping off a snappy salute before hurrying through the swinging doors in back of the operations space.

*Ah,* thought Alqahiray, *he moves with a song in his heart and spring in his step.* He tightened his lips to keep from laughing. Stupid boy; he would wear his arm out with all that saluting! There would be no more Walids in Alqahiray's life.

Two soldiers stood guard near the open heavy, soundproof steel doors leading into the spaces. He made a mental note to increase the security leading to this deep underground complex.

It seemed to him that if it was this easy for them to reach the operations space, then others could also. Of course, few had his knowledge of the command post; he helped design it and oversaw the building of it.

Alqahiray stepped onto the raised platform that held his chair. He tossed the still-burning cigarette at the nearby trash pail and missed. Alqahiray pulled himself up into the high control chair in the center of the platform and patted the arms twice as if welcoming himself to an old and familiar place. He pulled another cigarette out and lit it. Within minutes, the familiar blue cloud of acrid smoke encircled the hero of the revolution. He recalled how he had sat right here when they sank the American destroyer USS *Gearing*. His idea, his plan, and his revolution. No one else would have figured out how to lure the American warship into Libyan waters and then sink it.

He took another deep drag. He hoped he could restore Jihad Wahid to its proper course. His eyes studied the intelligence screens lining the tops of the walls around the compartment. The gigantic digital screens allowed him to start with the first, and as his eyes moved from one to the next, he began to interpret the current situation as it unfolded, screen by screen, with ever-increasing resolution. The first screen showed the Mediterranean Sea and the littoral countries surrounding it. Red diamonds reflected the location of enemy ships, and red brackets told him where enemy aircraft were operating. Each symbol had an arrow pointing in the direction of travel with a number on the arrow identifying the speed of the contact. In the southern desert of Algeria, a red square flashed alongside a similar one flashing in southern Morocco. *What are those?* he asked himself.

The second screen showed the North African coast and about 100 kilometers of surrounding sea. The third refined the presentation to show Algiers, and the fourth reflected an outline of the Libyan coast. The remaining three rotated presentations with various situations ranging from the Red Sea to hundreds of miles into the Atlantic. The key to good military operations is having a firm grasp on situational awareness. He pursed his lips as he took in the information on the screens.

A bank of seventeen six-inch-wide lights glowed a mixture of red and green above the intelligence screens. A red light meant the American satellites, identified in bold black Arabic letters beneath the light, were out of range of Libya. The green lights identified those overhead surveillance systems currently watching the new Barbary Republic. If only the Chinese had given him one of their laser weapons, this constant surveillance would be a thing of history. Even the information warfare data the Chinese provided to change the geopositional satellite output to lure the American destroyer into their waters was gone. The Chinese had put a self-destruct program in the software weapon they sold to him, ensuring he could never use it again without their help.

*They have their own problems trying to control North Korea.* The threat of North Korea invading South Korea was supposed to have been a feint to occupy the Americans while he consolidated his hold on the whole of North Africa. Well, the Chinese had their hands full now. The North Koreans had invaded. The fly the Chinese thought they had under their thumb had flown away. Though America was deploying most of its forces to repel the invasion, there remained the United States Sixth Fleet in the Mediterranean—a smaller Sixth Fleet than years ago, but still strong enough to destroy everything he had worked to achieve.

He blew a cloud of smoke toward the first screen where his attention had settled. The fact that the American Marines occupied Algiers had been broadcast on state radio. Still, seeing it on the screen sent a surge of anger rushing through him. If Walid—the traitor—had remained loyal, this never would have happened. He would have ordered the Algerians to let the Americans go. But, no, the weasel-faced twit wanted power for himself, under the guise of true Islam. To hell with Islam; the future of this effort rested in the might of the armed forces. It rested on his shoulders.

Two broad red arrows pointed from the north coast of Morocco into the interior of this Atlantic coastal country. Then the arrows curled back, turning west to cross the Atlas Mountains that separated Algeria and Morocco, their sharp tips heading toward the important Algerian town of Oran. Oran: the Mediterranean city occupied by the remnants of President Hawali Alneuf's army. The Algerian objective would have been achieved, if only they had successfully captured the Algerian president. The Americans had rescued the democratic icon of Algeria, who kept a never-ending tirade of BBC rhetoric flowing from London. Where was their spokesman to twist their own story across the airways?

Alqahiray touched the right arm of the chair and chose the three-sequence combination of buttons to activate the mouse. He clicked on the northernmost arrow. Blinking words "Spanish 1st Infantry Division" lit up beneath the arrow. He slid the mouse over, clicked, and a list of Spanish military units scrolled down the screen, identifying several armor battalions and other known military elements associated with the arrow. The word *more* blinked beneath the last unit. *More!* This was not good!

Spanish forces moving into Algeria?

"What is that, Sergeant?" he asked the soldier technician manning the force status console to his left.

"What, sir?"

"The Spanish units moving across Algeria."

"Sir, a day after you were wounded, Moroccan units invaded Cueta. Cueta, like its sister city of Melilla, is a Spanish-owned city-state just inside the Mediterranean side of the Strait of Gibraltar on the North African coast. As you know, my Colonel, Morocco has always claimed Cueta, much like Spain claimed Gibraltar from the British. Spain landed its forces at those two cities and moved into Morocco a week ago. They have since moved eastward along the pipeline leading from our oil fields. Our army has abandoned its attempt to stop them from joining the loyalist forces of President Alneuf in Oran."

"Yes, I remember the incident, Sergeant. I ordered the Moroccans to retreat!"

The sergeant stood and looked around at the other console operators, who immediately looked down at their computers or became busy with something else. He swallowed. "Sorry, my Colonel. The word never reached them or, if it did, they refused to obey. The events . . . the events surrounding the assassination attempt on you clouded the orders, sir. Colonel, I do not believe the order was ever sent."

The Spanish needed to stay on their side of the Strait. Alqahiray knew what they were doing and where they were going. Eighty percent of the natural gas Spain used came from Algeria. Pumped via a pipeline complex, the gas traveled from Algeria, through the Atlas Mountains, across Morocco, and then beneath the waters of the Strait of Gibraltar to the Spanish city of Algeciras. From Algeciras, the gas was distributed by pipeline, truck, and train throughout Spain. Alqahiray knew without that petrol, Spain's economy would come to a standstill and the immense strides it had made economically would be set back decades. He had to convince the Spanish they had nothing to fear. Or should he? He slid the problem into a recess of his mind. It might benefit the new nation to have a weakened Spain across the Strait. He made a mental note to revisit the strategic implications of shutting down the pipeline.

He moved away from the Spanish invasion and focused for the first time on the small symbol in southern Morocco. "The symbol showing a hostile element in southern Morocco? What is that? Do loyal Moroccan units still exist? I thought they had all surrendered or been annihilated."

"Yes, Colonel, Morocco is ours. This is the Americans. They have taken a vacant airfield and established a base there. We know they have helicopters, but we are still trying to determine the number of troops and what, if any, other types of aircraft are operating at the site. Units that have approached their position have been attacked by Cobra attack helicopters."

"So, our forces have yet to reach the airfield itself?"

"No, sir. The helicopter gunships keep turning them back."

"I don't believe that. Helicopters cannot stop a concerted army effort. What do we have out there? A bunch of cowards? Who is the senior officer here?"

"I am, Colonel," answered an older, gray-haired major, who moved out of the shadows where he had been observing everything silently to stand near the edge of the platform.

Alqahiray wondered where the officer had been since he had returned. He stared at the man. He knew him. He was a Walid lackey. Must be. Otherwise, he would have fawned over him as the others did. A loyal officer in charge would have been the first to meet him upon his return; instead, he had to call for him. One more loose end to tie up later. He mentally added the major to his list of things to do. More important things required his attention now. He turned to the displays, smoke shifting and weaving around his head from the movement.

He must sew up the ripping seams of Jihad Wahid before dealing with the den of traitors who ousted him. The Spanish were a big threat, but Alqahiray believed the larger threat lay with the reopening of the Strait of Gibraltar, allowing the Americans unfettered access to the Mediterranean. The thirty-

day smart mines, laid by the Algerian Kilo submarines, failed
to keep the American aircraft carrier out of the Med, but they
had slowed passage and in some cases stopped other vessels.
He had counted on keeping the American Navy out of the
Mediterranean long enough to consolidate his position and the
establishment of the Islamic Republic of Barbary and North
Africa. He had not counted on the United States Sixth Fleet
being able to mount an offensive with its limited number of
ships. His intelligence officers had eagerly agreed with him
when he had doubted that America would be able to deploy a
carrier battle group in less than three weeks.

Alqahiray stroked his chin a couple of times and twisted the
ends of his mustache. *The Islamic Republic of Barbary and
North Africa.* The Islamic moniker would serve as an additional
shield against the heretical West, who would fall over itself to
make sure that everyone knew this wasn't a war against Islam.
The good news was that no one in the Moslem world would believe it.

He inhaled and grinned as he recalled how the Algerian Kilo
submarine torpedoed and sank an American destroyer, a destroyer that had intentionally put itself in front of torpedoes to
save the aircraft carrier USS *Stennis.* As much as he hated the
Americans for killing his parents, he respected the bravery of
the skipper who gave his life and the lives of his crewmen in
battle. *You may hate your enemy, but warriors must respect
bravery.* If the Kilo had stayed and fought, it might have survived instead of being blown up by its own mines.

"Major Bahar, I did not see you when I came in," Alqahiray
said menacingly to the Libyan officer standing beside the platform. He watched the major in his peripheral vision. "I am surprised you would still be here."

"I believe the colonel knows that I would be no place else. I
have been standing here, Colonel. Welcome back. We are
pleased your wounds were not serious," he answered, his voice
calm and methodical. "It is truly Allah's miracle that has healed
you so fast. As you can tell, the troops are happy over your return."

"And I presume you are, too, Major." It was hard to tell with
Bahar what he truly thought. The man's face never betrayed his
feelings. That was another reason Alqahiray distrusted the officer.

Bahar bowed his head in an exaggerated nod. "Of course, Colonel. We are all pleased."

He moved the major's name up a couple of notches on his list. "Thank you, Major." He pointed to the map of Morocco displayed on one of the intelligence screens. "What can you tell me about this?"

Bahar looked up at the place on the screen that Alqahiray had highlighted. "Yes, sir. That is a small abandoned airstrip in the Moroccan desert. The Moroccan Air Force used it decades ago in their fight against rebels in that area. It has been abandoned for many years. Last month, a new American Amphibious Task Force, led by USS *Kearsarge,* arrived off the Atlantic coast of Morocco. They mounted an airborne assault and captured the airfield from the weeds and sands that defended it. The airfield is near the border with Algeria. The unopposed assault took less than a day. Afterward, with the exception of an unknown number of helicopters and troops, the remainder of the assault force reboarded the amphibious carrier *Kearsarge* and sailed with it through the Strait of Gibraltar a week ago."

"Why would they want to put troops there? There is nothing there. It is nothing but sand and grit and heat."

"Colonel Samir believed they have either vacated the airfield or are preparing to vacate. An American ship passed through the Strait of Gibraltar yesterday and turned down the coast of Morocco. We think it is hurrying to a position off the coast so that the Americans can abandon the airfield.

The Marines are at the airfield to rescue Americans stranded in southern Algeria. Reports from Algeria show two of the rescue helicopters were destroyed by our forces when they touched down near an oil drilling site." He reached down and touched a button. A red light lit up inside Algeria about 400 miles from the captured airfield. "Here. According to the last report, two days ago, the American Marines and their evacuees disappeared into the Sahara in two humvees and an old oil rigging truck. They are attempting to drive out with their evacuees. We lost contact with both them and our forces, which were pursuing them, two days ago."

Alqahiray grunted. "Good. Let the desert bleach their bones as it has bleached others who have tried to conquer it."

Major Bahar nodded.

Alqahiray pulled another Greek cigarette out and butt lit it from the one nearly burned to the filter. He then tossed the still-burning butt toward the ash can, missing again. Major Bahar followed the track of the cigarette and watched it roll onto the floor. He took two careful steps to the right and ground the cigarette out. His face showed no expression. *A mask,* thought Alqahiray as he observed the officer. Bahar gazed up at the colonel.

"Major, order the Moroccan forces to take the base back. There cannot be many troops there, and with the ship in no position to help them, they are stranded. How foolish and stupid can the Americans be to leave a sacrificial lamb like this! Well, let's take their offer to our new republic." He laughed. Did the Americans think they could come with impunity and establish a base inside the Republic of Barbary and North Africa? "Send the orders immediately!" He slammed his fist down on the arm of the chair.

Major Bahar nodded and saluted. "Yes, sir. It will be done."

The sound of combat boots marching down the corridor echoed off the tile floor outside of the operations room, capturing Alqahiray's attention. The sound brought back memories of how they marched him, wounded and bleeding, into his home in Tripoli, where they held him prisoner for nearly four weeks. The roles were reversed now.

Six soldiers turned the corner. Two half dragged, half pushed a short, dumpy man between them. The sleeves were torn on the man's suit, and specks of blood dotted the ripped white shirt. The tie lay askew across his right shoulder with the knot pulled down several inches below the top two opened buttons, exposing another double chin and a chest full of white hair. Two officers in gray uniforms walked between four soldiers outfitted in camouflage utilities. Alqahiray recognized the two officers in gray as intelligence aides to Samir, an added bonus with the capture of President Mintab. The eyes of one of the intelligence officers shifted back and forth as if looking for an escape. Even from across the room, fear gripped the man's face, a caged desire to run evident in legs that seemed to bounce slightly. A bullet in the kneecap would stop those thoughts. The eyes of the other officer, standing ramrod straight, met Alqahiray's stare. Alqahiray's eyebrows bunched. The man should be frightened, ready to beg for his life like his comrade. Alqahiray took another deep drag on the harsh Greek cigarette. Here was a man deserving of respect. Too bad he had to die.

Alqahiray looked away from the intelligence officer and back to President Mintab, the man in the suit. Mintab must have fought, thought Alqahiray, from the condition of the man's clothes and the bruises on the side of the short man's face. He had more spunk than he thought.

Four soldiers remained in the corridor, guarding the two intelligence officers as two others shoved the civilian prisoner around the consoles to the raised platform where Alqahiray sat. Alqahiray stood as they approached. The nearby guard tightened his grip on the AK-47 and slammed it into Mintab's back, knocking the man to the floor. Mintab moaned. He spread his arms out and began to push himself up onto all fours. The operators concentrated on their consoles while snatching quick glimpses of the terror near Alqahiray's platform.

Alqahiray sauntered down the metal steps, the sound of his boots echoing slightly in the quiet of the operations room until he stepped onto the rubber antistatic mats that covered the raised metal floor. He stopped over Mintab who had managed to pull himself up onto his hands and knees. Alqahiray put his boot lightly on Mintab's back.

Mintab looked up at the Libyan mastermind. He begged quietly, "Please, please, Colonel."

Then, again, his first impression was correct. The man had no spunk. No pride. Even when Walid and Samir had overthrown him in the operations theater, he had retained his pride. A true man maintains his honor, even in the face of adversity. Most politicians would find that a hard concept. Mintab was no different.

Alqahiray lifted his foot a few inches and stomped as hard as he could on Mintab's spine, knocking the older politician back onto the floor. "Hello, Mintab, my friend. Remember me?"

Mintab nodded, his head forced away from Alqahiray. His arms and legs, spread apart, shook on the rubber matting.

"Who designed and planned Jihad Wahid? Who brought you from obscurity to lead the political effort?"

Mintab turned his head toward Alqahiray; his face rested on the floor a few inches from the colonel's boots. The out-of-shape politician clenched his eyes shut as a wave of pain racked his body. He lifted his head slightly to stare up at Alqahiray. Tears trickled out of dilated, bloodshot eyes. The blue lighting cast shadows across the deep recesses of Alqahiray's eyes, creating two dark caverns on the colonel's face where normal men's eyes would have been visible. Blood trickled out of Mintab's nose to drip on the rubber matting, building a small puddle beneath the man's head.

"Please, please, don't," whimpered Mintab. "I did not know. Walid never told me."

"Walid never told you what, Mintab?" Alqahiray nudged the man's face with the edge of his boot. "What did Walid never tell you?"

"That you were okay," Mintab stuttered. "That you were still in charge. I am still loyal to you, my Maadi. I love you. Please, please believe me. If I had only known the circumstance. These men—"

Alqahiray laughed. "Mintab, you are such a poor liar. Even I could think of a better argument. Or does fear cloud your political mind?"

Mintab slid his left arm beneath him, and pushed himself up to a near sitting position. He might be able to talk his way out of this. "No, Colonel Alqahiray. I am still loyal to you. Walid forced us to go along. None wanted to. Our loyalty remained with you, the leader of the revolution."

Alqahiray drew his foot back and kicked Mintab. The president rolled once, landing on his stomach. Mintab moaned, his hands over his face, blood running out between his fingers. Alqahiray stomped the frightened man's back twice. Mintab jerked his hands away from his face, spreading his arms out. Alqahiray brought his boot down, planting it neatly in the small of Mintab's back. He put his full weight on the boot and twisted the heel, causing Mintab's head to involuntarily bounce off the thin matting as the boot dug further into the nerves of the spinal column. The man's arms flapped ineffectively as he fought to reach the tyrant's leg.

Alqahiray heard the air rush out of Mintab's lungs and smiled as his captive fought to catch his breath. Alqahiray laughed. He moved his foot to the top of Mintab's back, leaned forward, and put all his weight on the foot holding the prisoner down, keeping him from drawing a breath, enjoying the squirming beneath his heel. Mintab fought to free himself, fighting for air. The guards laughed.

Sergeant Adib, who led the group, drew back his foot and kicked Mintab in the side, drawing a cry of pain from the man and forcing out the last air in the man's lungs. Alqahiray leaned away, taking his weight off Mintab. The gasping sounds of Mintab searching for breath brought a wider smile to Alqahiray's lips. *Not a healthy sound,* thought Alqahiray.

"You should have taken better care of yourself, President Mintab. Maybe if you had visited me and seen for yourself, I might be inclined to believe you. However, not one word have I heard from you since your speech at the United Nations declaring the entire North African coast a new nation—which, by the way, was very good. Too bad for your health that you neglected to stick with making speeches. You politicians are alike; so fluid-flowing wherever you think the waters are best for you. Saying whatever will help retain the power you so cravenly desire and possess. What are you now? The interim president of the Islamic Republic of Barbary and North Africa? How impressive, Mintab! No, don't say anything. I am truly impressed how far you have risen in such a short time. Would it surprise you if I told you that I thought someday that I would be the president or prime minister of the Islamic Republic of Barbary and North Africa?" He leaned over the man. "No? I didn't think it would. And where are your cohorts who shot and kidnapped me—Walid and Samir?"

Mintab raised his head; his lips moved silently a couple of times before his head fell back onto the floor. Tears mixed with the blood flowing from his nose. Torn lips had turned his teeth a sickly red, causing them to appear black in the blue light.

The ammonia smell of urine reached Alqahiray, causing his nose to wrinkle.

Mintab finally realized he was going to die. If he knew where Walid and Samir had fled, he could bargain. Maybe he could delay. "I don't know, Colonel. I don't know. I saw them last night when we met to discuss the situations . . ." he said weakly, gasping the words out. *Think, Mintab,* he said to himself. *Make something up to give him. Anything to save your life.* However, fear, pain, and fatigue clouded his mental faculties, and he felt himself fading into a deep blackness.

Alqahiray put his foot on Mintab's head and shifted his

weight onto it and smiled as Mintab's weak struggle to free himself ceased. "Shut up, traitor!" he shouted. "You have pissed yourself, Mintab. What real man pisses himself, even when he knows he is going to die? You missed seeing how heroes die. When the junta died, not one of them pissed themselves. They stood straight and strong, waiting for their deaths, knowing their deaths were good for the country," Alqahiray lied. "You should have been there. You would know how to accept death." He pulled his boot away.

Mintab's consciousness returned as his lungs took in deep breaths. *"Ya* Colonel," Mintab whimpered, his eyes remaining closed. "I think they have gone to the naval base at Benghazi." He knew Walid talked a lot on the telephone with the admiral at Benghazi. Surely, that was where they had fled.

"You do, do you?" This he would check out. Admiral Asif Abu Yimin, the old man, was there. The admiral would offer protection to Walid and Samir. He looked down at the figure beneath him, watching the chest heave in and out. Mintab buying time. He would do the same thing. He shook his head, acknowledging that Mintab was lying. The politician had no idea where the two were, and if he were Walid or Samir, he would not trust Mintab with his plans, either.

He looked at Sergeant Adib and snapped his fingers. Alqahiray held his hand out. The sergeant unbuckled his holster and pulled his pistol out. He pulled the slide back, slipping a bullet into the chamber. He passed the loaded weapon to the colonel. Alqahiray moved his foot and put the pistol against Mintab's head.

"Any last words, Mintab?" And, before the man could answer, Alqahiray pulled the trigger. "I guess not." The sound echoed once before the soundproofing on the walls absorbed the noise. The smell of gunpowder mingled with the strong, acrid smoke of the smoldering Greek cigarette as it burned another mark on the arm of Alqahiray's chair.

The sound of breaking china jerked Alqahiray's attention toward the kitchen. The gunshot had surprised his new aide returning with their tea and pastries. Alqahiray smiled, then glanced down for a moment at Mintab's body.

Alqahiray blew the smoke from the barrel. He turned to the sergeant and smiled. "One should always have a last word prepared." He moved aside to avoid the spreading puddle of blood. "Get him out of here."

Alqahiray glanced toward Major Maloof. The tea tray hung from one hand. On the floor, broken cups and spilled tea stained the thin, worn carpet near the kitchen door. Hot tea soaked the young officer's pants leg.

"Major Maloof, you must be more careful. Go get more tea, and don't be clumsy this time." He stepped up to the chair and grabbed his cigarette. Frightened aides were useless. It would be a short tour of duty for Major Maloof.

White-faced, Major Maloof hurried back through the swinging doors into the small kitchen behind them.

Sergeant Adib turned to the two guards, pointed to the body on the floor, and jerked his thumb toward the hallway. They grabbed Mintab by the ankles and dragged him across the floor and through the door. The dead man's head bounced along the matting and off the step leading from the upper level of computer consoles to the next. A trail of blood marked the passage. Activity in the operations room slowed, then stopped, as operators watched the execution and subsequent disposal of the man known as the president of their new republic.

"And, for these two, Colonel?" Sergeant Adib asked, tilting his head toward the two intelligence officers.

Alqahiray tossed his lit butt at the nearby ashtray. He stared at the two traitors, amused at how the tall one unabashedly returned the stare. He returned the stare until the prisoner broke eye contact. Alqahiray shook his head. "Ah, Sergeant Adib. We shall take them with us to the laboratories. I think these two are volunteers for our project to bring the Western powers to their senses and help Jihad Wahid."

Sergeant Adib nodded and saluted. *"Aiwa, ya* Colonel."

Alqahiray looked around the operations room. Those at the consoles returned their concentration to the computer screens as his gaze turned toward them. Alqahiray smiled. Another lesson for the masses. Anyone can build respect if they work hard enough at it, but the conventional way just took too damn long. Fear built loyalty very quickly. He noticed that the twelve computers they had started Jihad Wahid with nearly a month ago had grown to twenty. What other new initiatives had Walid and Samir started while they had him incarcerated?

He walked back up the steps and shoved himself into his

chair, pulled another cigarette from the dwindling package, and lit it. Things were going very well on his return. If he could find Walid and Samir, he could nip this little insurrection in the bud and concentrate on the important issues of consolidating power within his new country and assuming the strong leadership it needed. He glanced toward the two prisoners near the steel doors. Well, at least he had Samir's able assistants.

The events along the North African coast that rattled the overall plan of Alqahiray to unite the Arab countries from Morocco to Sudan as an empire was being overshadowed by his hunt for those who had overthrown him four weeks ago.

Major Maloof returned with fresh cups of tea and several croissants. He held the tray while Alqahiray took a couple of pastries and stirred his tea. Maloof stared at the large bloodstain near the foot of the stairs and the trail leading from it. The two empty cups rattled slightly as Maloof held the tray.

"Ahsan? Ahsan, you listening?" asked Alqahiray.

Maloof jumped. "Sorry, Colonel. My thoughts wandered."

Alqahiray leaned forward and poked him roughly in the chest, nearly causing Maloof to drop the tray again. "Ahsan, I have had enough of people's thoughts wandering. Don't wander too much, or you may never wander again. Understand?" He leaned back and crossed his legs.

"Yes, sir, Colonel. Sorry, Colonel. It won't happen again." Maloof took a half step back, just out of the immediate reach of Alqahiray. The cups rattled noticeably on the tray as Maloof fought to bring the trembling under control. He shut his eyes, concentrated, and breathed a sigh of relief when he heard the rattling stop. He smiled and opened his eyes. Alqahiray was leaning across the arm of the chair, holding the edge of the tray and smiling at him.

"Is that better, Ahsan?" Alqahiray released the tray and leaned back in his chair. The rattling started again. "Of course not, Ahsan. Of course not." He waved the man away and watched as his new aide—a short-term one for the job at this rate—hurry across the floor and through the kitchen doors. The lesson with Mintab would be a strong one for his new aide. The fear racing through Ahsan would temper any disloyalty—for a time. Eventually, fear is replaced with complacency, and from complacency comes a feeling of security. Security creates a source for rebellion.

Major Bahar stepped in front of the stanchion. "Colonel, the orders have been passed." He nodded toward the kitchen. "I will talk with Major Maloof and explain his duties as your aide." He turned to leave, stopped and, with his hands behind his back, faced Alqahiray again. "Ahsan is a good boy, sir. He will serve you well." Bahar paused before he added, "And loyally."

"Good, Major. Let's hope others do so as well," he replied, staring hard at Bahar.

"Of course, my Colonel. We are your loyal subjects," Bahar replied, lowering his head respectfully.

Alqahiray took a sip of the hot tea. "This tastes so much better drinking it here. Hot tea is never a good drink when caged, Major Bahar." He patted the arms of the chair. "Now tell me about the rescue the Americans attempted in southern Algeria. Why have we not heard from them? What forces do we have there, and what forces did they have?"

"We have a small force of twenty Algerian soldiers. A captain is in charge, Colonel, but I do not know his name. I can find out if it interests you. A small force of American Marines survived the destruction of their rescue helicopters. We had an arrangement with the Taureg Bedouins in the area that the nomads may have the site, the equipment, and material after the Americans were captured. The Americans were to be turned over to us, with the exception of one."

"That sounds reasonable to me, Major," Alqahiray answered. Then, after a slight pause, he added, "One? Which one? Not one of the Marines?" He would never give up an American military person. The propaganda opportunities were too great.

"No, sir, not a Marine," Bahar answered, his lips in a tight smile. "A blond girl; they want a young blond girl the Tauregs have seen at the compound. Probably for their slave trade. Blond girls bring many camels, and I understand such auctions can go on for weeks. The seller can become a rich man with a blond woman."

Alqahiray smiled. "I would like to see this vision whose looks bend an entire tribe to our cause. I don't understand why they didn't just sneak in one night and take her. Why go through this bloodshed?"

Bahar shrugged his shoulders. "I don't know, Colonel. What I know is that she was part of the bargain."

Alqahiray nodded. He would have liked to have had the Marines as his prisoners, but he realized it was not to be.

"But our forces and the Marines have disappeared into the desert? It is too bad, but even I cannot control the Sahara when it demands a sacrifice. I fear we have heard the last of both the Americans and our own. The Marines would have been a nice display for the world press. The Americans won't know what happened to them any more than we do, so we shall wait and see if that knowledge can be used to our benefit."

"I would submit, *ya* Maadi, that forcing the Americans out of Algiers is a higher priority."

Alqahiray slid down from his chair. He would decide the priorities, not Bahar. He tossed the lit cigarette toward the ashtray, scoring a hit. Bahar's eyebrows rose slightly. Several cigarette butts of varying lengths surrounded the ashtray. This was the first one to go in since the colonel's return.

"You are right, Major. Driving the Americans out of Algiers is more important. We must show the world we can defend our new borders."

"And the Spanish?"

Alqahiray glared at him. They both knew the new country had limits to its capabilities, regardless of the rhetoric. He ignored the question.

"I am going to the laboratories, Major Bahar. I have a plan for ridding ourselves of the Americans in Algiers and off our coast. You stay here. For your own sake, ensure my orders are transmitted this time; properly understood and executed. Understand?"

Major Bahar nodded, his arms crossed behind his back. "Of course, my Colonel. I will have a report when you return."

"Good. We must reassert our grip on the situations confronting us. I will need to talk to our Navy and Air Force leaders. Have we repaired the video teleconferencing equipment while I've been gone?"

Major Bahar nodded. "Yes, sir. In fact, we now have two computers with their own teleconference capability," he said, pointing out two huge workstations outfitted with small cameras above the CRT. Small microphones were mounted on the side of the workstation.

"Where did we get these?"

"From our friends in China, where they now make these computers."

"Good. I will be interested in seeing how this computer version VTC works. Schedule one for this afternoon with the Navy and Air Force. Make sure Tripoli Naval Base is included. I want a separate video teleconference afterward with Admiral Asif Abu Yimin in Benghazi."

"I will try, sir. Not all the command posts have the video cameras installed yet."

"Then tell them to install them!"

Major Bahar stepped aside as Alqahiray stomped toward the steel doors. As the colonel passed, Major Bahar glanced into the ash can. He was right; it had been the first one to score.

Sergeant Adib, a few inches taller than Alqahiray, with his broad shoulders about twelve inches wider and a stomach two inches smaller, fell in step behind the Libyan leader. Muscles rippled beneath the starched, creased uniform. The expressionless face of Sergeant Adib, offset by a sharp forehead and chin, accented wary eyes that wandered from side to side watching, waiting. His whole gait reminded some of a lion on the prowl, looking for prey and prepared to leap without warning. Operators looked away to avoid eye contact with the two men. Alqahiray might be the more mercurial, but Adib was the more dangerous.

Along the top of the operations room, two more of the seventeen surveillance warning lights changed from green to red while three of the red ones flicked to green. Twelve remained a constant red.

"Bahar, what is this? Why are twelve of them red? We never have so few enemy satellites in range for this long!"

"I do not know, sir. Colonel Samir—"

"It is *Major* Samir. I did not promote him. He is still a lousy major."

"Sorry, sir. Major Samir said he thinks the Americans have moved their satellites to where they are fighting in Korea." He pointed at the light array. "It is only because of the new orbits to support the Americans in Korea that we even have these few. There are times when we have gone for hours without enemy intelligence coverage."

As if hearing Bahar's pronouncement, all the lights went red.

"Like now, Colonel Alqahiray," Bahar said, nodding toward the lights.

Alqahiray stared at the lights, waiting for one of them to turn green. He stared silently for nearly five minutes before turning to Major Bahar, smiling. "This is great news, Major."

One of the lights flickered to green.

*It never changes for Libya,* thought Alqahiray as he stepped to the steel double doors. *The Americans always watch us. However, that watch used to be continuous, with a twice-monthly exception of nineteen seconds!* Those nineteen seconds had provided the window of opportunity for them to change the GPS satellites to reflect a five-mile error and cost the United States one of its newest destroyers. Things were going to change in the years—no, months—to come as he wielded more power and influence against the Europeans than the Americans could bring to bear. Korea was sucking them out of the Mediterranean. It was keeping China from attempting to manipulate his own plans to gain control of the Mediterranean Sea.

America's own misplaced values and beliefs in a higher ideal would always hinder America. Words, words, words. That was all it was, anyway. Even Americans doubted the values their government spat out to the world. America was on its way out like the old, vanished Roman Empire. Everyone but them could see that. Their influence in Europe waned with the passing of the Soviet Union. When the big bear threat to Europe disappeared in the early nineties, Europe believed it lost its need for America. *Foolish and naive they are.* He smiled. The events of September 11 would never have happened without the laws that allowed so much uncontested immigration and visas—all for the sense of fairness. Fairness kills. Always protect your own first, and to hell with what others think.

The French, another group of pompous fools, would love to see the Americans go. The French illusions of past grandeur would remain just those: illusions. America had two areas where it wielded great influence: its economy and its military might. That military might disappeared yearly as less and less attention was paid to what most Americans believed to be unnecessary: a strong national defense. America was destined to forever relearn history. The continuing success of the North Koreans in pushing the South Koreans and their American ally south would cause the United States to abandon the Mediterranean. If he could just hold out until Sixth Fleet was sucked away.

That would leave the United States with only its economy as the remaining strategic resource of influence. After he consolidated his power, Alqahiray would degrade that influence. America did 65 percent of its trade with Europe. Two of the three major ports they needed to keep the trade going were Algeciras, Spain, and Livorno, Italy. There was little he could do about Rotterdam. Eventually, maybe, but not now. His plans for those two other cities would bring Europe to its knees. Alqahiray saw this epiphany in the few moments it took him to reach the steel doors of the operations room. In those few steps, he laid the genesis for his grand strategy in shoving America out of the Mediterranean and back across the Atlantic.

"Colonel," Sergeant Adib said, interrupting Alqahiray's thoughts. "What do you want to do with our prisoners?"

Alqahiray looked at the two officers who stood eight feet from him, their backs against the wall.

"We are going to take them with us, Sergeant Adib."

He turned to the two prisoners. "Are you two going to welcome me back?"

The two officers stood side by side. The one on the right seemed to be at attention, the military creases of his shirt and trousers as sharp as if he had stepped into a freshly ironed uniform. *He and Adib must use the same laundry,* thought Alqahiray. The prisoner met Alqahiray's stare eye-to-eye without flinching. Alqahiray refused to play stare-down, especially with men destined for the lime pit.

He moved his attention to the other man. The smell of ammonia, the smell of fear surrounded this prisoner. It made Alqahiray's lips curl in disgust. He hated cowards. All men hate cowards. The prisoner's matted black hair glistened with sweat, and his eyes, when he locked up briefly, shone with moisture. Sweat stains beneath the armpits spread down both sides of the wrinkled gray uniform shirt. Why do cowards piss themselves?

"Well? I said, are you going to welcome me back?"

The brave one spoke first. "Welcome back, Colonel." He bowed his head once in concession to the senior officer.

"Please, Colonel. I haven't done anything. I am loyal to the cause," begged the other, his eyes wavering between the colonel and the floor.

"What is the cause, you pitiful thing of a Libyan officer? What is the cause? Tell me!" he screamed.

The man flinched, drawing his hands up in front of his face. "We are the cause, Colonel. Islam is the cause. The Arab nations are the cause," he stuttered to the amusement of Alqahiray. The man brought his hands down slightly and looked up.

Alqahiray slapped the man, knocking him against the white stucco wall of the corridor. "You heretical fool! *I* am the cause!" he shouted, poking himself in the chest repeatedly. "*I* am the cause, and you forgot that, didn't you. You thought if you rid yourselves of me you could control Barbary?" The slap caused pain to shoot through Alqahiray from his wound. He shouldn't have hit him so hard. Stars danced around the edge of his vision. He must remember he was still recovering from a bullet wound.

"No, sir. No, *ya* Maadi. I have never thought that," he whined as he slid down the wall to squat with his hands above his head. Incoherent mumbling drifted up from the man. The thick black hair hung listless along the sides of the man's face.

Adib leaned forward and whispered, "Are you all right, *ya* Colonel?"

Alqahiray ignored the question. He turned to the other officer, paused as he watched the man raise his head slightly and tighten his cheeks for the expected blow. Alqahiray smiled and dropped his hand. "I doubt it would do more than just cause my hand to turn red and hurt my shoulder again." Alqahiray pointed to the crying man on the floor.

The soldier never moved but remained at attention, refusing to succumb to Alqahiray's motion for him to look at his comrade.

Alqahiray shrugged and pulled another Old Navy cigarette from a packet and lit it.

"Come, Sergeant Adib. Let's take these two fine intelligence officers to the laboratory." He turned to the brave one. "I think you will find it enlightening, Captain. You are brave now, my friend. I hope you don't disappoint me. I want to see how brave you are in the days to come. I truly believe you want to support the revolution, and I have a way in which both of you may redeem yourselves. And if you should succeed and live, then you may have your freedom to return to the cause." He laughed.

Alqahiray turned left and marched down the hallway. Fluorescent lights shining off the white walls gave the hallway a pristine, bright look, reflecting the leader's shadow moving along the wall as he walked.

Sergeant Adib moved to where the prisoner squatted, drew back his boot, and kicked the feet out from under the man.

"Don't hit me. Please, don't hit me," the man cried, curling into a fetal position.

"Get up, imbecile. You coward. Or I shall personally shoot you myself." He reached to his side and unbuttoned his holster.

If the frightened intelligence officer knew what was to come, he would have remained on the floor and allowed Sergeant Adib to kill him. The prisoner scrambled to his feet. Tears ran down his cheeks as he whimpered softly.

Adib motioned. The guards shoved the prisoners down the hallway as they followed the tall, lean sergeant through the corridor. The whimpering made Adib angry. He would ask Alqahiray for permission to kill the coward.

# TWO

⚓

**PRESIDENT CRAWFORD RAN HIS HAND THROUGH HIS HAIR.**
The gray had become prominent over the sandy brown strands
during the past few months. He wanted to show more gray, as-
sociating himself better with the population sector that poured
out in record numbers to elect him for this second term. The
key had been his health care bill. He had begun to allow a few
gray strands to show. He leaned closer to the mirror for a moment before shaking his head. However, he hadn't intended to
leave office as gray as Clinton.

"Mr. President?"

President Crawford turned away from the brass wall mirror
in the Oval Office. "Sorry, Bob," he said to the secretary of
state. "My mind wandered slightly. Could you repeat what you
said?"

"Yes, sir, Mr. President," Bob Gilfort, the silver-haired secretary of state replied. He understood the pressure on the president of the United States. Not only did the man have combat
operations in Korea and North Africa ongoing, but two days
ago, his wife was admitted to Bethesda Naval Hospital. Publicly, the word was exhaustion. Actually, she tried to take every
pill in the medicine cabinet in the White House living quarters
and would have succeeded if the maid bringing fresh towels

hadn't stumbled upon her. The psychiatrists diagnosed acute depression.

"The French are tying up our nominee, Admiral Walter Hastings, as Admiral Prang's replacement. We are pushing the political buttons as much as possible to expedite the replacement. The French want to leave it the way it is, with their French General Jacques LeBlanc as the head of NATO's Allied Forces Southern Command. They are fighting us every inch of the way."

"Can't really blame them for that, can we?" President Crawford asked in a melancholy tone. "According to the British prime minister, the combined British and French fleet north of ours is now the primary naval force in the Med. They have two carriers; we have one."

"Their two carriers don't have one-tenth the firepower of the *Stennis*. They're baby carriers, Mr. President!" Roger Maddock interjected.

"Say it as you will, Roger, but the Europeans don't seem to feel they need us. They know as well as we do our focus is on Korea while their focus is on the turmoil and threat this new country of Barbary and North Africa presents them. We don't have the influence we did ten years ago. They respect us, but they resent us . . . a conundrum. I think it is another fallout of globalization and . . ." His voice trailed off.

Roger Maddock, the secretary of defense, leaned forward from his seat on the couch. "Mr. President, we must stick to our position on the senior military officer of Allied Forces Southern Command being an American," he said firmly. "As we have discussed, the primary military force in AFSouth is the United States Sixth Fleet and the United States Third Air Force. The last thing we want is someone other than an American in that position. Can you imagine the impact on our leadership if Sixth Fleet comes under the command of a Frenchman? You can't trust the frogs as far as you can throw them."

President Crawford walked back to the straight-backed chair with the presidential emblem embroidered on its seat and sat down. "Don't French-bait me, Roger. The French are a very independent people and one with whom we have had a long and historic tie. I know you have had some bad experiences with them in the past, but when all is said and done, they are usually there beside us when we need them. They stood by us during

the war on terrorism. The truth is that when we needed our allies most, they were there. The French maneuver to promote
their own interests just as we do to promote ours."

Roger leaned back. *Yeah, I'll give them their Evian water,
champagne and good wine.* "Yes, sir, Mr. President. But we still
need to stand firm on our position that the senior military officer for Allied Forces South should be American."

"And we will."

"That's what we're doing," Bob Gilfort added, reaching
down and straightening his pants cuff so it flipped inside of his
crossed legs. "The British have edged back into our camp. At
yesterday's meeting of the NATO Security Council, the British
ambassador endorsed Admiral Hastings, Roger."

"I know," Roger said testily.

Gilfort turned to the president. "Mr. President, I am one hundred percent sure Admiral Hastings will be confirmed. Our
NATO allies understand the military might needed for the
North African crisis rests with the United States. With the offensive going our way in Korea, we may even be able to redirect the carriers to the Mediterranean."

"Thanks, Bob. I hope you are right about Admiral Hastings," President Crawford replied. He leaned forward, his elbows on his knees, and put his head in his hands. "But what if
Hastings's appointment continues to stay mired in European
politics? We need an alternative position, a close-hold one. An
alternative developed while we have the time. We don't want to
be in the position where we are running around at the last minute
trying to decide which way we go. We need an alternative we
can live with and support."

Roger and Bob exchanged a quick glance as the president
shook his head back and forth.

"Sir, not to be accused of French-baiting again, but the
French also know we have our hands full with Korea. They are
viewing this as an opportunity for them to grab authority they
shirked during the Cold War. Now—"

"Roger, never allow your emotions to get wrapped around a
position. It makes it nearly impossible to back away. I agree
with some of your perspectives on the French. Still, we have to
understand their thoughts, their strategy, and their interests. A
strategy that promotes French interests is the same as ours pro-
moting American interests."

"I had a pleasant phone call with the British minister of defense earlier this morning, Mr. President," Roger continued. "The gist of the conversation is that the British have heard—rumors, of course—that if Korea doesn't wrap up soon, we may have to pull all of our forces out of the Mediterranean to meet force requirements over there. I diverted discussion on that topic." Roger Maddock looked down at his notes. "On a second topic—the British Fleet joining Sixth Fleet as a combined naval force—he agreed to discussions. Last week in our conversation he diverted me by saying it was too soon. This is a positive change to my weekly recommendation during our telephone discussions. I believe our longtime ally, Great Britain, is about to return to our side."

President Crawford pursed his lips in thought. "I talked with the prime minister a couple of days ago, and he inquired about the future of American military forces in the Mediterranean and Europe. I think the British concern is the French. Just as we have long historical ties with both countries, their historical ties with the French have been ones of animosity and conflict."

"Do we have any idea what the British thoughts are behind the scenes?"

Bob Gilfort uncrossed his legs to put his coffee cup down. "Need to ask them. The British sport of diplomacy has always kept them far out front of their true capability of national power. Wish we had similar resources."

"Touché, Bob," President Crawford mumbled. "I know the State Department gets less than one percent of the budget, but Congress is the culprit, not the administration. What we should have done is fought harder for State's funding. If we had, then we would have not lost the influence we have overseas."

Bob nodded, ignoring the opportunity to object. The State Department was always the loser in congressional funding, even though diplomacy was listed along with economics, military, and information as an element of national power. "The big loss has been our inability to be a presence in all the international venues we should have been. Noblesse oblige—if you have the power, then you must accept the responsibility and do it in such a manner that your allies never think of you as smug or arrogant."

"Our European allies sometimes view us as a Johnny-come-lately to the international scene," Roger added, "even though we have been a world power since World War I. That's over one hundred years. Sometimes I get the feeling at meetings with them that they believe they know how to run the world—had more experience doing it—and if we would just listen to them, everything would be all right."

"I wonder if the British and French understand what our strategy is for North Africa? I wonder if they know how we are turning the tide on the ground in Korea?" Bob Gilfort asked.

"We haven't seen the tide turn yet, Bob."

"Mr. President, we are not losing in Korea," Roger said, agreeing with the secretary of state.

The president looked up. "No, Roger, and we aren't winning, either. With the military force we have already in Korea, there should be little doubt about winning, but even with a larger force than theirs, we cannot seem to drive those sons of bitches back across the thirty-sixth parallel.

"But, we have stopped their advance—"

"And we won't as long as we keep our military forces diverted with the ongoing events in Europe and North Africa. We need to focus on Korea. We may even have to mobilize—I hate to use that word and do not want to see it in the press—more military forces to Korea."

"Mr. President, we have activated National Guard units in—"

"Roger, we are doing all the politically correct things we need to do. The polls show the American people are firmly behind us. How long they are going to maintain this support is probably directly tied to when CNN begins twenty-four-hour coverage of body bags coming off military transports arriving at Dover and Travis Air Force Bases."

"You should see the grief I am getting from certain senators who oppose our actions in Korea and who take strong exception to their hometown boys and girls—National Guard units—being called up."

The door opened and Franco Donelli, the president's short, out-of-shape national security advisor entered. "Morning, Mr. President, Bob, Roger. Sorry, I'm running a little late. I was going over the morning intelligence summaries." He crossed to a chair beside the president and sat down. "They seem to be getting thicker and thicker every day." He crossed his legs, putting the left over the top of the right knee.

"Wonder why that is?" Roger sniped, earning him a disapproving glare from the chief of staff. Lately, Franco had taken to arriving late for most meetings with the president. Roger would never have tolerated this from a subordinate. He wondered why the president put up with the arrogant fool.

"Franco, glad you're here. I want to discuss what I think we need to do," the president said, interrupting Roger and Franco before another blowout occurred like the one two days ago. Just what he needed along with everything else would be *Washington Post* and *New York Times* headlines about the secretary of defense whipping the national security advisor's ass in the middle of the White House. *We are supposed to be the cool, calm heads of the American political system.* Crawford looked at Roger, who still jogged two or three miles every other day and worked out with weights on the odd days. Franco, on the other hand, had problems keeping up with him when he walked. So many things the press could latch onto right now, including his wife, which he would protect physically from such a prospect.

"Yes, sir?" Franco asked.

"Gentlemen, what is our strategy for these crises? No, better yet, what is our grand strategy for the United States?"

"It's to win the war in Korea and the crisis in North Africa." Roger Maddock answered.

Bob Gilfort started to say something, thought better of it, and remained quiet, waiting for the president to have his say.

"No, Roger. First, it is not a war in Korea. It is a combat operation. To me, a war is a nation fighting for its survival. None of us believes either of these crises will affect America's survival. What they do affect is America's leadership in this century. Since World War II we have led the world in two areas: economics and military. I mean, look at how nations and global businesses determine their wealth. They determine it in U.S. dollars. Even nations when looking at their gross domestic production, GDP, do it in dollars. We have had no competition. We won the Cold War by outspending the Soviets and doing it by forcing them to spend their money on a noneconomic productive source. Defense! We were able to do it without affecting the overall health of our economy and kept a strong enough military that we drove international terrorism back within their own national borders. There is only one other currency that even reaches the shadow of the American dollar."

The president stood and walked over to his desk and picked

up a pencil. He reached up and straightened his red tie. "Today, we have nations and businesses comparing their wealth against the U.S. dollar and the euro. The euro is our competitor. Military might? Yeah, we are still the only superpower in the world, and we should retain that title until at least the year 2030— probably even to 2050. I don't see another country, with the exception of the Chinese, trying to compete with our military, but right now we have a carrier battle group and two amphibious task forces tied up in the Mediterranean. The Army is tied down in Bosnia with nearly a whole division. And the Air Force? We have already taken them effectively from the European scene and redeployed them to Korea! If I could only move the Army as fast as I can the Air Force."

President Crawford sat down at the desk and began to drum the pencil on it. "What I want to do is reduce our military presence in Europe and use Powell's overwhelming might doctrine in Korea." He held up his hand. "I know what you're going to tell me. If we pull out of the Mediterranean and Europe, it will be very hard if not impossible to return." He sighed. "For the time being, we will continue on and see how the new developments in Korea turn. If the tide turns with the lying little bastards retreating back toward the thirty-eighth parallel, then we won't take the remainder of the military and naval presence out of the European and Mediterranean Theater. But if it stalls or they advance even one mile, then we will go forward with an unilateral pullout of American forces. I have no intention of losing in Korea. Our reputation and the confidence of the world in the United States rests on our ability to meet commitments and display the fortitude to stay the course. So, that is what confronts us."

Bob Gilfort leaned forward after several seconds of silence. "You mentioned grand strategy, Mr. President. What are your thoughts on the grand strategy for the challenges we are going to face in the coming months?"

President Crawford opened his mouth to answer, stopped, and hunched his shoulders. "Don't know myself, Bob." He picked up a folder in front of him and tossed it across the desk. "Right there is where all this started. Right here is the catalyst that started the second war of the twenty-first century." He tapped the folder with his index finger. "General Stanhope, director of the National Security Agency, dropped this off yesterday during our meeting. It shows how the USS *Gearing*—the most modern warship of the United States Navy—was lured into Libyan territorial waters by an information warfare attack against the geopositional satellites that provide navigational data to ships at sea." He leaned back in his chair. "This new class of destroyers—what does the Navy call them?"

President Crawford shut his eyes, and there was the USS *John Rodgers.* He always knew the military was trained to do what the skipper of this Spruance-class destroyer did, but he never really believed anyone would. To sail a warship between the aircraft carrier USS *John Stennis* and approaching torpedoes, knowing he was going to die, took a special type of person. He doubted he could have willingly sacrificed himself. Politics was not a profession where self-sacrifice was the norm, and a drowning politician usually tried to take those around him with him. President Crawford reached up and tweaked the bridge of his nose. The spot where the growth had been removed weeks ago was nearly healed. He wondered briefly what type of man Commander Warren Lee Spangle had been. What went through the captain of this destroyer's mind as he waited on the bridge, watching four torpedoes bear down? President Crawford had called the widow the day of the destruction of the USS *John Rodgers* and the loss of all who sailed her to offer his condolences and the thanks of a grateful nation. But words could never replace the husband and father who disappeared in seconds of madness.

"DD-21, sir," Roger said.

"What?"

"The answer to your question, sir. The *Gearing* was a DD-21-class warship. The latest destroyer class of the United States Navy."

His thoughts refocused, President Crawford leaned forward and tapped the folder again. "This DD-21 sank the patrol boat that launched the surface-to-surface missiles as well as the submarine and two Libyan fighter aircraft that attacked it. The battle damage from the short fracas sank the *Gearing,* and we had no resources within reach to rescue those sailors until three days after they abandoned ship and drifted in the waters off the Libyan coast. We couldn't even convince our Italian ally to send helicopters or ships into the Gulf of Sidra to pick them up." President Crawford clasped his hands together and folded them over his chest in a prayerful position.

"Everything seemed to escalate from this incident, gentlemen. The two ships in Gaeta, Italy, were hit by a car bomber; one admiral killed and another wounded. North Korea invades South Korea. So, where is the plan connecting all these events? Is it a Chinese operation to consolidate the Korean peninsula by keeping us occupied in the Mediterranean, or is it an Al-Qaida plot to keep us occupied in Korea while they consolidate the entire North African coast? Or, are the two even connected? I don't know." He sighed. "And, what, pray tell, do we do if China slows down or stops international trade with us? I mean, where in the hell is our heavy industry today? There's little of it left in America."

The three men exchanged quick looks but kept quiet. Lots of questions and few answers.

After a few seconds of awkward silence, Bob Gilfort leaned forward and asked, "Mr. President, may I get a copy of General Stanhope's file for review?"

President Crawford reached forward and shoved the file to the edge of the desk so the secretary of state could reach it. "Let me know what you think after you read it and, Bob, keep it between you and Roger. The director told me a lot of sensitive sources were used to obtain this information, and he would like to protect these sources this time."

Bob Gilfort reached forward and pulled the folder to him, flipped it open, and rifled the pages quickly before handing it to the secretary of defense.

President Crawford shook his head. "We have to wrap up the North African crisis as soon as possible; rescue the hostages in Algiers and withdraw from North Africa. Meanwhile, Bob, Roger, start laying the groundwork with our European allies to withdraw from Bosnia. We need that division in Korea. I want to put the best picture possible on how we do this, because I believe how we handle it will have long-term impact on our role and responsibilities as the world's leader. Our global influence in future years depends on America's performance in the months to come."

"As everyone knows, my orders to General Leutze Lewis, the new commander of our forces in the Mediterranean, is to disengage along the North African littoral. Disengage and prepare to sortie from the Mediterranean to join Joint Task Force Offensive Eagle off Korea. I have told him I want us to avoid further escalation of hostilities in the North African littoral. No offensive action from our side is to be taken. If you are right, Roger, and the tide is turning in Korea, then we will redirect forces from there to the Mediterranean. Until then, my orders to General Lewis remain in effect; take no action that expands our entanglement with this mess in North Africa. Just get our citizens out of there and pull out."

"Obviously, the British are aware or have some inkling of your plans, sir. They are right, in a way. If Korea doesn't show signs soon of winding down, then the United States is going to have to withdraw from the Mediterranean and from Europe. The Europeans are going to have to worry about the Balkan peacekeeping operations. They will scream and shout, no doubt. Additionally, we are going to have to withdraw the remainder of our troops out of Europe except for a small number. We will leave an infrastructure—several garrisons active—behind to support, what we will say, is for our return after completing the military operations in Korea. Between us, I doubt Europe will ask or want us to return. Our forward presence in Europe and in most of the Pacific remains baggage from the Cold War. We can use current events as an opportunity to reduce our overseas presence when Korea is over and bring our forces home where they belong."

"Mr. President, this will kill Admiral Hastings's NATO nomination," Roger objected.

"Mr. President, I believe our allies will understand our withdrawal of forces but—" Bob Gilfort began.

"We have to ensure these moves aren't misinterpreted as a return to isolationism," Franco added.

"What about Israel? Without a forward deployed infrastructure, there is no way we can provide timely military support to Israel, if needed," Roger argued.

"Mr. President, I think September 11, 2001, negates any policy of isolationism. We have to remain engaged. Remnants of Al-Qaida still remain out there, plotting to kill more Americans and destroy Western civilization."

"Gentlemen." President Crawford rubbed his eyes a few times as he answered. "I don't intend to tell the allies we are disengaging or even withdrawing our forces until we have unwrapped ourselves from North Africa with the exception of one. I will tell the prime minister of Great Britain. We have a phone call scheduled for later today."

"What if—"

"I know, Franco," President Crawford interrupted, holding his hand up toward his national security advisor. "It is a chance we take that he may decide to share this information with the French or Germans. Personally, I don't think he will. Most of the British are aghast over the Royal Navy steaming with a French battle group and having no overt links with the United States Navy. Plus, the fact that they are under the command of a French general pisses them off. I think we have an opportunity to throw a wrench into the European Union and it's anti-American stance, and this will do it. Back to the matter at hand. Withdrawal from the Med."

"If we withdraw Navy and Air Force elements from Europe and the Mediterranean, we will redeploy them immediately to Korea. Bob, the game plan will be once we start to execute it, you will inform our European allies about us withdrawing our troops from the Balkans. I will call our two favorite leaders in Paris and Berlin to tell them the necessity for such an action. I believe they'll understand. I'll tell the prime minister when we talk later today." President Crawford shut his eyes as he pinched his nose again. He felt drained. He had had less than a couple of hours' sleep last night, and since this started, the longest period had been six hours. Even he knew the toll was showing. An opportunity to lie down provided little sleep. Current events mixed with concern about his wife and the knowledge that what actions he took could mean to the future of the United States whirled through his thoughts. Looking up, he said, "Sorry, Bob, you were saying?"

"If we fail to reestablish a presence in Europe when the Korean conflict is over, then we lose what influence we enjoy in NATO and on an individual basis with some of our more important allies. Never before in our modern history have we needed to increase resources in our diplomatic service. If we are reducing military presence, then we must increase diplomatic presence and engagement. Otherwise, our leverage as a world power will suffer greatly," he pleaded.

"Always that chance, Bob. I didn't say we wouldn't return to Europe. I'm not even saying we will leave the Mediterranean. What I am saying is that if we have to pull our forces out for Korea, then they may not want us back, and we may even reach the conclusion that America's best interests are better served elsewhere. It is something we will have to think about during the months to come." The last two years of his second term were supposed to be devoted to establishing an enduring legacy for his administration, not fighting some godforsaken war—oops! Military action—in Korea and watching Americans die on both sides of the globe.

Franco picked up the black notebook off the floor beside his chair. "Mr. President, the polls show the American people are still behind you—"

"Franco, they will still be behind us when we leave Europe. They will not be behind us if we lose. Americans hate losers, and they hate to discover themselves in that position. We have never been losers in our history, and we do not tolerate losers or losing well. The American people will never forgive an administration that promulgates an image of our country that is less than one that stands above the rest. We must win in Korea." Crawford looked at the secretary of state. "Bob, have you had any success with the Chinese in getting them to use their influence with the North Koreans?"

Bob shook his head. "They continue to remonstrate that they have no influence. They tell us they are in talks with the North Korean leadership. Candidly, they offered an informal and nonattributable comment that further successes on the battlefield will cause the North Koreans to cease this misadventure. I believe they truly do want the North Koreans to stop this action and that they are working behind the scenes to get them to return past the thirty-eighth parallel."

"See, gentlemen, even our most favored trade partner and world nemesis recognizes we have to have combat victories in Korea for the combat operations there to cease."

"We are having combat successes, Mr. President. We are driving them back."

"You mean we *were* driving them back, Roger. For the past two days, it seems to me the offensive has been stalled a few miles north of Seoul. How far have we driven them back? Sixty miles? I wouldn't say the North Koreans are in full flight."

"What is it you propose, sir?" Bob asked, glancing at Roger.

"We do control the air," Roger offered.

"Just what I said, Bob. Continue our offensive, even if we are only inching forward, and end the North African operation. I don't want us to have to withdraw. It sends the wrong message to the world. We will not forget nor forgive the Libyans for sinking the USS *Gearing*. We will extract our pound of flesh from them, but we may have do it later. We have lost four warships in the European Theater and not one off Korea, and the action is hotter in Korea. Roger, you have two weeks to wrap it up."

"We have only lost two, Mr. President," Franco interrupted.

"Four warships, if you count the two in Gaeta, Italy, who had their sterns blown off by a car bomber."

"Not blown off, damaged, Mr. President," Roger corrected.

"Two weeks! Mr. President, we still have fifty hostages being held God knows where by the Algerian rebels, and intelligence reports that Libya is in the middle of another coup. If we pull out in two weeks, we could leave a war behind us."

"A war that Europe will have to handle," President Crawford said softly. "This is what I want you three to do, and I don't want to read about it tomorrow in the *Washington Times* or *Post*. I want it close-hold. I don't want someone else working this. I want you three to work it. I want a strategy that does just what I said with the best possible domestic and global spin on it. I want the world to see America as the military superpower it is. We know that if the wrong spin is placed on this withdrawal from Europe, it will be viewed as a major chink in our armor as the world's lone remaining superpower. That is one reason, Bob, you will do whatever is necessary to win Admiral Hastings's approval by NATO. I want him in place within the next two weeks. But, Bob, I want a backup position in the event we are unable to get him confirmed before news leaks that we are considering pulling out of Europe."

He pointed his pencil at Franco. "You, I want preparing the press releases and chronological order of events to ensure a proper spin on our withdrawal from the Balkans. Franco, I know how you love to play spin doctor. This time, do the good job that I know you can. While I doubt all of you agree with me, I view how we do this in the coming days, weeks, and months as determining America's future as the world leader. And, Roger, it is four we have lost. Two sunk and the two Sixth Fleet ships in Italy the car bomb damaged. They can't get under way on their own power, can they? So, they are lost to us."

Franco nodded and scribbled furiously as he made notes.

"And keep those notes with you. Don't leave them lying around your desk like all the others."

"Yes, sir."

"This may also affect our economic leadership, Mr. President," Bob Gilfort added.

"Yes, Bob, it may. I would say little would hurt our military superpower status, whether our forces return to Europe at their current level or we keep them in the United States. We may go to a rapid deployment idea the Army and Air Force have developed or start a rotating deployment schedule among service elements like the Navy does with its blue-gold crew concept."

The president stood and began to pace. Roger called it his "professor" trait. "Even with funds we diverted to force through my health plan, we are still the world's only superpower. I don't buy this Republican bullshit of it being a hollow force. It isn't, and our military are proving it."

He waved his hand, making a point. "What most people don't realize is that when we finished World War II, we finished it as the only country to come out of it with a healthy economy. Roosevelt's policy brought us out of the Depression and gave our economy a healthy shot in the arm. That healthy post–World War II economy made the U.S. dollar the bellwether for determining global wealth and economic health. No other currency has ever competed with it . . . until now. We may say publicly positive words about the euro, but the euro is a threat to American economic hegemony."

He pulled a dollar bill out of his pocket and held it up. "The euro is already used by major global businesses as a comparative currency with the U.S. dollar. This small piece of currency"—He waved the dollar bill—"has held world confidence for more than seventy years. If something happens to cost the U.S. dollar this confidence, the euro will gleefully ease right into its place. We will find ourselves in the same predicament the British did after World War II when they had no option but to watch the U.S. dollar replace the pound as the international currency of choice. Make no bones about it. The euro is a threat, which is another reason I intend to lay before the prime minister of Great Britain a proposal the British lion will find hard to turn down." He paused for a moment. "Ironically, we thought the euro was dying in the first ten years of its existence. I figured at any moment during those years to see European governments pulling away from the concept and returning to their own currency, but here it is nearly twenty years later, and the euro flourishes and threatens our economic hegemony."

He tossed the dollar bill on the desk. "I don't need to tell you what will happen to America's leadership if global confidence is lost in it. Worst case is the euro will become the primary currency for determining world economic health. If that happens, we will find our economy not just in a gradual decline but in a rip-roaring recession as people and nations trade U.S. dollars for euros. Keep that in mind as we go down this road. Other world powers in the past have had this same challenge, and none of them survived it. We will, and you must keep that foremost in your consideration. America can survive these challenges to its military might, but the underlying economic threat is far more sinister and dangerous. Bluntly, we can lose the Korean conflict and even the bulk of our military involved in it, and we would still remain the world's only superpower. However, if we lose our economic hegemony, then America begins a quick descent from its place as world leader and we will slowly return to isolationism. We will become just one more player at the table of global stakes with little influence as we follow Europe's lead. No, gentlemen, it is better to lose an entire Army division or Navy battle group than for the world to lose confidence in our economic banner.

"I am not going to allow that to happen. We are going to come out of this crisis stronger economically and militarily. How? That is what I need you to come up with: a plan that takes us through this critical period in American history. A period that can just as well mark the decline and fall of America's leadership. When I finish with the prime minister, we will have thrown some discord and discontent among our European allies and that, gentlemen, is what we need as we extricate ourselves from these military actions."

The three men, energized, assured President Crawford they could do it.

"Good. Franco, what is the latest on Senator Patton's call for a War Review Committee? Jesus! You'd think a senator would have enough sense not to call it a war. That's another thing,

Franco, you get word out to the Executive Branch that these are not wars we are involved in. They're *military operations*."

"Yes, sir. I will ensure it is done before lunch, Mr. President."

"Good," Crawford said, nodding. He tossed the pencil to one side. He ran his hand through his hair again.

Bob Gilfort's eyebrows bunched slightly as he watched the burdened president grab the pencil again and start to drum it on the table. Times like these made him thankful his own thoughts of trying for the presidency years ago never rose beyond the *should I or shouldn't I* point.

"Mr. President, Senator Patton will use this War Review Committee to investigate your handling of the two crises. What I have discovered is he will place the sinking of the USS *Gearing*, USS *John Rodgers*, and the other military setbacks in both North Africa and Korea directly on the doorstep of the administration. Being kin to General George Patton doesn't hurt his agenda or credibility. He enjoys great popularity with the American people and will use this highly visible committee to further his own presidential aims. With the presidential race less than two years off, this is a great opportunity to slam-dunk the administration and earn some free press for him."

The president rolled his chair back and stood, crossing his arms. He voiced his thoughts to the three men as he walked back and forth. "I think the American people will see through his charade as a political gambit, don't you?"

When no answer came immediately, President Crawford stopped and faced Franco. "You don't, do you?"

"Mr. President, I am concerned if the wrong spin is put on it, the attention of the media will be more on him and his committee and their interpretation of the crises. This attention will provide Patton a forum to shout to the American people that the administration failed to act properly. I have this nightmare of the news media screaming how our failure to maintain military readiness caused the deaths of these American sailors. How cutting the defense budget was directly . . ." Franco paused and in a low voice that slowly rose in tempo said, "I have this nightmare of Senator Patton dancing around the White House screaming, 'Killer,' with CNN broadcasting it to the nation as he dances. Mr. President, he will twist and maneuver the committee to every advantage to make you and this administration look bad . . . how you shirked America's global and national responsibilities." Franco took a deep breath and then softly added, "Of course, sir, I am trying to put the worst face on it."

"Well, you're doing a damn good job, Franco. I would hope it wasn't the best face. And I can't imagine Senator Patton dancing around the White House." President Crawford looked at Bob Gilfort and Roger Maddock and smiled. "Makes the mind boggle with the thought of Patton with his two hundred pounds plus twisting and turning around the White House."

"May be, sir," Franco added softly, "But twisting and turning with words is what Patton does best."

The president nodded. "I know, Franco. What do you gentlemen propose we do to lessen the impact of this committee?"

Bob cleared his throat and set his cup of coffee on the low coffee table in front of him and Roger. "Sir, I would recommend calling the Democratic leadership in both houses and put pressure on them to delay this committee until after the conflict. You have enough on your mind. Shift some of this political battle to the Hill, where it belongs."

"I have already talked with Senator Hill and Congressman Ford. They have already begun to rally our forces," Franco added.

"Maybe I should call the Senate majority leader, Senator Miller."

Franco's eyes widened and he shook his head roughly. "No, sir. Don't do that! If you call him, when the media discovers it—probably within minutes after you hang up—they'll interpret it as weakness in the administration, of you caving in to the Republicans. That nose of Senator Patton will be twitching with the smell of blood. He'll intensify everything he's doing in a leap for the jugular."

President Crawford smiled. "Franco, I thought he was already going for the neck. You have this nightmare of Senator Patton dancing around the White House. I have one of my head on a stake in front of the Senate with Patton and his cronies chanting while wearing blue-painted faces and dancing around it."

"Shouldn't have watched that old movie *Braveheart* the other week, sir," Roger Maddock said, drawing a short round of laughter from the men.

"Thanks, Roger. Sometimes those old movies relax me." President Crawford touched the spot on his nose where Bethesda surgeons had removed a small growth a month ago. The gesture made him think of his wife for a few seconds, shut up in the Navy hospital only six miles away. He sat down again. *Up and down, up and down,* he thought. *So many things to do to run this nation.*

"Okay, Franco. You win. I won't call Paul yet. However, I will keep the option open. Why don't you see—low level, of course—if you can get him to call me."

"Yes, sir, Mr. President." Franco did not intend to call Miller's office. He would let the president's request simmer for a couple of days and by then, President Crawford would have either forgotten he asked Franco to have the senator call or the War Review Committee would be dead.

"We still need to develop a course of action, a strategy, on how to handle the War Review Committee. It starts next week."

"Mr. President," Franco said, "we need to take the initiative away from Senator Patton. And we can do it by displaying the strength of character that has been the hallmark of your administration."

"How do you propose we do this, Franco?"

"I know we discussed this last week, and I know you opposed it at the time, but I would like to ask you to reconsider relieving Admiral Cameron." Franco held up his hand when he saw President Crawford open his mouth to speak. Out of the corner of his eye, he saw Roger Maddock uncross his legs and lean forward.

"Sir, we can take the initiative away from Senator Patton by relieving Admiral Cameron and bringing him back. You do that, you take the teeth out of that committee for a time because the media will focus on the admiral."

"You relieve him, you'll piss off every patriotic American in the nation," Roger Maddock said angrily. "The man has lost his wife in a terrorist attack, and you want to use him as a political sacrifice!"

President Crawford shook his head and raised his pencil toward Donelli, who began to speak faster, running his words together like a machine gun, ignoring the secretary of defense's outburst.

"Hear me out, please, Mr. President. Admiral Cameron was

the senior Navy person in charge when the USS *Gearing* was attacked and sunk. It was under his leadership the ship was conducting the Freedom of Navigation operation within Libyan territorial waters. It was under his leadership that the USS *LaSalle* and that other ship—what was her name?—USS *Mount Whitney*?"

"No, Franco," Roger said, his voice betraying irritation. "*Simon Lake*. USS *Mount Whitney* is the flagship for the Second Fleet."

Franco waved his hand, dismissing the difference. Second Fleet, Third Fleet—too many Goddamn fleets in his book.

"And USS *Simon Lake* were attacked and sent to the bottom," Franco finished.

"Weren't sent to the bottom," Roger corrected testily. "The car bomb damaged their sterns, causing their sterns to settle on the bottom. Both ships are raised now."

"And the Navy recognizes Cameron's responsibility. Last week, after Cameron finished burying his wife, he visited the chief of naval operations, who personally informed him that eventually he was going to have to explain the events surrounding the sinkings. The only reason the Navy hasn't recalled him to Washington is because of the current combat operations ongoing in Korea and North Africa. If we do this, it isn't going to surprise Cameron. He is a career Navy officer. They expect to be relieved when something goes bad while they are in charge. It is part of their heritage. It's a Navy thing, Mr. President. We may even disappoint him if we don't relieve him! We use this Navy tradition of responsibility as part of our administration. Show the American people we can make the hard decisions, even when it goes against our grain."

President Crawford held up his hand. "Enough, Franco. You have asked me twice to relieve this man. He may have been in charge when"—He waved his hands in the air—"all this happened. But the man lost his wife and right now is leading the Navy efforts in that theater. There are a lot of things I do for the sake of the administration, but I like to think it is done with America's best interests at heart. I will not sacrifice a military person, regardless of their rank, for the purposes of relieving some political heat."

Then, softly, the president continued. "Besides, we are hurting for flag officers to lead our military operations. Why would

I bring him home if we don't have someone who can relieve him? The Navy just retired a rear admiral SEAL for something he did, and you want me to sacrifice a man who lost his wife in a terrorist attack that was trying to kill him? The press would slaughter me, and Senator Patton would grin all the way to the stake. And we both know who would be tied to it."

Franco looked at Roger Maddock, who was nodding furiously in agreement with the president. "Roger, Admiral Pete Devlin is on Cameron's staff, right?"

"I believe so. He was the commander of the Naval Air Forces in the Mediterranean but has been moved up as the second-in-command of Sixth Fleet."

Franco turned to the president. "Mr. President, this has been more of an air campaign than anything else in the last two weeks. If we relieve Cameron, then we order Devlin to take over."

Roger ran his hand through his hair. Did this man ever listen to the president or anyone else other than his own sly and devious mind? "You're wrong, Franco. The air operations are backup and defensive in nature right now. We have Marines occupying Algiers. The good news is the Army has rescued the Marines who were stranded in southern Algeria along with the American and allied evacuees who were with them. The only remaining American land operation in North Africa is the Algiers occupation, and as soon as the remaining American hostages are located and rescued, they will be departing."

"Even better, Mr. President. Since the Marines have the lead in the theater, then bringing back Admiral Cameron to face responsibility for the devastating attacks in the Mediterranean will not hurt the ongoing military operations."

Bob Gilfort glanced at the two antagonists in the room. He'd give Roger odds-on favorite in a free-for-all—probably with all of them—except for the president, who had a few pounds and inches of height on the buff secretary of defense. Times like these made him wish the draft or some sort of service to one's country had been retained in the United States. None of them in the room had any military experience. Bob knew Roger prided himself on the six years of listening and learning from admirals and generals and even captains and colonels who trekked in and out of his office on a daily basis. Bob nodded at the thought, causing Franco to think the secretary of state was agreeing with him.

Smart men and women never hesitate to learn from others, even those who many times they considered intellectually inferior. He knew he and Roger had their differences—professional, from Bob's viewpoint. Unfortunately, Roger was one of those people who found it hard to separate a professional difference from a personal one.

Bob had military friends, too. He knew admirals and generals managed multiple disciplines. You didn't put an Air Force general in charge of solely air or an admiral in charge of only sea or an Army or Marine Corps general in charge of just ground. Today's joint service flag officers were multidisciplined, as they like to say. Look at what they did, putting an Army general in charge of the Joint Task Force African Force. Admiral Cameron ran the earlier joint task force to conduct an evacuation operation, but when the evacuation became a hostage situation, the Joint Chiefs of Staff had renamed it African Force. As missions changed, usually joint task force designations changed. It helped to refocus military units on the tasks ahead.

"Admiral Devlin may be a good relief for Admiral Cameron, but Admiral Devlin has only been a two-star for less than a year, and if you fleet him up, as the Navy says, then you raise him to three-star. He may not be able to handle it," Roger objected. *Christ!* Was he going to have to go back to the Department of Defense and face his warriors with this news? It had taken him his entire tenure as secretary of defense to develop the level of confidence and trust they had in him now.

"Sure, he can handle it, Roger," Franco argued. "Have you looked at his record?"

"No, but—"

"Well, I have. He is a combat hero from Desert Storm, led air strikes against the Taliban in '01, and survived a shoot-down by the Iraqis in 2002."

"Well, maybe but—"

"Wait a minute, you two," President Crawford interrupted, holding up his hands. "Drop the issue of relieving Admiral Cameron. At this time, I am not going to circumvent the Navy's own investigation. Franco, if the Navy determines Cameron needs to be relieved, then we'll look into replacing him. But, I want the administration above this investigation. You are worried about me calling Paul Miller, but on the other hand, what would the press do if I personally ordered Cameron back before the Navy finished its own investigation?"

"Mr. President—"

"Enough, Franco. This time I am overruling you. What the press would say is that we are running scared of the War Review Committee and are using Cameron to keep lions off of the administration."

Franco shook his head. "No, sir, that isn't why we would bring him back—"

"Sure it is, Franco. You'd do anything to twist and mislead—" Roger added.

President Crawford held his hand up to stop the two. "We need to go on to other issues, gentlemen."

Roger shut his mouth, forcing himself to swallow the words he was about to shout. He drummed his fingers on the arm of the couch. *Someday, you little wimp,* he thought. Bob gently reached over and touched the secretary of defense's knee, which had begun to bounce up and down, shaking the couch. Catching Roger's attention, he winked.

"Mr. President, it is a very small risk we run if we bring Admiral Cameron back, but if we spin this—"

Roger's eyes narrowed. *Christ! Doesn't the man know the word stop?*

"Franco, I don't want to spin it. I don't want to throw a good person to the wolves to save our administration some embarrassment. I have enough on my mind without adding human sacrifice on top of it. Let the Navy handle it."

Franco leaned back. Roger took an audible breath, surprised, amused, elated that the president finally stood up to "Little Caesar."

"Yes, sir, Mr. President. You are right. It is something I should have thought of but didn't," Franco said, nodding in agreement. He was satisfied. He had gotten what he wanted. Within two days, he would have the Navy recall Cameron. The president and the administration would stand above it. They would refuse to intervene, saying the internal investigation by the Navy takes precedence, and they could argue effectively that the War Review Committee directly interfered with Cameron's rights. Oh, yes, he could milk this one. President

Cameron was right about keeping the administration above the investigation. Donelli never hesitated to change his own plans and ideas when better ones emerged or his own career dictated. He was the master of the spin and looked forward, in a perverse way, to the coming confrontation with Senator Patton much like a boxer looks forward to his or her next bout. He could balance the Cameron relief with orchestrating some sort of awards for the commanding officer of the USS *John Rodgers* and its crew. *What was the man's name?* He should remember it; it had been mentioned in the papers nearly every day.

Crawford nodded once and tossed the pencil on the desk. It rolled a few inches before coming to a rest against his coffee cup. "Good. We still need a plan on how to stall Patton's game. Franco, that is your job, so instead of trying to find a Christian to feed to the lions, go out and develop a solid counter to the War Review Committee." He stroked his chin. "Something legal, with a patriotic twist on how this committee hurts our men and women in Korea and the Mediterranean."

Franco nodded. "Yes, sir, Mr. President. I have put myself on your schedule for later today to discuss several options. A media blitz demonizing the War Review Committee as being ill timed along with being unpatriotic is an option. Should we also think about awarding some of these heroes the Medal of Honor?"

"Good, you're thinking on the right track, Franco. Find us two of three, but Franco, make sure they truly deserve the award. I do not want to denigrate the highest military honor in the nation because of politics."

The president rose and walked around to the front of the desk and leaned back against it. He crossed his arms. "Gentlemen, that about concludes everything but one tiny, tender item. My wife." He looked down. The president's voice broke slightly. "As you know, she is suffering from severe depression. Severe enough that if it had not been for the maid the other evening, I would be a widower today." President Crawford's throat tightened. He cleared it a couple of times. "Sorry," he said, looking at the three faces staring at him. "She has been in Bethesda for two days. It is only a matter of time before the press discovers the real reason for her admittance. In about ten minutes, I am going to Bethesda to see her and explain that I intend to go before the American people and tell them why she is in the hospital. I know she will understand and will allow me to do that. I think there is enough of the old Helen in her that she'll realize that it is better to be forthright about her condition."

"The press—" Franco started, leaning forward.

"The press will be sympathetic, Franco," President Crawford snapped. "Not all reporters are demons and devils. Most are common Joes and Janes who go home at night and take their clothes off just as we do. I remember a press club dinner I attended when I was a congressmen. Veteran Sam was there. He was old even then, and we can count ourselves lucky he's retired again and only comes out a couple of times a year to snipe at us. What I wanted to say was that Sam was one of the speakers, and he said something I have never forgotten. It was a simple thing we learn as children and probably forget as we spin and twist the English language so we can be elected. What he said was, 'Always tell the truth. If you don't we'll'— and he was referring to the press—'find out.' And, he is right."

"Telling the truth means never having to remember anything," Roger interjected.

Bob Gilfort, quietly scribbling in his notebook, looked up. "I think you are right, Mr. President. If you can convince your wife, Mr. President, and if she is able to be by your side when you tell the American people her problems, you will invoke the sympathy of the entire nation."

"That's right," interjected Franco, hardly bothering to keep the excitement out of his voice. "And, it will detract from the War Review Committee. It will put Senator Patton on the defensive. Anything he says against you, sir, will be seen as being unsympathetic to your personal problems. You should go on television to tell—"

"Franco, most times I really value your insight into the political process," President Crawford said softly. "Like you, I enjoy analyzing the polls every morning and trying to steer our administration along a course so we leave a legacy for the history books. But, if you have one fault, it is that you have the sympathy of a viper. Right now," President Crawford's voice rose, "I couldn't give a rat's ass about whether my wife's condition stifles the War Review Committee or not. What I care about is one very simple thing," he said, his voice breaking slightly. "I care that when my wife walks out of Bethesda and takes those twenty steps from the hospital to the car, that she isn't bombarded by news reporters who, through no fault of their own, upset her. So, I am going to tell them! And I am not going to mention the War Review Committee. I am not going to mention the combat operations in Korea or the Mediterranean. I am not going to mention anything other than how I would appreciate everyone's consideration for my wife as she meets this personal challenge in the days, weeks, months, and possibly years to come."

"Yes, sir, Mr. President, I didn't mean—"

"Franco, I know you didn't mean to make it sound so callous. You're just a product of your own imagination. You've been in politics so long that everything has to have a spin, a political value, for it to be useful. There is no doubt that if we lost both of these combat operations you could turn them into victories."

"Mr. President, I am truly sorry about Mrs. Crawford."

President Crawford walked over to the window and, with his hands behind his back, peered out at the Rose Garden. "You know, she used to enjoy walking through the Rose Garden. Said she always wondered how many other first ladies had walked the same paths. I wonder if she wonders how many first ladies walked where she is walking now."

He turned to face the three. "I appreciate you allowing me to share my personal concerns with you. It is unfortunate that as the president of the United States that personal problems are always in the public domain. Bob, thanks for reminding me that Helen's personal problems are, in fact, hers, and if she should have any concerns with me addressing those to the American people, then, of course, I won't."

Franco made another short note in his book. If President Crawford told the American people about his wife's depression, and he had the Navy relieve Admiral Cameron, then Patton's War Review Committee would be swept from the front pages. The War Review Committee would be page-three news behind the other two. By the time Patton could garner the press attention he needed, the two military operations might be over. The day looked brighter every minute.

"Thank you, gentlemen. Franco, double-check my schedule

for today. I am going to Bethesda, and I intend to take as long as necessary. So we may have to reschedule our meeting this afternoon."

Bob Gilfort and Roger Maddock excused themselves and departed the Oval Office. They walked side by side, turning the corner and leaving the immediate vicinity of the Oval Office.

"What do you think Franco will do?" Roger asked, watching Bob for a reaction.

Bob stopped, cocked his head, and looked at Roger. "Roger, you asking me my opinion?" He touched his chest.

"Yeah, I guess I am," he replied.

Bob smiled and took the secretary of defense's arm, turned him slightly toward him as they continued walking down the hallway. Old paintings of famous men and events lined the golden hall where a plush red plaid rug softened their footsteps.

"Well, Roger, I think this is one of the first times you have asked my opinion since we began seeing opposite sides of the Korean and North African problems."

"Bob, you want me to eat crow. I am sorry. There, I have eaten it. Now, tell me what you think Franco is going to do. You always seem to have better insight on these political games than I do."

"I think Franco is setting himself up to get the ax from Crawford. I have known Crawford a lot longer than Donelli has. Donelli is a spin doctor and a lover of polls. He will do anything to manipulate a poll. He misinterprets Garrett Crawford's political interests as a personal bond. Regardless of what others may think, Garrett has a high integrity level, and Franco will cross the president one of these days, and it will be Franco's failure to realize that not everyone thinks like he does that will cost him. Good chance that you and I will be spectators at the tower when the executioner's ax comes down. So, try not to laugh when it happens. Meanwhile, Franco is off to manipulate the polls."

"So, how is Franco going to do this manipulation?" Roger asked. He shook his head. "Bob, I'm getting a headache. Tell an old farm boy what you think Franco is going to do."

Bob laughed. "Roger, you aren't an old farm boy. You're from New York and not upper New York state. You're from New York City. Manhattan isn't it?"

Roger grinned. "Brooklyn, but we raised tomatoes on the rooftop."

"I would have thought you would have caught it. Franco is going to have the Navy relieve Cameron."

Roger stopped and stared at the secretary of state, who grinned at him. "But the president said to leave him alone."

Bob shook his head. "No, the president didn't. What the president said was *he* wasn't going to relieve Cameron. He told Franco he was leaving it to the Navy to make that decision. Franco will interpret that to mean he can act to have the Navy do it. He will leave that room convinced our beloved president told him to have the Navy relieve that poor admiral in the Mediterranean."

"That's not what I heard the president say."

Bob bounced his head a couple of times and bit his lip for a moment as his grin widened. "Unfortunately, Roger, it is what I also heard the president say. He agrees with Franco. Garrett Crawford didn't become president of the United States by being a poor politician. He has integrity, and he won't relieve the warrior, but in his heart he believes that what he is doing is right for the American people. Garrett also wants to put distance between him and what may prove to be an unpopular act. It will prove useful to the administration because it will declaw Patton and his cronies for a while."

"I don't know why I didn't interpret it that way." Roger ran his hand through his thick shock of hair.

Bob shook his head. "No reason for you to, unless your job responsibilities were the same as Donelli's."

The two men stopped at the end of the hallway. Roger stuck his hand out and shook Bob's. "Thanks, Mr. Secretary of State, for enlightening me."

"You are very welcome, Mr. Secretary of Defense," Bob replied, giving Roger a respectful nod. "Oh, by the way, Roger, I have already told the president. If Franco knows, it is because the president told him. However, since we seem to be healing any wounds between us, I want you to know that I will be leaving the administration at the end of the year. The president and I decided yesterday that it would be best for the country and the administration to delay the announced departure until after these crises are resolved."

"I am sorry to hear that, Bob. Any reasons that you would care to share?"

He laughed, "No specific reasons, Roger. I will be seventy next month, and I think I would like to spend some more time with my children and grandchildren and just take life a little easier."

# THREE

⚓

"WATCH THAT CAR, BEAU!" CAPTAIN DUNCAN JAMES shouted, throwing his hands over his eyes in mock horror.

"Christ, Commander, where did you learn to drive?" laughed Lieutenant Heather J. McDaniels, more affectionately known as HJ, as she bounced off the right rear door when Beau swerved.

"Can I take my hands down now?" Duncan asked jokingly, spreading his fingers wide to peer between them.

"Hey, you two, it you don't like my driving, get out of the car. I can't help it if these Italians have no rules-of-the-road skills," Lieutenant Commander Beau Pettigrew replied. He stuck his head out of the window of the tiny Fiat. The hot, dry Naples wind blew his blond hair off his forehead. "Hey, Buddy, you run out of flicker fluid?" He pulled his head back inside the car. "Don't they know what turn signals are for?"

"Did you see that? I know he doesn't even speak English and he flicked me off! I can't believe it!"

Duncan pulled his hands down. He and HJ laughed. Beau joined them. "I guess it's better than being gridlocked in Washington, which in two days we'll be."

"HJ, tell me again how those magic jocks from Bethesda healed that shoulder in only four weeks. When we were pulled out of the drink by the Brits, I figured you'd be evacuated to Rhein Main or even back to Bethesda. What were they called? Nano . . . what?"

HJ leaned forward, grabbed both men by the necks, and shook them playfully a couple of times. "It may be too complicated for a couple of old Navy SEALs to comprehend."

"I told you we should never have taken her to Capri with us. Besides, I'm not old; he is," Beau said, jerking his thumb toward Duncan.

"I think it was that second bottle of wine."

"You mean the one before she pinched that Italian waiter on the butt or afterwards?"

"Hey, come on, guys, he had nice cheeks."

"I can't say I go around looking at men's butts," Beau said, whipping the steering wheel to the right. The car barely missed another Fiat and started another round of car horns from the midafternoon traffic. "You know, I could get used to driving here. Reminds me of the back roads of Coweta County."

"Go ahead, HJ," Duncan said. "I'm not sure I understand how this nanotechnology works."

"Makes two of us," HJ replied.

"Three," added Beau. "Yeah, yours, too!" He reached forward to press the horn, and his arm hit the windshield wipers, sending them whipping back and forth, smearing dust across the glass. "Damn," he said, pulling the lever forward, sending a spray of water across the windshield to form a thin veneer of mud with the dust.

"Bethesda National Naval Medical Center sent what I would call a futuristic medical team to the naval hospital at Naples. I remember vaguely reading about this in magazines years ago. Once, while I was kicking back my heels in Washington, they assigned me to attend a briefing given by the Mitre Corporation out at McLean."

"Just what we need; futuristic Navy doctors. Now, there's something that makes your putter stutter. The only thing that could be worse would be futuristic lawyers," Beau added. "Get out of the road, creep! Where do you think you are? Baltimore, Maryland?"

"I know where Mitre is," Duncan said. "I drove by their headquarters every morning when heading for I-495."

"It appears Mitre has been one of the pushers for this technology. What the doctor said is that nanotechnology is the science of assembling individual molecules and atoms to build things. In this case, what they built were tiny surgeons. They took a hypodermic needle filled with yellow fluid and shot it into my shoulder wound. Apparently, this fluid had millions of tiny nanorobots designed to repair tissue, destroy bacteria and infection, mend the bones, and build more nanorobots if needed."

"Ah, go on with you," Beau said, his voice betraying his doubt. "You mean they shoot little robots into you, and those things in four weeks repaired a broken shoulder, torn blood vessels, and sewed the skin back together?"

"Something like that. It was a clean break on the shoulder; more a crack. I still have those little buggers in me. I was told they would eventually biodegrade—that's the word they used—and go out of my system via the normal means that everyone uses to discard food when they are finished with it. Dr. Abercombie said the nanoboys and nanogirls, as he calls them—personally, I prefer nanoboys and nanowomen—would eventually biodegrade and pass out of my body. Until they do, I guess you can call me Biowoman: scourge of the male race, hero of the underdog, and shopper extraordinaire. You ever notice that anywhere you go there is always something you can buy? Christ! Isn't life great?"

"I think you're right. I prefer nanowomen, too," Beau added and laughed.

"From what I have heard and others have seen, nanowomen are just about right."

Duncan laughed. "See, Beau, I told you I saw HJ peeking when you were showering the other night. But not to worry; it was a *short* shower."

"Caught me, Captain. I apologize, Beau. It was just that there were no comedy shows on TV, so I needed a *short* laugh." HJ laughed.

"Very funny. You two are definitely not *short* on humor," Beau replied. "Look, that's the turnoff to Capo, right? That looks like the guard shack."

"Yeah, but you've got to go—Oh, Christ, Beau!" Duncan shouted, grabbing the dashboard in front of him and gritting his teeth, eyes wide.

"Shit!" screamed HJ as she dove for the floor.

Beau turned left against the cars coming around the traffic circle where five roads met. He dodged the first two before whipping into the road on the left leading to the front gate of the American Navy headquarters in Naples. Car horns erupted in unison. Duncan heard two cars collide. He glanced out the back window to see traffic around the circle slow to a standstill.

"See, I told you two I'd get you here safely."

"I'm glad the car is in your name. You turn it in to the rental agency at the airport."

"What time does our aircraft leave?" HJ asked.

"We have a sixteen hundred hours show for an eighteen hundred hours go," Duncan replied. "We're about an hour early."

Beau slowed the car as they approached the gate. Two armed Marines in full battle gear and carrying M-16s moved toward the car. One approached with his hand up, cautioning them to stop while the other stayed back. Duncan noticed the one in the rear had his finger on the trigger and the barrel positioned in such a way that he could bring it up quickly.

Beau stopped the car and the Marine leaned down. "ID cards, please, sir."

Beau had his out and showed it to the Marine. The Marine looked in the window at Duncan and HJ. "Sorry, sir, ma'am; I need to see yours, also."

Duncan raised his hips and pulled his wallet out the left rear pocket. HJ tugged opened the large purse she carried and showed the gate guard hers.

"Thank you, ma'am."

Duncan held his up, too.

"Excuse me, Captain," the Marine said after scanning Duncan's ID card. "CTF Sixty-seven chief of staff asks that you come see her as as you report aboard."

Duncan shoved his ID card back in his pocket. "I don't suppose she passed on what she wants to see me about, Corporal?"

The Marine shook his head. "No, sir. This was passed through the sergeant of the guard, and I was told that I could look forward to extra duty if I missed you."

"Okay, thanks, Corporal."

The Marine took one step back and saluted.

Beau eased the car through the gate. Inside, on the right, covering the entrance, was a sandbagged machine gun pit. Hidden from sight, the machine gun backed up the Marines at the gate. Terrorists trying what they did at Gaeta when they car bombed the USS *LaSalle* and the USS *Simon Lake* would find pissed off Marines here.

"What do you think she wants?"

"I don't know. Probably to say good-bye and good riddance. Of course, she may want to discuss that incident with you the other night." Duncan slapped Beau on the arm.

"What incident?" HJ asked. She leaned forward. "Beau, have you been a bad boy again?"

"It was a minor one."

"I wouldn't call an Italian husband trying to shoot you a minor incident."

"He overreacted about me talking to his wife."

"Someone tried to shoot you for talking to his wife?"

"HJ, sometimes there are minor misunderstandings."

"Tell her the truth, Beau."

"Yeah, tell me the truth."

"I have."

"What Beau neglects to mention is that this conversation took two days and nights before her husband tracked them down in the middle of their *talking.*"

"I didn't know she was married," Beau explained.

"Didn't the wedding band on her left hand give you any indications?"

"Look, Navy regulations state that it's not adultery if the lights are out and you don't know each other's name."

"Beau, I think your Navy regulations changed a few centuries ago," HJ said, slapping him playfully on the back of the head and ruffling his blond hair.

Beau eased the car into a parking space marked for rental cars, turned off the engine, and pulled the emergency brake on.

"You want me to come with you?"

"No, I'll walk over and do the necessary good-byes. You two sign us in to the flight, and I'll be back shortly."

Duncan unwove his big frame from the car. The bones in his right knee ground and popped as he stood. He waited a few seconds for the pain to subside. Beau and HJ scrambled out the other side.

"You ought to have Dr. Abercombie look at that knee. I bet one shot of nanofluid could cure it," Heather J. McDaniels said, raising her arms over her head to stretch as she walked to the rear of the car. Her eyes twinkled with mischief.

She opened the trunk, pulled their seabags out, and set them on the pavement.

"If you do, have them put some up here," Beau said, tapping the side of his head. He grabbed two of the seabags and tossed them on the sidewalk in front of the car.

"I'll see you in about fifteen minutes." Duncan walked off, turned to the left, and headed toward the huge C4I—command, control, communications, computers, and intelligence—building that dominated the small U.S. Navy compound located on the opposite side of the Naples International Airport.


**BEAU AND HJ SAT DRINKING BEER AT ONE OF THE PATIO** picnic tables in front of the entrance to the small airport lounge, their seabags stacked behind them. They saw Duncan, raised their beers, and toasted him from under the huge multicolored sun umbrella raised over the austere white table and benches. He noticed they weren't smiling.

"Thanks, shipmate," Beau said.

"Nice job, Captain," HJ added, raising her beer toward him.

"I guess you heard," he said as he reached the table.

"Here, have a beer," Beau said, reaching down beside him and pulling a cold one from the brown paper sack beside him.

Duncan popped the top.

"So, what is the story that caused the air terminal to scratch us from the freedom flight to the States?"

"No easy way to tell you. We are going back to the fleet." He took a deep sip. He was surprised to discover the news barely bothered him. How it affected these two was the question. They both had reasons to return to Washington. With Beau, it was anything in a skirt, which was one reason they never sent him to Scotland. For HJ, her mother was being a pain. She had been bugging the hell out of her congressman and senators ever since she discovered her daughter had been wounded. It embarrassed the female SEAL no end, but Duncan had written the obligatory answers that seem to satisfy those esteemed members who represent the American public. He never knew what the tall shipmate said to her mother after the first letters arrived, but the one from the senior senator that followed two days after the congressman's was the last one he received. HJ had been apologetic, but Duncan knew if roles were reversed, he'd probably do the same thing to find out what in the hell was going on with his daughter—if he had a daughter.

As it was, Duncan and his wife had never had kids. No specific reason. Maybe they were never interested enough to go to the right medical people to find out who needed the help. Now it didn't matter. A week before North Africa blew up in the face of the United States, his wife had moved out one day while he was at work, leaving with a boy toy from the local Safeway grocery. Then, while he was sneaking off a submarine with Beau, HJ, and two SEAL teams to go into Algeria to rescue President Hawali Alneuf, she had returned to their home in Reston, Virginia, and cleaned the place out, only to return a couple of days later and move back in. The one remaining, nagging question was whether she intended to go through with the animal cruelty charges she filed against him when she discovered the dog in the old luggage trunk in the garage. He felt bad about the pet.

The night before they flew out of Dulles for the Sixth Fleet and the amphibious warship USS *Nassau*, Duncan had returned from a night of heavy drinking to discover their pet dog dead from a hit-and-run driver. He planned to bury the animal the next day, so he placed the body in a trunk in the garage rather than leave it where scavengers could get to it. Reston wasn't the country, but it was close enough to attract undesirable wildlife. Duncan left so abruptly the next day, he forgot the body in the trunk. He had mixed feelings about her finding it. She swore he intentionally killed the dog. When he returned, he would make it right with her, and the two of them could bury the whole thing unopened somewhere in the hills of Maryland. He shivered slightly over the idea of the smell that would whiff out of that trunk if opened.

"Beer too cold?" HJ asked, drawing Duncan out of his thoughts. She tugged the left khaki pants leg up and planted her foot flat on the bench. She rested her beer on her knee.

HJ was an attractive woman, Duncan thought, but the recent experience inside Algeria had aged her. She was pixie cute, something not usually associated with a six-foot-tall woman. Her apple-green eyes accented the sparse freckles around the sides of her snub nose. The one thing different from when he first met her that day, which seemed eons ago, in Rear Admiral William Tecumseh Hodges's office, was the sparkle seemed somewhat diminished in those eyes. That was to be expected. Her experience as a prisoner of the rebels would kill the spark in anyone's eyes. At six feet, the dark wavy brown haired warrior was a couple of inches taller than Beau.

"Why are we returning to the fleet, and where in the fleet are we returning to?" Beau asked, leaning forward on his elbows.

Beau was a thirty-nine-year-old bachelor, while Duncan was heading fast for his first divorce.

Beau's Nordic face, accented with neon-blue eyes, topped by waves of flowing brown hair turned blond by the hot Italian sun contrasted with Duncan's scarred, middle-aged, wrinkled face and too-broad nose between brown eyes framed by rapidly disappearing gray-speckled hair. Duncan ran his hand across the top of his head, wondering which would win the race for possession of the top; the two receding hairlines or the growing bald spot at the back of his head. He reached down and tried unsuccessfully to find that small pinch of middle-age spread he discovered before they left Washington. Beau's mischievous ways, unnatural boyish good looks, and being a most eligible bachelor drew women like moths to a flame. Duncan rubbed his chin. Of course, Beau was more than ten years younger— eleven, to be exact.

"We are going to the aircraft carrier, USS *Stennis*, where the other team members are waiting for us." Duncan took a sip of Beau's beer and handed the can back to his number two. "Sorry," he said, grabbing his own.

"Other team members? You mean Monkey, McDonald, Gibbons, and all of them?"

"That's right, HJ."

"Let's not forget my partner in pain, Ensign of the Fleet Bud Helliwell," added HJ, raising her beer. "And a small sip for him." Bud and HJ had been wounded together in the same combat action. She finished the beer and crushed the aluminum can before tossing it into a nearby trash can. "See what those nanowomen can do when they're surging through your veins?" she said, doubling her fist and flexing her bicep.

"Doesn't count if you don't crush it using your forehead."

"What happens after we arrive, boss?" HJ asked.

"You two remember Bashir?"

"Yeah. How could we forget that overweight smuggler? By now, he should own most of Algeria. He seemed related to everyone in the country."

"And, Beau, don't forget that laugh of his," HJ added. "I wanted to sew his mouth shut by the time we parted company. He laughed when he was amused, he laughed when they were shooting at us, and he was laughing when he left us on that wooden dock where the rebels trapped us. If it hadn't been for that old water carrier, we'd still be fighting."

"He also found a doctor in the middle of the desert to give you his last batch of antibiotics, HJ," Duncan added. He tipped the can back and drained the last few drops of beer.

"True, Captain. If he hadn't, I probably would have died, you think?" HJ pulled another beer from the brown paper bag beside the picnic table.

"No, I don't think you would have died, HJ," Beau said, standing to toss his empty can into the trash. "God doesn't want you, and the devil won't have you. You're going to live to a ripe old age and punish the world by having too many offspring."

"May only have one."

"One may be too many. Go ahead, Duncan. What, pray tell, do we owe to our friend Bashir that caused the United States Navy to cancel our freedom flight back to civilization?"

Duncan pulled the tab, opening the fresh beer. Beau took the empty Duncan had set on the table and tossed it over his shoulder. The can hit the rim of the trash can, bounced from one lip to the other, and fell in.

"Two points; *dos puntos,*" HJ said, taking two fingers and dipping them in the classic basketball sign. She took her foot down and straddled the bench, placing her beer between her legs.

"Seems he knows where those American hostages are in Algiers, but he won't talk to anyone but us."

"Us?"

"Well, me, to be specific."

Beau grinned and threw his arms out. "There you are, Duncan. HJ and I can head back." He looked at HJ, who grinned and nodded. They clicked their beer cans together. "We'll be thinking of you, boss."

"Well, you'll be thinking of me while with me. The higher-ups believe we SEALs are better qualified to rescue the hostages after Bashir tells us where they are. The sooner we free those hostages, the sooner we detach ourselves from Algiers and head home. Let them fight it out among themselves on who controls that country. Sometimes you just have to give war a chance. The other thing"—Duncan looked around to make sure no one was within listening distance—"is that two days ago, the rebels executed a hostage. They are threatening to kill one every forty-eight hours unless we remove our forces from Algiers."

Beau ran his hand through his sun-bleached hair. HJ wondered how in the hell he could continuously ruffle that thick blond hair and it would just fall back into place as if he had never touched it. He was also a pain in the ass sometimes—a male chauvinist, her libber friends would call him. However, for all the joshing they did with each other, she had grown confident in her friendship with the senior officer. Not a romantic closeness, but shipmate close. That strange, intimate bond between shipmates and buddies was something that seldom occurred between the sexes in peacetime, but it was amazing what bullets and blood mixed with fear and adrenaline created. She wondered what they would say when she told them she had decided to get out of the SEALs.

"They want us to go in and rescue the hostages?"

"They know that I am qualified in hostage rescue. They also know that you are, too, Beau." He looked at HJ. "As for you, my fine Navy SEAL who has yet to do a true exercise, they heard about your nanowomen, and they want all hundred thousand of you to go with us."

HJ slapped her arm, looked down at it, and whispered, "I told you little shits to behave and keep quiet. But, no, you've got to tell the world our secret." She looked at the two of them. "Oh, no!" she shouted. HJ straightened her arms and bounced erratically on the bench for a few seconds, drawing grins from the two men. "I never should have hurt their feelings," she said, draining her beer.

"Another item of interest. Rear Admiral William Tecumseh Hodges has quietly retired."

"What!" Beau said, standing up. "Our fearless leader in Washington?"

"What does that mean?" HJ asked.

Duncan shrugged his shoulders. "Could mean a lot of

things. Hodges met for an hour with Admiral Farmer, chief of Naval Operations, last week. Afterward, Rear Admiral Hodges announced his retirement for undisclosed personal reasons. Less than two days later, he went on terminal leave."

"Does this mean they will move Admiral Goodwin from Coronado to take over the Navy's SEALs?"

"Can't. He is in a joint billet, and you aren't allowed to transfer out of those until your tour of duty is up. He just got there eight months ago. Besides, he has forward deployed to Korea to take charge of the joint Special Operations forces being sent there."

"No, they fleeted up the deputy, Captain Ray Jordan, as the interim head. I know Ray. Good man. Seriously wounded during the Liberian Crisis and never fully recovered from the wounds. Same operation that Bud was wounded in. Ray has lots of medical problems associated with those wounds that never seem to get resolved. He had another surgery just last year. The good news is that Jordan knows what we SEALs in the field need to do our jobs. The bad news is I don't think he'll be able to handle the job long with his medical problems, and he has all the tact of a sledgehammer when it comes to Washington politics."

"Not like you, the master of tact," Beau added with a wink. "And better not let the Navy look at those knees of yours," Beau added.

Duncan slapped his right knee. "They feel better every day I don't run."

"Running keeps you fleet of foot and in great shape," HJ added.

"I have always thought being fleet of foot was not exactly a good quality for a military leader to brag about."

"Wasn't Hodges watching your place for you in Reston?"

Duncan guffawed. "He sent me periodic updates on what my soon-to-be ex-wife was doing to it." He took a long swallow of the beer, the coolness of it lost to the hot afternoon sun. Duncan moved slightly to the right into the shadow of the umbrella. A slight wind whipped up the brown dust from the ground, causing the three to squint their eyes for several seconds.

Beau tilted his head, drained his beer, and crushed the can before tossing it into the nearby trash can. "I would sure like to know why they retired him. Everything I've read in the *Stars and Stripes* newspaper says we are hurting for flag officers in all the services. The Department of Defense has even convened special officer and enlisted promotion boards this week for all four services. The newspapers are saying the military is considering recalling military retirees to fight. Then, we go retire the head of the Navy SEALs! Now, what's wrong with this picture? He had to have done something terrible to piss off the CNO to retire him."

"The news will leak, Beau, and then we'll all know." But Duncan already knew the reasons for the forced retirement of Admiral Hodges. The CTF Sixty-seven chief of staff had the personal-for message sent by the chief of Navy Operations to all flag officers, revealing the reasons. Rear Admiral Hodges had colluded with several others—who had also been retired—to make sure women failed to make the grade in the SEALs. The discovery by Navy leadership resulted in a closed-door admiral's mast and a quick retirement announcement by Rear Admiral Hodges. Captain Ray Jordan was a placeholder while the Navy scrambled to identify a new admiral to assume the leadership mantle. What Duncan figured without the chief of staff telling him was the woman Hodges wanted to fail had been HJ McDaniels. The pieces of the puzzle fell into place as he walked from his office to the picnic area in front of the terminal. Hodges had led Duncan to believe he was heading to a joint exercise with the Spanish, but it had turned into a rescue operation of the last democratically elected president of Algeria. He knew now he had been chosen because Hodges expected Duncan to be angry and vindictive over being told by the Bureau of Naval Personnel to retire from the Navy by August. Hodges, a master of the political art, had insisted that Duncan submit a positive endorsement on HJ's performance, thinking that would further anger him. Hodges must have thought Duncan would be so angry he would sink the women in the SEALs initiative. You can only play negative politics so long, and it boomerangs against you. Here it was August; he was still on active duty, HJ had performed admirably and heroically in combat, and Hodges was gone. And here he sat, licking his lips and enjoying life. A smile escaped.

"Ain't funny, boss." Beau opened another beer. "What other good news do you have for us?"

"Apparently, all Selected Early Retirement Board nominees—such as myself—have been unilaterally deselected."

"You don't have to retire?"

Duncan reached down and wiggled another beer free of its plastic holder. He shook his head. "No. According to the message, a stop-loss action has been initiated Navy-wide. SERB results are canceled, and selections will not be reinstated. So, if they want to forcibly retire me now, they will have to wait for another SERB to meet. At this rate, I could be drawing Social Security by the time I walk out the Navy's door."

"You look old enough to draw it now."

"He does not, Beau," HJ said, grinning. "But it is nice having a father figure around."

They laughed.

"As long as it isn't a grandfather figure."

"Give it a year."

"There is a COD due about an hour from now," Duncan said, referring to the small two-engine propeller-driven airplane used by aircraft carriers to ferry passengers, mail, and small parts between shore and ship. "It's going to do a hot landing; shove us on board and fly back to the *Stennis*. The new commander of Joint Task Force African Force, General Lewis, and Commander U.S. Sixth Fleet Admiral Cameron want to talk to us before we move ashore."

"I thought Cameron was back in the States."

"I did, too. I read in *Stars and Stripes* that he buried his wife. I really expected them to relieve him. Having an Army three-star come in and take over may mean the powers that be plan on jerking Admiral Cameron out of theater soon."

HJ put her beer down on the bench and coughed twice; spittle hit the two men. "Sorry. I was trying to talk and drink at the same time."

"I know. I have the same problem with chewing gum when I'm walking." Beau made an exaggerated show of wiping his face.

"Why do you think they will relieve him?" she asked.

Duncan shrugged his shoulders. HJ noticed the ripples his biceps made in the tight khaki shirt. Amazing, she thought, that a forty-eight-year old man could be in such great shape.

"The Navy is not very forgiving when it comes to command. Our tradition heaps responsibility on its leaders. When they succeed and win, they are praised. When they lose, they are removed. For whatever we want to say about Admiral Cameron—and I, for one, believe him to be a great leader and an outstanding Navy officer—he was in charge when three ships in his command were damaged or sunk. It is only because the USS *John Rodgers* was sunk west of Gibraltar that he doesn't have the responsibility for it. Commander in chief, U.S. Naval Forces Europe controls the waters west of Gibraltar. I think of it as luck and good leadership when you have a good command tour, for everything that happens, whether intentional or serendipitous, becomes the commander's responsibility. Yeah, they will eventually call him before the green table. They usually relieve the HMFIC, convene a court-martial, and let the bones fall where they may."

"HMFIC?"

"Head Mother Frigger in Charge."

"Frigger?" Beau asked, cocking his head to one side. "Are we becoming politically correct in our old age?" He rummaged around inside the brown paper bag.

"But, they didn't relieve him. If that is what they normally do, why didn't they relieve him?"

Duncan stood, lifted his seabag, and threw it across his shoulder. "I think it is because of the North Korean invasion on the other side of the world, HJ. We lack the senior officers to command two major conflicts; so, for the time being, Admiral Cameron stays here. I have read some of the editorials and newspaper articles that lay the blame directly on his lack of leadership. I would submit anyone in the same position would still have been caught with his or her pants down. We had no warning, no idea the attacks were coming. If we had, he would have been ready."

"Why didn't intelligence warn us? Where were the CIA when we needed them?" HJ asked, lifting her seabag.

"Staring at their computer terminals, probably," Duncan said. "It's not like we have the intelligence apparatus we had at the end of the twentieth century. Too many funding and personnel cuts."

Beau folded the top down on the sack. "Empties," he said to them.

Beau grabbed his seabag. "Empty," Duncan said and tossed

his can into the trash before starting toward the door marked Departures.

"No. All he has gotten is a little time. When this winds down enough, they'll come for him. According to the chief of staff, Rear Admiral Pete Devlin, the former commander, Task Force Sixty-seven in charge of Naval Air Forces in the Mediterranean, has been fleeted up to deputy commander, United States Sixth Fleet. Captain Dick Holman turned over command of the USS *Stennis* to his XO and has assumed Devlin's old title. The chief of staff of CTF Sixty-seven, she has been given command of all the shore and support responsibilities. So the changes they are occurring and, taking a step back and looking at them, those changes don't bode well for Admiral Cameron."

Duncan opened the door. "Well, team, should we go sign up for our scenic flight back to the fleet? And remember, there are no bathroom facilities on the COD, so get rid of that beer you drank before we board, or you're going to have a rough ride out."

# FOUR

⚓

**ALQAHIRAY STOPPED ABRUPTLY. HE GLANCED BEHIND HIM.**
Sergeant Adib and his soldiers had the two intelligence officers
sandwiched between them, shoving and pushing the two down
the lighted corridor. What a great opportunity to see how his expensive Russians had paid off. He turned and continued his
walk, enjoying the sounds behind him.

Two hundred yards farther down the corridor, Alqahiray
stopped at the door to a gigantic freight elevator. A divided steel
door opened in the center, with the top half drawing up as the
bottom half slid into a receptacle. "I thought we would take this
one since there are so many of us. I would hate our two guests
to be forced into a smaller elevator without much company. Not
that I believe they would try to escape, being loyal Libyan soldiers. Right? After all, we are already a couple of hundred feet
underground."

"No, Colonel, not me," a high, trembling voice replied.

Alqahiray looked at the whimpering prisoner, who nearly
tripped drawing back. He chuckled. "No, I don't believe you
would."

Even when he was shot, Alqahiray believed he maintained
his composure. Bravery and honor ran together. Cowardice and
dishonor were unforgivable, two states to which no military of-

ficer should ever succumb. He thought of Walid and Samir, and a fresh wave of anger flooded him. His shoulder still ached from the abuse he allowed himself to indulge: beating Mintab and slapping the prisoner.

They crowded into the freight elevator. Alqahiray reached forward with a small key and turned a lock on the controls. He withdrew the key and pressed the button for the lowest area of the compound. The keys should have been the one thing Walid took when they confined him to his house. Walid knew about the keys, but he never demanded them or tried to take them. Alqahiray considered it just one more sign of incompetence on the part of his former aide. Four floors down, the elevator stopped, and they stepped into another white world—a white world dominated by the sweet pine smell of disinfectant.

Across from the elevator, four large double-paned observation windows, reaching from a foot above the floor to the ceiling, ran along the corridor, allowing the visitor to look without entering. On the other side of the windows, six men in long, white frocks moved silently around the laboratory. Long, white rubber gloves reached past their elbows, and each wore protective helmets that snapped seamlessly onto the white frocks. Microscopes, centrifuges, and a bunch of unknown scientific devices decorated the numerous tables.

"This way," Alqahiray said to everyone, knowing he was the only one of the group to have ever been here. Only a few trusted sources knew this secret. Walid and Samir had been two of the trusted ones.

They moved down the corridor. Inside the laboratory, one of the scientists moved parallel with them until they reached the end. When Alqahiray disappeared behind concrete walls, the man entered the cleansing cell and turned the knobs on the controls. A strong jet of steam blasted him from several different directions, killing anything that might be on his protective suit. It shut itself off automatically after a half minute. The scientist opened the shower door and immediately stepped into another shower stall. Green foam shot out from several nozzles strategically located to cover every aspect of the suit. The man shut his eyes as ultraviolet lights saturated the small room for forty-five seconds. The suit kept the strong, acrid smell of disinfectant from burning his nostrils. Of course, the mild sulfuric acid would have burned him without the protective garment. When the ultraviolet lights went out, he opened his eyes, reached up, took a mobile showerhead off a hook, and self-administered the disinfectant into the hard-to-reach spots such as the crotch and under the arms. Satisfied, he hung up the showerhead and moved to the third stall. Pressurized air blew against him, forcing the air back toward the second stall, keeping the air from the laboratory trapped inside the entryway.

The scientist waited until the door shut between him and the first two stalls. Jets of steaming water came on automatically and washed the green solution off. Finished, he stepped out of the shower to a nearby bench and began methodically removing his outfit. The protective clothing went onto the floor, leaving the man in his underwear. Another scientist standing nearby, wearing thick plastic gloves, reached down and tossed the gear into a nearby container.

"Don't want that to remain here long, do we, Vasilev?"

Vasilev Malenkomoff removed the underwear and tossed it into the same container.

Alexei tightened the cover and stepped back. "A quick shower, and you can join our friends," he said.

Vasilev stepped into a normal shower stall. He turned on the shower, slapped the dispenser lever several times, took the soapy antibacterial solution, and lathered himself from head to toe, not forgetting between his legs, his butt cheeks, and his toes. Carefully, he scrubbed every inch of his body before washing his hair thoroughly three times. Only then did he step out of the shower into a dressing room, where his normal clothes waited. Ten minutes it had taken to shower down. Five minutes later, he walked out of the sterilization chamber and down the same corridor where Alqahiray had disappeared. A few seconds and two doors later, he turned the knob and stepped into the conference room to find Alqahiray and the others staring at the chart hanging across the front of the room.

Vasilev had studied the charts thoroughly in the six months they had been quarantined deep underground. In that time, none of them had seen the sun, watched television, or made a telephone call to the loved ones left behind. If it had not been for the chess set and the well-stocked library, every one of them would have been slobbering idiots by now. Vasilev was glad Popov was still in the laboratory. His quick observation of the Libyan colonel convinced him that the plan to confront Alqahi-

ray about their imprisonment—which is how they had come to
think of it—would be very dangerous right now.

The chart showed the location of underground tunnels that
ran the length and breadth of Libya, a tribute to Qaddafi's paranoia. The Libyan tyrant had built tunnels running from Libya's
eastern border to its western border with smaller branches span-
ning points south and detouring to the cities of Benghazi and
Tobruk. A single set of railroad tracks ran along the right side
of the main tunnels. Turntables at the end allowed the two trains
assigned to the military underground complex to turn around
quickly. The main tunnel ran from the eastern border with
Egypt to within two miles of the western border with Tunisia.
A small, two-lane road paralleled the railroad tracks to permit
military vehicles as large as tanks to transverse unseen. Solar
energy powered the lighting and the ventilation, but conventional gasoline and diesel engines powered the trains and the
vehicles. He imagined the atmosphere inside the tunnels thick
with exhaust fumes, regardless of the ventilation scheme.

"Professor Malenkomoff, how are you, my kind friend?"
Alqahiray said, stepping forward, his hands clasped behind his
back. He ignored the outstretched hand of the Russian scientist.

"Very well, Colonel," Vasilev Malenkomoff replied, wiping
his hand on his white smock. "We heard you were wounded and
not doing too well. It seems what little information allowed
down here has been somewhat misleading." He smiled.

"I am sure your background in glorious Russia has taught
you the fickle nature of politics when making a new country."

"That it did, Colonel. What brings you down here? We have
not seen you in months. If we had known you were coming, we
would have prepared."

Alqahiray took a deep drag from his cigarette and noticed
the Russian scientist wrinkle his nose. *More and more these
Westerners are beginning to think like Americans. A little smoke
is good for the constitution, regardless of what Satan scientists
say.*

"Perfectly all right, Professor. I need to know how we stand
on your project. Are we ready?"

"The final warheads were completed two weeks ago per our
agreement, Colonel," Vasilev replied. The scientist moved to
the far wall and pressed a button. Blinds aligned along it slid
smoothly upward, revealing a large hangar nearly two stories

below them and stretching for a hundred yards. Two rows of missiles, tied down on flat trailers, faced each other. The ebony cones gave them the ominous look they deserved. Arabic numerals along the side of the missiles identified the serial numbers of each one. In sequential order, Alqahiray counted from one missile to the next.

"Twelve missiles, Professor?"

"We did have sixteen, Colonel, per your directions, but system checks revealed four with either definite or suspected malfunctions. Considering what you want to do with them, I thought it best to exclude them from the final results. Your soldiers removed them weeks ago."

Alqahiray looked at the scientist. *What a dumpy little man,* he thought, *an ugly man with more hair on his eyebrows than on his head. A stupid one, too. Amazing what the promise of money could achieve.*

Vasilev ran his hand through his thinning hair, ignoring the scrutiny of the taller Alqahiray. The colonel could think whatever he wanted. The ten million American dollars, safely squirreled away in a Swiss bank, waited for him or his wife to use their coded numbers. Though his wife and family had little idea where he was, he had no concern. This was not the first time he had disappeared. A scientist in mother Russia did what he or she had to do to make a living. He knew of others who had trusted fanatic Palestinian causes, and he knew two who disappeared while working for the radical Greek 17 November terrorist group. Every bit of the recruitment effort, including his role in bringing in the culture, had been transcribed and documented. The papers rested in a safe-deposit box in London. Someday he might need them to create a pension for himself and Valerie.

Professor Malenkomoff turned slightly to face Alqahiray. "And, you are thinking, Colonel?" he asked, risking the very confrontation he meant to avoid.

"I am thinking, Professor, how many of the missiles are ready?"

"They are all ready, Colonel." Vasilev paused, bushy eyebrows turning into a prominent V as he pursed his lips. "Are you sure you want to use them, Colonel? I know what we agreed, but what these warheads carry has great potential for getting out of control. We have been very careful here, and still we lost one of my most valuable assistants for no other reason than a momentary lapse of judgment, a moment of carelessness."

Blood rushed to Alqahiray's face. *Stupid foreigner.* If the missiles were ready, then Malenkomoff and the others' usefulness was over. These Russians had cost his country more money than they could afford to bring the biological culture to this laboratory. The knowledge these men possessed endangered the new nation. They would never be permitted to carry the knowledge of what they have done out of here, and he never intended to pay the remainder, anyway. *Soon, Professor. Very soon.*

At that moment, Vasilev saw the truth etched in the man's face. They would never be permitted to leave. They knew too much.

"You have been well paid, Professor. What I do with what I paid is up to me, not you."

Vasilev knew he walked a thin line of mortality along the wrong side of good sense with this madman, but he found himself unable to stop. He waved his hand as if shooing away a petulant child. "That's up to you, but I want to be out of the country before you use them."

Alqahiray grunted and scanned the room. "Where is the testing chamber used for the animals we sent you?"

"Why do you want to see that, Colonel, if I may ask?"

"Just show it to me. It is obvious that if the Soviet Union had survived, a professor with your litany of questions would not have."

Vasilev shrugged his shoulders and put his hands behind his back momentarily to hide the shaking. "Ah, the testing chamber, you want? Follow me." He dropped his hands and hurried past the despot as he moved down the hall.

"Sergeant Adib, bring everyone." Alqahiray ordered.

They followed Professor Malenkomoff away from the observation platform, farther down the hall, until they reached a darkened laboratory. "Come on in. It's safe. The testing chamber is on the other side of those windows," he said, pointing across the room. "And those windows are double-paned with a vacuum separating the two plates. You are very safe here."

He flipped several switches, and fluorescent lights flickered briefly before illuminating the room on this side and the testing chamber on the other.

Alqahiray moved to the double-sealed windows and peered inside. Two dead animals, a dog and a sheep, lay on the floor. He wondered briefly—something he didn't do too much—how long they had been dead and imagined what the smell must be like inside the testing chamber. The head of each animal was pulled back, constricted in death. Bloody tongues lolled out of their mouths, and dried blood surrounded their eyes. The feet of the dog faced the window, and Alqahiray could see where the skin had ruptured on the paws and the white of bones showed. Dried spots of blood dotted the floor where bloody paw prints marked the dying staggers of the collie-sized dog.

"Not a pretty sight, Colonel?" Vasilev asked, watching Alqahiray's face for some sign of reaction. His confidence grew in the familiarity of the laboratory. He noticed Sergeant Adib and his men move away from the windows. Alqahiray seemed to find the scene interesting.

"How long did it take for them to die?"

"The longest survivor was the sheep. The ewe lasted nearly two days. The dog took only six hours until the first symptoms appeared. He died less than twenty-four hours later." Vasilev lied. He took a couple of paces down and lightly touched the window. "Convulsions, skin ruptures, involuntary eruptions of blood from the eyes, nose, ears, anus, and through the urine. All of that within eight hours. Both were blind by the first day. Ten hours, and they found it hard to move. No, Colonel, it was not a pretty sight." He dropped his hand, and thoughts of his wife flooded his mind. The epiphany of what could happen to his wife and to mother Russia if—when—this bug was released caused Vasilev to reach out and steady himself. Whatever led him to believe his deadly work would remain in Africa or the Middle East? One word: *money*. Money he expected to get and realized now he would never see. His momentary confidence faded as a glimpse of his future flooded his consciousness.

"And the assistant who died?" Alqahiray asked, his eyes turning on Vasilev. "Professor, are you all right? I asked you about your assistant."

"Sorry, I felt faint for just a moment." He straightened up. "Karol's first symptoms appeared within twenty-four hours. We thought it was a cold or influenza. By the time we realized what it was, it was too late."

"How long did it take him to die?"

"Not too long. We administered a lethal dose of morphine and eased him out of his pain. By then, he was unconscious and unaware of what was happening. We bagged the body, and with the reluctant help of some technicians who came to check the missiles, we burned it in the furnace used for destroying biological waste. Once the symptoms appear, it is too late to stop the disease." Vasilev paused for a couple of seconds as he considered carefully what he said next. "Colonel, I would appreciate it if you would see fit to award an honorarium for his family. Karol had a wife and three small kids. They live near Odessa." He glanced at the colonel. "She doesn't know, of course, what has happened to him." Why ask such a question if he knew they were going to die? He hoped the answer would show he was wrong, and Alqahiray intended to live up to the Libyan end of the agreement.

"Thank you, Professor. I will consider it when this is over." Alqahiray took a few paces away and tapped the glass. "Double-glazed, you say? Safe?"

"Yes, Colonel, double-paned. Perfectly safe. We even maintain a slight negative air pressure inside the room to keep anything airborne confined to the test chamber."

"Your friend, what was his name? Kuri? Yuri?"

"Karol, Colonel."

"You killed him, Professor? Your friend?" Alqahiray held up his hand to stop Vasilev's protestations. "No matter, Professor. The truth is, we really have no idea how long it takes for this virulent strain of anthrax you developed to kill a human?"

"Not exactly, Colonel, however, we know enough to say that within forty-eight hours of exposure, they will begin to die." Vasilev rubbed his arms, which felt cold. It took concentration to keep his knees from folding. They were as good as dead from this madman. How they would die was the only question. "The two animals showed how long," he stuttered. He swallowed, willing the constriction from his throat. He covered his mouth and coughed twice before continuing. "Colonel, once exposed to the atmosphere, the bacteria will stop reproducing, but every breath will inhale the spores, infecting everyone who breathes. A minimum number of spores is all that is needed to activate the disease. We believe that within thirty-six hours after release, unconsumed spores exposed to sunlight will become inert. They won't wither and die right away, and they won't last forever like natural anthrax. They will wait patiently until disturbed. Sunlight will kill most of the spores, but some will remain active carriers for a long time. Some may last indefinitely, if they land in dark areas and hidden spaces. Natural anthrax takes years to disappear from an affected area."

His confidence returned as he lectured on his specialty. No way he was going to tell Alqahiray that this wasn't weapons-grade anthrax. It was a virulent strain of naturally occurring anthrax that he and his team had refined. "Direct contact with these spores months after the missile is fired will still cause the anthrax to germinate. We thought of that and genetically engineered a safety valve so that after the weapon is used, this strain of anthrax will decay more rapidly than the natural strain. That will allow you to go into an exposed area within two months with minimum risk of catching the disease." Professor Malenkomoff smiled, fighting to keep the smile from breaking. He had spilled information about the anthrax strain he never intended to reveal. He had an idea how the colonel would react if he figured out the anthrax with their genetically engineered shelf life made these weapons useless within the next six weeks. The warheads had already sat idle in the hangars for nearly that same length of time. Of course, the sterile nature of the warheads probably prolonged the viability of the anthrax.

"The man with the wife in Odessa, Karol, he was the biological engineer who created this strain of anthrax." Vasilev hurried on, hoping to divert the colonel's thoughts from the biological missiles. "We owe him for his sacrifice to your plans and your country, Colonel."

Alqahiray stared at the scientist. *Mad. They are all mad,* he thought. *What in the hell is wrong with the Russian? He acts as if he expects me to cut his throat . . . which I may do later, but not now.* "Professor, I said we do not know for sure how long a human will live once exposed. Right?"

Malenkomoff nodded. "Right, Colonel. We do not know for sure."

Alqahiray motioned toward the testing chamber. "Is it safe inside?"

"Probably not. We figured it was hardly worth the time to go through the precautions to remove the animals. We had too many other things to do, and the cold temperature inside delays decomposition sufficiently. We thought—"

"You talk too much, Professor."

Professor Malenkomoff nodded and turned away. His knees felt rubbery. "You are probably right, but you need to know what you are dealing with," he said, realizing he was pushing the colonel, both wanting the madman to rant and rave, while praying Alqahiray would burst into praise for what they had done and release them. Sure, he did this for money, but none of them ever expected the missiles would be anything more than a political weapon for diplomatic advantage. A professor once told him that naïveté was a common trait among scientists. He was right.

"How do you insert the biological agent once you have the test subjects inside?"

Malenkomoff moved closer to the window and pointed to the far wall of the room at a small, gray metal panel with nozzles installed in the center of it. "Those nozzles are connected to a container filled with anthrax spores. Like an aerosol spray, we shoot a controlled amount into the space. Inhalation anthrax is a sure killer. Knowing how much—"

"Thank you, Professor," said Alqahiray, holding up his hand in front of Malenkomoff. "And that container is still connected?"

Malenkomoff nodded. "Yes, it is still connected." Sweat broke out on his forehead.

"I am going to help you, Professor. We are going to find out how long it takes to work on a human subject."

Vasilev shut his eyes. So, this was how Alqahiray intended to pay them. How long would he allow them to live, once he knew the truth?

"I have two volunteers for the experiment. Stay and learn how we do things in the new order." He motioned to Sergeant Adib.

Vasilev nearly laughed with relief. His knees buckled slightly. Vasilev caught himself on the six-inch sill that ran along the observation windows.

"Professor, you must get more rest," Alqahiray said, amused over his astute intuition that the Russian had thought he was to be the test subject.

Sergeant Adib shoved the two prisoners forward. The frightened officer whimpered. Alqahiray smiled as he stared into the man's eyes. There was little reasoning behind those eyes, just fear and panic. The man's ability to rationalize clearly had long since fled. This was the one to watch. You never knew what a frightened person would do to survive. Alqahiray stared at the other officer and smiled. For the first time, he saw the man's jaw muscles ripple. Fear was not a stranger to the intelligence officer. Alqahiray admired the soldier. Another time, another place, they would have been comrades, but he shoved away the fleeting thought to allow the man to live. Everyone has something to fear, and he had found it for this one. Unlike the other intelligence officer, this one knew what was coming. The stubborn military pride would crumble soon. Alqahiray was curious how long it would take before the man broke. He wanted the pleasure of knowing again that he had succeeded.

"You know what this is?" Alqahiray asked, pointing over his shoulder to the test chamber.

Sergeant Adib moved to the side of Alqahiray and raised his AK-47, so the barrel pointed at the two prisoners standing about six feet from his hero.

A whimper greeted his question.

"It is where you are going to contribute to the survival of your country. It is where you will show us the effectiveness of our weapon. It is where you will atone for your sins and prove your loyalty to your country and, by that, your loyalty to me. You will stay in this test chamber for three days, at which time you will be freed."

Adib nodded. Soldiers on each side of the prisoners grabbed them by the arms.

"Of course, Colonel. Whatever you want, Colonel. I will show you. Please, believe me."

"Professor," Alqahiray said, ignoring the whining. "If you would show us how the door works so our newest test subjects can enter the chamber, I would appreciate it."

Vasilev moved the soldiers aside to step in front of Alqahiray. "Are you crazy? Do you know what this will . . ." The question tapered off as Vasilev realized the stupidity of his outburst. Sergeant Adib shoved the barrel of his gun into the Russian scientist's stomach, knocking the breath out of him and knocking him against the wall. Vasilev looked down at the gun and stared, expecting any moment for the sergeant to fire his automatic weapon. The vision of his abdomen splitting open caused his stomach to tighten.

"Professor, stop the acting." Alqahiray chuckled, his hand reaching out to press the barrel of Sergeant Adib's weapon down. "You knew what we were going to do with the stuff you made. You must have known we would use it. I am just helping you with your testing. A dog? A sheep? No, we need to know how it will work against the enemy. I want to make sure the money paid you was worth it. I would hate to think we have been misled. Be thankful we have human volunteers for this portion of the experiment."

Vasilev's head swam, and little stars danced in front of his eyes as blood drained from his face. The mercurial nature of the Libyan madman could easily see him as another test subject. The man was mad, of that he was sure. Alqahiray never had intended to allow them to leave here alive. He bit his lower lip to remind himself to keep quiet. He must think of himself and the others. Would what Karol died for save them? He rubbed his upper left arm, where two weeks ago, he had had the last injection of the series.

Alqahiray smiled. "You didn't really think I would use this weapon, did you, Professor?" He laughed. "Oh, you pathetic fool. I would never have spent this much money if I didn't intend to use what I paid for." Alqahiray nodded at Sergeant Adib.

Vasilev shook his head. Alqahiray was right. He never expected anyone would be mad enough to use this weapon. There were too many unknown variables. He figured anyone using such a weapon would know it endangered his own survival, if not from the agent, then from the world, once they identified the source. The anthrax fear had been beaten into the Western mind with the terror of letters mailed in America after the attacks on the World Trade Center and the Pentagon. Nearly fifteen years later, the mere mention of the word *anthrax* still sent governments into a panic. If they thought this madman had this biological weapon, this laboratory would be reduced to cinders. The American military even vaccinated their soldiers against the disease at the turn of the century until their Congress ordered it stopped. That was many years ago. Even with the anthrax scare of 2001, they only restarted the vaccination program for a few months and then stopped it.

Vasilev stepped back. "You're right. I never expected you to use it. I expected it to be used as a negotiating point to obtain your independence."

"Oh, it will, Professor. This weapon of yours will be a negotiating factor in obtaining our independence. A factor called fear and respect." He nodded toward the testing chamber. "Enough of this useless chatter. Show me how we put our two prisoners into the chamber, and then you can go back to your other work. *That is, you can go back, Professor, until we have finished Jihad Wahid, when you will join our two intelligence officers in the chamber, along with the rest of your team. I will have no need for you by then.*

Vasilev moved to the heavy metal door and worked the switches to open the chamber. Certain that the air pressure would keep him from being exposed to any anthrax spores remaining in the isolation chamber, he swung the door open. At another time, he would have enjoyed the sight of the soldiers moving backward, away from the opening.

"You are safe. All dead decay in the same manner, only some at a quicker pace." Maybe the spores were dead or maybe just dormant, waiting for new victims like some alien life form. Earth was more dangerous than most realized.

Alqahiray motioned to Sergeant Adib. The fear the soldiers showed amused him. Allah protected him from such earthly dangers. He nearly stepped forward and through the door into the unsealed room, thinking how it would enhance his followers' veneration of him. Allah may protect him from earthly dangers, but why tempt Allah's patience? The guards shoved the two prisoners toward the door, motioning them forward with their AK-47s.

"Don't hesitate, my fine friends of Major Salim. It matters little to me whether you are wounded or not when you enter the chamber. Sergeant Adib is fully prepared to administer bullets to the legs, knees preferably, and then have you dragged into the chamber."

Several of the soldiers exchanged glances over the idea of dragging the two prisoners into the anthrax chamber.

The brave one swept his gaze around the room, locking eyes with every soldier. "Watch me closely, fellow Libyans. What you see here will someday be you." He took the limp hand of the broken officer and led him through the door into the chamber, the whimpering and cries becoming louder as they entered.

Vasilev slammed the door shut, spun the lock, and tugged on the handle a couple of times to ensure the door was secure. On the other side of the vacuum-sealed windows, the two prisoners appeared out of the narrow entranceway. The brave one positioned his comrade in front of a nearby bed and gently pushed him down on it. He turned to the staring faces arranged along the windows. He gazed at them briefly before lying down on another bed and putting his arm across his eyes. The intercom system between the two areas was open, allowing the two prisoners to hear everything said on the other side.

"Professor, I want a camera running the entire time until they die. Then contact Sergeant Adib, and he will send someone for the disc. I am interested in how your research has paid off." He turned and stared at the two prisoners. "I am interested how long bravery survives in the face of a slow death."

**VASILEV WATCHED ALQAHIRAY AND THE SOLDIERS LEAVE.** He had made no safety mechanism to leverage such a situation. The stuff in London would stay in the safe-deposit box for years before the British government declared the owner missing and the contents state property. By then, the discovery would be of little use to him and his colleagues. He walked to the control room and peered inside at the others working. Alqahiray had no way of knowing that their work had been finished over two months ago. What they had been working on now was their own survival.

He looked over his shoulder. They still had time and access to do something with the missiles. Or to try to do something. Alqahiray intended to kill them. Why should they leave anything for the madman? Alqahiray would move the missiles soon. With luck, they could disarm most of them without the colonel knowing. They would have to hurry. The colonel might be crazy, but he was no fool. Before the colonel was overthrown, guards used to be permanently down here. Since then, their presence had grown so sporadic that a couple of weeks ago, they ceased altogether. Eventually, the madman would realize he had no guards here, and when he did, their flexibility would be at an end.

He pressed a buzzer. Inside the sterile, pressurized compartment, everyone looked over to the control room. He picked up the microphone. "Yuri, Fedorov, Alexei, Stepkolov, Hova, and, of course, you, too, old man, Popov. Please, come out. I will meet you in the conference room." He put the microphone back in its rack and heard Popov say, "See, I told you when the madman came through the elevator it would mean more work for us. Vasilev! I want more money. This old communist needs more capitalistic dollars for working so far from the sun of the workers, from the beautiful motherland."

Vasilev grinned weakly, watching for a couple of seconds as everyone moved toward the exit. It would be ten to fifteen minutes before they finished the sterilization process. Time enough to make a fresh pot of coffee and open the hidden bottle of vodka. He smiled at the tirade Popov would give once he saw the vodka. The man thought the last of the fiery, clear liquor had disappeared weeks ago. It would be a welcome relief for the task ahead. How do you tell a group of people they may die? He was surprised he accepted the fact so calmly. Maybe when you accept death as inevitable, you shrug it off, refusing to believe it.

He hurried into his office. A small gray safe sat on the floor behind his chair. The one thing he kept from Alqahiray was that Karol died developing a vaccine for this strain of anthrax. The work killed Karol, but not before he was nearly finished. Vasilev and the others had completed the work. Vasilev had had to argue forcefully to make the other scientists take the shots, but once they saw minimum reactions to the vaccine, they finished the series. It had taken three weeks to complete the immunization. They had hurried the process because of Karol's death. Hova Vaitsay had had the worst reaction. The Hungarian ran a fever for two days and had such diarrhea Vasilev had ordered bags of saline solution to compensate for the dehydration.

They should be immune, but he would not know for sure until they were exposed, something he would prefer to avoid. The other secret kept from the Libyan colonel was that the concentrated strain of anthrax they had developed was not much different from normal spores found in nature. He wondered if the immunization shots veterinarians normally take would prove effective with this strain. He thought they would, but without inhumane testing, he would never know. He looked up. Well, that wasn't true. Two subjects were now in the containment test lab.

Vasilev took the tray of test tubes filled with the clear vaccine and set it on his desk. He pulled two hypodermics from a nearby medical cupboard and laid them on a tray along with two of the tubes. He turned toward the testing chamber. He knew it was already too late for the two officers, but at least with this, maybe they would have a chance. He should have lied to Alqahiray and told him the chamber was still infected. The last few minutes with the Libyan leader had been sad ones where he had to enter the side chamber and spray the anthrax spores into the space where the two prisoners waited. He should have had a neutral solution on hand, but he never considered that something like this would happen.

They must atone for their crimes and atone quickly. Those missiles had the range to reach as far as halfway up the Italian boot, maybe even to Rome. With the mechanism to disperse the spores at ten thousand feet, four missiles could contaminate the whole of Italy, including the islands of Crete and Sicily. It would be a crime equal to if not surpassing Hitler's.

Popov was first out of shower row. His eyes widened at the sight of the vodka bottle. "What a great and wonderful asshole you are, Vasilev! Remind me later to bloody that bulbous nose of yours." Popov reached forward and grabbed a water glass from the table; it disappeared within the huge, hairy hand. "Oh, how the stomach yearns for mother Russia, but if mother Russia is not here, then its clear water must do." His deep bass voice echoed off the walls.

Vasilev poured a generous shot of the fiery liquor for Popov, who hoisted the glass in a one-sided toast and drained the vodka. Behind him, the four Russian scientists followed by the taciturn Hungarian, Hova Vaitsay, stepped, one after the other, through the door. Hova would do anything to escape this confinement. Vasilev had no doubt the thin, greasy-haired Hungarian would work furiously when he told him what needed to be done. The man missed the puszta plains of eastern Hungary as much as he missed his Valerie. The others would argue, but Hova would dive into the challenges they would face in the next few hours—a day, if they were lucky. There was something strange and secretive about the Hungarian scientist. At-

tempts to draw out Hova had always been met with evasion or
silence.

As long as the two Libyans remained alive in the test chamber, Vasilev knew the Libyan madman Alqahiray would leave
them to their work. He turned and stared at the missiles below
them and thanked the lax security that left them alone. When
everyone had poured a small shot of the fiery liquid, he proposed a toast and then began to outline his plan.

# FIVE

⚓

**DUNCAN GRABBED HIS CARBINE AS HE THREW HIS SMALL**
combat pack across his shoulder. "Let's go!" he shouted over
the engine and propeller noise of the CH-53E Super Stallion
helicopter waiting on the flight deck of the USS *Stennis*. Eight
hours ago, he had been sipping beer at the military airport in
Naples. Now he was leading two teams of SEALs back into Algeria because his friend, Bashir, refused to tell anyone else the
location of the American hostages. He waited a couple of seconds before joining the other seven members of the team as
they ran toward the helicopter.

General Lewis, the commander, Joint Task Force, had all but
accused Duncan of being the reason that Bashir wouldn't tell
Bulldog Stewart where the hostages were being held. What the
hell was an Army general doing in charge of a Navy–Marine
Corps mission? They could carry this jointness shit too far.

If he didn't shoot the fat Bedouin smuggler, Beau might.
Duncan tossed his pack into the back of the helicopter and
leaped aboard. He did a quick calculation. If they had made that
freedom bird at Naples, he, Beau, and HJ would have been
somewhere over the eastern Atlantic right now, sipping free air-
line drinks and watching some nondescript movie as they dozed
off. Yeah, he might just have to beat Beau to the Bedouin.

Beau, HJ, and Bud Helliwell rolled in after him. Bud had his cast off, fracture instead of broken arm, he argued. Duncan was glad to see the mustang Navy SEAL, even though he doubted the fracture story. HJ and Bud had been talking nonstop since the two had linked up again after the rest of the SEAL team arrived on the carrier two hours earlier. Strange how a little over a month ago, he had to separate the two when they first met on the USS *Nassau*. Bud had been adamantly opposed to a woman SEAL, and HJ offered to rip his lips off.

The two were wounded, fighting back-to-back, at the death village. *Death village* was how Duncan and the others referred to a small inland Algerian agricultural village where they had stopped to refuel Bashir's rusty truck. None of them could pronounce the Arabic name for the village. Dead bodies had swayed from streetlights, and stacks of others executed by the rebels lay on top of each other along white plaster walls streaked with dried blood. Halfway through refueling, the rebels discovered them. The SEALs, the Algerian palace guard, along with Bashir and his smugglers, found themselves fighting for their lives. HJ and Bud had fought a covering action only to be overrun and wounded. HJ had been captured. She was within minutes of being raped when Duncan and the other SEAL members had rushed the room and freed her. Duncan could only guess how the event traumatized her. She had refused evacuation to the National Naval Medical Center at Bethesda.

HJ elbowed Bud in the side lightly, pointing to Beau leaning his head against the bulkhead of the helicopter, his eyes shut. The two laughed, with HJ mumbling something to Bud. Duncan thought her lips formed the words "Moroccan Watoosie," a bar near the hotel, which Beau enjoyed for its mature floor show.

You couldn't separate HJ and Bud. Nothing bonded like combat and surviving death together. Every time you crossed paths—four weeks or four years later—it became a family reunion.

The crew chief of the helicopter stood in the open doorway, pointing and pushing the SEALs toward their seats. Duncan threw himself into the nearest webbed seat and shoved his pack beneath it. He rubbed his right knee. The cartilage grating against the bone had caused it to swell again. One of these days, some doctor was going to notice, and that would be it. What was he talking about? Here it was the second week of August. Before the world had gone to shit in a hand basket, he would have been forcibly retired by now. Probably when this mess was over, they would send him packing, but until then, he would work his butt off.

He touched the short message received when he arrived aboard the carrier and before he had spoken with General Lewis. His wife had returned and moved back into their house in Reston. She blamed Duncan for their troubles, but the affair with the Safeway boy toy seemed to be over. The Virginia Society for the Prevention of Cruelty to Animals had a civil warrant waiting for Duncan, accusing him of animal cruelty. He felt bad about the dog. He should have shown more remorse and buried the dog in the front yard when he discovered it. Then he could have put a gigantic tombstone directly over the mutt's grave, and his wife could slap flowers on it every day, for all he cared. He should have known that drowning one's sorrows in alcohol only made things worse. It definitely did for him. Unfortunately, he still cared for her.

He watched as the members of the team piled aboard. Everyone, with the exception of the new chief petty officer, had been with them when they rescued President Hawaii Alneuf, the last freely elected president of Algeria. It was amazing how resilient the human body is, especially when you're younger. Every one of them had suffered a battle wound of some sort during the week they evaded the Algerian rebels to rescue President Alneuf.

Monkey and McDonald crawled aboard, their heavy M-60 machine guns hefted across their shoulders. Monkey had suffered minor legs wounds from wood splinters caused by a rebel grenade exploding on the old pier from where they were making their escape out to sea. His large refrigerator-like frame blocked the door, causing McDonald to step back, hurling friendly insults, until Monkey crawled aboard. Everyone called him Monkey because of the thick dark hair covering him from his head to the tops of his feet. A thick mass covered the muscular arms of the giant.

"He's got hands that would make a proctologist envious," Beau had remarked about Monkey. He did have huge hands,

Duncan thought, wondering briefly how such a large finger could insert itself inside a trigger guard.

He recalled the scene at the village when they had stopped to gas Bashir's Volvo truck and found themselves under attack by rebels. He and Beau had been racing down the hill after rescuing HJ to see Monkey fighting two of the attackers. The huge Navy SEAL held one by the throat with his left hand, about a foot off the ground, as a second attacker charged. Duncan recalled the effortless way Monkey had backhanded the charging rebel, knocking him to the ground, as he broke the neck of the one he held and, in a smooth motion, pulled his knife to dispatch the one scrambling up from the ground. For such a large man, Monkey moved gracefully in dealing death.

McDonald was the handsome one of the group and the shy one. Gibbons enjoyed ribbing McDonald about being one of many long-lost grandsons of Errol Flynn. McDonald seldom talked, but he was a demon with the heavy machine gun. His thick black hair and thin mustache gave him the Errol Flynn look that earned him Gibbons's attention. He had been the only one to come out of the rescue mission with just minor scratches and a couple of relatively shallow shrapnel wounds. His time in the *Stennis* hospital had been limited to a couple of hours, before they released him.

Gibbons had had a rough ride. The Afro-American had been blown off the boat during the sea battle with the Algerian Kebir patrol boat. It had been Monkey who leaned over the side and pulled the drowned man back on board and administered the lifesaving CPR that brought Gibbons back to this world. One more example, Duncan was sure, that sealed the special friendship these two men from Newark had for each other. He knew Gibbons wouldn't be far from Monkey. The two were inseparable.

Bud Helliwell, the mustang ensign, had broken his arm during the battle at death village. At the time, his arm had been covered in blood, and Duncan thought the wound was worse than it was. Only later did they discover the blood had come from minor but numerous shrapnel wounds caused when a grenade blew up near him. Bud seemed fully recovered. Duncan doubted the mustang was telling the whole truth about it being a hairline fracture, but he felt better having a SEAL with Helliwell's combat experience along, even with a broken arm.

The new senior enlisted sailor, Gunners Mate Chief Alonzo
Wilcox, stood on the other side of the open door of the helicopter, waiting until everyone was aboard. Satisfied, the thin,
wiry Afro-American chief crawled inside and gave Duncan a
thumbs-up. Duncan nodded. Chief Wilcox slapped the crew
chief on the shoulder and took one of the canvas sling seats
across from Lieutenant Commander Beau Pettigrew, accidentally bumping Beau's combat boot with his as he sat down.

Beau leaned forward and uncrossed his arms. He bent over
and shoved his pack under the canvas seat. Duncan slapped him
on the shoulder and grinned. He depended on the brown—now
blond—haired, blue-eyed Adonis from Newnan, Georgia. They
both knew that Beau's chances for making full commander had
improved significantly with the war in Korea and this crisis in
North Africa. Admiral Hodges, the head SEAL at the Pentagon,
expected the Navy to pass over Beau Pettigrew, but Admiral
Hodges was gone, a victim of Pentagon intrigue. Being politically astute was important for a military officer assigned duties
in Washington, but most were less than qualified for the political intrigue common among the professional cannibals who in-
habited the jungles of the Potomac.

Duncan believed but could hardly prove that Beau had been
targeted to be passed over for promotion because of misplaced
personal jealousy the admiral carried for him. Whatever Duncan had done to earn the admiral's ire, had been sufficient that
during last year's Selected Early Retirement Board, the admiral
had reached out and touched Duncan's name. The January letter ordering Duncan to retire by August—this same month as he
sat here in this vibrating piece of military hardware put together
by the lowest bidder—had arrived at his house with no prior
warning or expectation. He believed the problems between him
and his wife started about then. The letter had hit him hard and,
down deep. It took a couple of months for him to come to terms
with the letter, and during that time, the angry depression he
suffered probably drove her into another man's arms. Duncan
shut his eyes for several seconds. If only he could change the
past.

HJ reached out, touched Beau's knee, and gave him a
thumbs-up. The noise of the helicopter vibrating through the
open door made normal conversation impossible. HJ had been
the biggest surprise when Hodges had called Duncan and Beau

to the Pentagon to order them to the *Nassau* Amphibious Task Force. HJ was the first woman to complete Basic Underwater Demolition, BUDs, training at Coronado. The admiral had ordered Duncan to give her a good report when they returned from what was supposed to have been a bilateral training exercise with Spanish Special Forces at Gibraltar. It had been today at Naples when he realized the admiral had really expected him to sink her, if not because of her performance, then because of the animosity between him and the admiral. As it was, his report had validated the presence of qualified women in the Navy SEAL program, but only if they were qualified physically and mentally, and that meant not lowering standards one iota. He imagined the groans and curses echoing through the halls of the Pentagon when his letter hit the desk of William Tecumseh Hodges. Captain Ray Jordan, the acting head of the SEAL community, would do the right thing. He would add his own comments and forward it to the chief of Naval Operations who would make a decision—usually a fair, equitable, and right decision for the Navy. The big challenge would be political, because most of the women who would apply would fail, and then you would get the PC do-gooders involved. He didn't want to think about it.

Duncan recalled HJ's capture. She had only been a prisoner for about thirty minutes before Duncan, Beau, Chief Judiah, and Gibbons had overrun the rebels, but in those minutes, he could only imagine the horror of what she went through. He recalled how on the water carrier that stole to escape out to sea, before the rebel Kebir patrol craft caught up and began shelling them, how he had tried to talk with her about the short captivity. She had lost her temper. She told him that every woman in the military knew something like this could happen, and it was up to her to handle it. He presumed she shoved the incident to some deep recess in her mind to never discuss or visit again, but if she had, then she had done something he knew he could never do. On the other hand, he worried too much about her.

Chief Judiah had died on the mission. He and the Algerian palace guard commanding officer, Colonel Daoud Yosef, had stayed behind on the pier to blow it so Duncan and the others could get the slow-moving water carrier away with President Alneuf. It had been a loose plan, calling for the two men to set the explosives, run to the end of the pier, and jump, whereupon

Duncan and the others would reach into the water and pull them aboard. The explosion had happened, but when the smoke cleared, the two men were gone.

Duncan had no way of knowing that both Chief Judiah and Colonel Yosef had been Israeli Mossad agents. When the two men had activated smoke grenades at the pier, Israeli frogmen had appeared and helped the two destroy the wooden pier before escaping to an Israeli Gal submarine loitering offshore.

The sound of repeated bongs broke over the noise of the vibrating props. "General quarters, general quarters. All hands, man your battle stations. This is not a drill. This is not a drill."

The helicopter blasted skyward off the flight deck of the USS *Stennis*, throwing the crew chief toward the open door. Duncan leaned forward against the seat belt restraints and grabbed the petty officer's arm. At the same time, Chief Wilcox caught the man's leg in the crook of his arm.

The crew chief nodded at Duncan and the chief, bracing himself against the sides of the helicopter. Chief Wilcox released the man. The crew chief weaved his way forward as the aircraft bounced through the air, changing altitude and direction to increase the distance from the huge aircraft carrier.

Beau leaned over to Duncan, putting his mouth near Duncan's ear. The two bounced against each other as the helicopter weaved and jumped through the air. "What in the hell is going on?" he shouted.

"I don't know!" Duncan shouted over the noise of the weaving CH-53.

The helicopter dropped, causing everyone to feel a moment of weightlessness as their bodies fought to catch up with the machine. They were slammed forward as the helicopter jerked sharply to the right. The heavy CH-53E reversed direction and began a steep, rapid climb. G forces jerked them back against the canvas straps. The passengers' bodies pressed down on the web seats. The unlucky ones with the crossbar between their legs had the metal forced up into their crotches. Monkey and McDonald wrapped their legs around the M-60s, keeping the heavy weapons from knocking them senseless as the g forces tried to rip them from their hands.

"Damn, that hurt!" Beau shouted, shoving himself up slightly off the metal bar.

The helicopter jerked left, throwing everyone against the

bulkhead. Then it leveled out, increased speed, and began a rapid move forward.

The young crew chief, Duncan figured early twenties, staggered back, holding onto the overhead metal railing until he stood in front of Duncan. A long wire trailed along the floor, running from a socket behind the cockpit to the earphones he wore. He held a push-to-talk mechanism in his hand.

"What's going on?" Duncan asked the man, speaking slowly and forming each word with his lips deliberately.

"Captain, they have gone to general quarters in the battle group."

"I heard the call to general quarters. Now, tell me why."

"Two bogies inbound toward the battle group."

"Bogies?"

"Yes, sir. Algerian warplanes, but this is the third general quarters we've had in two days. I think it's another bust for those in combat," the crew chief said, referring to the officers and sailors manning the aircraft carrier's Combat Information Center."

"What does that do to us?"

"Captain, the bogies are between us and Algiers. We are bingoing west and will cross the coast farther down and approach Algiers from that direction."

"Okay, keep me up to date," Duncan said, recalling that the coastal area to the west belonged to the rebels, and like most nonaviators, he believed that one well-placed bullet could send a helicopter down. The Sea Stallions were the best for this mission, and the extra armor added to the floor stopped all but the heaviest of hand-carried weapons.

**TWO MARINE CORPS F/A-18 HORNETS FROM THE MOON**-lighter Squadron turned together to the right, completing another figure-eight pattern to the east of the carrier battle group—one of three Combat Air Patrols conducting twenty-four-hour-a-day coverage. Chris Miller and Panope Lassiter had been on their CAP station thirty minutes when the *Stennis* Battle Group sounded general quarters.

"Alfa Papa Leader, this is November Bravo," came the call over Chris and Panope's headset as the *Stennis*'s air intercept controller called Chris.

"November Bravo, Alfa Papa," Chris replied.

"Two bogies inbound battle group. Full power, come left to two zero zero, descend to one two zero. Bogies bear one niner zero on course three three zero. Speed three five zero knots. Altitude one zero zero," the AIC broadcasted, telling the two hornets, known as Alfa Papa formation, that the two unidentified enemy aircraft were on a course of three three zero at ten thousand feet, heading toward the *Stennis* battle group. The two unidents were traveling at 350 knots.

"Alfa Papa two, let's go. Left turn, afterburner on. Weapon systems on!" shouted Chris to Panope.

The two F/A-18s turned in unison, and as Chris descended, Panope increased speed to take position on the left, slightly to the rear, as he followed the formation leader down.

"Alfa Papa formation, November Bravo," called the AIC. "Bogies twenty five miles; course three three zero, altitude one zero."

On the open privacy frequency between the two Marine Corps pilots, Panope keyed his mike. "Chris, think this is another false alarm?"

"Probably. You know how nervous those sailors are back on the bird farm."

"Lose two ships in two months, and I'd be nervous, too."

"Alfa Papa formation, come right two zero five."

The two Hornet pilots eased their fighters to the left five degrees and steadied up on the new course.

"Bogies, twenty miles; course three three zero and descending."

"Descending?"

Chris glanced out of his cockpit at his wingman. There were only two reasons aircraft at that altitude descend. One was to land on the carrier and, if they were going to do that, they would have approached the bird farm through the approved corridor; the other reason was to launch air-to-surface cruise missiles.

"Alfa Papa, this is November Bravo; request afterburners and max speed."

"Roger, Alfa Papa formation already on afterburners; increasing speed to Mach one point two."

Twenty miles at the speed of sound would be covered in less than a minute. The thrust shoved the two pilots back against their seats. Their heads pressed against the backrests. The sunlight obstructed the heads-up display on the cockpit windshield. Chris glanced down to verify weapons status. The status box showed all six Sidewinders active and ready. As they exceeded the speed of sound, silence enveloped the two pilots. Behind them, the normal flight noise followed, never quite catching up but chasing them nevertheless.

The AIC kept the information on the bogies rolling across the airwaves until she said, "Alfa Papa formation, slow to four hundred knots. Bogies are directly ahead five miles, two thousand feet." Her voice sounded nervous, Chris thought. *I would be, too, if I was sitting on a ship the size of two football fields waiting for missiles to be launched.* In the back of his mind, he expected to intercept two of their own aircraft as they did during yesterday's bogus intercept. A loud boom rocked the two aircraft as they slowed below the speed of sound and the noise caught up.

"I see them, Chris," Panope said. "They are below at our eleven o'clock."

Chris banked the aircraft slightly to the left to open his view. The sunlight reflecting off the two silver fuselages highlighted the bogies.

"Got them," Chris said. He flipped the radio switch to the *Stennis*. "November Papa, we have the bogies in sight. Beginning rear hemispheric approach. Request weapons free."

Several seconds passed as the Hornets began a smooth approach behind the two bogies.

"Alfa Papa, weapons free after identification pass."

"Identification pass! What does she want us to do? Give them a chance to shoot us down?" Panope asked.

Chris shook his head. "No, they just don't want us to shoot down one of our own. Let's go, Marine. They're probably Navy, and nothing gives me greater pleasure than to scare the piss out of a couple of swabbies."

The two aircraft continued their approach, leveling off three miles behind the unidentified aircraft. From their position, the sun blinded them, making it impossible to tell what the aircraft were or even if they were American. It would take several seconds to clear their vision.

"November Papa, request ELINT information on the bogies."

"Alfa Papa, we have no electronic signatures on the approaching bogies. No IFF or radar."

Chris's eyebrows bunched as the Marine captain tried to figure out who would be so dumb as to approach a carrier battle group with no IFF. If they shot them down and they were Navy, they deserved it, if for no other reason than being dumb and stupid. He shook his head, wondering with amazement how ignorant people can be.

"Activating fire control radar at this time," Chris announced.

Both Hornets' fire control radar painted the two bogies in front of them. "That should get their attent—" said Panope. "What the heck, over!"

Contrails from under the wings of the right bogie shot out. The two Hornet pilots watched helplessly as two Exocet missiles dropped from the Mirage aircraft. Almost immediately, the enemy aircraft on the left fired two more. *Four goddamn missiles! Shit!*

"November Papa; this is Alfa Bravo. I mean Alfa Papa to November Charlie. Shit! *Stennis*, you got missiles inbound. I say again, four cruise missiles inbound. Request permission to splash the bandits. Bandits identified as Mirages, believe them to be Mirage F1s." The Mirages' movement to the right brought them out of the bright sunlight. Even as he asked, Chris and Panope locked their fire control radar on the two Mirages in front of them.

The two Mirages separated.

"Fox one!" shouted Panope.

"Fox two!" echoed Chris.

"Fox three; Fox four," Panope shouted into the helmet microphone, as four Sidewinder missiles erupted from beneath the wings of the Marine Corps fighters. Following the missiles in, the two pilots depressed the cannon trigger, filling the air behind the enemy aircraft with twenty-millimeter shells.

The Mirage F1 on the left turned left and climbed; the other dove right, heading toward sea level.

"Alfa Papa; November Bravo. Splash the bandits! Repeat again, you have weapons release authority. Splash the bandits."

"Thanks, *Stennis*!" *Somewhat late,* thought Chris as he watched his Sidewinder make a long turn to follow the descending aircraft. The dark contrail of the air-to-air missile marked a corkscrew path as Chris's Sidewinder sought to connect with the fleeing Mirage F1.

"Roger, November Bravo. Bandits have split. We are engaged."

"Panope, you take the bandit to the left. I've got the son of a bitch going sea level."

"Alfa Papa, November Bravo; be advised formation Delta Papa en route your position," the AIC reported, indicating a formation of F-14 Tomcats were being vectored toward their engagement zone.

Chris clicked his mike twice, acknowledging the AIC. The AIC would keep the other formation out of the air combat maneuver zone if she believed any chance existed of a blue-on-blue incident. He had his hands full with this engagement. He expected the battle group to perform as they did during exercises. You fight like you train. He just wished they had had sufficient funds to do more training before they sortied with only two days' notice to the USS *Stennis*. At the time, the aircraft carrier had been in the Atlantic, heading full speed toward the Mediterranean in reaction to the Libyan sinking of the USS *Gearing*.

The two Hornets banked apart. Chris dove toward the weaving Mirage, which had come out on a southwest course, taking it toward the Algerian landmass. The Sidewinder banked right, but electromagnetic scatter caused by the proximity to the sea broke up the electronic lock. Chris watched helplessly as the missile hit the water, exploding harmlessly about a quarter of a mile behind the Mirage. "Damn!"

Burning flares erupted from the rear of the Mirage. Chris knew the pilot was trying to obscure the infrared sensors on the missiles, but he had no worry. At this angle and this close to the sea, missiles were useless. He reached down and flipped open the toggle protecting the trigger to the single cannon of the F/A-18. The Hornet shook from the vibration caused by the thicker air as he descended, passing one thousand feet in an attempt to align the aircraft behind the bobbing Mirage. He glanced at the altimeter reading on his heads-up display. Seven hundred feet and still heading down. A new surge of adrenaline brought his senses to heightened awareness as his hands tightened on the throttle and the trigger. He felt the trouser legs tighten as compressed air squeezed his legs, reducing blood flow in the extremities to increase blood available to the brain. A simple device designed to help pilots stay conscious when pulling multiple g's. Simultaneously as he descended, Chris fought the turbulence of the lower atmosphere as he attempted to align his cannon on the Mirage. The heads-up display registered the decreasing height, a soft beeping sound alerting him to the low altitude.

Chris flipped off the afterburner. Too much danger of it flaming out as he descended closer to sea level.

He fired a few rounds of the twenty-millimeter shells and watched the tracer round pass harmlessly over the top of the Mirage. He corrected and fired again. Unexpectedly, the Mirage pulled up, causing Chris to undershoot.

The Marine captain banked to the right, believing the Mirage to have pulled right. His head whipped back and forth as he searched for a visual on the enemy aircraft. The last thing he wanted was to pull out and discover the enemy had rolled into position behind him. One thing he noticed when the Mirage pulled up was the absence of air-to-air missiles. Even as he searched for the enemy aircraft, he realized the absence of air-to-air missiles meant these two Algerian pilots had charged the battle group fully expecting to die during their mission. No fighters went out against the force these two did with just air-to-surface cruise missiles and expected to survive. Look what happened to those two Iraqi Mirages during Desert Storm back in 1991.

He rolled the Hornet to the left and immediately picked up the Mirage on his air intercept radar. The enemy was climbing for altitude, rolling right as he ascended, but as soon as Chris flew past, the enemy pilot rolled left and started a fast, controlled descent back to sea level, all the while working toward the Algerian landmass. He hoped the battle group gave permission for hot pursuit, if the enemy aircraft crossed the coastline. Their new orders were simple: "Avoid Algerian territory and national waters," but he and his adversary were fast approaching both. "Avoid further entanglements" had been the second order. How in the hell did you avoid further entanglements when you had troops on the ground? "Answer me that," he mumbled, his eyes searching the sky.

He could ask, but one thing he had learned in his six years in the Marine Corps was never to ask a question if you really do not want to know the answer, because whatever answer you get, you won't like.

The maneuver gave the Mirage pilot breathing room, opening up the distance and giving the Algerian pilot a hope for survival. Six miles separated the two, and the Mirage pilot was only ten miles from shore.

"Splash one bandit!" cried Panope. "You should have seen it. A missile right up the tail. A July Fourth fireworks if I ever saw one. That's one Al-Qaida shithead who won't need his Preparation H tonight. Christ, Chris, I am now an ace."

"Shut up, Panope, and get your ass over here!"

"On my way, Chris! . . . *Oh, Roll me over in the clover—*"

"Panope, I'm still fighting. Shut up!"

"Alfa Papa, November Bravo; one confirmed kill. Bandit offscreen. Other is closing shore, eight miles from coast. You have permission for hot pursuit. Delta Papa formation one minute from your position, approaching from the east, altitude five zero."

"Roger," replied Chris. He rolled the Hornet left, ascended a thousand feet, flipped on the afterburner, and in seconds closed the distance to four miles. The Algerian coastline filled more of his vision than the Mediterranean Sea. He glanced quickly to the east and up, half hoping to spot the Tomcat formation entering the combat zone at five thousand feet. He jerked his head to the front, his attention riveted on the enemy aircraft weaving below him. He rolled the Hornet to the left and dove against the slower Mirage.

He fired his cannon as he passed the enemy aircraft and thought he saw one of the shells hit the rear of the plane. He flipped the Hornet right, pulling over a g as he turned for another pass. Chris lost visual on the Mirage. His head whirled from side to side as he fought to regain visual position on the bandit. Chris glanced down at the radar and saw no sign of the enemy. The only place it could be was behind him. "I've lost him!" he shouted into his helmet microphone.

"Behind you, Chris. He's behind you!" shouted Panope. "Get your ass out of there! Up, man. Go up! I'm coming."

Shells from the Mirage's cannon passed down the left-hand side of the cockpit. Chris pulled the Hornet straight up, rolling into a loop, and as he passed overhead, the enemy passed beneath him. The pilot of the Mirage looked up, flicked two fingers at Chris, and then banked the Mirage right. *Balls,* thought Chris as the Mirage disappeared from his vision again. If he had been the pilot of the Mirage, he would have bingoed across the shoreline and disappeared into the land scatter. Instead, the Algerian pilot had opted to take advantage of Chris's maneuver and attack the superior fighter aircraft. *Balls,* Chris thought again. *Or just another fanatic lusting after those virgins in paradise.* Well, he was going to give the enemy pilot his wish.

In the middle of the loop, Chris flipped the Hornet down and around, bringing the fighter out right side up and directly behind the Mirage. He fired his cannon, seeing the trace lace the tail of the aircraft. The Mirage swung from side to side, attempting to evade the cannon fire. Chris slowed the Hornet to match the speed of the slower Mirage and started rocking the aircraft, matching the Mirage swing for swing. On the second swing, Chris depressed and held the cannon trigger, firing as the Mirage crossed his nose. He caught movement out of the corner of his eye as Panope pulled up alongside of him.

Chris glanced through the cockpit at his wingman flying about seventy feet to his right. He nodded, and the two of them laid down a wall of continuous twenty-millimeter cannon shells at the fleeing bandit. The shells tore through the rudder, the engines, the small rear wings, and blasted the top of the cockpit off. One moment the Mirage was serving as a target and the next, a huge fireball blinded the two F/A-18 pilots. The Mirage, minus its tail, tumbled downward out of a cloud of debris, a huge black trail of rolling smoke marking its fall. Chris and Panope pulled up on their throttles, taking their Hornets up and over the conflagration before turning together to commence a clockwise circle of the area. A minute later, the remains of the burning Mirage hit the shallow sea about a half mile from the shore, rolling repeatedly across the surface before exploding again. No ejection seat burst forth. Chris gave a thumbs-up to Panope as the two of them gained altitude and turned toward the battle group.

**EXOCET, FRENCH-MADE ANTISHIPPING MISSILES SOLD** widely during the 1980s to Third World nations, have a warhead with over 360 pounds of high explosives. Two Iraqi Mirages "unintentionally" launched Exocet missiles against the

USS *Stark* in May 1987, killing nearly forty American sailors and nearly sinking the American frigate in the Persian Gulf. During the Falklands war in May 1982, Argentina's aging Super Etendard fighter aircraft sank the British destroyer *Sheffield* and the British support ship *Atlantic Conveyor* with Exocet missiles. *Thank goodness it's August and not May. May is not a good month for warships,* thought Chris.

The two F/A-18 Hornets sped ahead of their sound wave toward the battle group in vain hopes of catching the missiles. The Exocets had automatically descended to ten meters' altitude, losing themselves from aircraft radar against the sea scatter of the Mediterranean.

"Captain, we have four missiles inbound. Target is USS *Stennis*," said the Tactical Action officer to Captain Richard Holman. The acting captain of the USS *Stennis*, Commander Tucson Conroy, stood beside the new commander, Task Force Sixty-seven.

Holman reached up and buttoned his helmet. "Tucson, you're the captain. It's your show," he said, fighting the urge to take control and fight his ship. It was the hardest thing he had done since being forced to assume command of the U.S. Naval Air Forces in the Mediterranean.

Tucson nodded. "I know," he said, his reply acknowledging both the positional authority he held and the turmoil he knew Dick Holman was experiencing.

"*Stennis*, this is *Ramage*," a voice blasted over the secure circuit. "I have missile track zero six two for action!"

The second-class petty officer sitting beneath the speaker reached up and turned the volume down.

"*Stennis*, this is *Yorktown*," crackled the speaker overhead. "Missiles away!" The Aegis cruiser was not waiting for direction from the carrier and, as far as Holman was concerned, that was fine with him. He rubbed his hands on his khakis. The *Yorktown* had been detached from the *Nassau* Amphibious Task Force and assigned to the *Stennis* soon after they inchopped the Mediterranean. Its air defense might and Aegis sensor capabilities provided the *Stennis* Battle Group the defense in depth it needed. *Where is the USS* Hue City? he asked himself, referring to the other Aegis-class cruiser in the battle group. Dick Holman turned to the surface operator console and scanned the battle group layout, searching for a few seconds until he saw the other Aegis cruiser. Good, they overlap each other's weapons systems.

"Splash one inbound!" shouted a voice across the airwaves.

"Identify yourself!" the TAO screamed into his microphone.

Tucson Conroy reached forward and touched the young lieutenant commander on the shoulder. "Stay calm, Commander. Stay calm."

Dick Holman turned away and walked briskly to the EW console. He glanced at the AN/SLQ-32(V)3 electronic warfare system, where dotted lines marked the three remaining missiles tracking inbound toward the carrier.

"Three still coming, Skipper," he said more to himself than to Tucson, who heard his warning.

The air operator sitting at the Naval Tactical Data System spoke up. "Commander, that would have been USS *Ramage*, sir. The radar image of their missile connected with inbound track zero six two."

The TAO turned to the operator. "Thanks." His voice was calm but firm. "Keep the operators on the circuit identifying themselves. We need to keep a clear picture."

"Sir," she said. "I show three inbound videos at speed Mach point eight. Time to impact two minutes."

"What happened to the *Yorktown*'s shot?" asked Holman as he started to crawl up into the captain's chair, remembered he wasn't the captain any longer, and stopped himself. He stroked his hands on his khaki trouser legs. It was hard to keep quiet and let someone else fight his ship. He glanced at the chair. He wanted to sit there silently and watch the well-oiled combat team fight the ship, but, by God, it was still his ship, and he was finding it hard to keep quiet. Why in the hell did Admiral Cameron promote him to CTF Sixty-seven and make him transfer command of his carrier to his XO? His stomach tightened as he waited for the answer. Several seconds passed, the missiles continued to close, and Dick Holman was surprised to discover he was holding his breath.

As if hearing him, the speaker blared. "*Stennis, Yorktown*; missile miss; I repeat missile miss. Second and third shots in the air at target zero six three."

The NTDS operator rolled her mouse to the video designated as zero six three and hooked the inbound missile. She glanced at the displayed data on her NTDS console. "Inbound zero six one; time to impact one minute four seconds! Zero six three and zero six four; time to impact one minute ten seconds."

In combat, even seconds counted. Holman worked through the amazement of how combat and war seemed to slow time. A minute seemed longer when you were fighting for your life. The odds of them stopping the three remaining Exocet missiles were against them. Aircraft were ineffective this close.

"Splash!" cried the NTDS operator, her voice obtaining a high note. "Track zero six three off scope!"

"*Stennis, Yorktown*; zero six three destroyed. I repeat zero six three destroyed."

"*Stennis, Hue City*; I am moving to your port side to engage the inbound. Estimate three minutes to position. Am unable to engage missile."

Holman recognized the voice from the USS *Hue City* as that of its commanding officer, Captain Horatio Jurgen McTeak, fondly known as Buc-Buc. "Not enough time," Holman whispered to himself in reply to Buc-Buc's broadcast. He breathed a sigh of relief. The Aegis cruiser *Hue City* was trying to steer herself between the *Stennis* and the remaining two inbound missiles. The heavier firepower of the *Hue City*, positioned directly in the path of the Exocet missiles, would probably destroy the last two. The cruiser brought with it not only its surface-to-air missile vertical launch systems but also two Close In Weapons Systems—CIWS—designed for such enemy attacks. But he wanted no other situations like the USS *John Rodgers* on his conscience. Not another surface warfare sacrifice done for the good of the battle group, which was what Dick considered the *Stennis*. He and the *Stennis* were one as long as he was the commanding officer. But he wasn't CO now.

The USS *John Rodgers*, an aging Spruance-class destroyer, had maneuvered herself between the USS *Stennis* and four inbound torpedoes when the battle group reached the Strait of Gibraltar five weeks ago. The *Stennis* had been saved by the bravery of the officers and sailors on the USS *John Rodgers* but at the cost of the destroyer and all those who sailed her. Not one body had been recovered from the fireball that engulfed and destroyed the ship. Holman had personally written the Medal of Honor citation for Captain Warren Spangle, commanding officer of the destroyer, and had it endorsed by Admiral Cameron. It was one of the last things Admiral Cameron did before he was relieved yesterday and flown off the carrier toward whatever fate awaited him in Washington.

"*Stennis, Hue City*; decoy effective—track zero six one. I say again, we have successfully decoyed track zero six one. It is inbound our way. You can say good-bye to that son of a bitch!"

"*Stennis, Ramage*; sir, I cannot fire without endangering the carrier. The last missile is directly in line with me to you."

"*Stennis, Yorktown*; same here, over."

Tucson Conroy, commanding officer of the USS *Stennis*, picked up the microphone. "Battle group, this is *Stennis*, Charlie Oscar speaking."

The doors to Combat bounced off the bulkhead as Rear Admiral Devlin, the new commander United States Sixth Fleet, burst in. Devlin had stayed as long as he could in the Sixth Fleet staff Combat Information Center. He needed to be nearer the action. This was only his second day as the new Sixth Fleet commander.

General Lewis, the commander of the Joint Task Force African Force, had called both him and Admiral Cameron into his stateroom late yesterday. To the surprise of Devlin but not Admiral Cameron, the Army general broke the news that Admiral Cameron had been ordered to return to Washington. Admiral Cameron was to answer questions about the terrorist attacks, the sinking of the USS *Gearing*, and his own leadership responsibilities. Devlin demanded to be relieved along with Cameron. General Lewis ignored the request and, in front of the man who took them to war, the general read an order from chief of Naval Operations reassigning Devlin as commander, United States Sixth Fleet. Devlin and Holman had yet to find an opportunity to discuss the events.

"*Hue City*, continue your approach. We estimate missile impact in forty-five seconds." He pointed to the TAO and mouthed, *Give me the speaker.* "*Ramage*, request initiate antisubmarine tactics in the event this is a coordinated event. *Yorktown*, take position five miles off my port side and provide air defense."

Tucson raised the microphone to his lips. An involuntary but audible sigh escaped Richard Holman as Tucson's voice traveled over the circuit. "Men and women of the *Stennis*, this is the commanding officer speaking. We have an inbound Exocet cruise missile. We'll see if our Close In Weapons System, the Vulcan Phalanx, works. Prepare for impact." He paused for a second before keying the 1MC again. "I expect everyone to do your duty."

Tucson hung up the microphone and turned to Dick Holman and Rear Admiral Devlin, who had invaded his space. He remained standing beside the captain's seat. He knew the turmoil going through his former skipper's mind, but this was his command now, his space, and he knew they knew.

"Admirals," he said, granting Dick Holman the higher, unpromoted rank, "I would recommend grabbing something and holding on."

The 1MC of the ship blared with a boatswain whistle from the bridge of the huge aircraft carrier, followed by the voice of the officer of the deck. "Stand by for missile impact port side. All hands, brace for impact. Time: twenty-five seconds."

On the flight deck, sailors ran from the port side, fleeing to the starboard side and safety, some diving into the walkway that encircled the massive flight deck. The crackle of the depleted uranium shells of the two CIWS mounts on the port side gave new urgency to their dash for safety. The CIWS only fired at targets within its five-mile limits.

"What happened to the last two missiles?" Pete Devlin asked. He had been in the passageway running to the *Stennis*'s Combat Information Center when the electronic warfare suite about the USS *Hue City* decoyed one of the remaining two Exocets.

Before Holman could answer, the sound of an explosion off the port side echoed through the spaces. The ship actually rocked to starboard slightly from the impact.

Devlin grabbed the side of the captain's chair. He saw Holman start to fall and grabbed him as he lost his grip. The impact barely shook the ship, but it still managed to catch Holman off balance. Amazing what an aircraft carrier can take. During World War II, the last time aircraft carriers endured air attacks—until the North Koreans tried it last week—they took multiple hits and still continued to launch and recover aircraft. The USS *Stennis* dwarfed by three times the size of old World War II carriers.

The TAO pulled his headset off his ears and turned to Tucson. "Captain, CIWS hit the target off the port beam, causing it to spin before exploding on our port side near the aft elevator. Damage control parties are on scene, and we should have initial reports soon."

"How many casualties?"

The TAO shook his head. "Unknown at this time, Captain."

Admiral Devlin leaned toward Dick Holman. "Dick, let's clear the area. I want the battle group relocated fifty miles farther out while we assess damage." Devlin pointed at the forward bulkhead. "To the northwest. The shift will complicate further enemy actions and put more water between us and the shore."

"We may be giving them what they want, Admiral."

"So? What's fifty miles to a carrier?"

Holman nodded. "Yes, sir, I will order the battle group north fifty miles and establish a new operating area—a MODLOC—for us." He reached forward and touched Tucson Conroy's shoulder. "You hear?"

"Aye, aye, sir. Will do," he replied.

"Captain," said the TAO, "so far, no casualties in the attack. Damage appears to be minimal, and damage control has already extinguished the fire the missile caused. But so far, we have fourteen wounded. I will have medical's report as soon as they provide it."

"Roger, Commander. Tell the battle group we are moving north." The commanding officer of the USS *Hue City* was the senior surface warfare officer in the battle group. Usually the senior SWO was assigned the duties of commander, Task Force Six-zero, with overall tactical authority over the warships in the battle group. In this case, Buc-Buc had been passed over in favor of Commander Tucson Conroy, a fellow SWO but one rank junior. The proximity of commander, Task Force Six-seven, and commander, Sixth Fleet, caused Admiral Cameron to appoint the commanding officer of USS *Stennis* as the commander, Task Force Six-zero. The Iron Leader had insisted on keeping the elements of command together.

"Define a new operating area about fifty miles from here, clear it through me, and Sixty-seven and we'll broadcast it to the fleet. But turn the fleet north now." He turned to Dick Holman and Pete Devlin. "Orders under way, sir. This will give us time to assess the situation and, if the enemy wants to mount another attack; they'll have to come farther out."

Tucson reached over and lifted the headset off the TAO's ears. "Keep us at general quarters for the time being. Do not secure from it unless I personally authorize it. I am going to the bridge to survey the damage from there and then will probably go on down to the impact area, once damage control efforts have eased." Tucson knew his presence would disrupt the damage control parties around the elevator, so he chose reluctantly to delay going to the damaged area.

He turned to the two observers. "Would you gentlemen care to join me?"

Dick Holman let out a deep breath. "Tucson, you don't know how hard it was to keep quiet. You did an outstanding job."

"Skipper, I think I know, and I appreciate you letting me fight the ship."

"I feel the need for a strong cigar. May I offer both of you one? They are Havanas."

Devlin nodded. "I think I could use something stronger than a cigar, but a Havana sounds good . . . only later, not right now."

"I'll pass on the cigar, Captain."

"Good job on fighting the battle group, Captain Conroy," Pete Devlin added. "You didn't have much time to react, and your forces pulled it off as the true professionals they are. I'll let you and Dick go shake out the jeebies, while I return to discuss this with my staff. Dick, we need to talk about the recent changes after I have a meeting with General Lewis. At least we were blessed with him staying in the commander, Joint Task Force—CJTF—ops space."

"That may have been more a case of him not knowing how to find his way around the carrier." Dick grinned. Then he realized he had an overwhelming urge to urinate.

"I'll be on the bridge, sir," Tucson Conroy said, turning toward the ladder leading upward from the center of the Combat Information Center.

"Admiral, I'll call as soon as we know the extent of damage. Even a small cruise missile like an Exocet can do a lot of damage if it hits the right area," Dick Holman said. "We need to see how much damage. It doesn't sound too bad. If what Damage Control passed is accurate, we should have the flight deck up and running within the next hour. If it is worse than the initial report, we are still going to have the flight deck up and running in an hour. We have no choice. I have aircraft out there with nowhere to land. It's too far to Sigonella, the Spanish and French probably won't react well if we bingo our fighters to their soil, and the French and British carriers are incapable of taking our aircraft on board."

"We could land them at the Bouhiemme International at Algiers. We own it right now," offered Pete Devlin.

Holman nodded. "Let's hope we don't have to. If you will excuse me, sir." He turned and made a beeline for the head located just outside Combat.


**THE HELICOPTER CREW CHIEF WORKED HIS WAY TOWARD** Duncan. Duncan took his earphones off as the young sergeant bent down. "Captain, we will be crossing the coastline in about two minutes. We are about ten miles west of Algiers, sir. Captain Cochran, the pilot, asked me to tell you two enemy aircraft fired air-to-surface missiles at the *Stennis*. Apparently one hit the carrier."

"Do they know how much damage?" asked Duncan, shouting over the noise of the rotary engine overhead.

The young Marine shook his head. "No, sir. We haven't been told to divert yet, but the captain is considering staying in Algiers after he lets you off."

Duncan nodded. "Let me know if you get any additional information."

"Aye aye, sir," he replied and then weaved his way slowly back to the cockpit.

"Duncan, why is it that whenever I am with you, *excretus occurus*," said Beau.

"*Excretus occurus?*"

"Yeah, shit happens. I'm going to stop going places with you if you don't rid yourself of this unlucky cloud that keeps following you."

Monkey, who had been scanning the sea out of one of the small, oval windows in the cargo bay shouted, "We're over land!" He hated flying. The sooner they were off this traveling bucket of low-bidder bolts the better.

The helicopter rocked slightly as the CH-53 swung left onto an easterly heading toward Algiers. Captain Cochran pushed his aviator sunglasses back onto his nose. He tugged his flight gloves tighter and wiggled his fingers. Only six more months before he would have been out of the Marine Corps, and now he had been told he was in for the duration. Duration of what? He had a job lined up, flying helos between oil rigs and the shore along the Gulf of Mexico, and would probably lose it because of this.

The crew chief leaned over Dale Cochran's shoulder. "Captain, I told Captain James. He wants to be kept abreast of any additional information you get."

Dale nodded. "Yeah, if they tell us anything," he shouted over the noise of the helicopter. "I have been calling for the past five minutes and have yet for them to answer. I know they're not sunk because I hear others talking with them."

His fellow Marine Corps copilot, Captain Luke Blair, pressed the intercom button. "Maybe they have more on their minds right now than a lone CH-53, flying unprotected over hostile territory at an outrageously low altitude toward a city occupied by its own forces." He gave Dale a forced smile, widening his eyes as he showed his teeth.

Luke, ever the clown. "Thanks, Butt Hole. Just what I need. Pleasant thoughts to occupy my mind." Dale jerked up on the controls, causing Luke's head to snap back and the crew chief to nearly fall. "Remember, I have the force with me."

"And, may the force remain with you," Luke replied.

The crew chief reconnected his intercom. *Dumb air jockeys,* he thought. He grabbed the bar behind the pilot to steady himself. Four years in the Marine Corps had prepared him for this. At least, he hoped so. He connected his harness to a nearby clip so he wouldn't fly all over the cockpit if the pilots decided to outdo each other, jerking the heavy helicopter all over sky. He liked the two men, but every so often, the two forgot they were Marines and acted like college jerks. He hated the idea of being in the helicopter with them when they decided to play *Animal House* in the air.

He heard a *ping* and glanced around the cockpit, looking for the source. It was an unfamiliar noise. He leaned forward to ask the lieutenants if they heard it. The bullet caught the sergeant under the chin, penetrated upward into his brain, where it lost momentum and bounced around inside his skull, turning his brain to jelly. The forward motion of the crew chief turned into a fall, and his body fell onto the two shoulders of the men. The safety harness held him up. Red blood and brain mush jetted out of the sergeant's nostrils, ears, and mouth to cover the two men.

"What the hell!" shouted Dale, trying to wipe the stuff off his neck and flight suit. There was a brief moment of wondering what the stuff was on his gloves before realization hit him like a sledgehammer.

Two more pinging sounds echoed in the cabin. They were being shot at. Dale pulled back on the throttle, pulling nearly a g before easing back as he fought to gain altitude. He heard the noise in the back as the SEALs were thrown back and forth against their harnesses. The shift in weight influenced the trim of the helicopter, causing him to overcorrect. The engines missed a beat and with it, so did his heart. If he had teeth in his ass, he'd be chewing a hole in this seat right now.

Luke pushed the dead crew chief off them and grabbed the throttle, ready to take over if something happened to Dale. The body of the crew chief swung back and forth on the safety harness. Luke felt the engine miss also. His stomach tightened, and he had an overwhelming urge to pee. He looked down at the controls.

"We're loosing revs, man. We're loosing revs! Hydraulic pressure dropping. Damn!"

"Find a place for us to put down!" Dale shouted as he banked the helicopter south, heading away from the coast, trying to avoid enemy fire.

"Shit, man, you can land anywhere here. It's all gawldamn desert!"

"Tell *Stennis* we're going in, then warn our passengers we're ditching."

A minute later, Luke was back in his seat. "Did you tell them?" Dale asked. The power to the engine was missing and stuttering every few seconds before returning to full power. One of those bullets must have hit the engine, he guessed.

"Naw, they were sleeping. I thought why wake them and tell them my bestest friend in the world, Captain Dale Cochran, United States Marine Corps, has gotten us shot down where we are going to have to crash in hostile territory where enemy forces are going to capture us, pull our toenails out with red-hot pliers before cutting off our balls and stuffin' 'em in our mouths. Naw, I didn't wake them." He shoved himself into his seat and put his headset on.

"Screw you, Luke."

"Hey, man, don't talk nasty. I wasn't the pilot who was flying when we got shot down. It's your career in tatters now." He stopped and pointed. "There, Dale. There's a good place. At least it's got some cover."

As if hearing Luke, the engine coughed several times and then quit. Only the autorotation kept the main rotor turning, slowing slightly the rush of the helicopter toward the earth.

Dale stretched his neck to see where Luke pointed. Luke was right—thank God—because they had little choice now. The softer sound of the wind buffeting off the round nose of the helicopter filled the silence created by the loss of power. The smell of burning oil filtered into the cockpit. A flat area within a small depression, surrounded by rocks and tall bushes slightly to the right of where Luke pointed seemed better to Luke. He pulled the stick to the right and was grateful when the heavy helicopter slowly pivoted toward the new landing site. Dale glanced briefly at the flight control instruments. Temperature was pegged all the way into the red. Oil was the same. Shit! The only thing not in the red was the altitude. It was fifty feet, and the needle was moving downward like a second hand on a clock.

The huge helicopter came in hard and fast. The wheels slammed into the ground, bouncing the Super Stallion back into the air several feet before it hit again, rocking from side to side. Dale thought at first it was going to flip over, but at the last second the helicopter righted itself and settled. He and Luke flipped the switches, securing the revolving rotor. He hit the extinguisher button, flooding the smoking engines with $CO_2$. The important thing was reducing the chance of fire. No doubt, the enemy would be here *muy rapido*.

Duncan unstrapped as soon as the helicopter quit rocking. "Beau, get out there and secure the area. Be prepared for anything." Bending over, Duncan moved to the cockpit.

The two pilots were unstrapping from their seats. "Captain, guess we'll walk the last ten miles, sir," Dale said. He jammed his gloves into his flight suit and tossed his headset onto the seat.

He and Luke unstrapped the crew chief and lowered the body down to the deck.

Duncan reached down and put two fingers against the young man's neck. "He's dead."

Dale picked up the body by the shoulders. "Grab the legs, Luke. We're not going to leave him."

Duncan moved out of the way as the two pilots carried the third member of the CH-53 team out of the cockpit and out of the helicopter. He looked around, saw a couple bottles of water, and grabbed them. They would need them if they were going to hike ten miles while evading these fanatics. Outside, Beau's familiar voice, shouting something to HJ and Monkey, was followed by the familiar sound of gunfire. He tossed the two bottles of water out the door, grabbed his carbine, and leaped from the helicopter. Black smoke from the damaged engines rose into the sky. *Might as well be flares,* he thought as he unlimbered his carbine and rushed to the lip of the depression where they had landed.

He rolled up against Beau, pointing his carbine over the lip. Across a paved road about five hundred feet from their position, a line of Algerian rebels charged. Must be at least a hundred of them. A gust of wind blew sand into his face. If he survived this, he was never, ever going to another beach for the rest of his life. He pulled the trigger, his bullets joining the others, as he blinked his eyes, clearing the sand from them.

# SIX

⚓

**VASILEV PULLED A CLOTH FROM HIS WHITE OVERCOAT** and wiped the sweat from his forehead. He leaned away from the warhead, turning slightly on the mobile platform to see what progress the others were making on the other missiles. Four missiles down, Yuri stood on tiptoes at the top of a stepladder, his head inside an open bay of a warhead. Two missiles farther, Fedorov grinned as he held up a canister in a toast toward Vasilev. Vasilev waved in acknowledgement. They both started down the ladders at the same time.

Two other Russian scientists pushed a cart down the middle space separating the twelve missiles. Yuri leaned out of the compartment and nearly fell, but he grabbed the lip of the hatch at the last moment to regain his balance.

"Be careful," Hova Vaitsay, the Hungarian scientist, warned from the base of the platform.

"Be careful, Yuri," Vasilev added softly. "If anyone hurts himself here, there will be no one to help him."

Grimacing, Yuri climbed down the stepladder to join the other two at the cart.

Stepkolov reached over and took Professor Vasilev Malenkomoff's canister. The heavy white gloves held the biological component of the warhead carefully as the second man on the cart, Popov, opened the security chamber. Yuri and Fedorov impatiently waited their turn. The canister fit perfectly into a hole designed for the deadly warheads. Hova stood a few feet away, looking ready to run if anyone dropped the steel-encased canisters.

"The longer we stay here in the missile storage facility, Vasilev, the more danger we are in. If that madman catches us here, he will kill us."

Vasilev nodded. "Yuri, what other options do we have? I asked him yesterday that we be allowed to leave. What happened? He refused to let us even go to our own rooms. We are confined to the laboratory, according to that evil-looking sergeant that stayed behind for a few minutes." Vasilev sighed, held his hands out, and with a resigned look met the eyes of the other scientists. "And I think we all know why."

"He is going to kill us, isn't he?" Stepkolov asked, taking the canister from Yuri and putting it in the cart.

"I don't think he intends to pin the Order of Lenin on us," Popov said.

Vasilev shrugged his shoulders. "We don't know he is going to kill us for sure," he said unconvincingly. "Could be we are being confined for security reasons." He looked at the other faces.

Popov snorted and spat on the floor. "If you believe that, comrade, you are a fool." Popov was a dedicated, unreformed communist. Of course, a communist who knew the value of money and had leaped at the chance to earn a few Yankee dollars doing clandestine work. "I will tell all of you, comrades. When they return to move these missiles, they will remove us if we are still here." He wagged a finger at them.

"Then we should go now," Hova suggested.

"How are we going to go?" Stepkolov said sharply. "There are only two ways out of here. The elevator or stairs leading up or the tunnels behind those heavy doors. The elevator and stairs are guarded, and we don't know the combo to the hangar doors."

Vasilev sighed deeply and audibly, the noise echoing within the large hangar.

"Maybe I am overreacting. Maybe they will honor their agreement. Maybe we will get our money and return to mother

Russia to lead a long and prosperous life with our loved ones," said Yuri.

"And, maybe we, too, will have forty virgins waiting when he kills us."

"Don't be ridiculous. We are fools. We made a deal with the devil, and now we are paying. We allowed the smell of money to cloud our common sense. Why do you think Vasilev talked us into taking Karol's anthrax vaccine for the last two weeks?" Fedorov asked.

Popov ran his hand through his unruly shock of graying hair. "He will kill us. It is something I would do if I was a madman and not just an extraordinary ex-Soviet scientist. Fedorov, my boy, if you had been observant like the scientist you are, you would know this, too. He cannot afford for the world to know we have done this, even if he never intends to use the weapons. No one must know the true story behind how Libya produced biological warheads. Do you think Russia or Hungary would step in to help us? They don't even know we are here, and if they did, they would run to their NATO allies and tell them. NATO would tell America and, like Afghanistan, they would come after Libya with a vengeance."

"Three more," Stepkolov interrupted, leaning back and nodding toward the holding chamber. He wiped his hand on a moist sterilization cloth.

"Stepkolov is right. We need to be working, not talking," Vasilev said. "There is always the chance that he will live up to his bargain."

"You are living in a dream, comrade. We must be prepared in case he doesn't."

"Here, Stepkolov. With this one," he said, handing the scientist his canister. "You only need two more."

Stepkolov took the canister from Fedorov. "Be quiet for a moment and let me put these away," Stepkolov growled. "If I drop one and it breaks . . ."

Hova took another few steps backward.

Popov laughed. He took the one from Fedorov, stared at Hova, and dropped the canister. The clang of metal hitting the concrete floor echoed off the walls. Even Vasilev jumped back like the others.

Hova ran toward the ladder stairwell leading to the platform overlooking the missile chamber.

"Hova, you coward!" laughed Popov, his bass laughter echoing through the cavernous chamber.

Hova stopped with one foot on the ladder. He turned around but remained at the foot of the ladder.

"Stop clowning, Popov," Vasilev said angrily.

"If these things were that fragile, they would never survive a missile launch and would shower their contents on the missile crew . . . which, come to think of it, would not be such a bad idea." Popov picked up the canister and tossed it a couple of times into the air, catching it each time. "If warriors were put in peril when every weapon they launched could blow up and kill them, then we would have fewer weapons. Right?"

"Popov, stop it," Vasilev said, reaching over and snatching the canister in midair from the communist. He handed it to Stepkolov, who quickly put it inside the cart.

Popov laughed. "I think the stress is affecting your humor, Vasilev."

"There! That's it! This cart is full . . . six canisters. We can move it upstairs with the other one and come back for the last two," Stepkolov said. He turned and shoved Popov. The huge man tripped a couple of steps backward before regaining his balance.

"Hey, what was that for, comrade?"

"That was for scaring the shit out of me, comrade, and acting stupid."

Vasilev put his hands on the heavy cart and began to push. The others grabbed a side, and soon they had the contraption at the door of the elevator.

"Come on, Hova Vaitsay. Give us a hand," Popov said, taking an exaggerated breath. "See! No anthrax. Arggg!" he shouted, grabbing his throat. "I was wrong!"

"Stop it, Popov."

Popov took his hands from his throat. "The Hungarian is a coward, Vasilev. If we are going to die, then we should at least be men about it. Personally, the best way of dying is in the arms of a beautiful woman. At least then I could go out of this world a babbling idiot, but a babbling idiot with a permanent smile across my face."

"Screw you," Hova said as he joined the group around the cart. They shoved the anthrax-loaded cart into the elevator.

"We still have two more to do," Popov said. "We don't really need the cart. Leave me and Yuri to do them."

"No, we will work together. I know," Vasilev continued. "Numbers four and twelve are the only two left. We will empty one of the carts and come back for them."

"We are playing with our own deaths," Stepkolov said.

"As we have for the past months, comrade?"

"We have an agreement with the Libyans," Yuri added, straightening his smock. "Once we finish this project, they are to allow us to go. I cannot understand why they would not."

The confines of the freight elevator muted Popov's heavy bass laughter. "Why are Vasilev and I surrounded by fools? Of course, they are going to renege. Even if we weren't the most costly item in their defense budget, we know too much. Vasilev is right. We have some money already in offshore accounts. We have to figure out how to escape. Once in Europe, then we can demand Alqahiray pay the remainder he owes. Of course, when he fires those missiles and they go *pfffft*, with the worse thing that happens is a city full of shit-filled pants, we may have to wait a couple of years for him to cool off."

"He may send an assassin team after us," Hova said.

"Yeah, and he may rape your mother, my Hungarian plains cowboy."

"Two more hours, and we will render their missile capability to nil. At least, if we die, then we die knowing we have stopped them from visiting death on innocent women and children," Stepkolov said.

"Now we become patriots and humanitarians?" Popov asked.

The elevator stopped at the laboratory level. They pushed the cart down the hallway past the testing chamber. Vasilev stopped and looked inside at the two captive Libyan officers. Both sat on the edge of their cots and stared back. He doubted the vaccine administered yesterday would be effective. You needed about a week for the antibodies to reach a level where they stood even a small chance of protecting you. Once anthrax spores were inhaled, you were dead without immediate treatment. The vaccine was only effective if you had taken it long before being exposed. He had also given them antibiotics, but he doubted they would be effective.

The tall, thin officer held up his hand and waved. The other ignored Vasilev and the other Russians. He lay on the bed curled in a fetal position. *The way life works sometimes,* Vasilev thought, *the brave ones die and the cowards live, only to die later.*

Popov continued to deride the others on their naïveté about the situation. Vasilev had been naive until yesterday, when the colonel showed his true colors. The two men inside the testing chamber would die. The vaccine and the antibiotics were too little, too late. He knew the intelligence officer who waved knew this, too.

He heard the suction sound the door leading into the laboratory facility made when it opened. The negative air pressure inside pulled the air from the hallway into it. Vasilev hurried down the hallway and around the corner in time to watch the door shut. Oh, well, the three inside were sufficient to dispose of the biological agents. He and the other three would wait outside the main facility to pass the canisters through a small box-like window designed to pass small items back and forth. It saved the drudgery of suiting up every time they needed something from outside.

Vasilev walked down the hall to where Alexei, suited and inside the laboratory, was removing the canisters, one by one, and placing them on the counter. The small Cossack had the unenviable task of draining off the aerosol pressure from the small canisters and then disposing of the spore tubes into a small furnace in the back. Vasilev knew from the many hours spent inside how the heat would make Alexei's job uncomfortable. The unventilated space depended on undependable air-conditioning to keep their body temperatures down. He waited patiently until the last canister was on the table. This was their second trip since they started last night. He looked at his watch. Aboveground, the sun would have been up for nearly two hours, and the temperature would already be climbing toward the nineties on its way past a hundred. They would be cutting it close to finish the last two.

The noise of the elevator doors behind him opening startled Vasilev, causing him to jump. He turned as the doors widened. Hova came around the corner and joined them.

Sergeant Adib stepped out, along with six other Libyan soldiers. Vasilev wondered briefly if the man had changed his clothes, or if his uniform had a special chemical to keep it creased so perfectly.

The soldiers carried AK-47s with the exception of Adib, who had, somewhere since yesterday, traded his AK-47 for a Beretta. Vasilev stepped forward.

"Welcome, Sergeant. I guess you have come to check on the two test subjects?"

Adib nodded curtly. "Yes, I suppose I have, Professor Malenkomoff—among other things."

Vasilev Malenkomoff heard the huge noise of the freight doors to the missile hangar opening. "Is something going on?" he asked, stepping toward the windows overlooking the hangar.

Adib ignored Vasilev to peer into the window, where Alexei worked methodically in his heavy, white, protective suit. "What is he doing?" he asked, waving the pistol.

Vasilev stepped up beside the taller Adib, feeling the inadequacy of his smaller size. "Oh, Alexei? He is cleaning away the results of our experiments and decontaminating the room as much as possible. You never know what can happen if you don't keep track of every item of work when you are engaged in such a dangerous job as ours. Without these special precautions, every one of us here could have anthrax spores on our clothes. Don't you agree, Sergeant Adib?"

Sergeant Adib took several steps to the right, putting a few feet between him and Vasilev. "You may be right, Professor." He waved his Beretta at the scientist. "Have the other scientists join us on the floor. We are going to move the missiles to their deployment sites. Al Maadi has decided to show the West our righteousness and resolve by hanging the sword of Damocles over their heads."

"I don't think you need weapons here, Sergeant. The two soldiers are quite unable to resist."

Adib waved his gun again. "These weapons are for our protection, Malenkomoff."

They walked down the hallway toward the freight elevator leading toward the main missile hangar. At the test chamber, Sergeant Adib and his men stopped to look in at the two intelligence officers.

"Can they hear me?" he asked.

Vasilev picked up a nearby microphone. "Press this button

here and they will be able to hear you. Keep it pressed, and you can hear their reply."

Adib took the microphone and pressed the speaker button. "Good morning, sirs," he said. "Colonel Alqahiray sends his regrets on being unable to see how you are doing this morning. He wishes to ask how you feel. He also wants you to know that he does intend to visit you in the days to come. He wants to witness how the disease progresses." Adib laughed.

"Your mother must have mated with a sorry, flea-bitten camel, Sergeant, to raise such an imbecile," said the intelligence officer, who sat impassively on the edge of his cot.

"Don't try to anger me, sir. I never had a mother. What would you like? Me to come in there and face off with you one on one? Of course, you would love to see me angry, but in this instance, Captain, you are the stronger one. You have a power inside there that protects you from me. Unfortunately, it won't protect you from it."

"Please tell your Al Maadi that I extend my personal invitation for him to visit inside with us at any time."

Adib tossed the microphone to Vasilev.

"Where are the other scientists?"

"They are coming."

As if hearing Vasilev's answer, two of the scientists who were inside the laboratory walked around the corner.

"Welcome, Sergeant," Popov said. "And I see that you have had your morning supply of razor blades for breakfast?"

Adib glared at the communist, but before he could respond, Popov continued. "I suppose you are here to escort us to our quarters. For that, we thank you. We need a chance to rest, a nice shower, and at least to change our underwear before we leave. Vasilev, is that a spore I see on your collar?" Popov reached up and flicked an imaginary speck from Malenkomoff's collar.

Adib raised one eyebrow. Vasilev saw the Libyan sergeant's lips curl in disgust. In that instant, he knew only orders from Alqahiray stopped this man from killing them. Adib wanted to hurt them, he could tell. What orders had Alqahiray given him?

"We must go below," Adib said contemptuously. He reached out and pressed the button on the elevator. He started to step inside, stopped, and turned to Vasilev.

"Professor, where is the scientist who was inside the laboratory?"

"It will take Alexei a few minutes to sanitize himself and change out of the decontamination suit, Sergeant. If you would like him to come with us, then we will have to wait a few minutes."

Adib shook his head. "No, that is all right." He turned to one of the soldiers. "Mamud, go back to the laboratory and wait for the scientist in there to clean up."

The young soldier ran down the hallway, his steel-toed boots scuffing the tile floor, his AK-47 held against his chest. *How much younger they seem with the passing years,* thought Vasilev, as the elevator doors closed. Where would Adib do the dirty deed? Down below? If so, not before the missiles disappeared onto the tracks in the tunnel that connected the room to the vast underground complex running the length and breadth of Libya. He had no idea where the missiles would go, but he knew that once they were aboveground, their presence would soon be discovered.

"What are you thinking, Professor?" Adib asked as they stepped out of the elevator.

The smile disappeared. "Oh, sorry, Sergeant. I was taking pride in what we have accomplished in the six months we have been here. I do not think anyone else could have done what we seven have done . . . God rest Karol's soul," he said.

"You should be proud to be a part of this moment," Adib said, agreeing.

Vasilev estimated a hundred soldiers swarming over the missiles now. He watched as they hooked up one after the other to a small tractor and pulled them toward the huge hangar doors leading to railroad tracks farther down the corridor. Three soldiers, one with a clipboard, stood at the doors, crossing off numbers from the side of the missiles. Vasilev knew each missile was predestined for a specific missile site. Which one, he had no idea, but eventually they must go aboveground to fire.

He saw missile number twelve roll toward the door. Death departed on this one. He glanced around the room but failed to see number two. It had already gone. Those two missiles were still functional. It was in God's hands now; there was nothing he could do. His focus now turned toward saving their lives. The hangar doors could be opened from inside or outside, but you had to know the combination to the keypad to open them. Around midnight, when they began the slow process of disarming the warheads, Vasilev had spread a light coating of talcum powder on each of the keys. Four keys controlled the door, and with the substance on the keys, they could tell what four were used. Of course, what they couldn't tell was the order in which the keys were pressed. They could escape, if they remained free.

Six hours passed with Adib moving constantly around the hangar while the guards—and Vasilev thought of them as guards—watched the seven scientists. Vasilev also noticed that the thin pretension that they were part of the event had faded during that time. The guards' weapons never wavered from pointing at them. Popov's weak bladder earned a few derisive comments from the guards as they continually escorted the aging scientist to and from the bathroom. One of the soldiers at the hangar door reached over and pressed the buttons of the keypad when the last missile being towed out of the hanger passed the doorway. Vasilev couldn't see the numbers the soldier pushed, but he noticed the fingers went up, then down, then up twice. The screech of the hinges and the hydraulic mechanism drowned out the whispered conversations. What if the cipher lock had two combinations? One for opening the door and another for closing it? He shook his head. If it required two combinations, then they would never hit the right one to escape. That is, if they were permitted to live long enough to escape.

Vasilev wiped the sweat from his brow. Without the missiles, the facility brought to mind the stories of underground execution rooms beneath the KGB buildings in the old Soviet Union. He glanced over at Popov and saw fear there. He nodded at the elderly communist, who raised his eyebrows in response and winked back. They both probably had the same thoughts. Vasilev wondered to whom a communist prays when he is about to die.

Sergeant Adib and four more soldiers came over to Vasilev and the others.

"Congratulations, Sergeant Adib. A most smooth and professionally run operation. How long will it take the missiles to reach their deployment site? And when do you think we can expect to see them fired?" Sometimes, an offense is better than a defense. *Pretend we are still on the team,* Vasilev said to himself.

"I think those are questions for which you have no need to know, Professor."

Popov stepped forward. "Come on, Adib. We are not fools. Do you intend to shoot us?"

Hova stepped behind the four scientists in front.

Adib laughed. "Of course not. You have been instrumental in helping Barbary achieve greatness. Colonel Alqahiray has asked that we confine you until after we have completed the operation."

"See! I told you they would honor their part of the bargain," said Yuri, his words trailing off as he tried to rein in his unexpected outburst.

*Don't say anything about the vaccine,* prayed Vasilev.

"Of course, the colonel is interested in how the test subjects progress as the anthrax works."

*The gods are smiling on us.*

"Well, of course, comrade," Popov said. "We are taking copious notes and observations. This morning, the smaller of the two shit himself. Later, we will pull his pants down to determine how much."

Adib pointed to the elevator. "Shall we go see the two officers who volunteered for this experiment?"

Minutes later, group stood outside the closed testing compartment. Alexei joined them from the other side of the room, where he had waited for their return. Vasilev and Alexei's eyes met for a fraction of a second, acknowledging that the scientist had completed his disposal of the anthrax warheads. The two prisoners were in the same spot they were six hours earlier.

"There is no known cure for this strain of anthrax, is there?" Adib asked, looking directly at Vasilev.

Vasilev met the man's stare and looked directly into his eyes. He had read somewhere that when people lie, they are unable to meet your eyes or return your stare. "No, Sergeant, there is none," he said, meeting the man's eyes. "Those men are dead in there. Already the one curled up has lost control of his bowels. The disease has reached the point where it is causing internal hemorrhaging. This is a very virulent strain of anthrax."

Adib looked inside the testing chamber.

"I pity those who are exposed to it," Vasilev continued as he moved up beside the Libyan sergeant. "The brave one, as Colonel Alqahiray called him, has been spitting up blood since early morning," he lied. "So far, he seems to be fighting the disease, but even that fight will ebb away as the anthrax spreads, taking control, flooding his lungs with blood and sending pain racking through his body with each breath." *Maybe the antidote was effective in such a short time.*

"That is good news, Professor. The colonel believes that observations can be better kept if you are with the men."

"What!" Popov shouted. "That is outrageous. We will die if we are put into the testing chamber."

*Don't overdo the theatrics, Popov,* Vasilev thought, shutting his eyes briefly.

Hova fell to his knees. "No, don't do that. I don't want to die. Please, shoot us instead."

"But, you promised!" Yuri shouted, ignoring the pleading Hungarian.

Adib laughed. "Are you so naive you think we would let you go? However, I am a merciful man, so I will give you a choice. You can go into the testing chamber walking, or I can have my men shoot you in the knees and then shove you into the chamber. Either way, you are going." He waved the new Beretta pistol in front of them and looked at it. "I have been wanting to see how this weapon works. It belonged to the one whom you call courageous," he said, pointing the weapon at the intelligence officer, who was watching the proceedings from the edge of his bed.

*Pistols symbolize authority,* Vasilev thought. *Adib is very proud of how much he has grown in importance since yesterday.*

Stepkolov stepped forward. "I, for one, would rather be shot out here than go in there. I have seen what this strain will do."

*Good,* thought Vasilev. *Make it seem we are not eager to go in there. Be careful, Stepkolov, don't get yourself shot.*

"We can accommodate you, Russian." He pointed the pistol at the Russian, his finger beginning to tighten on the trigger.

Vasilev stepped in front. "There is no need, Sergeant. We will go. Stepkolov, help Hova to his feet."

Adib lowered the pistol to his side and snapped his fingers. The barrels of the AK-47s pointed at the seven men. "It is time, gentlemen," he said, pointing to the entry door. "Enjoy your observations." He chuckled.

Vasilev touched Popov on the arm. "Come on." He tugged open the door and led the way inside.

"But why? Why are they doing this?" cried Hova Vaitsay.

Moments later, Adib and the guards watched as the scientists joined the two intelligence officers. Adib bent over the intercom. "Professor, I will leave a couple of soldiers to oversee your welfare. If you need anything, be sure to call. Tea, milk, bread. Anything." They saw him laughing, but the perverse sergeant hung the microphone up, thankfully releasing the button.

"What do we do now?" Alexei asked Vasilev.

"We wait. The guards will tire of watching us, and when they do, then we go."

"We are going to die. The vaccine will not work," the petrified Hungarian said softly.

"Be brave, my coward," Popov said, pulling Hova Vaitsay to him and engulfing the Hungarian within his gigantic arms. "Besides, it is me who may kill you if you keep whining. What would your mother say if she heard you now?"

Hova buried his face in the man's chest. The closeness muffled the whimpering.

The intelligence officer rose from his cot. He reached out and put his hand on Fedorov to steady himself. "There is a way out of here?" He asked, his voice coming in gasps.

The vaccine had failed to work on the officer, Vasilev knew without having to examine the man. The small blood vessels around his eyes had burst, flooding the orbs with a solid wall of red. Blood outlined his gums, staining his teeth with red smears that reddened his lips.

"Hey," hissed Popov. "This one is dead."

"It works faster than we thought," Yuri added, as they inhaled the spores floating around the room.

"Do you think the vaccine will be effective?"

"Of course," said Vasilev with as much conviction as he could muster. If it weren't, then by the time they reached the tunnel, they would all be in the same shape as the remaining survivor from yesterday. Fedorov helped the surviving Libyan lie down on the cot.

Vasilev looked out the window. Two Libyan guards stood watching them. He knew the Libyans well enough to know the two young men would soon tire of the spectacle and wander off to see what else this floor held. With luck, they might even enter the laboratory.

**"IT'S ONE UP, ONE DOWN. THEN TWO UP,"** VASILEV mumbled to himself as he searched the keys on the combination door lock. His head was inches away from the keys aligned with the first five numbers along the top row and numbers six through zero along the second.

Behind him, the other scientists watched nervously, frequently glancing toward the elevator leading down from the platform above to the missile chamber where they stood. The windows on the platform above remained empty.

"It's three o'clock," Yuri said softly, his whisper echoing in the room. "They are probably sleeping."

"What if they follow?"

"They won't, Alexei," Popov answered. "Even if they did, do you think any of them are going to get in the elevator with the Libyan soldier who is dying in it?"

"We should have left him in the facility," Hova Vaitsay said. "And the dead man we should have left where he died."

"Why? The one in the elevator is going to die anyway, comrade. And the dead man in the hallway will keep those guards away like nothing we could have done. I doubt they know that anthrax is not a communicable disease. They will come charging around the corner when they hear this door open. When they see their former comrade dead in the middle of the hallway, they will slip and slide, fighting to turn around rather than stumble across the man. Their lives will flash across their minds as they fight each other to be the first off this floor. As for the one in the elevator, what if one of those Libyan guards is brave enough to follow us? Do you think he will get in the elevator with a dying anthrax victim who is moaning, blood spitting out of his mouth, and shitting all over himself? No, comrade, this way his death will be our freedom. Besides, by the time they discover us gone, he may be dead."

"Be quiet, please. Popov, your voice echoes like an opera singer. Try not to talk. Now, the numbers are two, six, five, and four, but I don't know in what order they go," Vasilev said to the group.

"One up, one down, and then two up?" Fedorov asked.

"That's what I saw."

"That's not what I saw," Yuri said.

"Let me try it. I used to work for . . . never mind. Let me try it." Fedorov shoved Vasilev out of the way. He looked at the keys, tried twice, and on the third attempt, the sound of the bolts sliding back greeted his attempt. "Child's play," he said, smiling at the head scientist. "You see, the second number has to be six. It's the only number on the second row. Since the human fingers like to dance in rhythm—"

"Okay, okay, okay. You are one brainy guy, Fedorov. Now move out of the front of the door so we can get the hell out of here," Popov said.

Vasilev pressed the Open button above the cipher lock. The loud sounds of hydraulic gears engaging the huge hangar door woke them to the precariousness of their situation. The scientists ran to the center of the doors and edged as close as they could to it as the two sides slowly moved apart.

"What are we going to do once we get on the other side?" Yuri asked, almost shouting over the noise.

"Take one of the vehicles parked outside. We drive north until we hit Tripoli."

"Sure, Vasilev, but do you think the Libyans are going to allow us to walk right out of the next door? There may be guards."

"Stepkolov, you're right, but there are ventilation shafts along the tunnel. All we have to do is find one leading into Tripoli or near Tripoli and then climb out."

Vasilev reached up and pressed the Stop button. "Come on. It's wide enough to slip through." He turned sideways and slid into the huge tunnel on the other side.

"Right! We are just going to drive up the middle of the Libyan military tunnel, find a ventilation shaft, climb out of it . . . and then what?" Yuri mumbled as he followed Vasilev through the opening.

"Why, we hail a taxi and take it to the Russian embassy," Popov offered as he squeezed his bulky body through the small opening.

"If we make it," Hova Vaitsay added. He looked back at the hangar, the glass-enclosed platform above the empty, cavernous room, and waited a second or two to see if the guards appeared. Then he ducked through the door and followed Yuri.

"Oh, shut up. We're further along now than we were an hour ago," Fedorov said as they followed the first four.

Three open-top six-passenger vans and a small truck were parked about a hundred feet down the tunnel. Yuri scrambled into the driver's side of one of the vans, grinning from ear to ear as he jingled the keys left in the ignition. "We are lucky, and they are too confident."

Within minutes, the van, with the other six crammed into the five remaining seats and watching the open doorway behind them, zoomed off down the lighted tunnel, heading toward Tripoli a hundred miles away.

Vasilev's fear that the Libyans would catch them before they reached the Libyan capital was wrong. He had no way of knowing the four Libyan guards discovered the two dead prisoners within minutes of recognizing the sound of the hangar doors opening. The fear of anthrax was only outweighed by fear of what Colonel Alqahiray would do to them for allowing the foreigners to escape. By the time the van was a half mile into its escape, the four frightened Libyan soldiers were racing up the stairs leading to the surface and away from Alqahiray. The disappearance of the scientists was discovered late that afternoon—nearly twelve hours after they drove off—when Sergeant Adib made his rounds. By then, Vasilev and his fellow scientists had already abandoned the van and crawled out of the tunnel through an air vent on the outskirts of the Libyan capital. Just as Popov had predicted, six of them took an early-morning taxi to the Russian embassy, while Hova Vaitsay abandoned his fellow scientists for the Hungarian embassy.

The captain of an Aeroflot airliner, scheduled to depart at noon from Tripoli, angrily confronted the embassy personnel, who escorted six special passengers to the business section, delaying their flight to Moscow by an hour. Fifteen minutes after Vasilev, Alexei, Yuri, Fedorov, Stepkolov, and Popov strapped into their seats, the wide-bodied airliner took off. Popov was already on his third vodka by the time the wheels locked into the undercarriage.

At the Hungarian embassy, the military attaché hastily wrote a synopsis of what Hova Vaitsay, member of the Hungarian Intelligence Service, debriefed. His bosses had listed Hova as missing months ago, having lost contact with him after he disappeared into the desert with the Russian scientists. Five minutes after the encrypted message was transmitted from the Hungarian embassy's secret, soundproof, lead-lined room deep in the bowels of the formidable building on Gamal Abdel Nasser Boulevard, it arrived at the Hungarian Intelligence Service Headquarters in Budapest. The American CIA agent, assigned as an exchange officer for the Hungarian agent stationed at Falls Church, read the message. He had lived in Washington through the biological attacks of the early twenty-first century. He knew well the implications of what Hova Vaitsay had relayed. The Hungarian Army general at the intelligence center sent a shorter encrypted message to the Hungarian NATO representative in Brussels.

Ten minutes and eight thousand miles later, the Hova message, along with the CIA agent's personal validation assessment of Hova's reliability, reached the duty officer in Falls Church. This time, the deputy director of the CIA had not been out jogging when the critical news arrived.

Deep underground, one hundred miles south of Tripoli, Colonel Alqahiray screamed at Sergeant Adib and shoved Major Ahsan Hammad Maloof, his terrified aide, out of the way. While he was launching his tirade over the escape of the scientists, tasking had already been transmitted from the chairman of the Joint Chiefs of Staff to the commander of Joint Task Force African Force.

The tasking message was short and to the point: "Take out the missiles before they can be launched." General Sutherland, the commander in chief, European Command, called the chairman and asked him to go through him with future orders and quit jumping the chain of command. He did it very tactfully.

The crisis in Korea still held the attention of the small, overworked JCS staff, but the immediacy of two anthrax warhead missiles being prepared for launch against Europe caused a new focus. The chairman leaned back in his chair, pinching the top of his nose and blinking several times to clear his eyes. For him, it would mark the sixth night in a row he had not been home, and home was only six miles away. Though none had complained, he knew most of the staff had been here much longer; the couches in the various cubicles and rooms had gotten a lot of use in the past two months.

He stood and strolled to a map of the Mediterranean. He wished he had the resources to help the remaining United States Sixth Fleet units that would have to deal with this. The only thing he could do was detour a couple of Air Force B-52s with their air-launched cruise missiles to help. He would like to have sent another reconnaissance asset to the area, but every available recce bird was in the Pacific Theater of operations. After several seconds of thought, he turned to his aide and told him to get his British counterpart on the STE secure telephone line. The plan agreed upon between the president and the prime minister would have to be moved up. It helped that he and General Alexander Suttle-Temple had a long personal friendship from their days when he was commander, European Command, and supreme allied commander. He would leave it to the secretary of defense, Roger Maddock, to iron out the niceties of the political end with the minister of defense. He'd call General Sutherland later and explain why he circumvented the chain of command.

The door to his office burst open, and the vice chairman, accompanied by the Joint Staff Operations director, Vice Admiral Sterling Jones, walked in with broad smiles across their faces.

"They're retreating."

"Who?"

"The North Koreans, General. The Eighty-second Airborne with the First Marine Division outflanked the Korean lines and have been rolling up the bastards. They are breaking and running."

For the first time in two months, the chairman grinned. "About time for some good news." He paused for a moment. "If this works—"

"No, if about it, Chairman. The Chinese called the State Department a few minutes ago, trying to take credit for the North Koreans retreating."

General Eaglefield nodded. "Then as soon as possible I want two of those carriers with their battle groups heading toward the Mediterranean."

"Should we also send an Amphibious Task Force?" Jones asked.

"Of course. Meanwhile, keep the *Kearsarge* and her Marines locked in place for the time being, but tell them to be prepared to execute original orders of supporting the Korean Theater."

"Congratulations, sir," the vice chairman said, saluting General Eaglefield, then along with Vice Admiral Jones the two hurried out of the office as the joint director for command, control, communications, and computers walked into the chairman's office.

"You heard?"

Lieutenant General Moses Davis nodded. "Congratulations, sir. Does this change the other plan?"

General Eaglefield shook his head. "No, the forces are in place. You know what you have to do. Unless you hear otherwise, Moses, make it happen."

"Yes, sir. Everything is rolling along smoothly so far. I have talked with Colonel Dusty Cooper, and he assures me his men are ready to execute Tangle Bandit." The gray-haired African-American ran his hand across his short crew cut. "Sir, maybe we should tell Task Force African Force—"

"No. This is a special operation, and we will keep it that way. The less who know, the safer our people are."

"It's still dangerous."

"I know." He nodded. "And we will probably sustain casualties, but it is something we have to do."

# SEVEN

⚓

**THE SUN RISES QUICKLY ALONG THE FLAT, SCRUB-**
covered terrain of the Algerian coast where the edge of the Sahara desert teases the Mediterranean shores. The occasional
shots fired by the rebels, dug in across the highway, failed to
cover the continuous sound of smooth surf mixing with the
slight wind coming off the night desert. Duncan wiped the
moisture from his eyes and licked his dry lips. Like the other
members of the team, he had been awake through the night.
Twice the Algerian rebels had tried to overrun their position,
but the casualties inflicted by the battle-hardened SEALs had
soon dampened any desire for further attacks. Daylight might
change the rebels' reluctance when they discovered there were
only ten of them: eight Navy SEALs and two Marine Corps
helicopter pilots. Every Marine was a rifleman, even if the only
weapons were Navy-issued Colt forty-five pistols.

The razor-sharp edge of sunlight flowed like a fast-moving
tide, racing across the beach until its sharp, bright rays flooded
over him and the others, quickly burning off the night cold with
unbridled heat. Minutes before, he had his knees drawn up,
bunching his flack jacket against his torso to conserve heat
from the night's near-freezing temperatures. Now he unbuttoned his collar, straightened his body, and rolled up his

sleeves. The process of unlayering began as the temperature raced upward like a great stallion bolting from the gate. Around Duncan, the others began to do the the same, welcoming the warmth after a night of shivers. The smell and sounds of the sea seemed at odds with the heat, lack of humidity, and rough sands of the desert.

Duncan looked for Chief Wilcox and spotted him lying along the top of the incline leading up from the small depression where the CH-53 Super Stallion had crashed. The man's carbine-14 pointed over the top toward the fanatical Algerian rebels. The two Marine Corps pilots squatted at the bottom near the body of their crew chief.

"Captain," Gibbons whispered from his right.

Duncan turned his head toward the radioman SEAL positioned on the ground near the rim of the depression they had defended through the night. The damaged Marine Corps green CH-53 Super Stallion sat silently behind them as if it could take off whenever they wanted, if he ignored the bullet holes, which told the true story. Bullet holes peppered the sides from the sniping, periodic fire, and the two rebel attempts to overrun them. Bullets zipped over their heads and played rat-a-tat on the fuselage throughout the night. Even if they had wanted to sleep, the noise would have kept them awake. When no other charge followed the second attempt, Duncan figured the rebels had decided to wait until daylight. He had everyone keep their heads down and let the rebels waste their ammunition sniping and firing over their heads. Beau had expressed amazement when no mortar rounds followed the attack. The only thing they could figure was the rebel forces confronting them were not military. "Probably civilians," Beau offered. "Kind of a light infantry equivalent," Duncan agreed.

"What you got, Gibbons?" Duncan asked the New Jersey native who was holding the handset of the backpack radio.

"Sir, the Marines just called. Rescue helicopters are airborne and on their way."

The smile on the man's face belied the slight tremble in the SEAL's voice. Duncan understood. You don't stay pinned down overnight, praying for rescue, without anxiety building up. He felt it himself. Navy SEALS were not used to being pinned down. They fought better on the move. That was what they were trained to do: fight on the run.

"Okay, pass the word your way, Petty Officer Gibbons, but tell everyone to still keep their heads down. Rescue is on its way, and we don't want anyone shot this close to going home."

"Home, Captain?" Gibbons smiled.

"Anywhere they aren't shooting at us is home today, Petty Officer Gibbons."

Duncan scrambled crablike to the left until he rolled up against Beau, bumping the lieutenant commander on the shoulder with his body.

"Well, good morning to you, too, boss." Beau slid a couple of spaces away. Not because of being upset but to reduce target opportunity for the rebels who might have an improved advantage this morning. "To hell with Washington; I've changed my mind. I want to go to London."

"Good morning to you, too, Beau. The Marines are airborne out of Algiers . . . should be here shortly. We need to be ready to board as soon as they touch down. London? Not because of why I think you want to go there?"

"London? Strictly pleasure, boss. As for the helicopters, this boy will be one of the first on board. How's your knee?" Beau reached up and wiped the sand from the side of his cheek. "You know," he said before Duncan could answer, "as much as I like you and have enjoyed this deployment, remind me when we get back to ask for a transfer. We are developing different opinions on what makes a fun deployment and what doesn't."

"Here they come!" shouted Monkey from the western side of the depression. The giant rose to his knees just below the edge of the rim, cradled the heavy M-60 machine gun, and fired a long, low-sweeping burst across the plain and the highway that separated them from the rebel positions. For the rebels to get to them, they had to cross that asphalt and a few hundred feet of flat sand terrain, making them easy targets with the sun up.

Duncan touched Beau and pointed ahead. His number two flipped off the safety and pushed his carbine over the top.

Duncan slid down the side of the bank, leaving a wake behind him in the sand. He hit the bottom and ran to Monkey's position. Bud Helliwell arrived at the same time. Both men crawled the few feet to where Monkey blazed away.

Looking over the rim, Duncan watched as about twenty Algerian rebels turned and scrambled back across the road. To the right about one hundred yards, a lone rebel sniper kneeled on the asphalt, his cheek pressed against the butt of the gun as he took aim at Monkey. Duncan pushed the giant SEAL, causing the big man to fall on his side. A burst from the M-60 blazed harmlessly into the air as Monkey, rolling down the hill, shouted, "What the fuck, Captain!"

The bullet ripped a long crease in the sand where a moment before Monkey had kneeled. Duncan fired a shot at the sniper, causing the rebel to roll across the few feet of road and disappear into the dip on the other side. The sniper's bullet clipped a small rock between Duncan and Monkey, ricocheting through Bud's shirtsleeve to nick his left arm. Blood welled up to soak the upper sleeve.

"Damn!" Bud shouted, looking down at the wound. "Why in the hell can't I go on a mission without someone shooting me?"

Monkey crawled across, flat on his belly, using his elbows and knees on the way to the top, all the while holding the M-60 above the sand.

Duncan slid down a couple of feet to where Bud had rolled onto his back. The mustang officer raised his head as he held his wounded arm. Duncan lifted the arm, ripped Bud's shirtsleeve, and prepared to apply a pressure bandage.

The bullet had made a long crease, ripping the outer skin as it zoomed away toward the empty desert.

"It's nothing," Duncan said, looking closely as he turned the arm back and forth. "Bullet only grazed you, Bud." He handed the SEAL officer the square white bandage he had pulled from his side pocket. "Here, hold this on it until the bleeding stops."

Bud took the bandage and pressed it against the three-inch-long slash. "Bullet hell, Captain. Look what you did to my shirt! Do you know how much they cost nowadays?"

"Shows your tattoos better without the sleeve, Ensign," Monkey offered, taking a quick glance before turning around to face the rebel positions. Monkey's attention focused to the front, his hands tight on the M-60, ready to turn back any other charges by the rebels. He licked his dry lips. The secret to desert survival was to drink as much water as you could, if you had it. If you didn't, then you rationed and hoped and prayed you stumbled on a source of water soon. All rationing did was delay inevitable dehydration; it wouldn't stop it.

"Monkey, as big as you are and as small as I am, why don't

you—never mind," Bud said, realizing what he meant to be a friendly exchange might bring bad luck on the sailor.

"I'll buy you a new shirt, Bud," Duncan said, then slapped the mustang officer on the good shoulder. "How many Purple Hearts now?"

"One is too many, Captain."

"Captain," Monkey said.

"Yeah?"

"Thanks, sir."

Duncan reached up and shook the man's ankle. "Monkey, who the hell would carry you if you got wounded?"

The three men grinned. Those never in combat believed it a grim, solemn, fearful event with unrelenting anxiety. In fact, combat seldom lasted long. But while it lasted, it was a mind-numbing, fear-bending, pants-filling, praying-for-life event filled with the smell of cordite, blood, and sweat bent to a belief that the hot gun jerking in your hands would save your life. Few knew how close to the surface emotions rose during combat. When the fog cleared and the bullets stopped, black humor, prayers, or tears, or all three emerged from the grateful alive even amid the screams and cries of the dying. Laughter was as common as tears after the worst of battles.

HJ squatted at the bottom of the incline where the three men lay. Duncan hadn't noticed the woman SEAL move to a backup position behind them. Something was bothering her. He couldn't quite put his finger on it, but her answers during the night had been one-word replies and only then after two or more requests. He didn't believe she was scared, but she was new to the SEALs, and her only time in the field had turned into a combat situation.

"Captain, helos in three minutes, sir," she said, relaying the word from Gibbons.

Then, again, maybe he was wrong.

Duncan slid down the sandy incline, leaving a desert wake behind him.

Beau, crouching, rushed over from the other side, his carbine pulled tight across his chest. Behind him came McDonald, Chief Wilcox, and the two pilots, Captains Dale Cochran and Luke Blair. "What's going on, Duncan?"

"Helos inbound. We may have to fight our way into them."

"Captain," Dale Cochran said, "we are taking the body of our crew chief with us."

"Of course, Captain. Did you think we would leave him behind? SEALs have never left a body, and we aren't going to start now."

"No, sir, I didn't mean . . ." the young man stuttered. "I just wanted—"

"Don't worry about it. Beau, put McDonald about twenty feet to the right of Monkey. Use the two M-60s in crossfire to keep the rebels' heads down when the helos arrive. No heroics," he said, pointing at Beau. "HJ, you and Chief Wilcox, I want you at the helicopter door. Beau and I will provide cover fire for Monkey and McDonald. Once we're on—no hesitation—jump aboard and let's get the hell out of here."

Bud opened his mouth to argue.

"No argument, Ensign. On board the helicopter is where I want you."

"Aye, aye, sir."

"How about us?" asked Captain Luke Blair, the Marine Corps copilot.

"Gentlemen, as much as I know it will irritate a couple of Marines, you two are to be the first aboard. Brief the pilot ASAP how we are boarding. I want us airborne thirty seconds after he sets down. Take the sergeant's body with you."

Gibbons, bent over at the waist, came running over to where the five squatted and did the same, cradling his carbine across his knees. "Captain, I have the lead pilot on the radio. You want to talk?"

Duncan nodded and took the mike from Gibbons. "What's his call sign, Gibbons?"

"Viper Four Seven. And, it's a her."

"Viper Four Seven, this is James One," Duncan broadcast, using his last name as a call."

"James One, this is Viper Four Seven, we are four Cobras and one heavy inbound your position," said the female voice.

Duncan pointed at Beau and motioned to the top of the depression. Beau touched HJ, and the two hurried away at a crouch with Chief Wilcox following.

Duncan held his hand out, trying to stop the two from following Beau. He had assigned HJ and the chief to defend the landing area.

"Expect to arrive in two minutes."

He dropped his hand and turned his attention to the approaching helicopters. "Roger, Viper Four Six."

Over the sound of the radio, the noise of approaching rotors filled the air. Duncan and the others turned toward the east, shading their eyes, looking for the light green silhouettes to mark the helicopter formation.

Machine gun fire erupted from McDonald and Monkey at the edge of the depression. The loud explosive fire of the heavy machine guns mixed with the slightly louder approaching rotor noises.

"Come on!" Beau shouted, his voice barely audible above the increasing decibels of battle. He pointed HJ toward the right, where Monkey fired. He crawled to the left side of McDonald. Chief Wilcox went up the center to take position halfway between the two machine gunners.

"Here they come!" shouted Monkey.

"Viper Four Seven, be advised we are taking fire. Zone is hot. I repeat, zone is hot!" Duncan shouted into the microphone.

"Roger, we will clear the area around you to give the heavy an opportunity to land. We have you marked, James One. Break flare," Viper Four Seven said. Then, after a couple of seconds, she asked, "You are still near the 53? Confirm."

"Affirmative, we are north fifty feet from the 53. Shallow depression several hundred yards this side of the highway."

"Roger, I have you in sight."

Dale Cochran pulled a flare from his kit and ran to the front of the damaged helicopter. He pulled the tag and tossed the flare about fifty feet on the other side of the disabled Super Stallion. The red smoke rose straight into the air for about twenty feet before the light desert breeze pushed it northward. He shaded his eyes and searched the sky for the Cobras; the approaching noise told him they were inbound. They sounded as if they were overhead. Airplanes and helicopters are hard to spot when cruising at low altitude. A reflection of the sun off one of them caught his attention to the east. The two inbound, thin, cross-sectioned Cobras were flying so low they resembled two huge motorcycles driving across the desert. Sand blasted out and away from the underbelly of the two assault helicopters as they zoomed toward the embattled position. A hundred yards out, the two deadly choppers shot up to about fifty feet altitude.

Before he could warn anyone, the low-flying Marine Corps AH-1 Cobra gunships blasted by overhead, the rotors blowing sand into the air and temporarily blinding Duncan and the others. Hands flew to faces in a late attempt to protect their eyes.

"Viper Four Seven, you just blinded us."

"Roger, we have you now, James One."

"God!" Beau said. "How many times does she need to confirm us?" He blinked his eyes as he rubbed them, trying to get the sand out.

Rockets from the other two Cobras roared overhead, heading toward the rebel positions. Explosive impacts sent asphalt, beach, and bodies tumbling into the air.

A second pair of Cobras approached on both sides of the small depression, their twenty-millimeter chain gun cannons blasting the area where rebel fire was originating. The small-arms fire tapered off and stopped. Above the noise came the heavier rotor sound of the approaching heavy. Duncan spotted the first pair of Cobras circling to the east, preparing what he thought was going to be an east-west run along the beach against the rebel positions.

"That's a Super Stallion!" shouted Captain Dale Cochran, his shout drowned out by the noise. "I'd recognize the sound of my own aircraft anywhere." He turned his hand upside down and wiggled his fingers at Luke, giving the Marine Corps hand sign for a CH-53. A hand with the index finger pointing over three curled fingers with the thumb cocked as if making a pistol symbolized a Cobra.

Duncan couldn't hear what Dale was shouting, but the first thought he had when he glanced back at the two Marine Corps pilots was they had had too much sun. Luke Blair had his free hand shaped like the pistol he held in his right, pointing the finger at Dale Cochran, while Dale, with a large grin on his face, enthusiastically wiggled his fingers upside down in reply.

More twenty-millimeter cannon fire filled the air. The smell of cordite and smoke from something the Cobras had destroyed blew across the depression, causing Monkey and McDonald to slide down from the rim. Beau scurried across the bottom of the depression, his body bent beneath the smoke rolling over the position.

"You win the prize, Captain," said Beau. Even as he said it, the slight north wind blew the covering smoke away from them and back toward the Mediterranean Sea.

The Cobras broke apart, one making a tight turn to the north over the rebel position and the other south passing about a hundred feet west of the SEALs. Duncan saw it first and keyed the microphone to warn Viper Four Six. "Viper Four Six," Duncan started.

HJ pointed. No one had time to say anything. The contrail from a handheld surface-to-air missile rose above the rim, heading toward the Cobra gunship on the left, looking like a comet crossing the sky.

"Oh, no!" shouted Luke Blair, the Marine Corps copilot of the damaged Stallion. "Climb, mutha fucka, climb!"

Flares exploded from the rear of the Cobra milliseconds apart as the gunship fought for altitude. The bright magnesium flames overshadowed the heat signature of the Marine Corps gunship. The missile locked on the third flare, drawing it away from the gunship to explode harmlessly meters behind the small helicopter. The Cobra stood on its tail as Duncan, amazed, watched the Marine Corps fighter pilot in the gunship climb. A second missile burst over the rim. The Cobra on the right zoomed overhead, heading for the area where the missiles originated, its cannon firing continuously. The other two Cobras appeared over the depression, sending sand again into the air and blinding them. Decoys dropped in a constant stream from the gunship in a vain attempt to stop the missiles.

They heard the missile hit. It punched into and through the rear rotor, blowing the tail off the Marine Corps gunship. The Cobra seemed to stop and hover in midair for a second before it began a twisting, uncontrolled tail-first fall out of the sky. The gunship burst into flame. Duncan saw the two crewmen; the gunner in front and the pilot sitting slightly above the crew member in back. Held motionless by centrifugal force, the two crewmen could do nothing but wait for impact. Fire enveloped the cockpit.

*What do you do in the last seconds of your life, when you know it's about to end?* thought Duncan.

The gunship hit the ground a hundred yards to the west and exploded. No one said anything.

"Viper Four Six, James One; Cobra down two hundred feet northwest our position."

"James One, Viper Four Seven; that was Viper Four Six. Area is too hot. Heavy is being recalled."

Duncan looked at the microphone in his hand. They were aborting the rescue. It felt as if a fist had hit his stomach, even as he knew the Marines had no choice. It would do little good for the heavy to land, only to have them all killed by a surface-to-air missile.

Rebel shouts and yells drew their shocked attention toward the direction of the enemy. "Here they come again!" shouted Monkey and McDonald together.

"Beau, you three get up there and help Monkey and McDonald. Not you, Gibbons," Duncan said, grabbing the radioman by the sleeve as he turned toward the battle sounds. "I need you here to work with the helicopters."

Beau, HJ, Bud, and Chief Wilcox ran to the edge of the depression and scrambled up the incline again. Aligned along the edge, they brought their weapons to bear on the attacking rebels. The sounds of *"Allah alkbar"* filled the air as the Islamic fanatics charged. Many had already made it across the highway during the fighting with the Marine helicopters. Encouraged and morale fueled by the crash of the United States Marine Corps gunship, they came en masse.

"Like shooting candies from a baby," Beau offered.

"What the hell is that supposed to mean, Commander?" HJ asked irritably. "Candies from a baby?"

"Hey, Lieutenant, you use your metaphors, and I'll make up mine."

"At least get them right, sir," she said, gritting her teeth as her carbine jerked against her good shoulder. HJ saw two rebels go down. "That's two sets of balls less."

Beau fired several shots at a group of rebels to the right and was rewarded with them diving to the ground. "Your mind is in the gutter, young lady."

"At least I have a mind." She was not going to allow herself to be taken again. HJ rose to one knee and fired at several rebels crawling toward them fifty yards to the left. A bullet caught one in the head, flipping the man up and on top of two rebels behind him. She fired a controlled burst, as the two pushed the dead man off them, hitting one in the right hand and the other in the left. The moisture on her cheek made her realize she was crying. She shook her head a couple of times and forced herself to stop. *Christ! Get a grip.*

"Must you keep showing off, HJ? Just because you were the number two on the Academy's firing squad," Beau said. His focus on the charging formation in front kept him from glancing at HJ.

"Rifle team," she said, her composure regained. "Firing squads were saved for freshman Saturday formations and those who exceeded the allowable demerits for the week. Personally, I preferred the whips and chains."

"I bet you did. And tight leather."

The crossfire from the M-60s began to have an effect. About one hundred yards from their perimeter, the surviving rebels turned and ran back toward the paved road, some crossing and disappearing into the depression on the other side.

"And spike heels, Beau."

"Hey, team!" shouted Duncan from below. "Viper Four Seven has identified where the rebels' vehicles are parked. They're going to blast the rebels to keep their heads low and give us time to get to the parking area. After that, we steal a truck and drive into Algiers. How the hell is that for a plan?" Duncan shook his head, realizing how unrealistic it sounded when said aloud.

"Duncan, who the hell came up with that idea?" Beau asked as he slid down the incline to where Duncan stood. He hit the bottom, squatted, and checked his carbine quickly, wiping the sand away from the ejection mechanism.

HJ and Bud Helliwell followed.

"Well, I did, to be honest. It seemed a better idea until I voiced it."

"I guess the next question is how do we get there without getting ourselves shot?"

Duncan pushed his soft hat back on his head. "Here is what we are faced with. The heavy can't land, and we can't stay here. We're going to run out of ammo before the Marines can clear the area, and we are already low on water. They may be able to clear the area later. The third reason we have to move is, according to Viper Four Seven, a rebel column is moving toward Algiers and most likely will arrive here by tonight. The other alternative, and I discussed this with Viper Four Seven, is that we fight our way to one of those trucks, hot-wire the son of a bitch, and hightail it down the road toward Algiers. Viper Four Seven and the other two remaining Cobras will escort us to the city. She has called for backup, and the USS *Kearsarge* has launched Harriers. The Harriers should be here by the time we get to the trucks."

"How far is it to the trucks?" Bud asked.

"A mile."

"A mile!"

"Yes, Beau, a mile."

The two CH-53 pilots overheard. "Are we planning on leaving the crew chief's body?"

"No. SEALs don't leave anyone behind. I told you that. But you two are going to have to carry him."

"Monkey, McDonald, Gibbons!" Duncan shouted. "Get down here."

Duncan pulled his handkerchief out and wiped his forehead. "Water. Without water, we wouldn't last today. According to Viper Four Seven, the trucks are west, so we are going to have to go a mile farther away from Algiers before we can turn around and head to the city."

"Captain," HJ interrupted. "Why don't we just head toward the city and have the helicopters provide protection? We can walk it."

Duncan shook his head. "It's a good twenty kilometers. Twenty kilometers of sand and rough scrubs cutting into our cammies and twenty kilometers of blazing sun. Between the sun and the enemy out there, we'd never make it." He shook his head again. "No, the trucks are our best chance. Right now, they are our only chance."

Duncan pointed behind him, past the damaged helicopter. "Viper Four Seven reports a shallow ravine about one hundred yards behind us that trails off toward the west. It should provide us cover until it peters out."

"So, when do we do it?" Chief Wilcox asked.

"We do it now," Duncan replied. "You pilots grab the crew chief's body. Chief, you and Monkey take point. Hit it."

They watched as the two SEALs, crouching, began a zigzag run to the south.

"Bud, you and McDonald bring up the rear." A hundred yards south of their position, Monkey turned and waved. They watched as he and Chief Wilcox disappeared into the shallow ravine spotted by Viper Four Seven.

Dale Cochran lifted the crew chief's body and draped it across his shoulder. Luke Blair held a pistol in his right hand and stood beside the man. "We're ready, Captain," he said, nodding at Duncan.

Duncan pointed to where Chief Wilcox had reemerged and squatted with his carbine. "There's your destination, Captains. Good luck, keep your head down, and keep moving."

The Cobras screamed by overhead, this time bracketing the depression and sending sand clouds blowing up along the edges and blocking the view of the Americans from the Algerian rebels. The sounds of their rotors beat the eardrums harshly and repeatedly. The two Marine Corps pilots hurried as fast as the weight of the dead crew chief permitted. Twenty-millimeter cannon fire tore up the rebel positions along sides of the road, while intentionally avoiding hitting the highway. The SEALs would need the road later.

Chief Wilcox waved them on, pointing toward the ditch.

"Okay, Beau, you take the cover position at the ditch. Bud, as soon as you see everyone in the ditch but Beau and the Chief, vacate toward us. We'll provide cover."

Beau nodded and took off for the shallow ravine that offered their only escape route.

"Come on, McDonald," Bud said, slapping the heavy machine gunner on the shoulder. The two hurried up the unprotected rim of the depression and threw themselves on the ground. Cannon and rocket fire from the gunships told Duncan that Viper Four Seven and the remaining two Cobras had engaged the rebels.

"Let's go, HJ, Gibbons," Duncan said.

The three of them, bent at the waist, ran toward Chief Wilcox and Beau at the edge of the ditch, zigzagging as they ran. As they neared, Monkey's head popped up fifty yards farther up. His M-60 machine gun positioned on the edge of the floodwater ditch, pointing toward where Bud and McDonald held the rear.

Duncan and HJ threw themselves to the ground and pointed their carbines back toward the depression. "Call them in," Duncan said to Gibbons, who squatted behind the two officers.

HJ pulled her brick out, pressed the Transmit button, and said, "Bud, vacate now. We have the cover."

A huge explosion filled the air from across the road where the rebels had dug in during the night. Another surface-to-air missile shot out of the smoke and sand around the rebel site to pass harmlessly skyward before arcing north in a circle to explode on the beach.

The two remaining SEALs zigzagged as they ran. Duncan, along with the other SEALs, watched the crest of the depression, expecting any second to see rebels appear over the top.

"Keep going," Duncan said, pointing down to the ditch.

Bud slid down the sand into the ditch.

Behind him and McDonald came Beau and Chief Wilcox. HJ pulled the men upright as they slid into a small ravine. The two pilots could be seen about fifty yards ahead. The crew chief's body now shared between the two men as they stumbled along the rough bottom of the floodwater ditch.

The ravine was a deep but narrow ditch created by the few rains that drenched the coastal plains of Algeria during the short rainy spring seasons. Duncan figured the ditch about seven feet deep and four feet across. It was enough to hide them but also closed in enough to permit them to be trapped. It took a helicopter to find this ditch even with them being only a hundred yards from it all night and the early part of this morning. Their survival depended on speed. It would not take long for the Algerians to discover the helicopters were a decoy. When that happened, the rebels would head back to the depression and come after them.

"We got everyone?"

"Yes, sir," said HJ, who had taken muster as they entered the ditch. "McDonald is ahead at point. Told Monkey to wait for us . . . separated our M-60s."

Duncan nodded. "Good."

"Bud, grab Monkey when we go by, and you and him bring up the rear. Chief, you get your butt up ahead with McDonald."

Wilcox rose to move out, but Duncan stopped him. "Chief, avoid any confrontation. With luck, the rebels may think we struck out on foot toward Algiers. If we avoid them for the next thirty or forty minutes and they keep chasing the ground beneath those easterly moving helicopters, we should have our truck and then—"

"I know, Captain. Then we pray for more luck." Wilcox grinned. The grin revealed a long scar along the right jaw.

"Yeah, more luck. But that's what we SEALs do best, isn't it, Chief?"

"What's that?"

"Make luck."

"Well, sir, then we better get busy generating some. So far, the factory ain't turned out a lot of it this trip." Chief Wilcox shifted his carbine to his left hand and hurried off, soon passing the two Marine Corps pilots with their burden. Duncan, Beau, and HJ followed with several feet of space between them, with the exception of Gibbons, who stayed near Duncan, keeping the radio available if needed. Monkey trailed with his M-60, constantly scanning behind them and along the rim.

Duncan took the handset and told Viper Four Seven they had made the ravine and were moving to the west. Viper Four Seven passed his intentions to fight the helicopters slowly eastward as long as they remained undetected. If, or when, the rebels discovered them, the gunships would return and provide air cover. Duncan agreed, signed off, and tossed the handset to Gibbons, who hung it on his belt, reached behind him, and turned the volume to its lowest setting. Last thing they needed was for the radio to blare out and alert the enemy to their position.

Thirty minutes later, the ditch widened as the sides decreased in height. The sound of battle continued unabated behind them. Smoke from the explosions around the depression, along the beach, and across the road obscured the desert between them and Algiers. Duncan sent HJ racing ahead to catch up with Chief Wilcox and McDonald. He didn't want them to wander out of the protective cover of the ditch. HJ returned within minutes with news that the ditch ended about two hundred yards from where the Algerian rebels had established their truck pool. She could see three trucks from the end of the floodwater ditch.

"You two stay here," Duncan said to the pilots. The two Marine pilots, breathing heavily from the exertion of the rough journey carrying the body of their crew chief, nodded as they fell against the side of the ditch. Duncan knew the Marines were exhausted. Carrying a body or wounded person a few feet to safety was one thing, but to carry one for a long distance required stamina and tenacity. It also required respect, honor, and a sense of duty to one's fellow warrior. He wouldn't leave one of his, and he expected nothing less of the Marines.

"Captain, we got three trucks. Chief Wilcox and McDonald are watching. I count three rebels, and they are squatted around a small fire, probably making tea."

Bud and Monkey appeared around the curve of the ditch behind Duncan. He motioned the two SEALs forward. The group squatted in the center of the ditch while HJ briefed again the setup at the truck park.

Ten minutes later, the group joined Chief Wilcox and McDonald at the end of the floodwater ditch where it disappeared like a paper fan spread across the face of the desert. This small portion of the Sahara benefited from the sparse rainfall. Scraggy scrubs fought for survival against a burning sun and whipping winds trying to fry or rip every bit of foliage from the ground.

"HJ, you, Bud, McDonald, and the chief take the left side. Watch for the red light on the brick. I want minimum fire. Take out the guards and head for the trucks. Bud, Chief, as soon as the guards are out, see if some fool left a key in one of those ignitions. HJ . . . No, Bud, you search them for a key. If we find a key, then whichever truck it fits is the one we take. Any questions?"

Beau raised his hand. "How about the rest of us?"

"Beau, you, myself, Monkey, and Gibbons will move to the right and take position between the trucks and the highway. We will provide cover in the event the rebels become aware of our presence. Let's hope they don't."

"Sounds like a plan, boss."

"Keep low, everyone, and use the bushes. If you get close enough, you should be able to take them out with minimum fire. I am going to call Viper Four Seven and have them increase their attacks to cover ours. Wait until you hear the Cobras' rockets and cannons increase in tempo and then, at your discretion, HJ, take the rebels out."

"Nothing will give me greater pleasure," she replied, moving off at a fast clip toward the exit.

Duncan wondered briefly if he had detected a slight tremor in her voice. He hoped HJ's experience at the hands of the rebels didn't cloud her thinking. Duncan had seen such a reaction in other warriors where desire for revenge and hate for the enemy overrode training and common sense.

But he said nothing as he watched the four move to the left, keeping their profile low as they moved from scrub to scrub. He glanced at the rebels laughing and chatting as they drank hot tea from small cups.

Gibbons handed Duncan the handset. He contacted Viper Four Seven and in a whisper told him their position. Viper Four Seven acknowledged the request to increase their attacks to cover the gunfire as they took the trucks. Duncan pointed to the right. The four followed as he led them along a line of scraggly bushes. Along the way, Duncan would point at one of the SEALs and indicate for the person to take position. Several minutes later, the four were spread along a rough, hundred-foot line with their weapons pointed at the unaware Algerians sipping and chatting around the low fire.

Duncan rubbed his knee as he squatted behind one of the small bushes. Swelling had increased in the back of the left knee. Every move resulted in the joints grating where the cartilage had long ago worn away, the curse of old age in a young mind's body. He waved them forward. Carefully, the four SEALs eased slowly from bush to bush as they decreased their distance between themselves and the Algerian rebels. The four reached a position between the first truck and the highway. If anyone arrived from the highway in the next few minutes, there was little Duncan and his team could do to avoid detection. He was amazed they had reached this far without the guards discovering them.

The noise of the Cobras making fresh attacks against the rebels increased in tempo, and when the attack came from HJ and her team, Duncan could not hear the gunfire. All he saw were the rebels standing to flee and falling over as the SEALs' gunfire tore through them.

"Let's go!" Duncan shouted.

From the edge of the ditch, the two Marine Corps pilots hurried forward, carrying the crew chief's body between them. Chief Wilcox jumped into the cab of the first truck, jumped down, and hurried to the second.

Bud was going through the pockets of the dead men, jerking the pockets inside out and going on to the next one.

"Got one!" shouted Chief Wilcox, waving everyone toward him.

"Let's go, everyone! Get your butts on board," Duncan ordered, looking around for Gibbons.

"Gibbons, come here!" Duncan shouted as he walked, carbine in his left hand, toward the truck.

McDonald passed them at a run, stopped, turned, and handed Duncan a canteen. "Found these back there, Captain. Water!" Duncan took it as McDonald continued his run to the truck. He tossed the canteens into the bed of the truck. HJ grabbed them and began passing them around to the others.

"Yes, sir," said Gibbons as he reached Duncan.

Duncan took the handset. "Viper Four Seven, this is James One. We have a truck. Two minutes, and we will be on the road."

"Okay, James One. Here is my plan. We will stay where we are and watch your progress. As soon as you take fire, we will rejoin and conduct a truck-helicopter formation—a new tactic for a new era."

Duncan clicked the transmit button twice, signing off the air. He handed the handset to Gibbons as they arrived at the back of the truck. McDonald had his M-60 across the top of the cab, while Monkey lay across the rear, his heavy machine gun poking through the left side of the wooden rails that lined the bed. HJ and Bud had the right side. Beau leaned down, offered Duncan his hand, and pulled the SEAL captain onto the bed. The dead crew chief's body lay in the center, and the two Marine Corps pilots, with their nine-millimeter Navy Colt pistols cupped with both hands, squatted on their haunches to the left of Monkey.

"Does this look familiar, boss?" Duncan asked.

"Except for the absence of sheep dung and the heavy odor they bring, it could be Bashir's truck." These same SEALs, with the exception of Chief Wilcox, had avoided capture by Algerian rebels through the efforts of the overweight Bedouin smuggler and his rusty Volvo truck. It had been Bashir who located a doctor for HJ after she was wounded in a small village somewhere west of where they were now. Duncan doubted they would have successfully rescued President Hawali Alneuf if it hadn't been for the big buffoon. He knew they would never have survived the mission without Bashir, and for that reason alone, he felt he owed the Algerian patriot and smuggler some sort of payback. But that was no reason for Bashir to endanger American lives by holding back information because he would only give it to him.

"Do they have anything else in Algeria other than old, dilapidated trucks?" Beau asked.

Chief Wilcox leaned out of the cab. "Captain, what now?"

"Beau, ride up front with the chief. This plan is a complicated one that you may have a tough time remembering, so take notes. Turn this truck east and at a high rate of speed—if this thing has it in it—head toward Algiers. Once you reach the city, stop."

Beau climbed down, cocked his head to one side, and nodded. "Let me make sure I understand this plan," he mumbled as he walked alongside the truck and opened the door to the cab. "Turn this truck toward Algiers and stop once we reach it. Yeah, I think I may have it," Beau said, looking up at Duncan with a broad smile on his face. He gave him a half salute and ducked inside the cab, slamming the door behind him.

Duncan, hunched over at the waist, moved to where McDonald stood, his M-60 pointing over the top of the cab. "Gibbons," Duncan said, straightening. "You stay near me." He pointed to his right where the wooden rails ended at the cab. "So I can use the radio if I need it."

Beau stuck his head out of the window. "Boss, is that a right or left turn?" he asked, joking before pulling himself back inside the cab.

The engine cranked, revving up as Chief Wilcox gave it the gas. The grinding sound of the gears, common to Russian trucks, gave warning to those on the bed to grab hold of something.

Gibbons slid to a squatting position, his carbine pointed through the middle gap between the three wooden rails. His fingers twitched as he grasped the weapon. The petty officer reached up and pulled his cap down over his eyes, shading them from the sun.

The truck jerked forward with no warning, nearly knocking them off their haunches. The wheels spun in the sand for a few seconds before finding grip. A minute later, Chief Wilcox turned the Russian truck right onto the potholed asphalt that passed for the major coastal road in Algeria. The gears ground as Chief Wilcox fought the awkward transmission to shift from low to second to third and eventually at the great speed of forty kilometers an hour into fourth. Any shock absorbers this truck had at one time had disappeared years ago.

Duncan pulled his cap down tighter on his head to keep it from blowing off and with the back of his hand wiped the sweat from his eyes. McDonald started to pull his hat off and tuck it in his back pocket, but Duncan shook his head and made the man keep it on. A few minutes in this sun could bake a man's brain, he thought, reminding him of his thirst. He took another long drink from the rebel canteens McDonald had found. A small green flag fluttered from the radio antenna on the hood of the truck.

"Here it comes!" Bud shouted, pointing forward.

On the right, the rotors of the crashed CH-53 appeared above the depression. From the vantage height of the truck bed, Duncan saw the Algerian rebel positions along the left of the highway. He waved. He felt foolish, but he waved. Surprisingly, several of the Algerians returned it. Sometimes a friendly wave is the best deception. An Algerian truck flying the green Islamic flag with a friendly wave confused the rebels long enough for the truck to zoom by their positions, continuing toward Algiers. One of the rebels jumped up and began screaming at the others. *Uh-oh,* thought Duncan.

Over the noise of the truck caused by faulty mufflers, Algerian rebels poured out of their holes, scrambling onto the hardtop, and firing at the truck. Monkey returned fire with Bud and HJ firing alongside him with their carbines. Duncan couldn't tell if they scored any hits, but the rebel fire soon stopped as the truck passed down a slight dip and around a corner.

HJ and Bud grinned at each other, turned, and gave Duncan a thumbs-up. *Thumbs-up,* Duncan thought. *This is August, and I am supposed to be retired. Instead, I am in the middle of some godforsaken country, while my wife and her boy toy tear up my house in Reston.*

Two Cobra helicopters appeared ahead and passed down both sides of the truck before turning and taking position about a hundred yards on either side of the truck.

"James One, Viper Four Seven; good job. We seem to have cleared the pack. Algiers is eight kilometers ahead. Colonel

Stewart is waiting at the outskirts, so recommend not firing on
the desert cammy uniforms ahead."

"Roger, Viper Four Seven. Thanks for the escort."

"Viper Four Seven, this is Ranger Two Six," the pilot's
voice flying the Navy's EP-3E Orion reconnaissance aircraft
interrupted. "You have bandits inbound from the south, ten
miles. Believe them to be Foxbat fighters. Could be some
Sukhoi mixed in with them." Sukhoi aircraft were vintage
ground attack variants made by the old Soviet Union.

"Ranger Two Six, identify yourself."

"Viper Four Seven, James One; we know Ranger Two
Niner. If Ranger Two Six any kin, welcome aboard, Friendly
Ranger," Duncan broadcast.

Ranger Two Six was the only remaining Fleet Air Reconnaissance Squadron Two aircraft left in the Mediterranean after
Ranger Two Niner, shot up by rebel fire, crashed in Sigonella
two days ago. The EP-3E, a four-engine versatile aircraft variant of the Navy's Anti-Submarine Warfare ASW P-3C Orion,
was the lone remaining signals intelligence reconnaissance aircraft in the United States Sixth Fleet inventory. With only
twelve available worldwide when this crisis in North Africa
started, the conflict in Korea had taken all from the European
Theater with the exception of these two. Two of the original
twelve had been destroyed by the Libyan Air Force when they
attacked Sigonella, Sicily, and Souda Bay, Crete. Ranger Two
Nine had crashed and burned on the runway of Sigonella after
being damaged by an Algerian surface-to-air missile. This lone
VQ-2 Aries II aircraft was all the Sixth Fleet had to support its
intelligence reconnaissance requirements in the Mediterranean.
Even the Air Force versatile RC-135 Rivet Joint had been ordered to the Pacific.

Duncan looked north out to sea, knowing just over the horizon the EP-3E was orbiting. Ranger Two Nine had saved their
bacon four weeks ago. He would have felt better if it had been
the familiar call sign of Two Niner out there. He had read about
the deaths of the aircrew and in a small church in Rome had lit
a candle that night in their memory.

Four weeks ago, Duncan and his SEAL teams had been
under attack by the Algerian Navy and Air Force while escaping to sea on an old water carrier with President Alneuf and Algerian Palace Guard units. While F/A-18 Hornets off the USS

*Stennis* had taken out the Algerian fighters, a Harpoon launched from Ranger Two Niner had erased the Algerian warship from the sea. If it hadn't been for VQ-2, the parent squadron of the EP-3E aircraft, Duncan and his SEALs might still have been treading water.

"Roger, James One. Enemy aircraft should be coming into sight now!" Viper Four Seven broadcast, bringing Duncan's thoughts back to the current situation.

Duncan shaded his eyes and searched to the south. "Heads up, everyone. Friendly Ranger says we got company inbound from the south."

Twenty-millimeter cannon fire stitched down the sides of the truck as two MiG-25 Foxbat aircraft suddenly dove on the bouncing, weaving truck. The two Cobras broke left and right, avoiding the cannon fire.

"Where the hell did they come from?" shouted Chief Wilcox, scrambling to bring his carbine to bear on the enemy aircraft.

Monkey rolled onto his back. The roar of the heavy M-60 machine gun rocked the truck, the shells filling the air as the two Algerian fighters roared overhead and began to climb.

Duncan keyed the handset. "Ranger Two Six. We confirm two MiG-25 Foxbats—and they came from the west, not the south."

"Roger, we'll calibrate our radars later. Be advised formation of four Fox 18s inbound your position. Expect overhead in two minutes."

"Ranger Two Six, Viper Four Seven; where are the Foxbats now?"

"Foxbats at altitude two zero," the EP-3E pilot replied, identifying the enemy aircraft at an altitude of two thousand feet. "They are in hard left-hand turn, aligning for another pass."

"Roger, thanks. Viper Four Five and Four One, hit the deck. Engage Foxbats with Sidewinders."

"Viper Four Seven, Ranger Two Six; be advised two F/A 18s inbound."

"Roger. And, when they get here, they are more than welcome to this engagement. Until then, we have a truck to protect."

Duncan balanced himself against the wooden sides of the

truck bed and scanned the skies, searching for the enemy aircraft.

"There they are!" shouted Beau, pointing toward the sea.

Duncan looked in the direction Beau pointed. The sun reflected briefly off their fuselages. The two aircraft were nearly wing-on to the ground in a hard left turn and appeared to be descending.

Static blasted from the radio, followed by the voice of Viper Four Seven. "Lock-on. Fox one!"

The Sidewinder blasted away from the pylon beneath the starboard wing of the Cobra, dipped briefly before the rocket fuel kicked in, and the missile shot forward. It weaved along its flight path as a sensitive, heat-seeking guidance system corrected the missile flight toward the MiG- 25s. The MiGs were so close together, it was impossible for Duncan to tell in the few seconds of the Sidewinder's flight which aircraft was the target. The Sidewinder seemed to oscillate between the two aircraft until its seeker window had only one target, then it drove through the tail of the lead Foxbat and exploded. Enemy aircraft pieces rained on the beach and the Algerian rebels beneath it.

The other Algerian fighter aircraft circus-rolled to the right, afterburners blazing out behind it as the aging aircraft turned straight up on its tail at a ninety-degree angle and zoomed toward altitude.

"We show only one enemy aircraft," said the voice from Ranger Two Six. "Good shot, Viper Four Seven. Let me see . . . there, check mark by your name. One confirmed kill."

Viper Four Seven clicked his transmitter button twice in acknowledgement.

"Viper Four Seven, Ranger Two Six; we have the other aircraft on scope and the two F/A 18s engaging at this time. I think you are home free now. Good luck, Special Unit One, or is it Big Apple? I can never remember all your call signs."

"Thanks, Two Six. You can call me anything you want as long as you keep showing up when we need you," Duncan replied.

"Roger. Tell Congress the next time you're on the Hill. The mission commander from Ranger Two Niner sends his compliments and as soon as they let him out of the hospital, he expects to be back in the saddle."

"My best to the Ranger Two Niner crew. We owe them." The good news about the crash of Ranger Two Niner was that the cockpit crew had kept the damaged aircraft airborne long enough for everyone but them to bail out. According to the news reports, the pilot even landed the aircraft, but the damage was so severe, it blew up as it stopped at the end of the runway, killing the three in the cockpit.

"James One, we will stay with you until Algiers, and then after we refuel, its back to recover our fellow Marines," Viper Four Seven interrupted, referring to the two dead pilots in the Cobra the rebels shot down.

Duncan eased himself down gradually, resting his back against the cab. Once his butt touched the bed of the truck, he straightened his leg and rubbed his right knee lightly, feeling the swelling. His thoughts turned to Reston, his wife, and a dead dog he forgot to bury. Maybe he was better off in Algeria. Bud and HJ were exchanging friendly barbs with each other about beer cans, women, blonds, bubbas, and hairy armpits. It seemed to Duncan that HJ was just going through the motions of the verbal duel. He missed most of the comments but nodded in recognition that the two had developed a close bond, hopefully, the kind of bond warriors need in battle. Ground combat was different from war at sea.

At sea, you had little choice. You fought because you were restricted to a ship engaged in combat. On the ground, it was a different story. You could always run, and running was a gut reaction that hit everyone who ever raised a rifle and fought. Why didn't more run in combat? Duncan knew. Most figured it out after a decade or so of military service. You didn't run because your comrades depended on you. You would let them down if you ran. You'd lose face with your fellow warriors, and few could live with the knowledge they ran and, by fleeing the carnage, left their friends. *Amazing,* Duncan thought, pulling his carbine across his lap and bracing his hand on the truck bed to steady himself as the truck continued its weaving and bouncing trek toward Algiers. *You may go into combat for God, country, and family, but you stayed because of a bond between you and those fighting alongside.* Sure, there were other things to help you overcome the fear: stiff, uncompromising training and your own self-expectations carried a lot of weight, but the real, primordial reason was you fought for those who fought alongside you. That was the intrinsic bond between warriors.

The truck hit a large pothole, bouncing all of them off their haunches. Duncan went a few inches in the air and landed hard on his butt. He heard Gibbons groan beside him. "You all right?" Duncan asked.

"I'm fine, Captain," Gibbons replied in a high voice. "But, I think the strap between my legs may be a tad too tight."

# EIGHT

⚓

DUNCAN SIPPED LUKEWARM COFFEE AS COLONEL BULL-
dog Stewart briefed the situation in Algiers and the latest developments. The Marine Corps colonel had been notified while
Duncan and his group were escaping along the floodwater ditch
that the USS *Kearsarge* Amphibious Task Force would not be
relieving the Marines occupying Algiers. The newly arrived
Task Force had been ordered to stand ready to make best speed
for the Sea of Japan off the coast of the Koreas. Duncan leaned
against a metal office desk as the colonel paced back and forth.

Bulldog had his orders to evacuate Algiers in the next seven
days. What the hell was going on, he wanted to know, and Duncan could only shake his head and agree. The world was falling
around their heads. Here they were stuck with some fifty-odd
missing American hostages, a major conflict—others would
call it a war—in Korea, and not enough personnel, weapons, or
ammunition to resolve both crises at once. All they could hope
for was to rescue the hostages and leave the North African coast
to its own solution. "Let the Europeans handle it" was a favorite
theme for the American newspapers, college professors, and
CNN. Of course, the European news media had their own per-
spective, broadcasting a never-ending cycle of rhetoric about

the world's only remaining superpower abandoning Europe just as radical Islamic terrorism had reached its borders.

Duncan put his cup down. "Sounds like a mess, Bulldog."

"It is, and it's our mess for the time being. We're not going to get the French and the British to help us."

"Thanks for giving us a couple of hours' sleep and a chance to shower."

"That was a narrow escape you had, Duncan. But we need what information this fat Bedouin has and hope we haven't pulled you out here on a wild-goose chase."

Duncan shook his head. "No, if Bashir says he knows where the hostages are, then he knows. I spent a week with the man in the desert last month when we rescued President Hawali Alneuf. He smells, his clothes are dirty, and he has a laugh like fingers down a blackboard, but the one thing he does know is information. He found a doctor in the middle of the Sahara who saved the life of one of my officers. Bashir took a large, dilapidated truck, which we expected any time to give up the ghost, and avoided rebels who were searching Algeria for Alneuf. Without him, we would never have escaped. No, I trust him." Duncan mentally crossed his fingers.

"Glad you do, Duncan. The man has been a pain in the ass. If it hadn't been for his claims and him knowing the names of you and your SEALs, I would have chucked him on the outskirts of Algiers and let him take his chances with the rebels."

Duncan nodded. "I think there were times as we sought a way out of Algeria that the same idea passed through every one of us." Duncan straightened, put his cup down, and looked at Bulldog. "Well, shall we go see my old friend?"

"The rest of your team is at the building where we have the Bedouin."


**"AH, MY OLD FRIEND, CAPTAIN DUNCAN JAMES,"** SAID Bashir as Duncan appeared through the door. A bright smile spread across the huge face of the Bedouin.

Colonel Bulldog Stewart, United States Marine Corps—and damn proud of it—followed Duncan into the small room.

"I am so glad to see you and so glad you were able to come." Bashir stood, his huge frame overshadowing the straight-backed chair behind him. The familiar *thobe* covered the large

man's body. The *thobe* was the traditional Arab desert robe designed to reflect the hot sun while allowing the air to circulate
within it.

"I have been kept locked up like a common bandit, waiting
for you to arrive, my friend." Bashir leaned toward Duncan and
whispered, "Your country must get psychiatric help for these
Devil Dogs." He tapped his head several times, his eyes shifting between Duncan and Bulldog, who stood near the door.
"There is something not quite right up here."

The small room in which the Marines had placed Bashir had
a single glazed window, and its sparseness was broken only by
a small wooden table and three chairs. A cot, strengthened with
boxes jammed beneath it, was arranged against the far wall.
Light, rectangular spaces on the white walls revealed where, at
one time, pictures had decorated the room. Duncan surmised
the pleasure he showed hid the anxiety Bashir had experienced
imprisoned here these past few days.

Duncan shook the two hands clasping his. "Bashir, you fat
bastard," he replied softly, a small grin breaking. "What the hell
do you think you are doing not telling the colonel where they
are holding our American citizens! You're lucky the Devil
Dogs managed to contain their patience this long. I think, my
friend, it is a new record for them."

Bashir's eyes darted to the colonel and back to Duncan.
"Ah, Captain, it is you I needed to see," he confided softly, licking his lips nervously as he shook Duncan's hand.

"Bashir, the colonel is trustworthy. Whatever you have to
say, you can say aloud. He isn't going to shoot you. But you
need to understand that we already have one dead because of
you." Duncan broke free of the clasp. "If you had told the
colonel the whereabouts of the hostages, we could have saved
him."

"No, he was already dead." Bashir pulled the long trail of his
full-length, dingy *thobe* from over his shoulder and wiped his
nose. He saw the questioning look Duncan gave him. "Oh, Captain, do not be angry with me," he pleaded. "The American
hanging from the light was dead before the rebels hung him.
They do not want to kill the Americans. They only want you to
leave."

"That's bullshit!" Bulldog erupted. "They kill innocent
women and children as if they were dogs."

Bashir jumped at Colonel Stewart's outburst, staring at the Marine colonel's sun-worn face. The sharp lines of the cheekbones and tight neck gave the Marine Corps officer a hard, nononsense look. Bulldog locked eyes with Bashir and slightly narrowed them, causing Bashir's gaze to whip back to Duncan. "Can we speak alone, my good friend?" he asked, glancing at the Marine Corps colonel again to find the piercing eyes glaring at him. Bashir attempted to whisper with a deep bass voice that trembled slightly, "Your friend scares me with his evil stare. I have heard of these Devil Dogs."

Bulldog narrowed his eyes further and deepened the furrow of his eyebrows, pulling the short hair on top of his head forward. The colonel's expression knowingly enhanced by the skintight face stretched across the skull and jawbones beneath.

"Bashir, my friend Colonel Stewart is in charge of all the Marines in Algiers." He waved his right hand in a wide circle. "He should scare you. Right now, the only thing standing between you and thousands of angry Marines is this man. Thousands who want to take you out and hang you like the American was hung from the streetlight."

Bashir burst into nervous laughter. "Oh, Captain James, you are trying to scare poor Bashir? I would never have come to find you if I thought the Marines would kill me. Americans do not kill civilians unless it is by mistake." He wiped the sweat from his forehead and then blew his nose on the tail of his *thobe*. When Duncan failed to reply immediately, Bashir looked up, his eyes wide. "They don't, do they?"

"We need your help, Bashir. If you know anything, tell us."

"I understand, my Captain, the frustration I brought, but I have a message for you that I was ordered to deliver only to you. You are a true friend of Hawali Alneuf, and the message is from him."

A message from the deposed president of Algeria? Alneuf was sequestered somewhere in London, where the British spirited him after they rescued them from the sinking water carrier. Duncan ran his hand over the top of his head and turned to Bulldog. The United States government would want to know what the message contained. Even an old captain being forced to retire like him could appreciate the importance such a message might hold. Could Alneuf have changed his mind and want to defect from the British to the Americans? Doubtful. All the man would have to do is grab a London cab to Gloucester Square and walk into the American embassy. England wouldn't try to stop him—or would it?

"Colonel, I'm sorry, but can I have a few minutes alone with this fat bastard?" Duncan asked.

"Captain, you hurt my feelings," Bashir said, touching his hand to his chest. "Twice you have called me fat. I am weight challenged and a few inches too short. Would they allow you to say such things in America?" The deep booming laughter Duncan and the other SEAL members had come to recognize and hate echoed off the vacant walls of the small room.

"I'll be outside if you need me, Duncan," Bulldog said. He curled his thumb at Bashir. He pulled his pistol out and examined it closely. "Let me know if you need a firing squad. So far, we have sold over five hundred raffle tickets for the pleasure."

They waited until the door shut behind them.

"Raffle tickets?" Bashir asked.

**OUTSIDE, BULLDOG STEWART STOMPED INTO A SIDE** room, where a couple of Marines from Second Radio Battalion sat hunched over in front of a receiver with a portable CD recorder beside it. He nodded at them, lifted his right hand, and whirled his index finger several times before pointing at the speaker. The corporal put the headset on and flipped a switch, piping the conversation between Duncan and Bashir onto a speaker. Bulldog leaned forward and turned it down slightly so he could hear without the speaker being heard next door. He would tell Duncan later. Well, maybe he would.

**"OKAY, BASHIR, WHAT IS THE MESSAGE, AND WHERE ARE** the hostages?"

"He is selling raffle tickets for the opportunity to shoot me," Bashir said incredulously. "I am telling you, Captain. The man needs help." He tapped his finger against his head several times.

"Bashir, you came here telling everyone that you know the location of the American hostages. You get everyone energized to rescue them, and then you shake your head like a petulant child and refuse to tell them, insisting on only speaking to me.

They had to go to Naples, fly me out to the aircraft carrier and then into Algeria, where I was promptly shot down. While you waited, an American was tortured, killed, and his mutilated body hung from a streetlamp within a block of the vacant American embassy. Tell me why you think they wouldn't want to shoot you."

"I know, I know, my friend. Nevertheless, believe me. The American died of illness . . . maybe a heart attack." He shook his head while his hand made a downward motion. Grabbing the tail of his *thobe* again, Bashir wiped his sweating face. "Your doctors will discover the truth when they do their autopsy."

Bashir pulled the chair he had been sitting in earlier under him and sat down. Duncan pulled a chair out from under the small wooden table, turned it around, and straddled it backwards, facing the huge straddle-legged Bedouin from across the table.

Bashir's booming laughter filled the room.

Duncan covered his ears. "What is so funny, Bashir? Someday that loud laughter is going to get you shot, my chubby friend."

"I am not laughing because I find this humorous, my Captain. I am laughing at the irony of having to give myself up to American Marines so I could find you." Bashir leaned forward and reached under the table, pulled out the hidden transmitter the Marines had installed, and palmed it in his hand.

"It seems your friends do not trust you, either, Captain James," Bashir said. He opened his fingers so Duncan could see the transmitter.

"They are doing no less than I would have, if I had thought of it." Duncan lied. *What the hell, Bulldog?* he thought. *We need this information.*

Bashir's huge hand folded over the hidden transmitter. "I will put it back after we talk. President Hawali Alneuf sends his respects to you and his apologies for abandoning you at sea in favor of the English. While he knows Americans rescued him, he also knows the Americans would never have supported him in returning to Algeria. He would have become a waiter in some Middle Eastern restaurant like the Vietnamese generals and leaders became waiters in American restaurants after the fall of Vietnam."

"Bashir, you misunderstand me. I could give a shit whether Alneuf hightailed it to London or took a job waiting tables in Washington. My job was to rescue him. We accomplished that mission at great cost. We lost a good chief petty officer, and you lost a professional warrior who could have led your country's war to reclaim Algeria."

Bashir chuckled and then burst into laughter. The big man rolled back and forth on the small wooden chair. It would not have surprised Duncan if the chair broke. He wished it would, and one of those wooden legs would impale the fat Bedouin. Bashir's double chin bounced up and down to a laughter that only a bass voice, a deep set of lungs, and strong emotions can bring out.

"Bashir, if you don't stop laughing, I'm going to rip your lips off." Duncan put his hands momentarily over his ears. The room was small, and the unusual voice this man possessed made the room shrink. He made Duncan think of that Italian opera singer from the '90s—the name escaped him—but with a beard, Bashir and the Italian could have passed for twins. "When this is over, you should consider becoming an opera singer."

The laughter stopped abruptly, and Bashir leaned forward to touch Duncan's hand. "But, they are not dead, my friend. Both Colonel Yosef and your chief are alive."

Duncan half stood from the chair. If they were still alive, then the rebels had them. If Bashir knew where they were, then he needed that information. SEALs never leave other SEALs behind.

"Where are they, Bashir? Are they with the hostages?" Duncan asked, leaning forward and putting a hand on the table.

Bashir shook his head. A deep sigh escaped him. "No, they fooled you Americans as they fooled us. Most times we feel Americans are naive, but in this instance, we both were taken by the Israelis."

"Israelis? I don't understand," Duncan said, crossing his arms on the back of the chair. If they weren't dead, then they were captives. No way the two of them could have escaped the pier and evaded the rebels for this long. And what in the hell did Israel have to do with it? Duncan's expression showed his confusion. It made no sense to him. Was this just more Arab rhetoric?

Bashir leaned forward and touched Duncan's arm. "Captain, they were Israeli spies."

Duncan sat back and grinned. After a few seconds, he leaned forward, crossing his arms on the back of the chair. "Right, Bashir. Don't give me that. You sound like the rest of the Islamic world. Whenever something happens, and you don't understand it, blame the Jews."

Bashir shook his head. He touched his chest and shook his head. "No, it is true. The British told President Alneuf that Colonel Yosef and your Chief Zackeriah Judiah were . . . are members of Mossad, the Israeli intelligence service. According to the British, your CIA knew about Chief Judiah but had an understanding with the Israelis to leave him alone."

"No way, Bashir," Duncan replied sharply. "Your Colonel Yosef may have been Mossad or whatever, but no way a chief petty officer in the United States Navy could have been. I have even put Chief Judiah in for the Navy Cross."

"Has he gotten it?"

"Not yet," Duncan said. "But, Bashir, these things take time."

"Then let's disagree on this for the time being, Captain. If he gets an award from your Navy, then obviously the British are lying." Bashir pursed his lips and bobbed his head a couple of times before shaking his finger at Duncan. "Of course, I have known the British to lie when it comes to furthering their own interests. And the French, the Italians, the Spanish, and even— be prepared—the Americans."

"Bashir, enough small talk. Where are the hostages?"

"First, my friend, the message from President Alneuf. I need your agreement before we go further. President Alneuf would like for America to occupy Algiers for two more weeks."

"Bashir, I can't promise that. The current position is that once we have recovered the hostages, we are going to leave. My government wants us out of here as soon as possible. We have other commitments elsewhere in the world. If you haven't noticed, we have a small war going in Korea. If Alneuf wants us to delay our departure, he needs to go through our State Department."

"He understands, Captain, and he assures me he is working the diplomatic end, but he has confidence in you. He needs the Americans to remain in Algiers for two more weeks. Only two more weeks, and then you can go. That cannot be too hard, my friend. Even if you recovered the hostages today, it would still be a week before you could pull out. All he is asking . . . all I am asking is that you delay your departure for two more weeks, until the end of August. If you cannot agree with me on that, then I cannot tell you where the hostages are. I will have to delay passing this information to you for a week."

Duncan placed both hands on the back of the chair and pushed himself back. "Why, Bashir, does he need American forces to occupy Algiers for another two weeks?"

"Because, Captain, President Alneuf is returning to Algiers. If he can return with his loyal forces to Algiers peacefully, then it gives him time to take control of the city without having to fight the rebels building by building for that control. He considers Algiers the center of gravity for the rebels. The force who holds the capital controls Algeria."

Duncan bit his lower lip. The safety of the hostages was number-one priority. Most likely, it was going to take two weeks, anyway, for the Marines to pull out. The USS *Kearsarge* and her escorts, steaming in circles west of the city for a couple of weeks, were heading west out of the Mediterranean. Two weeks from now, the Marine Amphibious Group on board *Kearsarge* would be off the Korean peninsula. The Marines in Algiers would embark the next week aboard the *Nassau* Amphibious Group, and he would not be surprised to hear they were being diverted to Korea. The rotation between the two Marine Expeditionary Units, to commence in two days, was dead in its tracks. Any promise to Bashir could be a lie. He raised his head and looked at the Bedouin across from him. For the first time, the mask disappeared from the man's face. Bashir needed him to agree. Even smugglers can have a tint of patriotism. The future of Algeria could rest on America delaying its exit for two weeks. One week was easy. Two weeks? He would be cutting it close. *What is Algeria to us, anyway?* Duncan asked himself. Any agreement he made had little validity and no substance. The American government marched much to its own drum and a piddle-ass captain in the Navy lacked authority to tie its hands. Besides, this was a State Department problem, not his. But lives were at stake, and unless he made the decision here and now, more could be lost.

Duncan wondered briefly if Bashir would really delay revealing the location of the hostages for another week if he failed to agree to Alneuf's terms. Lies were cheap, but they never remained hidden long and once revealed, they ruined credibility. You lose your credibility, you never regain it.

"Bashir," Duncan said softly, nodding his head. "One week is easy. Most likely, it will take about ten days for the Marines to pull out once the order is given. Even if we rescue the hostages today, which we want to do, it would take at least another twenty-four hours before a withdrawal could begin." Duncan shook his head. "Bashir, I can't lie to you. I don't have the authority or power to agree to U.S. forces remaining in Algiers for an additional two weeks. You have to understand that what I am giving you is a best-guess estimate for how long we will be in Algiers once we have freed our American citizens. It's just an estimate, an estimate I believe is accurate. I don't see us being able to extricate ourselves earlier than next week. That gives you ten days. Is there some way President Alneuf can expedite his return before then?"

The huge Bedouin bit his lower lip. When a couple of seconds passed and no answer came, Duncan continued.

"He needs to approach our government through official channels, Bashir."

"*Bien sur,* my Captain," Bashir said, a faint smile crossing his face. "I will pass your agreement to President Hawali Alneuf. I am sure he will be glad of the extra time. We knew two weeks was too much to ask. Ten days should be okay." Bashir's eyebrows arched. He pointed at Duncan. "You may even get an Algerian medal for your chest for this moment," he said enthusiastically, his pudgy finger jabbing at Duncan's chest. "The best Algerian medals are made of gold. If you get one and you don't like it, let me know. I can get a good price for you." The Bedouin raised his hands above his head, his fists clasped tightly and shouted, "Praise be to Allah, Captain Duncan James. You are a hero of—" He stopped in midsentence and brought his hands down.

He unfolded the fist with the transmitter in it. A tangle of broken plastic, wires, and a small triple-A battery lay in it. He glanced at Duncan, smiling like a young boy sharing a humorous secret. "Guess I squeezed too tight?" He held it up to his eyes. "Just as I thought, Captain. Made in China. But, then, why am I not surprised?"

"Sit down, Bashir, and tell me where the hostages are."

"Well, Captain Duncan James, I don't know specifically where the hostages are, but I know where the rebels enter and leave the passage that leads to them."

"You said you knew the location of the hostages."

Bashir waved his hands. "Of course, of course, I know the location of the hostages. I just don't know their exact location, but I know the path that will take you to them."

"You said you knew where they were."

Bashir shrugged his shoulders. "Most likely, it was a language difference between my English and your American. Wasn't it the great English statesman Winston Churchill who said that America and Great Britain were two great countries separated by a common language?"

"Bashir, the hostages?"

"We don't even have a common language, or a common—"

"Bashir!"

"Okay, okay. I can show you where the rebels sneak in and out of where they are holding the hostages." He laughed. "I know how you and your SEALs perform. It will be a simple matter to go through the sewers in the catacombs and recover the Americans. Who knows, Captain, you may even get a medal from your own government as well as from Algeria."

"Sewers? Catacombs?"

Bashir nodded, blowing his nose again on the tail of his garment before wiping away the sweat that seemed to continuously flow from his forehead and drip down the sides of his face. "Yes, but they are big pipes. You see, my friend, Algeria is honeycombed underground with catacombs that rival those of Paris and Rome. If a big earthquake ever happens in Algiers, the entire city will disappear into the earth. Yes, they are massive, these catacombs. Many have gone in and—"

"Bashir, if these catacombs are so big, how do we know we won't get lost trying to navigate this passage?"

Bashir shrugged his shoulders. "Ah, you know," he said, stroking one of his chins. "It has never occurred to me that you Americans cannot do this. Maybe President Alneuf should ask the French? They would do it."

"Bashir, I wouldn't ask the French to wipe my ass. They've been nothing but a pain lately. They have a carrier battle group two hundred miles north of ours and have yet to offer help. And the British haven't been much help, either, letting the French jerk them around as part of their battle group."

Bashir stuck a fat finger up his nose, twisted it a couple of times, and then wiped it on his *thobe*. "That is the French for you, Captain. They are more than willing to come and help Hawali Alneuf once you depart. The French have never forgiven themselves for losing their African empire. They are impressed with the empire they never had and the world power they never were. I sometimes think—"

"Bashir," Duncan interrupted. "Let's go. You're going to take us to this pipe that leads to the Americans?" He glanced at the glazed window high along the wall. Daylight was fading, and time was running out.

"Of course, but I must contact the president first and tell him of our agreement."

"We don't have an agreement, Bashir. Don't mislead President Alneuf by telling him the Americans have agreed to remain here. Tell him the truth. There is no agreement. There is probably another week or ten days for him to replace us, and make sure he knows that's just an estimate."

"Of course, Captain. Of course. What did you think I was going to tell him?"

"You can give Colonel Stewart the telephone number, and his communicators will patch you through to Hawali Alneuf," Duncan said, irritation in his voice.

"Oh, I don't need them for this, Captain. I will call him here."

"Call him?"

"Of course! How do you think we have been talking?"

"I figured by radio . . ." Duncan's voice trailed off.

Bashir grinned. "No, my friend, by cellular satellite telephone. He picks up the telephone at the Cumberland Hotel in London, dials my number, and my telephone rings. I pick it up and—*bravo*—there he is. When I want to talk with him, I do the same. It is amazing what new technology permits even in a rebellion where landlines are cut or being monitored. But, of course, you know we never really had telephone lines here. Before the advent of cellular telephones, it took eight years to get a telephone installed, and you had to know the right person. I remember—"

"Okay, okay, okay," Duncan said, waving his hands. "I give

up. I'll get Colonel Stewart, and we'll take you to your telephone. Then we want you to take us immediately to wherever this pipe is located."

"There is no need to take me anywhere, Captain Duncan James."

Bashir hiked up his yellow white *thobe,* revealing two huge, hairy thighs the size of Duncan's waist. A black strap encompassed an immense right thigh, holding a tiny cellular telephone inside a small holster. He pulled the telephone out and unfolded it before straightening his *thobe.* He saw the surprised look on Duncan's face. "You know how Americans are, Captain Duncan James. They would never search between a man's legs . . . especially a man of my size with a propensity for sweating. You should have seen the face of the young Marine when he was searching me. I asked him if he wanted to run his hands up between my legs to see what weapon I had there. His face turned so red. It was really quite funny." Booming laughter filled the small room, the sound easily audible to the Marines next door who were working furiously to restore the intercept audio. Colonel Bulldog Stewart stood over them, the veins in his neck visible as his whispered, angry commands drove the Marines.

**DUNCAN, BEAU, HJ, AND BUD HELLIWELL LAY IN THE** sand on the opposite bank, peering over the ridge. A huge pipe protruded from the other side several yards. A sparse maze of wild scrub and vines surrounded the rusting sewer pipe.

They were close enough to see anyone coming or going. The five-foot-high, ragged mouth of the rusting pipe jutted out over a small stream that flowed north toward the sea. A steady trickle of water and sewage ran out, making small splashes in the shallow, dirty water below it. The smell of fetid sewage occasionally reached their nostrils as the evening air blew in from the sea.

Duncan, Beau, and HJ crawled down from the top of the bank to the dirt road below them. Bashir, Colonel Bulldog Stewart, and several urban-armed Marines waited.

"During the day, they do not use it, my friend," Bashir said. "At night is when they come and go." Bashir looked at the sky. "Which will be here soon. The smell keeps the Americans away, who would never consider anyone using a sewage pipe as a means for access. The rebels are far from dumb. Don't you agree? But so unhygienic, I think." He blew his nose on his *thobe* tail and wiped his face.

Duncan noticed Bulldog Stewart's upper lip curl in disgust.

"Bashir, how do we know this leads to where the hostages are being kept?"

"My nephews—fine men every one of them; you have met and shared food with them, Captain—have trailed the rebels and recognized one of those responsible for kidnapping the Americans. His name is Mohammed. He nearly captured President Hawali Alneuf at the piers the first night when the rebels overran Algiers. He is a religious man but not one inclined to kill the hostages without good reasons, unlike his comrade Kafid, who Colonel Yosef—the Israeli spy—killed during their escape from Algiers."

"Israeli spy?" Beau asked, cutting his eyes toward Duncan.

"Bashir. The hostages, please." Duncan said. He found it hard to believe that Daoud Yosef was an Israeli spy, much less Chief Judiah. He saw the pier, the smoke, the explosion. Neither of the two, who had volunteered to stay behind and blow the pier so the rest of them could escape, could have survived.

"The hostages are somewhere at the end of that pipe. Unfortunately, the pipe could lead anywhere in the city. But you are Navy SEALs, and if anyone can find them, you can."

"Flattery will get you nowhere, Bashir."

"Can you trust this man, Duncan?" Bulldog asked, pointing at Bashir. "How do you know he isn't leading you to certain death?"

Bashir glanced between the two men. The Marine Corps colonel scared him. More so, since Duncan warned him he needed to be scared. He had read where even the Germans feared them and dubbed them Devil Dogs for how they fought. The rebels on one side with instant death and the fear of the Marines on this side convinced Bashir that it was time for him to go. He would see Duncan and the SEALs on their way before leaving the hospitality of the Marines.

Beau and HJ appeared behind the three men.

"Boss," Beau said. "We have the stuff the Marines promised." He held up two camouflage packs.

Duncan nodded, biting his lower lip. His misgivings about

going underground caused him to think of delaying the rescue. Thoughts of what the rebels might be doing to the hostages overrode customary caution. He recalled the war in Afghanistan, when his team had stumbled upon three prisoners who had been skinned alive, down to the bones of their skull, while leaving their eyes intact. He doubted they could have lived long after the torture had started, but it was a scene that had haunted him ever since. It was another reason he had forced an immediate attack against the rebel position where HJ had been captured last month. Al-Qaida still existed, and as much as they had done to wipe it out, it still thrived in the maladroit twists of fanatical minds.

"Got no choice, Beau," Duncan said, a slight sigh escaping. "You know how to organize the team. Looks like single file to me."

"Duncan, you ever seen the movie *Aliens*?"

HJ handed a satchel to Duncan. "Here, Captain. Inside you will find a couple of flares, flashlight, ball of string, and several florescent crayons for marking our way. In addition, a couple of spare D cell batteries when the ones in the flashlight give out. Gibbons has the rope. I told him to leave his radio with the Marines."

"Duncan, I still would like to send some of my Marines with you," Bulldog offered.

"Thanks, Bulldog, but we've worked together as a team and know how each other operates. I'd hate to try to incorporate your Marines and my SEALs without us doing some combined training first. Right now, I don't think we have time."

Initially, Bulldog had argued the rescue to be a responsibility of the Marines, and Duncan was more than willing to allow that. The SEALs had had little sleep in the past twenty-four hours. Here they were, twenty-four hours after arriving on the USS *Stennis*, preparing to go into the Swiss cheese–like catacombs of Algiers. Catacombs for which no one had an accurate map. Moreover, this was the month he was supposed to retire. Instead, the Navy extended him on active duty for "the duration," whatever that meant.

When the rescue plans were forwarded to General Lewis on the *Stennis* and the newly arrived one-star Marine Corps general on board the *Nassau*, the decision had been to use the SEALs. Duncan had superior training in hostage rescue, having taught the subject and refined the tactics used by the SEALs, the Marines, and the Army today.

Beau saluted—something he didn't do much. *Showing off for the colonel,* thought Duncan.

HJ held out a ball of string, two florescent chalk markers, and four extra batteries to Duncan. He took them, slipping the string, one of the markers, and the batteries back into the satchel before strapping the light-green pack to his belt. He took one of the markers and put it in his desert cammie shirt pocket.

"Colonel, I guess we had better be going while we have some light left. We have our bricks," he said, touching the small portable radio on his belt. "And I have this contraption your urban commandos loaned us," Duncan added, touching the keyboard on his wrist and swing-down eyepiece connected to his helmet. "As soon as we locate the hostages, we will call you."

Bulldog stuck his hand out. "Duncan, be careful and good luck. I have a quick-reaction force, ready to come when you call. All we need is for you to tell us where. We can be anywhere in Algiers within fifteen minutes."

"Thanks, Bulldog," he said, shaking the Marine's hand.

Duncan turned to HJ. He saw the battle going on inside of her as if she were transparent. Regardless of the front she put up, the assault by the Algerian rebels while she was a prisoner still churned her fears. She would go, he knew, but it was only willpower and tenacity that forced one leg in front of another. Lord help any rebel who got in her way. For the first time, he wondered if she would remain a SEAL when this was all over and they were back in the States.

Duncan walked up the bank. Chief Wilcox, Bud, Gibbons— without his radio—McDonald and Monkey, the two M-60 machine gunners, stood watching from below. A couple of Marines stood nearby. "Let's move out, HJ. Beau," he called. "Let's go."

Within a couple of minutes, the SEALs were crouched below the lip of the pipe. McDonald and Chief Wilcox bracketed the dark opening. The chief nodded at McDonald, and with the machine gunner covering him, Chief Wilcox swung the heavy flashlight beam into the tunnel. The beam revealed rusting ripples of metal along the sides of the ancient pipe before the darkness swallowed the light into the distant gloom. A small, fetid stream splashed around and over rotting debris before spilling out the worn end of the pipe. Wilcox nodded. McDonald slung the machine gun over his back, pulled the thin gloves tighter on his hands, and then pulled himself into the pipe. Chief Wilcox followed. Bud Helliwell hoisted himself up into the pipe, turned, and helped the others up. Duncan first, after he tugged his gloves tighter, followed by Gibbons, HJ, Beau, and Monkey. The flight gloves, loaned to the team, helped protect their hands from the sharp metal edges and the fetid matter that seemed to cake the interior of the pipe.

Ahead, at the very edge of the darkness, McDonald waited until everyone was inside before turning on the small miner's light on his helmet. The low-power light gave McDonald about six feet of visibility. Low visibility marked the way in grades of gray and black. Just enough for him to avoid most of the human waste and rotting material stuck or flowing along the fast-moving stream. But nothing stopped the horrid smell of decaying and fresh sewage that washed across the tops of their combat boots and filled the closed atmosphere of the Algiers sewer.

Colonel Bulldog Stewart turned to Bashir. "I hope for your sake they come back alive."

Bashir's eyes widened. He grabbed the tail of his *thobe* and wiped a fresh wave of sweat from his face. The large rings of perspiration under his arms stuck the garment to his skin.

Monkey, the last inside the pipe, glanced at the Marines and waved lightly before turning and disappearing after the others.

Bulldog turned to the Marine Corps officer standing slightly behind and to the left of him. "Captain, I want a squad here to guard that pipe. No one is to come out or go in with the exception of—"

The explosion knocked him into the captain, throwing both of them to the ground, sending them rolling partway down the bank.

Bulldog pushed himself up. His head hurt from the concussion, but he was conscious. Feeling no pain other than the ringing in his ears, he pulled the captain up. "You okay, son?"

The captain blinked his eyes a couple of times and nodded.

Bulldog left the recovering Marine and ran back to the top of the bank.

Across from him, clouds of dust rose from where the explosion had covered the pipe, burying it beneath a ton of rock, sand, and man-made debris. The explosion blocked the stream, creating a dam that stopped the water flow.

The Marine Corps captain appeared at the side of Colonel Stewart.

"Captain, get men down there and start uncovering that pipe. Call headquarters and tell them I want another platoon, right now!" He shouted, his finger emphasizing the order. Bulldog turned, searching for Bashir. Bashir had disappeared. "Where is that fat bastard?" he shouted as he unsnapped the holster, his fingers curling around the handle of the pistol.

# NINE

⚓

"I OVERHEARD AN OPERATIONS SPECIALIST AT THE SUR-
face console in the Combat Information Center call him Lu-
cifer," Rear Admiral Devlin said softly to Captain Dick
Holman, former commanding officer of the USS *Stennis* and
now the commander of Fleet Air Mediterranean. "Fits when
you consider his high and tight haircut, hook nose, and those
angry eyes he has, plus continuously shouting 'Hooah' to punc-
tuate his sentences."

"Well, Admiral, the Marines use 'Ooyah.'"

"Yeah, and the Air Force uses 'Fore.' Guess it goes well with
that bottleneck waist and bull-size chest. I would submit that
this is not the first time troops have stuck that moniker on him."
Devlin chuckled and then let out an audible sigh. "Even so,
Dick, pass the word to cut it out. As much as the nickname
seems suitable, it's inappropriate for the commander of our
Joint Task Force. Besides, there's not much difference in his
haircut and mine." Devlin ran his hand over his close-cropped
hair. "Of course, the chest measurements are a little different,"
he said, grinning. The lean physique of the new commander of
the United States Sixth Fleet was more a runner's profile than
the weight-lifting physique of General Lewis.

Dick pushed his chair away from the desk, leaning back on

two legs. "Aye, aye, Admiral. Speaking of our Army leader, General Lewis, where is he?" Dick glanced at his watch. "Not much danger of anyone confusing me or Kurt of being physical fitness gurus." He patted his stomach.

Captain Kurt Lederman, the Sixth Fleet intelligence officer, moved impatiently at the lectern, shifting his weight from one leg to the other. Kurt was slightly shorter than Dick Holman. Dick still had a full head of hair. Kurt kidded that his baldness was due to fast turns under the sheets. The image of the short, chubby intelligence officer's legs kicking for those fast turns drew laughter when the statement was first heard. Unfortunately, it was the only joke he knew, so it drew less laughter with each telling.

The commander, Joint Task Force African Force, moved to his own schedule, expecting everyone to be in place if and whenever he arrived. Seeing Dick glance at his watch, Kurt did the same—twenty minutes late. The average wait was fifteen minutes.

"I take it the USS *Hue City* and USS *Spruance* are well on their way east?" Dick asked the admiral. The *Hue City* was an older Aegis-class cruiser, while the USS *Spruance* had the distinction of being the oldest active-duty destroyer in the Navy. The first chief of Naval Operations in the twenty-first century had been one of her commanding officers in the mid-1980s. That was how old she was.

"I detached them when Kurt briefed me on the missile threat being deployed along Libya's coast." He glanced at the huge Navy clock on the bulkhead. "That was over ten hours ago. I suspect they are near the Strait of Sicily, since they were transiting at thirty knots plus. My orders to Captain McTeak, skipper of the *Hue City*, as the officer in tactical command of this Surface Action Group, is to establish an operating area fifty miles south of the Strait and wait for us."

"Leaves us with only the USS *Hayler*, the Arleigh Burke Guided Missile Destroyer, for surface-to-air protection if we are attacked."

"Well, Dick, that is why you have this big, shiny carrier with over ninety fighters on it—to shoot down anything that's flying our way. Besides, you can close up with the *Nassau* Amphibious Task Force, combine the Carrier Battle Group with it, and take advantage of the USS *Yorktown*'s coverage."

"The *Hue City* is the only Aegis cruiser I have available without pulling the *Yorktown* away from the *Nassau* Amphibious Task Force. Couldn't do that and destroy Task Force integrity." Pete Devlin leaned forward with Dick and continued in a low voice, "The *Hue City* is the only cruiser with the Linebacker theater ballistic-missile defense capability."

The Aegis-class cruisers of the United States Navy were the mainstays of defensive action against a ballistic missile launch by a rogue party. Developed over the 1990s, the United States Navy and the United States Air Force led the cooperative effort to develop a theater ballistic-missile-defense capability to detect and destroy a theater ballistic-missile launch. The United States Sixth Fleet had led the exercising of this tactical plan, but this would be the first time a TBMD action had been authorized and the first time it would be implemented without the Air Force side by side with them. The Aegis cruisers were total weapons systems designed to operate the full war-at-sea spectrum from detection to kill. The heart of its man-monitored/computer-controlled warfighting capability was the high-powered AN/SPY-1 radar system. The AN/SPY-1 was an advanced multifunction phased-array radar system. Every year saw the Navy fighting for funds to keep it fully modernized by changing and upgrading its capabilities as new, improved technological advances occurred. It was a twenty-first-century weapons system on an aging, twentieth-century platform.

"It's got the extended range Standard Missile on it, I believe."

"You believe right, Dick."

"For an airdale, Admiral, you're getting pretty good on this surface warfare stuff."

"I believe, Captain, those are wings on your chest, also." Admiral Devlin grinned as he pushed his chair back slightly, glancing at his shoes. "We both still have brown shoes on, Dick," he chuckled.

Until the late 1990s, the aviation branch of the United States Navy was the only warfighting branch allowed to wear brown uniform shoes, separating the aviators from the surface warfare officers and submariners who wore black. At the turn of the century, the Navy modified uniform regulations to permit every officer the option of wearing either black or brown shoes, but the tradition persisted with few surface warfare officers or submariners opting for brown. The option made black shoes prestigious.

"*Hue City* has the extended-range Phase II Standard Missile on her. The SM-3 replacement for the SM-2."

Dick shook his head. "You've got me, Admiral."

Devlin grinned. "I had a great teacher the past hour with Captain Derek Wild Cloud, the Sixth Fleet surface operations officer."

The admiral turned to the side and scanned the faces in the shadows behind him. "Derek, come here," he said, motioning a broad-shouldered Native American up from one of the metal armchairs shoved against the back bulkhead.

Dick grinned as the native Cherokee wrestled a moment with the chair trapped around the man's broad hips. No-Neck Wild Cloud was the nickname given by the wardroom to the former Naval Academy fullback.

"Yes, sir, Admiral," Wild Cloud answered as he approached.

"Tell Captain Holman the capabilities of the SM-3 missile."

"Morning, Dick," Wild Cloud said. "The SM-3 began replacing the extended surface-to-air SM-2 Standard Missile last year. As you know, the old SM-2 extended-range missile had a max range of a hundred nautical miles. The new SM-3 has taken advantage of new technology, a new propulsion system, and a smaller but more effective warhead to extend the range to nearly double that. The *Hue City*, but not the *Yorktown*, has the new SM-3 missile."

"I thought *Yorktown* had it, too," Admiral Devlin interjected.

"No, sir. She's still outfitted with the SM-2 extended-range missile, Admiral. The *Hue City* and USS *Hayler* have the SM-3. With this newest Standard Missile incorporated into the Aegis weapons system, the *Hue City* and *Hayler* should be able to detect, track, target, and destroy any ballistic missile coming within range of the SM-3."

"What does the USS *Spruance* have? Can she do anything?" Dick asked. "Would it be a good idea to shift our F/A-18 Hornets farther east to reduce time if the two ships need them?"

"Dick, I've been working with Commander Steve Cloth, the air operations officer, and we have been orienting the locations of both the Surface Action Group with the Combat Air Patrol fighters. Right now, if we had a TBMD launch, those two ships are our first lines of defense. The Hornets are the second. As for the *Spruance*, she has a limited number of SM-2 extended-range missiles within her vertical launch system, but her air-search radar capability is not much better now than when she was commissioned back in the '70s."

The command master chief standing near the *Stennis* commanding officer, Tucson Conroy, answered the telephone installed on one of the beams running from the deck to the overhead. He mumbled a couple of words, hung up, and whispered something to Captain Conroy.

Tucson took a few steps forward and tapped Dick Holman on the shoulder. "Captain, that was the general's aide. He's on the telephone and will be a few minutes longer. He passed on that he would like everyone to wait, that he wouldn't be much longer."

"Thanks, Tucson."

Admiral Devlin overheard the comment and nodded in acknowledgment to Dick. He turned back to White Cloud. "Thanks, Derek. Just needed a black shoe to enlighten us brown shoes on what we had out in front of us. Where is the Surface Action Group right now?" Admiral Devlin asked.

"As of a few minutes ago, they were entering the Strait of Sicily. Should be east of the Italian island of Lampedusa within the next couple of hours."

"Thanks, Derek," Devlin said, turning his attention back to the front and to Dick Holman. Derek White Cloud eased away from the table and fought his chair to sit down again with the crowd in the rear of the compartment.

"Have you heard anything from Admiral Cameron?" Dick asked.

"Not from him, but his aide, Clive Bowen, called from Washington on the STE secure line this morning. He needed some papers from Sixth Fleet to support the Board of Inquiry hearings scheduled to start next week."

Dick shook his head. He let the chair come down on four legs, resting his arms, hands clasped, on the metal desk where the two sat. Two empty chairs remained pushed beneath it to the right of Rear Admiral Pete Devlin. "They are really going to do this? We have a major conflict going in Korea, even if it does appear to be winding down. North Africa is seventy miles to the south and we—the Navy—are holding hearings about the events in Gaeta." Dick was referring to the terrorist car bomb-

ing attack against the USS *LaSalle* and the USS *Simon Lake*.
The semtex-laden Mercedes sedan had hit the two Mediterranean moored—tied sterns to the docks—warships, blowing
large enough holes to cause both to settle stern-down on the
bottom of the Gaeta, Italy, harbor. Sixty-eight sailors were
killed, and over two hundred were injured during the attack. At
the same time the car bomber was attacking the two ships, a terrorist team had attacked Admiral Cameron and the Sixth Fleet
wardroom at a social gathering in a nearby bistro. The terrorists
had killed eleven staff and family members while wounding
several others. Admiral Cameron's wife Susan had died in the
attack. If it had not been for the quick actions of the Marine
Corps colonel attached to the Sixth Fleet staff, Walt Ashworth,
more would have died.

"It was not a pleasant conversation, Dick. Clive tells me—
and keep this between us—the admiral has decided to make this
board as short as possible. Gordon wants to limit the negative
press the Navy will suffer from this, so he intends to preempt
the long-drawn-out Q and A by accepting full responsibility.
While we talked, Admiral Cameron was in the next office filling out retirement papers, asking the Navy for immediate retirement."

"Doesn't seem fair."

"Life isn't fair, Dick. We both knew—Admiral Cameron
knew—that eventually he would go before the green table.
Navy tradition and all that."

"I would think they would have waited until everything settled down. He, more than anyone else, is responsible for our
fast response to this crisis. It's not like they left us with much
to work with. If we had kept more foreign presence, we probably wouldn't be fighting this North African action now."

Devlin nodded. "You've hit the nail on the head about foreign presence. As for Admiral Cameron, he was responsible. He
wasn't at fault, but fault and responsibility are two different
things, though few people are able to separate them. Back in the
1980s, I remember a cruiser in the Caribbean accidentally
launching a Harpoon cruise missile. The thing whipped up out
of its canister on the amidships deck, arched over another warship sailing less than a mile away, and headed for the horizon,
never to be seen again. It just disappeared into the sunset. The
investigation revealed that two groups of electronic maintainers

were conducting two separate preventive maintenance checks: one in the Combat Information Center and the other on the Harpoon deck. For some unexplained reason, the two maintenance checks being done simultaneously caused a Harpoon missile to fire. No one's fault on board that ship, but the skipper, who was in the head at the time, was held responsible."

"Little bit different from this, Admiral."

"Same principle, Dick. You and I know that regardless of what happens, if we are the ones at the helm when it occurs, it is our responsibility. Admiral Cameron was the commander of the United States Sixth Fleet when the car bomb sank the two ships in Gaeta; when the USS *Gearing* was conducting a freedom of navigation operation and was sunk by the Libyans; and when the evacuees, guarded by the Sixth Fleet, were captured by Algerian Islamic fanatics. Not his fault, but Navy tradition and regulations place every one of those events under his responsibility. Being a Navy or Marine Corps officer is not for the fainthearted."

"I think it's a little different from what you say, Admiral."

"How's that?"

"I think we are reaping the seeds sowed over decades of cutting Defense budgets and now they need a scapegoat to divert the news media from them. This cuts across party lines. The Defense Department has always been the cash cow for the administration in power to fund whatever petty—or not so petty—project they come up with. Look how the president's chief of staff led the effort to cut our funding a few years back so the president could have his national health plan." Dick paused. "Sorry, Admiral. I know that a mishap board is a necessity to assess what went wrong and how our own performance and readiness affected events. But a Board of Inquiry? That's a little harsh, I think, which makes me believe the timing is political. One keyed to the negative press and drop in popularity that the administration is experiencing over its handling of the Korean and the North African crises."

"It'll work out in the end, Dick. I know Admiral Dixon personally, and I cannot see him standing idly by and allowing a Navy Board of Inquiry to become political." He shrugged his shoulders. "Of course, who knows what pressures he is under. With less than a three hundred ship Navy, there isn't much he can do."

"Admiral Cameron is an outstanding leader, an iron man in the Navy. He had a way of chewing you out, and instead of you feeling as if your career was over, you felt as if you had disappointed your father. Not many who can bring off that type of leadership."

"And he will be the same when the board finishes its findings." Rear Admiral Devlin took a sip of the strong coffee.

Mitchell, the shaven-head mess specialist, approached with a tray of freshly cooked raison coffee cakes.

Mitchell's usual banter, fighting off hands grabbing the fresh, hot pastries before he could set the tray on the table, was missing. One cake rolled off the tray and bounced on the tile floor. A week ago, the person responsible would have earned a caustic eye from the professional. Today, Mitchell continued his trek across the room toward the front table with nary a glance. The raisin cake lay on the floor until a nearby junior officer picked it up and tossed it into the trash can. A nearby mustang—an officer who worked his or her way up through the ranks—glared at the junior officer. Wasn't a damn thing wrong with that cake that a brush of the hand wouldn't have cleaned. It wasn't as if it landed facedown.

Mitchell nodded to the admiral and Captain Holman as he set the dishes in front of them.

"Thanks, Mitchell," Rear Admiral Devlin said, reaching forward and taking one of the hot cakes.

"You're welcome, sir," the petty officer said before turning and silently leaving the compartment.

"Mitchell isn't happy," Devlin said between bites. "But he still makes great pastries. No wonder Gordon kept him with him wherever he went."

"I think Mitchell has taken the departure of Admiral Cameron a little harder than most. If I was the general, I wouldn't have Mitchell cook for me."

Devlin swallowed. "This wasn't General Lewis's doing. I was in the room when Lewis broke the news to Cameron about being relieved and being ordered to Washington. Hard to believe, but Lewis was genuinely upset over Gordon being ordered back to Washington. If he wasn't, he put on a great job of acting.

"Probably because in his own mind he sees where something like that could happen to him."

Devlin took a bite out of a second coffee cake. He shook his head, pointed to his mouth, telling Dick to give him a second to finish this mouthful. Dick wished he had the Admiral's metabolism as he pushed a half-eaten piece of pastry away.

"No, I disagree. My communications officer, Paul Brooks—"

"He's your cryptologic officer, sir."

"My cryptologic officer, Paul Brooks, told me the general went up behind the green door and called the chairman of the Joint Chiefs of Staff directly, General Eaglefield, and asked that he rescind the order from the Navy. From what Captain Brooks said, the conversation got a little heavy, and from some of the language going back and forth, if the two generals didn't know each other, they do now."

"You mean the chairman refused a commander of a Joint Task Force his request? That's a new one. Most times, they give the benefit of doubt to the commander in the field."

"They should. Unfortunately, it doesn't always work that way. General Eaglefield not only refused Lewis's request, but from what Brooks was able to garner out of the conversation, the order came from high up."

"Meaning what?"

"Meaning either SecDef or the president ordered Cameron's relief. I would put my money on the president. General Eaglefield has Maddock wrapped around his finger when it comes to military strategy and tactics. It's only budget issues where Eaglefield bows to Maddock's wishes. So, maybe you are right about this relief of Admiral Cameron being more political than traditional."

"And we went through this whole convoluted thought process to figure it out."

"Eh! You're still a captain, remember."

The hatch to the Operations briefing room burst open, bouncing back to clang against the steel doorstop. Dick and Pete Devlin exchanged glances. They knew the sound. Navy hatches, designed for watertight integrity, lack the springs, pumps, and other accessories normal doors have to ease opening and closing. Hatches have nothing attached to stop their movement once opened. Sailors familiar with shipboard life soon learn never to stand behind a hatch and to open and close them slowly. Steel doorstops are welded to protect the bulkheads when the uninitiated send a steel hatch rocketing in a

180-degree scythe. General Lewis, on board over four weeks, had yet to learn the secret of moving gracefully from compartment to compartment. He attacked each hatch, each door, and each knee-knocker as if taking an enemy foxhole. Scuttlebutt had quickly circulated among the crew to treat the general like an aircraft carrier; stand clear of the hatches when he was maneuvering.

"Attention on deck!" Kurt Lederman shouted as Lieutenant General Leutze "Call Me Rocky" Lewis entered the compartment. Behind the Army commander of the Joint Task Force scurried his aide, Colonel Brad Storey.

Devlin and Holman stood as Lewis marched to their table and sat down. "Hooah, take seats," Lewis said as he pulled his chair to the table.

Colonel Storey, immaculate in his freshly starched, military-creased uniform, stood slightly to the rear of the general. He grinned at Rear Admiral Devlin before sitting down. Storey leaned back in his chair, his brown eyebrows arched for a moment as he mouthed a cheerful "Good Morning" to Dick. A future congressman or senator if he had ever seen one, Dick said to himself.

"Sorry to keep you waiting. I had some 'personal for' messages that just came in, talked with General Sutherland in Stuttgart, and had a quick conversation with the British battle group commander, Admiral Sir Ledderman-Thompson. They do go for the long-drawn-out names, don't they? I'll brief you later. Meanwhile," Lewis paused, glancing at Kurt Lederman. "Go ahead with the update, Captain, and we'll see if what you say agrees with what I've been told."

"Aye, sir," Kurt replied, miffed over being put to a test. He nodded to the graphics operator. The first view graph containing a geographical map of the western Mediterranean appeared on the screen.

"General Lewis, Admiral Devlin, a quick synopsis of our current status before addressing the emergency operation order received two hours ago."

"Make it a real quick synopsis, Captain," General Lewis interrupted curtly.

"Yes, sir. The Spanish Expeditionary Force that penetrated into western Algeria four weeks ago has relieved the besieged Algerian loyalist force at Oran as well as occupied the nearby naval base. They appear to be consolidating their position and establishing a logistics base before further advances—if they intend to advance. We believe they will. The presence of the Algerian loyalist forces lends legitimacy to the Spanish forces. The Algerian Navy units that had previously sought sanctuary in Malaga, Spain, are already beginning to return to Oran."

Kurt pointed on the map to the location of the eastern Spanish port of Malaga. "The Algerian Kilo submarine associated with the crash of Ranger Two Nine has been granted asylum in Malaga, Spain. Interrogation of its captain revealed that this submarine was responsible for the mining of the Strait of Gibraltar. The mines were programmed to deactivate after thirty days. This supports what Navy Intelligence had already determined. The mine threat in the Strait no longer exists. The Spanish are confirming the deactivation and will get back to us as soon as possible."

The intelligence officer nodded at the operator. "Next slide." Using a laser pointer, Captain Lederman highlighted on the map the Korean capitol of Seoul. "American forces have halted the advancing North Korean armor attack. American airpower has full air superiority over the peninsula and Operation Full Stop has commenced. For review, General, Operation Full Stop is a combined allied-force air campaign to obliterate the logistic pipeline running from North Korea to its forces engaged in the south. Simultaneously, United States Army armor and artillery divisions are commencing a major attack against the North Koreans, forcing them to use their precious ammunition and giving them no rest. Amphibious Task Forces continue to build in the Sea of Japan.

Kurt cleared his throat. "The USS *Kearsarge* has been ordered to remain on station with Task Force African Force but to be prepared to execute earlier order to commence a high-speed run around South Africa. When Full Stop terminates in approximately thirty days, the United States Navy and Marine Corps assets off Korea will have four full Amphibious Task Forces—nearly a division of Marines."

Kurt nodded again. "Next slide."

"Aha!" General Lewis said, grinning from ear to ear. "I win, Captain."

"Sir?"

"What you don't know," General Lewis said, standing so he

could face the assembled officers. "What none of you know, but I know you will be pleased to hear, is that about an hour ago, the North Koreans accepted the terms of peace as dictated by General Marks, Commander of United States Forces in Korea. The major attack that Captain Lederman just briefed went better than expected. Thought was that the North Koreans would slug it out and make us fight for every inch of territory." He laughed, drawing wide-eyed stares from a room full of people who had never even seen Lewis grin, much less laugh. "They broke! The North Koreans broke and ran. They were low on fuel, ammo, and food. As we sit here in the Mediterranean, a half world away, we have not only contained a major theater war, but we have won it. When we know more, we will share it, but for the time being, forces that are in the Mediterranean will remain here. General Eaglefield has already directed two of the aircraft carriers in the Sea of Japan to head here along with one of the Marine Expeditionary Forces. So, instead of losing forces and possibly having to vacate the Med itself, within a couple of weeks, we will actually increase our strength to a size capable of taking the North African littoral if we want."

It was one clap at first, followed by another, until the whole compartment erupted into thunderous applause. After a couple of minutes, it wound down, and General Lewis sat back down and motioned for Kurt to continue.

"Next slide." A photo of Algerian tactical aircraft appeared on the screen beside a small map of Libya. The three major cities of Libya—Tripoli, Benghazi, and Tobruk—were highlighted with red stars.

"We still have approximately thirty fighter-attack rebel aircraft unaccounted for." His pointer moved to the map of Libya. "The CIA and NSA report that Colonel Mumtaz Alqahiray has overthrown the current Libyan leaders and returned to power. Alqahiray has been identified as responsible for the North African crisis. Information from the National Infrastructure Protection Center at FBI headquarters has linked Alqahiray with the terrorist network Al-Qaida. Alqahiray is controlling the military and the government from somewhere south of Tripoli in a deep, underground bunker."

"They do love the underground, don't they?" General Lewis piped softly.

"The previous leaders, led by a Colonel Walid, have set up a provisional government in Benghazi. This will most likely spark an internal conflict within the new government, or at a minimum within Libya. Captain Paul Brooks will tell us more about Colonel Alqahiray and his location later."

"Next slide. The primary reason we are here today is to discuss the recent reports from the Hungarian Intelligence Service." Five lines of text against a green background filled the viewing screen. Kurt knew the secret of presentations was never to give viewers hard copies of the slide show. When you did, they spent their time going through the copies rather than listening to what was being said. The five lines of text were there to focus audience attention, not answer their unasked questions.

"A member of the Hungarian Intelligence Service infiltrated a Libyan project to build biological warheads. Six Russian scientists, along with the agent, were incommunicado in the same bunker where Alqahiray is holed up. The seven escaped, made their way to Tripoli, where the Russians went to their embassy, and the Hungarian agent worked his way to his. According to the Hungarians, Colonel Alqahiray personally ordered the attack that sank the USS *Gearing* and was responsible for the information warfare attack on the geopositional satellites used for navigation. This attack caused the USS *Gearing* to inadvertently penetrate Libyan waters, giving Alqahiray the excuse needed to attack her.

The laser pointer highlighted the first line of text, which read, "Twelve missiles—two armed."

"Twelve missiles were deployed last night via a system of underground tunnels built by the late Qaddafi. According to the agent, the Russians and he disarmed ten of the twelve missiles. That means two of the missiles have biological warheads on them."

Kurt moved his laser down a line: "High Probability of use."

"The CIA assesses Colonel Alqahiray will fire the missiles. The missiles are aimed . . ."

Kurt moved the laser down to the third line: "Italy, Spain, or Greece—Includes major island groups."

". . . toward Europe. The range of the Libyan Al-Fatah II, which is the follow-on to the original '90s Al-Fatah ballistic missile, is over one thousand nautical miles. This gives it the

range to hit anywhere along the Mediterranean coast. It can hit
Israel from the Libyan eastern border areas and Spain from its
western border. Nearly all of Italy and Greece are within
range."

Kurt moved his pointer to the fourth line. "A ten-kilo anthrax warhead designed to disperse the biological agent from
altitude is still active on two unlocated missiles."

"I think most of us have had our anthrax shots," Rear Admiral Devlin said, addressing General Lewis.

"Will they be effective against this strain of anthrax?" General Lewis asked.

"Dr. Jacobs!" Admiral Devlin shouted.

Captain Charles "Chuck" Jacobs, the Sixth Fleet surgeon,
stepped into the small cone of light near the front of the compartment. "Yes, sir, Admiral?"

"What is the status of our anthrax vaccinations?"

Chuck Jacobs shook his head. "Not too good, sirs. Most of
the old-timers have the vaccinations, and we are unsure if they
are still effective after such a long time. I would put the number of those, not only in the Navy, but in all the military services with vaccination shots at less than thirty percent, and most
of them don't have the four shots required to complete the program. General, as I am sure you are aware, the anthrax vaccination program requires an annual booster shot. I would doubt
if more than ten percent have the booster shot." Chuck Jacobs
had reviewed the immunization records by sorting them according to anthrax. The resulting computer readout showed that
only he, Clive Bowen, who had left with Admiral Cameron, and
the command master chief of the USS *Stennis* had kept their
booster shots up to date. Three people out of thousands on
board the aircraft carrier and the Sixth Fleet staff. Anthrax vaccine was in limited supply with the couple of pharmaceutical
companies making it unable to meet the demands of the civilian population in America and the American military.

"Without the booster shot, is the vaccination worthless?"
Pete Devlin asked.

"Don't know, Admiral. Not necessarily. The vaccination still
has some value; it's just the booster keeps that value at its
peak."

"What can you tell us about anthrax?" General Lewis asked.

"Not much more than nearly everyone here already knows.

Every one of us lived through the anthrax attack against America years ago." Then, for the next twenty minutes, the fleet surgeon reviewed the deadly disease, detailing how spore-forming bacteria caused anthrax commonly found in warm-blooded animals. How inhalation anthrax was the deadliest, but with the right combination of antibiotics administered early enough, even it could be cured. American intelligence agencies had discovered in the late 1990s that several terrorist-supporting nations, such as Iraq, North Korea, Iran, and Libya, had bioterrorist strategies centered on aerosol delivery of anthrax. A Defense Science Board report in 2000 warned that unvaccinated exposure to anthrax would result in a near 100 percent casualty rate. No one listened to the countless warnings by countless authorities before countless committees until that first anthrax-laden letter had hit Florida. Now, most Americans knew more about anthrax than they ever wanted to know.

Dr. Jacobs warmed to his subject as he paced the front of the briefing room, revealing how anthrax could be spread in three ways: through a cut in the skin, by ingestion while eating, or by inhalation.

Kurt Lederman interrupted to point out that a small explosive device in the enemy warhead would activate during the descent phase. The warheads are programmed to explode at approximately ten thousand feet. At this altitude, the explosion would spread the anthrax through the atmosphere in a thorough fashion that would ensure no one avoided inhaling the biological agent.

"In which case, everyone who breathes in those spores will contract anthrax," Dr. Jacobs said.

An interested Marine Corps officer in the dark shadows of the back of the room asked how they could recognize an anthrax attack.

Dr. Jacobs thought a few minutes before replying. "Anthrax is colorless, odorless, and tasteless. It's a spore, so if it gathers in one spot sufficiently enough, you can see it. Symptoms vary, depending on how it is contracted. Inhaling the spore will cause initial symptoms similar to the common cold or a mild case of flu, but you shouldn't have a runny nose. Experts say that it takes sometimes two weeks for inhalation anthrax to appear. Weaponized anthrax can appear in seventy-two to ninety hours after inhaling the bacterium. Severe breathing problems followed by the onset of shock will occur. Death usually results within forty-eight hours after the onset of the coldlike symptoms. So, if you have inhalation anthrax and think you are coming down with the flu, then you are already too late."

How can they recognize something like that, another officer asked. They could not go running around every time someone had a cold or the flu, shouting anthrax attack!

Dr. Jacobs shrugged his shoulders, suggesting that only by early recognition of a larger than normal number of coldlike symptoms could the presence of the biological agent be considered. If caught early enough, it was possible to save some lives. Most anthrax is susceptible to penicillin, but as early as the '70s, virulent strains resistant to penicillin had been identified. This would give them maximum dispersal range. It is possible to treat anthrax during this phase with penicillin or, if the strain is penicillin resistant, with another antibiotic.

General Lewis turned toward the Sixth Fleet surgeon. "So, if we have enough penicillin and similar antibiotics available, we could defeat these two warheads?"

He nodded. "If we had enough, General." Dr. Jacobs shook his head. "Unfortunately, we don't have that much antibiotics in Sixth Fleet to start the necessary preventive antibiotic course to protect everyone. Just isn't enough. And I doubt that the European countries will have enough. But what we do have is technology. We have a Zebra chip in our medical computer. The Zebra chip is a screening shield we use in medical on all blood samples. It contains biofingerprints of most contagious diseases and known biological warfare agents. It would be our quickest way to discern between an outbreak of flu and the presence of anthrax. That way, we can best determine who needs the antibiotics to stave off anthrax. Meanwhile, we will ask the Pentagon to rush us an increase in supplies."

"The entire Mediterranean coast is within range of the missiles, General," Kurt Lederman added.

"Do all our ships have these Zebra chips, Doc?" Pete Devlin asked.

Captain Jacobs shook his head. "No, Admiral. Only the *Stennis* and the *Nassau*, as far as I know."

General Lewis leaned back. "Gentlemen and ladies, we have to stop those missiles from being launched. That is the same thing that the chairman and General Sutherland, the European commander, relayed: 'Stop those missiles!' "

"Yes, sir," Captain Jacobs added. "If those missiles hit a populated area, then we can expect a ninety percent death rate. Survivors can expect a significantly shorter life span. Death by anthrax is an ugly, painful death. The lymph glands swell to immense size, racking the body with pain as the bacteria spreads throughout the body. The lungs begin to drown in fluids produced by the victim's own body. Dryer parts of the body such as the hands and feet have been known to crack and bleed as if a sharp knife had sliced through the skin in the more virulent strains. What I have described has been the common anthrax bacteria found in the ground and on farm animals, commonly referred to as woolsorter's disease because of its association with sheep."

"So, you think the warheads have an unknown variant of anthrax in them?"

"Yes, sir, General Lewis. The former Soviet Union had over nine hundred strains of anthrax in its military inventory, some genetically manipulated and some not. If the Libyans had these scientists working on anthrax warheads for six months, then, most likely, they have a genetically modified anthrax bacterium in the warhead. Common anthrax is too easy to replicate and reproduce for them to have spent six months developing it."

"Captain Lederman, what is the soonest the Libyans can launch those missiles?"

"Tomorrow morning, General."

"Then we need to be in position to launch a preemptive strike tomorrow morning. Can we do that, Admiral?"

"General, we are steaming west at twenty knots, but it will be late tomorrow before we pass through the Strait of Sicily. The *Hue City* and the USS *Spruance* are transiting through the Strait now."

Admiral Pete Devlin, his second day on the job as the commander of the United States Sixth Fleet, turned to the faces behind him. "Who's the command duty officer?"

"I am, sir," answered Commander Bailey, stepping toward the table but stopping a few feet away.

"Estimated time of arrival at the Strait of Sicily?"

"Ten hundred hours tomorrow morning, Admiral."

"That's unsat!" boomed General Lewis. "I want the battle

group in strike range by morning. When the sun comes up, I want us to be through the Strait."

Captain Jacobs stepped forward. "General, they won't fire those missiles before tomorrow night."

All eyes turned toward the medical officer. "Why is that, Captain?"

"Sir, anthrax is negatively affected by sunlight. Sunlight can kill the spores. The way anthrax normally survives is in the tissue of its victim or hidden from sunlight in the ground. If they launch those missiles during the day, most of the spores will be dead before they reach the ground. They have to launch at night for maximum effectiveness."

"Are you sure of that?"

"Unless they have developed a particularly virulent strain of the disease."

The officers turned to Kurt Lederman. "So, Kurt, how long do we have if the Libyans do what the doc thinks they will?" Captain Dick Holman asked.

"Sunset is twenty-one forty-five Greenwich mean time tomorrow," Commander Bailey added.

"Then, sirs, we have less than twenty-four hours to locate twelve missiles, plan, and launch a strike to stop those warheads," Kurt Lederman announced.

"We will do it. Right, Admiral Devlin?" General Lewis asked, hitting his fist on the table.

Pete Devlin shook his head. "We can handle the western portion of Libya with no problem. But from the center of the Gulf of Sidra, midway of Libya to the Egyptian border, we will need help from our allies."

"The chairman has diverted five Air Force B-52s with air-launched cruise missiles to support our strike. The aircraft are already airborne from Mildenhall Air Base in England."

"Yes, sir, General, and we have them arriving on station within the hour," Commander Steve Cloth added from the back row.

"The Italians and the Greeks are aware of the dangers," Kurt Lederman added. "An Italian battle group, centered on their aircraft carrier *Garibaldi*, is getting under way from Taranto tomorrow morning. They have a reconnaissance aircraft flying a mission along the CENTMED littoral in the hopes of pinpointing the location of the twelve missiles. The Italian battle group should be within striking distance of the central Libyan coast by early afternoon. The Greek Navy remains active off the east coast of Libya, and the Greek Air Force has already increased air patrols between Crete and Libya. The French and British battle group has been forewarned, but we haven't received any feedback from them . . . unless you have, General."

"I have. The Royal Navy battle group intends to break away from the NATO combined battle group within the next hour. They will join us somewhere near the north coast of Tunisia, and we shall become a coalition battle group. Admiral Sir Ledderman-Thompson said his duty officers would coordinate with ours."

Dick Holman leaned forward, resting his elbows on the table. "That's a pleasant surprise, General. I thought the British were hamstrung under their European Union agreements."

General Lewis stood up and shook his head. "There's more to the British action than just the preemptive strike for tomorrow, but I'll tell you about that later. The actions of the British battle group were decided at a much higher level than the military, the results of which you two deserve to know."

Dick Holman and Pete Devlin exchanged glances. Dick Holman had worked with the British warrior during the anti-submarine actions of the *Stennis* battle group following the sacrifice of the USS *John Rodgers* during their initial approach to the Strait of Gibraltar. The Royal Navy aircraft carrier *Invincible* Battle Group had been following only miles behind the American carrier battle group when it was attacked near the Strait of Gibraltar. Admiral Sir Ledderman-Thompson had ordered a destroyer and his antisubmarine helicopters forward to work alongside the American counterattack against the unidentified submarine attempting to keep the warships out of the Mediterranean. The Royal Navy would be a welcome addition, even if their only aircraft were the limited-range, vertical-launched Harrier ground support/fighter aircraft. The surface warships would at least have cruise missiles on them.

General Lewis interrupted Dick Holman's thoughts as he spoke to Pete Devlin. "Admiral, I would like a draft strike ops on my desk within the hour. Nothing fancy or firm, just an order of events." He turned to Kurt Lederman, standing in front of him, and pointed his finger at the Navy officer. "Captain, by

morning, I want to know where those missiles are. Get some reconnaissance assets airborne and active."

The three Navy officers exchanged glances with each other.
"General," Pete Devlin said. "We only have Ranger Two Six,
an EP-3E out of the Fleet Air Reconnaissance Squadron Two,
in theater. The Italians have promised to share any missile locations they get with us. They should be finishing their mission
any moment now."

Lewis put both hands on his hips, stretching the top part of
his extra-large-tall shirt across his massive chest. "Well, answer
me this, Pete, why in the hell doesn't the Navy have any carrier
capable aircraft SIGINT reconnaissance assets? Seems to me
you'd give up the shore-based capability before you'd forgo a
carrier-based capability. I would think shore-based would be
more an Air Force mission than a Navy." He glanced at Colonel
Brad Storey, who nodded quickly in agreement.

"That's a long story all the way back into the mid-'90s
about a fleet commander in chief who wanted so desperately to
find money for information technology upgrade that he forced
the Navy to cut the ES-3B program. Most of us with warfighting experience disagreed. When this is over, if the general
finds the subject interesting, we can spend a couple of hours
discussing it."

Lewis exhaled audibly and dropped his hands. "Well,
maybe. Right now, find the location of those missiles, and take
them out. If we can use allied intelligence and reconnaissance
results like we have the Hungarians, then do it."

General Lewis took a few steps toward the hatch, preparing
to leave.

"General," Kurt Lederman interrupted. "Before you go, sir,
Paul Brooks knows the location of the Libyan mastermind behind the missiles, behind the North African crisis, and who has
been identified as responsible for the sinking of the USS *Gearing*."

The cryptologic officer, his dark hair too long and covering
the tops of his ears, stepped up beside the intelligence officer.

"Go ahead, Captain Brooks," Pete Devlin said when he saw
General Lewis nod.

"Next slide, please," Paul Brooks said. A map of the Libyan
coastline replaced the textual slide. With his laser pointer, he

targeted an area about one hundred miles south of Tripoli. "The exact coordinates are—"

"I know the exact coordinates, Captain," General Lewis interrupted.

"Sir?"

"The question is how do you know the coordinates?" he asked, a little anger in his voice.

"Colonel Alqahiray loves his computers, General. It was only a matter of time until we became computer partners with him. Fleet Information Warfare Command at Little Creek, Virginia, pinpointed him yesterday. They infiltrated his command, control, computers, and communications—C4—link with an electronic warfare array activated along the coast of the Gulf of Sidra. Our initial assessment is that this EW array is responsible for blinding the USS *Gearing* while it operated in the area. It could have been responsible for the destroyer sailing into Libyan waters, suckered into—"

"Can you take them down?"

"The EW array?"

The general rubbed his chin for a second. "Yes, the EW array, but I was thinking more of getting inside his C4 net and either controlling it or blinding him."

Paul looked at the admiral. "Sir, we can task FIWC to take the C4 down just before we launch the attack. We take their C3 and computers down, Alqahiray won't even know an attack is under way until those cruise missiles pierce the floors of that underground bunker and blow him to hell and high water."

"Good. But I don't want you to do anything unless I tell you to. If I do tell you to take it down, I also want to remove the EW array." General Lewis looked around the operations briefing room. "I want no misunderstanding at this point of discussion. I am not targeting Colonel Alqahiray. I do not want to target him. But there are other things going on that not all of you are aware of. Captain Brooks, tell your FIWC to withdraw their electronic tendrils from the Libyan headquarters, but be prepared to launch a computer network warfare attack, if so ordered." His voice betrayed the tone of a conspirator.

"But General," Kurt Lederman interrupted. "We have his location. We can put a missile right down his throat. Kill the bastard responsible for this."

Lewis glared at the intelligence officer. Kurt took a step

away from the table, a little surprised at his own outburst. The blood vessels on the general's neck grew as the already tall flag officer seemed to expand in height. "Captain, there may be other operations going on that you are not privy to. A cruise missile would disrupt it and prove disastrous for everyone. I have said no hard targeting of this asshole. You understand?" He put his hands on his hips.

"Yes, sir," Kurt replied, his mind reviewing what the general had just said. He, as the intelligence officer, was responsible for the targeting phase of any military action. If another operation was going on in this theater, then it had to be a covert Special Operations Command action out of Tampa. Shit! How the hell was he going to identify what to target other than those missiles if he had no idea of everything going on in the Sixth Fleet area of operations?

Dick Holman looked at Admiral Devlin, who mumbled quietly, "Wait."

"Admiral, I will be in my quarters for a few minutes and afterward at the gym. Until then, gentlemen and ladies, remember the *Gearing* and the *John Rodgers*. It's time to take the message home, and we're the ones who are going to do it. Our victory in Korea sends the right message to these nuts."

"That was great, sir," Colonel Storey said in a soft but audible voice as the huge flag officer stepped through the exit. "Great morale-building, sir."

"I'd gag if it weren't so serious," Dick Holman said, listening to the exchange.

Kurt Lederman joined the two Navy officers. "Admiral, what is he talking about? Is there a military operation going on that I don't know about?"

"Kurt, Dick, I wish I could tell you more. In this one, you will have to trust me. Don't target Alqahiray. And, if any of those missiles are within fifty miles of his bunker, then check with me before adding it to the target list."

"But, sir—"

"No, buts, Kurt. No targeting, and I want no brainstorming as to why."

Kurt acknowledged the order, knowing as soon as he returned to his spaces, he was going to tweak the Naval intelligence circuits to find out what the hell was going on. By God, he was the intelligence officer. How the hell could he do his job if they were keeping secrets from him? He remembered the paper he was holding.

"Admiral, bad news from the beach," he said, glancing down at the folded paper in his hand. "Captain James and his SEALs entered the sewer system leading to the suspected hiding place of the rebels holding our American hostages. A few seconds after entering it, the pipe blew, sealing them inside the catacombs."

"Are they dead?"

"Don't know, sir. The Marines are removing the rocks and debris from the entrance as fast as they can. That will take several hours. Bulldog is rigging lighting so they can continue."

"Let me know when we find out the status. Without them, the hunt for the hostages must go on. Our plans still call for us to evacuate Algiers in seven days with or without the hostages. I had expected General Lewis to share that timetable at this briefing, but he either forgot or decided to keep it close hold, so keep that information to yourself until he releases it. Anything else, Kurt?"

"No, sir, Admiral, other than that Bulldog is not happy about the carrier abandoning Algiers while he has forces still engaged on the ground."

"He will still have the Harriers on board the *Nassau*. If something happens where he needs high-performance tactical aircraft, then we can launch them from our station off Tunisia. They can always recover at the Algiers airport," Dick Holman said to Admiral Devlin. "Of course, he doesn't know about the imminent attack on Libya."

"He doesn't really have a need to know," Paul Brooks added, walking up to the group.

"I disagree," Kurt added. "What if one of those missiles is aimed at Algiers?"

"Why would Alqahiray do that?"

"Why wouldn't he?"

The hatch burst open, and a master chief petty officer, who Dick Holman recognized as one of the Sixth Fleet Combat Information Center assistant watch officers, stepped inside. The woman looked around the darkened room, saw the briefing was over, and flipped on the nearby light switches. Dick squinted his eyes from the sudden glare of the fluorescent light.

The master chief rushed over to the four senior Navy officers standing near the felt-topped table. "Admiral, you are needed in Combat, sir. We have detected a missile launch out of southern Tunisia."

"A missile launch?" Admiral Devlin asked, surprise echoing in his voice. He glanced at Kurt. "You said they wouldn't be ready until tomorrow."

"I didn't, Admiral. Doc said that."

"Maybe they had others—nonbiological warhead missiles—already deployed?"

"No, sir. Only those twelve."

An intelligence specialist first class petty officer entered the compartment with a folder stamped TOP SECRET COMPARTMENTED TRAFFIC. He handed it to Kurt Lederman, who flipped it open and glanced at it before shutting it as he opened his mouth to speak. He stopped and flipped it back open.

"Well, I'll be damned! The Italians have located the missiles."

"Plot them out, and let's get the targeting orders out ASAP!" Pete Devlin ordered.

Admiral Devlin led the way, with Dick Holman hurrying to keep up. Kurt Lederman and Paul Brooks followed close behind. "I hope you're right, Kurt. If not, we are going to have a lot of dead people on our hands."

At the door, a first class petty officer materialized, nearly colliding with Admiral Devlin. He stepped back sharply and saluted. "Sir, a second missile has been detected. Fired from north of Tripoli, it is on a northerly trajectory."

"Jesus Christ," Devlin muttered as he pushed by the petty officer, nearly running as he headed toward the Sixth Fleet Combat Information Center of the aircraft carrier. "Where are the *Hue City* and *Spruance*?"

Dick Holman hurried to catch up with the athletic admiral. Kurt Lederman turned the other way and scurried up the ladder toward the intelligence spaces. Paul Brooks passed him as Kurt was keying in the combination to the hatch. He took two steps at a time up the nearby ladder, heading to the cryptologic compartment. The bongs of general quarters hit the super carrier as Paul stepped into the blue-lighted spaces of cryptology and information warfare.

# TEN

**DUNCAN SPAT OUT DUST AND DEBRIS, BLINKING HIS EYES**
repeatedly to clear them. "Anyone hurt?" he asked, coughing.
He pushed himself up from the metal side of the sewer pipe,
where the explosion had blown him. Duncan fumbled at the
side of his belt for his flashlight.

Beau shouted from the rear, "Okay back here! The explosion
was upward and outward. Speak up, everyone!"

"I'm okay," replied Chief Wilcox, as if not completely sure
he was. "But my face stings like hell."

Beau turned around and shone his flashlight in the chief's
face. "Well, there goes my night vision, Commander." He took
the proffered hand and pulled himself up. "And you look like
shit, Commander."

"Chief, if your face didn't hurt before because of how ugly
it was, it should now. You've a few scratches and cuts from the
explosion. Some blood below your left cheek, but nothing that
looks life threatening. A six-pack, some iodine, and three eight
hundred–milligram tablets of Motrin should take care of it."

"We're okay up here, boss," HJ replied from her position
ahead. "I can't see anything but dust back your way. Everyone
okay?"

"Captain, here it is." Gibbons held up the end of a small strand of wire. "Trip wire."

"What?" Duncan hit his ear. He had a slight ringing sound in both of them. "I didn't hear that, and I can't see anything until this dust settles. Beau, take a quick muster."

"That's what I'm trying to do."

"Gibbons hit a trip wire, Captain," Monkey relayed.

"And a hell of a trip wire, too," Beau said. He wiggled his jaw, relieving the pressure in his ears. Beau called out the names of the team, quickly going down the roster from memory. Gibbons, the combination radioman, medic, and SEAL. McDonald and Monkey, the two heavy machine gunners with their thirty-pound M-60s they lugged everywhere, reported okay. The two had refused to exchange these formidable weapons for ones better suited to tramping through the sewers. Up ahead, the only woman SEAL in the Navy with a Purple Heart, and at least a Bronze Star waiting for her, stood Heather J. McDaniels. Gibbons and Monkey called her Wonder Woman behind her back, until Chief Wilcox put a stop to it. Chief Wilcox had a few minor injuries to his face from the explosion, but the newest member of the team was already working his way forward, physically checking each member to assure they were all right. SEALs weren't known for being honest when they were wounded. Bud Helliwell, mustang and only original officer from the deployed SEALs assigned to the USS *Nassau* Amphibious Task Force, ran his hand along his recently healed arm and cursed. It looked as if the arm was injured again. He wiggled his fingers and decided it wasn't broken, it was just stunned, so he reported okay, though he had no feeling in his left thumb. But who needed thumbs? He had two of them.

Duncan found the switch on his flashlight and inched his way back toward the opening. He shone the beam back along the sewer tunnel. A ton of rock and soil covered the opening. He moved the beam to the bottom. The steady sewage drainage along the base of the tunnel had lost its exit and was beginning to rise. No danger yet, but it would become one if they stayed here. The foul liquid was already licking at the top of his combat boots.

"HJ, you and Gibbons keep moving, and keep an eye out for other trip wires. I don't want us trapped between the entrance here and some sort of exit ahead."

Duncan touched the side of the tunnel to hold himself upright. His hand slid down the side, coming away from the ancient bricks covered with a slime of fungi and crud on his gloves. He wiped it on his pants leg. "Don't touch the sides, if you can help it."

"Too late," came the reply from several of them.

"Well, don't bite your nails, fellows," HJ said.

"Who brought her along?" Beau joked.

"We need to move, Captain. This water has risen a couple of inches while we've talked," Chief Wilcox said. The chief pulled a fluorescent crayon from a pocket on his pants leg and made a huge X on one of the rocks that blocked the entrance. On the side of the sewer, he drew an arrow pointing in the direction they were heading, though at this point they only had one way to go.

Duncan pulled his crayon out and wrote, "Okay, heading out." When the Marines broke through the rocks sealing the entrance, they would at least know everyone was okay and the mission was still a go.

"Captain," Bud Helliwell said. "The infrared devices the Marines gave us don't work so good with no light or heat down here. About all I can see is the trickle of water and sewage along the bottom."

"We'll have to use our lights. Every other person uses a flashlight. The rest of you conserve yours until we need them and stay close to those using them. And keep those headlamps turned off."

The line of Navy SEALs moved forward slowly, the headlamps on the helmets off, as HJ, Chief Wilcox, Beau, and McDonald used their small flashlights to light the way. Duncan turned his flashlight off and slipped it back on the ring alongside his belt. He reached up to the right side of the helmet and pulled the small handle down. A thumb-sized computer screen appeared in front of his right eye. He pulled his left arm up and hit the lighted F1 key on the small keypad strapped to the forearm. On the screen, a schematic of the Algiers catacombs appeared, along with a small red dot showing their position. The problem with the software the Marines loaded was that they could only load the sewer systems that the Algerian Water and Gas Company knew about. The Algerian supervisor argued that only a tenth of the sewer maze had been charted, and only that portion where they had their lines. The Marine captain in charge of their Urban Warrior software had laughed when he outfitted Duncan, telling him how last year the Algerian Water and Gas Company lost two workers in the maze. Never found them and still paying wages to their families. Duncan hated to be inside anything. He disliked the ride in the USS *Albany* when the submarine dropped them off five weeks ago to rescue President Hawali Alneuf, and he particularly disliked being trapped under a foreign city surrounded by shit.

Duncan hit the F4 button to check if they had contact with the surface, but a red warning banner flashed, showing no connection existed. He knew it would. It was nigh impossible to establish an electromagnetic connection through God knows how many meters of soil, brick, and concrete above them. An image of a hundred thousand butts sitting on toilets adding human waste to the catacombs flashed through his mind. The circumstances gave Duncan a new appreciation for sewer workers, especially those in New York caught belowground during halftime of the Super Bowl when the flash flood of a million flushes rush simultaneously through the smaller pipes of the city that never sleeps.

Taking his mind off the possibilities of drowning from overhead action, Duncan pressed the F1 button again. The F3 button allowed them to pass information among themselves, but since he was the only one with the outfit, the button was useless. The keyboard was inconvenient. To use it effectively, he would have to lay his carbine down, and right now, the carbine gave Duncan a more secure feeling than the piece of modern technology the Marines used for urban warfare. The power pack for the contraption was strapped on his belt like a knife scabbard. The wires ran under his cammies, above his skivvies and T-shirt, to exit down his left arm. The Marine Corps captain, who insisted on telling and retelling the story of the two lost in the sewer catacombs of Algiers, warned Duncan to be careful, or the battery could become disconnected. Between the horror tales the Marine Corps captain told, he remembered to tell Duncan the battery had a useful life of five hours. Duncan had a second, backup battery in his small backpack. But he had no intention of being in the sewers long enough for the first one to go dead. He had been here nearly thirty minutes, and that was thirty minutes too long. If he suspected Bashir knew another way to where the hostages were being held, he'd strangle the weight-challenged Bedouin when he got out of here.

"Captain, we got a fork," Gibbons passed back.

"Ask the captain to check the map," HJ relayed.

"Of course, if we had been given a hard copy, we could move faster," Bud Helliwell added.

"Sure, Ensign. You have to get into the computer age, Mustang Bud, or you are going to be left behind," Beau said, slapping the sandy-haired ensign on the shoulder. "Besides, more fun exploring without a map."

"Bud, quit your whining. You want to ruin your reputation?" HJ asked.

"HJ, check those nanorobots steaming around inside you. I think they're building balls."

"Bud, why would I want something that would slow me down and cloud my brain? If I had balls, I would have the same problem you do—never knowing where my brains are."

"Cut the chatter," Duncan said. He searched the computer-generated map. "HJ, give Gibbons a hand, and see if you two can tell which fork the rebels used."

"I'll go, too," Bud said, wincing slightly as he put weight on his left arm when he shoved off the side of the sewer.

The two SEAL officers moved slowly through the confines of the pitch-black tunnel, their lights providing the only illumination. The curved bottom caused them to stumble periodically, making it impossible to keep their hands off the sides. As they plodded onward, the metal wall near the entrance gave way to older bricks and rocks covered with foul-smelling slime that stuck to their gloves. The sticky wetness of the substance was already soaking through the thin fabric. Finally, the slightly curved bottom of the sewer changed to a rough, flat surface with small potholes worn out by the steady flow of Algerian waste. The soft grunts of Duncan's team as they stumbled in the dark marked a slow progress. Duncan gave up trying to avoid the four to five inches of water and sewage flowing along the bottom of the sewer and started walking through it, hoping he didn't hit the wide puddles that grew around the larger potholes. For all he knew, these ancient potholes might be bottomless, drowning anyone who fell into them before others could save them. Duncan softly passed a warning to the others.

Chief Wilcox tramped through the center of the mess, step-

ping on the sides to push himself over areas where the water
spread out to the sides. The others, one by one, quit trying to
avoid the middle of the slow-moving sludge and started walking through it. The high sides of their combat boots saved most
from what could have been broken or fractured ankles.

Gibbons appeared out of the shadows ahead, standing between two six-inch waterfalls that poured from two man-sized
sewer lines that ran off in different directions and were about
four feet higher.

"What you got?" HJ asked.

He pointed at the left one. "I think this is the one they've
been using, ma'am."

Bud leaned over HJ's shoulder to see the tunnel Gibbons's
small flashlight illuminated. Bud shone his light down the other
one. "I can't tell the difference."

"I couldn't either at first, Mr. Helliwell, but look closely at
the bottom of the sewer. You can see scrape marks where their
boots have cleared the moss and crud away."

"Moss hell, try alien fungus."

"Either way, sir, they've been scuffed off."

"It's the left one, leading off to the north," HJ said, glancing
at the compass in her hand. She cringed slightly as Bud bumped
her healing shoulder.

"I wouldn't trust the compass too much, HJ. No telling what
around us could be affecting the needle."

"Bud, I'm not using the compass, and get off my back," she
said sharply, pushing the older but junior officer away.

"Oh, sorry. It was the only way I could see. I forgot about
your wound."

"It's healed but still tender to the touch," she lied, her body
shaking from the contact for several seconds. She gritted her
teeth, expecting someone to comment, and after several seconds passed, HJ relaxed. She didn't know why this was happening. She wanted to scream and run through the pipes until
she found a ladder or steps leading up. She didn't care where
they led; she just wanted out. She closed her eyes and took several deep breaths.

Gibbons reached in his pocket, pulled a fluorescent crayon
out and made an X on the far side of the left tunnel. "Looks like
we go this way, ma'am."

"Okay," HJ mumbled.

"What have you got?" Duncan asked as he appeared behind the trio.

"Left side, Captain," HJ replied, pointing to the tunnel. "Gibbons, show the captain the scuff marks." She let out a sigh of relief, feeling the emotional moment pass.

Gibbons pointed his flashlight along the slow-moving sludge line and highlighted the places where the growth of ages had been scuffed away. Duncan agreed with the second class petty officer's observation.

"Lead away, Gibbons, and be careful. There may be more booby traps in this tunnel. Keep an eye out for trip wires or anything else that looks suspicious."

"Hold up a minute, Gibbons," Bud Helliwell said. He leaned forward and, with his flashlight leading, he ran his hand along the edges at the top of the tunnel. "Here it is, Captain." He tugged on a loose brick, causing it to fall, splashing into the mess below and splattering it across the tops of their steel-toed combat boots and the bottom of their trouser legs.

A small square of plastique explosive hung from wires above them. "Seems to me, Gibbons, that somewhere ahead is another trip wire. And it doesn't necessarily have to be around your feet. It could be head or body level."

Gibbons shone his light down the new pipe, waving it slowly from side to side. "There it is," Gibbons said, holding his light steady at a point in the sewer tunnel about ten yards ahead. "You can barely see it, but it's there."

"Okay, Bud, you stay with the trip wire and make sure everyone steps over it. Gibbons, you lead the way, and be careful of a fallback trip wire ahead."

Duncan pressed F1 on his keypad, and the schematic of the sewer system lit up. "According to the schematic, this line runs alone for about a quarter of a mile before coming to an intersection with five other lines." He looked up. "This would be where I would put explosives. Be careful. Go slow, and keep a fine eye out for anything else."

Gibbons spat several times.

"What's wrong?" HJ asked.

"Nothing, ma'am. Just don't wipe your mouth with your gloves."

Beau stumbled up to them. "Boss, what are we doing?"

Duncan told Beau and Chief Wilcox about the explosives,

the trip wire, and the length of the sewer tunnel they were entering. "Another thing. It is possible that somewhere along this tunnel, we'll find where the hostages are being kept. Gibbons, you keep an eye out for any more traps, and keep tracking those scruff marks. If you go more than ten or fifteen feet without seeing a scuff mark or some indication we're still on the right track, then stop, and let's take stock of where we are and where we last saw the signs. Personally, I can't imagine the rebels using these tunnels other than for a short movement between their base and escape," Duncan said. His watch showed they had been beneath the city for over six hours. "I think we will find their base within the next hour, but let's find it without getting ourselves blown up. It's night above us, so we should have until morning to find the location."

"Aye, aye, Captain," Gibbons said. He put both hands against the wall of the new tunnel and pulled himself up into it. His carbine, strapped across his front, hung barrel down. If he encountered anyone, Gibbons would have little time to unstrap, unsafe, and fire. Duncan noticed the man's survival knife was strapped to his calf, making it easier to reach in close quarters. He touched the handle of his knife, strapped along his waist. The way they were moving in this small system, the hands were closer to the calf than to the waist. If the point man encountered anyone unexpectedly, the knife might be his only defense.

HJ and Bud followed. Duncan gave them several seconds' head start and touched Monkey. "Okay, Monkey, you're next. I hope you know not to fire the M-60 inside these tunnels?"

The dark hid Monkey's scowl. "Of course, Captain." The huge man pulled himself up and disappeared into the sewer tunnel.

Duncan turned to McDonald, who stood behind him. "McDonald—"

"I know, Captain. My M-60 is safed."

Duncan pulled himself into the pipe and, with his left hand guiding along the sides of the wall, he moved forward. A fluorescent O marked the trip wire. Bud stuck his hand out, touched Duncan, and pointed.

"Trip wire," Duncan mumbled to himself, as he stepped over it.

He heard the warning passed from SEAL to SEAL as the

others followed. Chief Wilcox was the last to enter behind
Beau, who followed McDonald.

Wilcox stopped briefly at the X Gibbons made and drew an
arrow pointing back the way they came. For a brief second, the
image of the lost explorer in the movie *Journey to the Center of
the Earth* flashed through his thoughts. The sterility of the
movie had little in common with the smell, the crud, and the
sewage that floated around them. A patch of gray fur bobbed on
the surface of the stream. *Dead rat,* he thought. Chief Wilcox
would be surprised if any of them survived this without a major
illness. He wiped his hands on his pants and hurried to keep his
position with Beau Pettigrew, who turned the curve ahead of
them. The words "trip wire" floated back to him. Chief Wilcox
saw the shining O as he lifted his feet. A fraction of an inch separated the toe of his boot from the deadly wire. Vigilance, not
speed. Somewhere ahead, more trip wires would be waiting. Of
that, he was sure. He stepped over the wire and deliberately
slowed his pace, knowing that as long as he kept the last man
in line in sight, he was okay.


**"WHERE IS IT?" DUNCAN ASKED QUIETLY, SQUATTING BE-**
side HJ, Bud Helliwell, and Gibbons. They had traveled two
hours since the fork in the sewers. He had decided to evacuate
the sewer at the first opportunity, believing they had missed the
rebels' hideaway somewhere along their search.

Monkey pressed his back to the slime, his eyes focused upward on the manhole cover above the ladder where the three officers and Gibbons squatted. Although he knew the dangers of
firing the M-60 inside the tunnel, the machine gun pointed upward. If anyone opened that manhole, they'd better open it with
a white flag flying.

"Look here, Captain. Scuff marks continue along the floor,
but look at the ladder." He brushed his fingers on a rung.
"Smooth. Scuff marks where someone has climbed up and
down it a lot," Gibbons whispered.

"Gibbons is right, Captain," Bud added. "Let me climb up
and see if I can hear anything."

"Sounds like a plan. Be careful," Duncan whispered.

Bud strapped his carbine across his back, grabbed the rungs,
and began to climb the twenty-foot-high ladder. The sides of

the pipe leading up narrowed as the ladder approached the top. Bud touched the manhole cover and pushed. Too heavy for one person to move.

Beau unstrapped his carbine and worked his way past Duncan, HJ, and Gibbons to the other side.

Monkey lowered his M-60. He couldn't use it now, even if someone opened the cover. He'd shoot Helliwell. Beau had a good angle past the climbing ensign. A narrow one, but even a limited angle of fire was better than none.

They watched quietly. Bud flipped on his small helmet light and with his knife began to move it around the edges of the cover. Duncan shifted his stance slightly. He couldn't tell what Bud was doing, but Duncan assumed the mustang was checking for trip wires. They had passed two others during the past two hours. One, they hadn't even seen until after the first two in line had luckily stepped over it. He estimated they were five to six miles from where they started. Eight hours underground and only such a short distance. He tried to recall the buildings that lined the banks of the drainage ditch where they entered. He fought the urge to power up the computer on his arm to see if he could find the outlay instead of relying on his memory. From what he recalled, there were several huge warehouses toward the center of the capital, located inside barriers of barbed wire. The port wasn't that much farther. He did not have a good feel for where they were. Maybe they were close enough to reestablish communications with the Marines. He pulled the eyepiece down that held the computer display. He might fail to recall how to search the onboard database, but all he had to do was hit the F7 key, and if they were in range, a data link would start to function with the Marines topside. The flashing red light at the bottom of the web page showed they were still out of range. He flipped the eyepiece down. How in the hell did anyone fight with all this techno-shit?

Bud climbed down. When he reached the bottom, he turned to Duncan. "Captain, I don't hear anyone on the other side, but I can tell the cover has been raised a few times. The lip is clean. It's probably cast iron, but I need help to lift it and slide it aside. It's a narrow fit up there, Captain. Monkey is going to have a problem getting his big butt through it. I need someone up there to help me lift it. I can slide it aside by myself."

"I'll do it," Monkey said.

"What if someone is waiting inside?" Bud countered.

Monkey shrugged. "Then I'll have to kill him." The huge Navy SEAL handed his M-60 to Chief Wilcox and, taking the steps two at a time, raced up the ladder. A minute later, the cover was up and aside. A faint light shone through the opening. Monkey stuck his head inside and gave the place a quick look. Then he spun around, spreading his legs apart and, holding on with his hands, slid down the ladder. "It's opened, sir. No one up there." He reached over and took his weapon back from Chief Wilcox.

"Okay, Bud, you lead the way. Get up there and take a defensive position. HJ, you follow. Gibbons, you're next. Monkey, you think you can get through that small opening?" Duncan asked.

Monkey stared upward, biting his lower lip as if deep in thought. "I think so, Captain. I was able to shove the cover aside. If Gibbons can get through it, I can, sir," he said confidently.

"Okay, you're fourth through the hatch. McDonald, you're fifth, I'm sixth. Beau, you and Chief Wilcox bring up the rear. Stay back a ways. If they drop a grenade down here, I don't want it taking all of us out."

"Always a bridesmaid and never a bride," Beau said.

Bud reached the top. HJ swung around the ladder and crawled up parallel with the ensign. She wrapped her arm through the rung to keep from falling and with the free hand held the stock of her gun.

"Okay, Bud, anytime you're ready."

Bud stuck his right hand through the top rung. He positioned his left hand a foot and half from the other. Wrapping one of his legs around the ladder, Bud shoved himself up and through the opening.

HJ scrambled up two more rungs and followed the mustang through the opening.

HJ and Bud were in a small basement room. It was about ten by twelve feet, with a solid, lightweight metal door leading out of it. A wooden table with four chairs scattered haphazardly around it was pushed against the far wall, along with what looked like a small coffee table near the door. Several small Arabic coffee cups sat on the tables. Pipes from a central heating system installed across the back wall ran across the overhead, up the walls, and out through the overhead. Paint peeled from where the walls met the unfinished ceiling.

Bud squatted near the table, his carbine unstrapped. He nodded to HJ before sprinting to the door at the end of the room. He put his ear to it, listened for a couple of seconds, and took a couple of steps back, glancing at HJ. Bud rotated his left shoulder, trying to ease the throbbing pain in the rotator cuff. He should have let Gibbons or Monkey take the lead.

"Anybody?" she asked softly.

Bud shook his head and gave her a thumbs-down. "Don't hear anything," he whispered.

HJ spun around and stuck her head and arm back inside the hole. "Come on up," she said, motioning to the others.

Gibbons hurried through and rushed ahead of Bud to retake the point.

Five minutes later, all the SEALs were in the small room. The single naked low-watt bulb hanging from the overhead seemed bright after over eight hours beneath the ground.

Gibbons and Bud covered the door. McDonald and Monkey quietly moved the coffee cups off the small table and turned it over on its side. They carried it to the hole and turned it so the top faced the door. If they had to make a quick exit, the table would provide some cover but not much from the feel of the cheap wood.

Duncan moved in front of Gibbons and put his ear to the door. Hearing nothing, he turned the knob. The door opened easily, revealing a dark hallway. Gibbons slid down to the floor and stuck his head out around the bottom of the door, did a quick 180 glance, and pulled back.

"Nothing, Captain. Set of stairs to the right. Light coming down it."

Duncan motioned Beau to his side. "Take Gibbons, and secure the base of the stairs. Don't go up until we get there." He hit Beau on the shoulder. "Go!"

Beau rolled out of the door, crossed the hall, and ran to the end of the stairs. Gibbons rolled around the door, keeping close to the near side of the narrow hallway wall. His eyes roved forward and back, expecting any moment to encounter resistance.

Duncan watched the opposite direction from the open door. He had no way of knowing where they were in the building. In fact, he had no idea what building they were in or even if they were still in Algiers. For all he knew, they could be in the center of the rebel command post surrounded by thousands of religious fanatics waiting for their Al-Qaida paycheck. In which case, the gold crucifix he wore around his neck wouldn't be much help.

He motioned to HJ and Monkey. "Go!"

HJ led as the two moved quickly into the hallway. At the same time, Beau and Gibbons arrived farther down the hall at the base of the stairs. Duncan motioned Chief Wilcox and Bud Helliwell forward. "Take position to protect the team at the base of the stairs. McDonald, come here. You remain inside the room in the event we have to make a quick exit. As we move forward, I want you three bringing up the rear in similar positions. Got it?"

"Got it, boss," Ensign Bud Helliwell replied, but he didn't like being a rear echelon guard. He was used to being in the front lines, where the action was. He hoped it was not because of the slight wound he received in the firefight with the Algerian rebels yesterday morning, or maybe the captain had noticed the pain he was having with his shoulder. He never should have said what he did about the Purple Hearts.

"What's wrong, Bud? Am I forgetting something?" Duncan asked, seeing the look on the mustang's face.

"Nothing, boss." He gripped his carbine tighter. "Well, maybe one. You aren't putting me in the rear because of that slight wound yesterday, are you?"

Duncan grinned. "Bud, I had forgotten all about it until you mentioned it. Now, don't go sensitive on me; I don't have time to give you a hug and a pat on the back. You got the rear because if we have to withdraw, then you three are going to have to provide covering fire. Your experience comes in handy if we are pinned or something up ahead happens where we need a quick reserve force. I am depending on you to do the right thing, even if it means leaving us and escaping with your life and the lives of the hostages." He reached over and patted the side of Bud's head. "There. That will have to do instead of a hug."

"Okay, Captain," Bud replied, grateful for the shadows that hid his embarrassment.

Duncan slapped him on the shoulder, failing to notice the mustang wince. "Go!"

Bud and Chief Wilcox eased out the door and moved down the hall several feet. Bud stopped halfway to the stairs and motioned the chief ahead. Duncan stepped out from behind them and walked carefully down the center of the hall to where the others had the base of the stairways secured.

A muffled scream, easily recognized as a woman's, from above, startled them. Duncan heard the safety clicks going off the rifles like a garden full of crickets. "Let's go," he said softly, tapping Gibbons and Beau on the shoulders.

The two SEALs moved quietly up the stairs. From above, further cries in English and what sounded like a struggle urged them forward. The three moved slowly and carefully. It would not do whoever was above any good if they hurried right into an ambush. Duncan caught the words "don't" and "kill," and the frightened crying of begging. Anger poured over him as he recalled the massacre they had stumbled upon in a small Algerian village west of Algiers during the rescue of President Hawali Alneuf. It had been at this village where the rebels had overrun HJ McDaniels's position. He glanced back at the female officer following and briefly wondered if the cries above brought back thoughts of her own experience. HJ's head was down.

At the top of the stairway, another set of stairs led up and away in the opposite direction. A door blocked the exit to it. The screams gave way to a low, mournful continuum of whimpers surrounded by periodic outbursts of masculine laughter. Beau held up one finger and motioned up the stairs. He and Gibbons hurried to the door. Duncan walked up the stairs as softly as possible, thankful for the railing along the side. His left knee ached. He touched it gently and felt the swelling. Just get through this mission, and he could retire. Go home, bury the dog, divorce the wife, and maybe lay a little whup ass on that Safeway lover.

Beau squatted, braced his carbine against the wall, and pulled a two-foot-long electronic cord from a waist-mounted power pack. On the end was a small camera. A small video screen on top of the power pack allowed the viewer to see what the camera saw. He pushed the thin fiber-optic camera and cord into the small space between the bottom of the door and the cement floor.

Duncan leaned over Beau's shoulder and watched the small

screen with him. Gibbons moved back slightly so if anyone opened the door, they'd be dead before they could shut it.

On the other side of the door was a small hallway about five feet wide, running north to south. Multiple doors opened off it, but only two in the northern direction sixty to seventy feet ahead showed light coming from beneath them. Small, unshielded lightbulbs, similar to the one in the basement room where they had exited the Algiers sewer, hung from three frayed cords providing faint illumination to the hall.

Beau twisted the cord, and the camera rolled to face the other direction. A door at the end of the hallway with an opaque glass facade marked the way out of this one.

Behind them, HJ and Monkey moved up to flank Gibbons. At the top of the stairs, McDonald unlimbered his M-60, pointing it up and away from those in front of him. Chief Wilcox stayed near the machine gunner while Bud creeped up beside HJ. Chief Wilcox pulled his fluorescent crayon and made an X on the floor beside the stairway, followed by an arrow. HJ saw the chief do this and raised her eyebrows at Bud.

"If we have to make a hurried exit, we don't need to be trying to reach a consensus on which way is out."

Beau looked at Duncan. "Looks clear."

A new series of screams sent chills up Duncan's back. Screams of pain quickly subsided as laugher echoed over the moans that followed.

"She's in this hallway somewhere," Duncan said.

Beau reached up and tried the knob. The door opened easily. Duncan and Beau braced themselves against the sides of the wall, expecting gunfire, although a few seconds ago, the camera showed the hallway empty.

Gibbons dodged past, accepting the verdict of the spy system. There was only so much a petty officer could take, having the senior officers jumping out in front of him. Point was his job this mission and, by God, the captain and the commander could follow.

Beau waited a couple of seconds, watching the opposite direction from where Gibbons moved.

Duncan motioned to the others to follow before he stepped into the hallway and leaned against the far side of the wall. The woman's cries and the men's laughter blocked what little noise the Navy SEALs made as they leapfrogged each other down the hallway. Gibbons dodged ahead toward the door leading out of the confined space. Beau tiptoed down the other way, checking the lighted rooms. He bent down and looked through the keyhole, shook his head, and moved to the second one. Monkey passed the officer, stopping opposite Gibbons, and nodding to his shipmate.

"Oh, my God!" the voice screamed. "Not again. No, don't, please. Oh, my God! I beg you, *don't! Argggg!*"

Beau pointed at the second door. Duncan touched him on the shoulder and whispered, "No weapons, if possible. The longer we keep our presence a secret, the longer we have to find the hostages. Use your knife."

HJ and Bud heard his warning as they appeared beside the two crouching officers.

Beau propped his carbine against the wall and began threading the spy camera under the small opening. Bud leaned against the doorknob side of the door. Monkey crept up and took a spread-legged position above Beau, reminding Duncan briefly of a scene out of a Rambo movie he saw years ago. All the man needed was a bandana.

Chief Wilcox stayed at the door, guarding their rear and keeping a backup watch on Gibbons. McDonald eased himself into the center of the hallway, ready to bring his M-60 to bear in either direction if the rebels suddenly appeared.

Duncan gently pushed Monkey to the side so he could see the small screen of the spy camera. A chair a few feet from the door blocked the small camera's view. Laughter from within complemented the three sets of legs the camera showed.

Duncan looked around at the team, ready to make his decision to rush the room. HJ's fingers curled and uncurled around the carbine, her finger already on the trigger. Her eyes blazed along with a heaving chest as HJ's anger threatened to overcome SEAL training. Duncan reached over and tapped her shoulder twice, causing her to shake her head. He pointed at her carbine and raised his eyebrows. She stared for a couple of seconds at Duncan before curtly nodding her head and removing her finger from the trigger. The spell was broken.

Duncan didn't know what she would do once inside the room. The camera failed to twist sufficiently to show what was happening to the woman; they all had different ideas, none of them good.

Beau twisted the camera. As it spun around to a new position, Beau caught a good glimpse of three pairs of combat boots. He pulled the camera out and looked up at Duncan. He held up three fingers and then four. He figured if they were doing what he thought they were doing in that room, then three of them were watching while the fourth was . . . well, doing what he thought was going on.

Duncan pulled his knife.

Bud put his free hand on the doorknob and turned it slowly. It was unlocked. He nodded at Duncan. Duncan gave a thumbs-up to everyone and then, nodding to Bud, he held up one finger, then two . . .

# ELEVEN

⚓

THE AEGIS CRUISER, USS *HUE CITY*, AND THE AGING DE-
stroyer, USS *Spruance*, were built from the same Spruance-
class hull, with the *Hue City* being four feet longer and
displacing six hundred tons more than the *Spruance*. Weapons
systems and mission focus truly determined whether these warships were designated a cruiser or destroyer. Cruisers focused
on antiair warfare as the primary mission, while destroyers his-
torically were allocated the antisubmarine missions of the surface fleet. As the number of United States Navy warships
declined, along with retention of critical manpower, warships
began to incorporate multiple-mission capabilities along with a
theory that a smaller crew could do the same work as a larger
crew. The USS *Gearing*, sunk by the Libyans at the beginning
of the North African crisis, was one of the first DD-21-class
warships capable of fighting a multidimensional war with two-
thirds less crew.

The USS *Spruance*, named for the World War II Navy admiral and hero of the battle of Midway, Admiral Raymond
Spruance, was the oldest destroyer on active duty in the United
States Navy. USS *Spruance* was commissioned on August 12,
1975. Her engine plants, electrical systems, and crew quarters
showed the forty-plus years of action. The number of empty

bunks revealed the number of missing sailors. The designers of this ship were ahead of their time. They had the forethought to realize the ship would outlast its 1980s weapons systems and technology, so they built empty compartments along with electrical conduits to accommodate whatever new warfare developments occurred.

This engineering forethought proved invaluable when Congress cut funding to build new ships, and the Navy was forced to keep aging warships on active duty. Technology provided the capability for the *Spruance* to continue a primary ASW mission while now possessing the capability to fight antiair warfare actions. The loss of the USS *John Rodgers* a month ago, when its commanding officer sacrificed the ship to save the USS *Stennis* from four enemy torpedoes, had reduced the Navy inventory of Spruance-class destroyers to six, all of which possessed technologically enhanced warfighting capabilities.

The Strait of Sicily separated Europe from the Tunisian coast by eighty-three choppy miles, a chokepoint in the center of the Mediterranean capable of severing the sea into two nearly equal halves. On a clear day, no ship sailed through the Strait without being visually logged from military observation points located on the high mountains on both sides of the Strait. The two-ship surface action group, with the *Hue City* leading two nautical miles ahead and to the south of the USS *Spruance*, had entered this Mediterranean bottleneck thirty minutes ago. The SAG sailed under the direction of the commanding officer of the USS *Hue City*, a four-striper by the name of Horatio Jurgen McTeak, who hid the mouthful *Horatio* and *Jurgen* under the nickname Buc-Buc. Not that he wasn't proud of his folks or didn't love them, but a name like Horatio had its own cross to bear in a Navy community, and no one ever pronounced or wrote Jurgen—it was pronounced *joor-gan*—correctly. The Jurgen name was a McTeak legacy passed down through the first-born of his family for four generations. Buc-Buc received a lot of badgering from his father when he failed to stick the Jurgen brand on his name, but when the second son was born and became known as Jurgen Thomas McTeak, his father, Thomas Jurgen McTeak, lovingly accepted the compromise. The Navy had not been a McTeak legacy. The original Jurgen McTeak had fought with the Union Army in the Civil War. Another one had been in Black Jack's expeditionary force in World War I, and his father had served in World War II and Korea as a colonel in the infantry. Buc-Buc was the first Jurgen McTeak to earn an officer's commission in the Navy. The McTeak family were proud of their Navy son. It was a family joke that if he had gone to a real college instead of the Naval Academy, he could have had a real degree.

His father and two elderly uncles enjoyed poking fun. The three of them, Army veterans, made the annual Army-Navy football game an exciting event in the McTeak household with beer, pretzels, grilled hot dogs and shifting insults flowing between the grill outside and the large-screen television inside. The game had become as much a McTeak family get-together as Thanksgiving.

Buc-Buc earned the nickname early in his childhood, unlike most military veterans who are honorably dubbed by their shipmates. It occurred during a grammar school incident with two bullies in his class.

The two, terrorizing the eighth grade, decided it was McTeak's turn to provide them with spending money. When he realized he was going to be unable to avoid a confrontation, he lowered his head and, like a battering ram, knocked the breath out of the bigger of the two. Then he turned and, before the other one could run, rammed his head into the boy's stomach, sending both scrambling away, crying. The incident was bigger in Buc-Buc's mind than in the school history. He received numerous invitations to speak at alumni reunions or schools he attended, places where a Navy captain was considered prime speaker material. One of those many places had been his old grammar school, and when he casually mentioned the incident, no one seemed to remember it, so he dropped the subject to never raise it again.

The principal remembered it. He remembered it with glee, for the two boys McTeak punished had been a growing problem. They seemed to teeter on the edge of misbehavior, always around the corner out of sight from authority. He had slapped his leg and said, "Gosh, darn," which was the strongest language Mr. Alonzo Abernathy ever used, causing his secretary to rush in to see if he was all right. After a moment of satisfaction, Mr. Abernathy recalled that rules were rules, and the rules for fighting called for suspension. He searched for a couple of days for an acceptable alternative before the three sets of parents attended a counseling session with him about the unfortunate incident. After allowing the three sets of parents to argue "My child is innocent," he let go a deep sigh and offered an alternative that they all reluctantly accepted rather than have their young angels suspended. The three boys spent two weeks in after-school detention. Two weeks in which the reformed bullies fawned over the new grammar school hero, who spent his two weeks ignoring them.

Mr. Alonzo Abernathy stuck him with Buc-Buc after overhearing a teacher say to a fellow teacher, "Sure, they started it. But we can't have this. Violence begets violence. What if every time we felt threatened, we lowered our heads and buc-bucked them. We'd have chaos everywhere." The nickname spread through his classmates, and no one called him Horatio again. Buc-Buc was the first of many accolades and awards Captain Horatio Jurgen McTeak would receive in the years ahead.

**BUC-BUC PACED OVER TO THE PORT BRIDGE WING FOR** the third time in fifteen minutes and hoisted the heavy Navy binoculars hanging around his neck. A couple of twists of the eyepieces, and the profile of the USS *Spruance* steaming three thousand yards—one and a half nautical miles—off his port side leaped into view. The thirty-two knots they used to zoom ahead of the battle group ruined any ASW capability for both ships, but the primary threat to them was air. Sixth Fleet had cleared the seas of hostile submarines with the lone remaining Algerian Kilo safely in port in Malaga. The lone remaining Libyan Foxtrot diesel submarine lacked the legs to reach this far north.

"Officer of the Deck," Buc-Buc said, sticking his balding head back inside the bridge.

"Yes, sir, Captain."

"Relay to the tactical action officer to slow the SAG to eighteen knots. And give me an updated estimate to our MODLOC." MODLOC: another Navy acronym seldom understood by even the officers and sailors who used it. MODLOC stood for miscellaneous operational details, local operations. It was a term to describe an assigned area of the sea where a ship or battle group, or in this instance the surface action group—the SAG—was to operate. They could burn holes in the sea, do exercises, race from one end of the box to the other, but the assigned area was the MODLOC, and they were expected to remain within it. The center of the MODLOC for the *Hue City* and *Spruance* was a hundred nautical miles southeast of Lampedusa just north of the one hundred–mile mark from Tripoli. Their mission was to take out any military threat airborne out of Tunisia or Libya. They were not to cross the thirty-fifth parallel.

"Skipper, TAO says thirty minutes at eighteen knots to the north boundary of the MODLOC."

"Very well. Keep me apprised." Buc-Buc looked at his watch. He loved this Omega, but had no illusions he was anything like James Bond. He had bought the expensive chronometer purchased in Norfolk from an antique dealer who specialized in Mariner paraphernalia. *Chronometer* was just another name for a watch, only it cost more. The stars overhead were beginning to fade with the emerging sunlight. The *Stennis* and its escorts would still be in darkness for another hour.

The sound of the reveille bugle at six o'clock marked the start of another workday. There was always someone near the light switch, eager to flood a sleeping compartment with harsh fluorescent light to arouse the occupants. The sound and fog of the morning showers caused moisture to settle on the tile floors as sailors rushed to dress and head toward the mess decks. The clanging of metal trays against the slide rails of the serving bar mixed with the morning chatter as mess specialists dished out breakfast. Like a sleeping bear, reveille brought the ship from its nightly hibernation to its full warfighting strength.

The thought of breakfast caused his stomach to growl. He could step into his at-sea cabin behind the bridge and order up his earlier. Of course, if he did that, the crews would know within minutes that the Old Man had used a privilege. It was amazing when he thought about it how, here he was in charge of one of the most powerful ships in the world, and morale could be affected by the little things he did in running it. *What were the days of Rock and Shoals like?* he wondered briefly for the thousandth time, referring to the laws that governed Navy captains during the period of sail and before the Uniform Code of Military Justice was passed after World War II. He grinned. *Probably too rough for me.*

He watched the gray silhouette of USS *Spruance* ease back

until she was off his port stern. Good. This cleared their weapons from mutual interference so they could better fight a 360-degree war.

"Bridge, TAO; captain still up there?"

"Captain, TAO for you, sir."

Buc-Buc stepped into the bridge near the 12MC speaker box and flipped the switch. With all the technology shoved onto this ship, the Navy still depended on a sound-powered communications system as the primary means for instant communications between warfighting stations. Sound-powered communications depended only on voice for power, thereby removing battle damage to the electrical system as a threat to internal communications. "Go ahead, TAO."

"Captain, we have two blips airborne out of eastern Libya. Computer assesses them as ballistic missiles—designated targets zero zero one and zero zero two."

"Officer of the Deck, sound general quarters. TAO, Sixth Fleet notified?"

"In process of doing so, sir."

"You have flight path yet?"

"Yes, sir. Target zero zero one launched zero six oh one hours from coordinates—"

"Don't give me coordinates, Commander. I never have time to figure them out. Give me geographical locations or names."

"Yes, sir. Target zero zero one launched from west of Tripoli near the Libyan-Tunisian border. Direction of travel is north by northwest."

Buc-Buc moved over to the navigation table, where the chart displayed the coast of Libya, Tunisia, the Strait of Sicily, Sicily, along with the southern boot of Italy and then farther west to encompass most of the Algerian coast. "Possible targets, TAO?"

"Intelligence officer says based on estimated range of the Al-Fatah III missile, the target could be Algiers."

"Or?"

"Or eastern coast of Spain."

"Why Algiers?"

"U.S. Marines are there, sir. Plus Algiers was identified by Sixth Fleet as a primary ballistic-missile target."

"I'm coming down, TAO." Buc-Buc stepped behind the

helm and swung open the watertight door to the stairwell leading between the Combat Information Center and the bridge.

"Captain off the bridge!" shouted the boatswain mate of the
watch as Buc-Buc stepped over the transom. The BMOW
stepped over and closed the hatch behind the captain. The
bongs of general quarters filled the approaching dawn skies.
From across the water, the GQ bongs of the USS *Spruance*
echoed through the bridge. *Great way to greet the morning,*
thought the young lieutenant officer of the deck as he lifted his
binoculars to scan the horizon for approaching traffic. The two
ships were approaching center of MODLOC at eighteen knots
and going to battle stations against hostile theater ballistic missiles. Complicating this was the fact they were in one of the
most heavily traveled areas of the Med for maritime traffic.

"How many ships we have on scope?" the lieutenant asked
as he lowered his binoculars. He took the life vest and helmet
the BMOW held out to him and quickly put them on, holding
the helmet momentarily as the navigator gave the range, bearing, course, and speed of the four contacts reflected on the
AN/SPS-55 surface-search radar. The OOD's job was to maneuver the ship in tandem with the USS *Spruance* through the
morning traffic maze of ships waiting for full daylight to tran-
sit the narrow Strait of Sicily.

**BUC-BUC STEPPED THROUGH THE OPEN DOOR INTO THE**
Combat Information Center. The quiet professionalism in the
blue-lighted compartment gave him satisfaction. A lesson he
learned from an old mustang captain during his first duty as an
Ensign on a now-decommissioned destroyer was that a quietly
functioning CIC was the sign of a well-trained warfighting machine. He refused to allow any shouting in his CIC.

"Captain in Combat," came from a voice from the shadows,
probably the CIC watch supervisor, who moved continuously
among the sailors, ensuring they were doing their jobs effectively and exchanging information rapidly.

"What you got?"

The TAO pushed the buttons on the holograph display and
with his laser pointer highlighted the two small missile symbols
airborne. The two missiles were still climbing. The operator,
sitting nearby, hit the keyboard. Behind the two missile sym-

bols, red flickering contrails appeared. Ahead of the missiles, a green line leaped from their noses and curved off into the horizon, showing the projected flight path.

"Zoom out a little," Buc-Buc ordered, leaning over the display to get a better view.

The TAO nodded to the operator, and in a second, the HD flickered briefly before returning. The missile symbols were smaller, but the green line from target zero zero one shot through Algiers, while the projected path of target zero zero two traveled southeast of their MODLOC over Sicily and through Naples and eventually disappeared into the Balkans near the Italian-Croatian border.

"Give me the red phone. TAO, you have targeting solutions on the missiles?"

"Sir, we have a brief window in four minutes for target zero zero one. Target zero zero two, we can take out in two minutes, but we will be in range for twenty minutes. Target zero zero one is the hard one, Skipper. She is traveling opposite direction from us at an awkward tangent. We have a three-minute window," he glanced at the clock. "And only three minutes in which to fire."

The assistant TAO, a young lieutenant, handed the secure phone to Captain McTeak. "Sixth Fleet, this is Charlie Oscar *Hue City*; come in, please." Charlie Oscar was the NATO phonetic for CO—commanding officer.

"*Hue City*, Sixth Fleet; go ahead."

"Sixth Fleet, this is Charlie Oscar *Hue City* speaking. Unless otherwise directed, I intend to engage two ballistic missiles launched from the Libyan landmass. Data transmission on Global Information Grid should show you same picture we have here. Request advice if other course of action desired. We have a two-minute window remaining for target zero zero one." Without waiting for an answer, he hung up the phone. Naval action was always based on an unless-otherwise-directed concept. Unless higher authority directed him to do something different, Buc-Buc would fight the *Hue City* as he saw fit. Buc-Buc knew that if Sixth Fleet did not want him to launch against the missiles, they would tell him in the next two minutes. Two minutes was a lot of time in combat.

Around Buc-Buc, the movement of arms and rushing sailors hurried through their portion of the theater ballistic missile defense—TBMD—plan. No one ran—another golden rule of Buc-Buc's on what made an effective CIC.

"*Hue City*, do you have projected targets yet?" came from the overhead speaker connected to Sixth Fleet.

A sailor handed a sheet of paper to the TAO, who quickly read the data, whispered a quick question, and received an equally quick reply. The TAO grabbed a blank sheet and wrote hurriedly on it.

"Sixth Fleet, data being transmitted via Global Information Grid even as we speak. Initial indications are one missile inbound Algiers and second heading toward Sicily or Naples."

The TAO held up a sheet of paper for the captain to read.

"Sixth Fleet, probability of SAM success is only sixty percent for the missile heading toward Algiers. We have an eighty-plus percent probability of taking out the northbound missile."

"*Hue City*, keep us advised. Good shooting. We are moving fighter aircraft between Algiers and inbound target zero zero one, but they will be out of range of your SAMs. You have free fire zone, sir. Admiral Devlin sends his compliments."

"Roger, out." He handed the handset back to the sailor standing beside him.

"TAO, how soon you ready?"

"We've been ready, Skipper. You just say when."

"Well, tell me how you intend to handle this dual problem, Commander," Buc-Buc said to the young lieutenant commander. Buc-Buc turned and crawled up into his chair, fighting the urge to shout, "Fire!" The captain's chair in Combat, like the one on the bridge, sat up high, allowing the skipper to see everything and everyone as they fought the ship. Conceivably, from the chair, the captain could fight and drive the ship during combat. Buc-Buc had fought computer-simulated sea battles before in a lot tighter situations than this. The only way future warriors learned their craft was to experience it. His major challenge was to remain calm, regardless of how fast his heart was beating and his blood was racing right now. A sailor slipped a cup of coffee into the cup holder on the right side of the chair before handing Buc-Buc a helmet. Buc-Buc looked at the coffee but was afraid his hand might shake if he tried to lift it. He glanced up at the TAO as he put the helmet on. Time to discover how well this officer performed in a real-life situation. Time to discover how well he performed, also.

"Captain, for target zero zero one, I recommend two two-missile firings; extended-range Standard Missiles with each of the pair fired at five-second intervals. Second pair to be fired ten seconds after first pair."

Buc-Buc nodded. "Okay, Commander." He glanced at the clock on the wall. They still had one minute until their weapons systems would be within range of the launched missiles. "Whatever happened to fire two, wait, watch, and then fire two more?"

"Captain, we are at max range for our missiles. If those missiles have biological or chemical warheads and one hits Algiers, we are going to have a lot of dead Americans and Arabs on our hands. If we fire two and wait until we see whether they hit or not, we will have insufficient time to fire the second pair."

Buc-Buc nodded again. "Good argument, Commander. Make it so." He nonchalantly waved his right hand at the TAO as he said it. It always made him think of Jean-Luc Picard of the starship *Enterprise* whenever he said that. "Second target?"

"Second target already assigned to USS *Spruance*, sir," the TAO said, knowing that in most ships, the TAO would never make a unilateral decision like this without the skipper's permission. But the captain of the *Hue City* was no ordinary skipper. He expected his officers to be able to perform both independently and as a team.

"Good work, Commander." Buc-Buc surveyed the CIC, searching for anything that needed his personal tweaking or involvement. A sense of pride in ship, sailors, and officers who manned her flooded his body. This, coupled with the electronic warfare decoy and shootdown of the Algerian Exocet missile two days ago, would bond the crew and the ship even more strongly together. He nearly grinned before immediately remembering they were in a combat situation.

"Well, let's get on with it and show the airdale Navy the value of a good black-shoe surface ship, shall we?" he asked in his normal, low, monotone voice. It was common in the military to share information on commanding officers. The number-one shared comment on Buc-Buc was to watch his lips and listen closely, because he rarely raised his voice above a normal conversation level. Buc-Buc nearly stood up as the excitement of the SAG actions beckoned him to take charge. The only thing he wanted right now was to shove the TAO out of the way—

although the officer was doing everything he should and doing it right—and take charge. He lifted his hands off the arms of the chair to keep from pushing himself up.

"Yes, sir." Anxiety washed over the TAO, who wanted to shout his orders in the microphone and who also fought to keep his feet still. Knowing the skipper was sitting calmly in his seat, acting as if this was another training exercise, and relying on the TAO to respond accordingly, the last thing he wanted was to let the Old Man see him get excited.

The TAO pulled his headset down and lowered the microphone. Buc-Buc picked up his and put it on under his helmet. A flip of the switch on the left arm of the chair allowed him to speak to all the major stations on the ship: the bridge, engineering, TAO, medical, and even the mess decks and navigation.

Buc-Buc looked at the clock for the umpteeth time, noticing the second hand had moved nearly halfway around the large Navy-issued timepiece. Time seemed to slow during combat. He spun the chair to the maximum forty-five-degree angle to better see the AN/SLQ-32(V) electronic warfare system installed against the forward bulkhead. Several round symbols identified surface vessels in the area, but no fast-moving V-shaped airborne symbols followed by a dotted trail showed what would indicate an inbound or passing aircraft. Of course, the AN/SLQ-32(V) had to be hit by the radar or telemetry signals for it to activate, and ballistic missiles had no radar. The internal gyroscope guided most of them. Cruise missiles had radar to permit use of topography guidance systems, but these were ballistic missiles. He knew that, but still he looked. The last thing he wanted was for one of their SAMs to accidentally take out an airliner.

"Captain, starting countdown," the TAO said. He flipped the microphone down. "All ships Tango Foxtrot, stand by for missile launch."

Buc-Buc loved it. Two ships sailing in tandem still calling each other with proper Navy tactical call signs. He would be hard pressed to explain to his high school buddies why he did it or how come he loved it. *Tango Foxtrot* stood for Task Force, and Task Force could be anything from one unit to multiple units.

The TAO looked to the captain a last time, even as the

countdown entered the single digits. Buc-Buc smiled slightly, winked, and nodded. The TAO turned so he could watch over the shoulder of the missile-launch operator. From the chair, Buc-Buc watched the numbers hit three—two—one, and then the operator turned the key. The *Hue City* shivered slightly as the first extended-range Standard Missile blasted out of a vertical launch tube located on the other side of the forward bulkhead where the AN/SLQ-32 was located. Five seconds later, the muffled echo of another blast shook the ship as the second missile left its launching pad. Two United States Navy surface-to-air missiles were on their way.

Buc-Buc remained quiet, listening to the TAO direct the action in the Combat Information Center as the ship prepared to launch the second set of missiles. On board the *Spruance*, their CIC would be doing the same thing: tracking and preparing to fire against the northbound missile. Buc-Buc flipped the switch to connect himself with engineering.

"Chief Engineer, Captain here. Are we at condition Zebra?" he asked, knowing they were. Condition Zebra referred to the tightest water and airtight condition on board the ship. Hatches dogged, doors shut and secured to effectively seal inside those who fought the ship from anything outside. Only the topside and bridge watches remained exposed to the outside elements. If combat damaged the bridge, an officer and sailors manning an aft bridge station belowdecks could take over control of the ship.

"Captain, we are fully secured."

"Chief, make sure that all ventilation is fully secured. We have a target heading our vicinity. We're not its target, but it may have a biological warhead, so set Condition William."

"Masks and CBW suits, sir?"

Buc-Buc had not thought of going that far. The suits were hot, uncomfortable, and the masks complicated clear communications. Chemical biological warfare was seldom exercised, but even though the war against terrorism had eased somewhat over the past few years, the threat of another anthrax or chemical attack still existed. He had exercised against the threat several times since they had sortied at maximum speed directly from their workup exercise off the Virginia Capes. It seemed so long ago. The USS *Stennis*, his ship, USS *Ramage*, USS *John Rodgers*, and the aging auxiliary ship *Concord* conducting a routine battle group workup. The USS *Seawolf* joined them halfway across the Atlantic. A routine workup allowed them to test their individual weapons systems and learn to work and fight together as a battle group. With only two days remaining in the ten-day exercise, the Libyans had sunk the USS *Gearing*, whose survivors eventually drifted in the Gulf of Sidra for nearly a week before an American submarine rescued them. He remembered the chills racing up his arms and how he shivered slightly in the ninety-degree ocean sun when he read Captain Dick Holman's message refusing to return to Norfolk as the skipper of the aircraft carrier USS *Stennis* ordered the battle group east, toward the Mediterranean.

And the fighters had arrived. Air Force KC-135s staged from Langley provided refueling zones along the route so additional squadrons of F-14 Tomcats and F-18 Hornet fighters could reach the USS *Stennis* halfway across the Atlantic. He rubbed the top of his nose. The USS *John Rodgers*. He nearly made the same decision Warren Spangle did when those Exocet missiles were inbound against USS *Stennis*. It was only then he fully appreciated what Spangle had done.

The low noise of CIC changed slightly as the air launch operator began marking the countdown to intercept by the first pair of missiles.

"Sir, masks and suits?"

Buc-Buc flicked the switch to respond to the repeated question that had caused him to recall the events leading to the *Hue City* being here at this precise moment to execute this precise mission. Maybe fate was something that always waited at the end of the tracks, and you never quite knew what you were going to encounter along the trip until it approached and passed.

"Yes, Chief Engineer. I don't want to, but we should. Be prepared to activate the water wash down system." The water wash down system was designed to spray salt water over every exposed part of the ship to wash away radiation following a tactical nuclear blast. It also served a purpose of cleaning away biological and chemical hazards.

"Captain, we tested it a few weeks ago, and it worked."

"Good. Once activated, I want it to run continuously until I order it turned off."

After receiving acknowledgment from the chief engineer, he

flipped the switch to the bridge. "Officer of the Deck, Captain; your bridge wing doors shut?"

"No, sir."

"Shut them, and I want all hands topside to don CBW equipment ASAP."

"Yes, sir. It will take a few minutes until—"

"Lieutenant, you may not have a few minutes. Hurry." Buc-Buc flipped him off before he had an opportunity to answer. *Stay calm. Show calm. Use it, don't lose it.* He caught the TAO's eyes glancing at him for a moment. *They are watching, and how you perform, Buc-Buc, is how they will react.*

"Captain," the TAO said, pointing to the scope. "One minute to impact."

"Attention all hands!" came the call through the 1MC announcing system. "Now don chemical-biological warfare gear. I say again, don CBW gear, and set Condition William throughout the ship. Report to Damage Control Central when William set."

"*Hue City*, *Spruance*; this is the Charlie Oscar. Is Captain McTeak available?"

Buc-Buc leaned forward and flipped the switch. "Go ahead, Louise."

"Captain, our surface search radar is showing two fast-moving ships heading our way, bearing two eighty, range sixty nautical miles. They had been masked by Lampedusa Island and are CBDR," Commander Louise Edwards, Commanding Officer USS *Spruance* said. CBDR was Navy short talk for constant bearing, decreasing range, which revealed that a contact was on a collision course with the detecting unit if either one or the other failed to maneuver.

The *Hue City* TAO took several quick steps to their surface search position. The young petty officer manning the console pointed to the two new contacts.

Buc-Buc glanced at the AN/SLQ-32 console and saw no ELINT reflections in that direction.

"Any thoughts on what they are?" he asked the CO, USS *Spruance*.

"Yes, sir. Our cryppies in the OUTBOARD electronic detection suite identify them as two Libyan fast-attack patrol craft coming out of Tunisia. Weapons systems include the older Styx missiles as well as Exocet."

"At sixty nautical miles, they are still out of launch range and out of our Harpoon range. Let's open up our distance, Louise. Settle *Spruance* back, and take station ten miles astern. If they fire, I don't want either one of our Close In Weapons Systems to hit each other."

"Roger, sir. Do you want us to take them as targets?"

The distant *whoosh* of a missile engine overlaid the low level of conversation in the *Hue City* CIC. Buc-Buc looked up at the TAO, who was deep in conversation on his intercom with another station and failed to notice his inquiry.

"We are firing the second one now," Louise Edwards relayed.

Five seconds later, the same *whoosh* sound rolled through CIC.

The *Hue City* TAO walked up to Buc-Buc. "Sir, we have firing solutions on the two approaching fast attacks. They are within Tomahawk range."

He nodded. "Louise, go ahead and prepare to take them out. We'll take them for now. You're backup. Your primary mission is to shoot that ballistic missile down before it reaches Sicily."

"Roger, sir. *Spruance* out."

Buc-Buc reached for the switch and was going to advise *Spruance* to don CBW gear, but he stopped himself. "TAO, have *Spruance* execute CBW procedures." Better to act through the tactical path than have the two COs give the impression they were fighting this action by themselves. *Remain calm, act involved, but let the crew use its training. They know what they're doing.* He crossed his fingers. At least he had confidence that they remembered their training, he told himself. *All you have to do, Buc-Buc, is remain calm and show confidence.*

"We have video merge, Captain," the TAO said, referring to the radar blips of their surface-to-air missile merging with the radar blip of the Libyan ballistic missile. Tactically, that was good. It indicated a direct hit. A few seconds later, the video return on the air search and fire control radarscopes disappeared.

A cheer went up in CIC. Buc-Buc unconsciously raised his hand and motioned downward to quell the cheer. The need for a quiet, professional CIC was more important. The battle wasn't over yet.

Over the southern landmass of Tunisia, the debris from the shootdown of the Libyan ballistic missile fell. The warhead shot outward, landing several miles from where the heavier parts of the two missiles scattered. Split open by the explosion, the warhead tumbled nearly fifteen thousand feet before impacting in the fields of an Arab farmer who was gathering eggs from the few chickens he had penned near his small one-bedroom hutch.

He dropped the basket and, stumbling over the roughly plowed rows, ran to the smoking, fourteen-foot-wide crater where tendrils of smoking metal stuck out. Cautiously, he touched one of the hot metal fragments, only to jerk his hand back, shaking it. Carefully avoiding the tangled warhead, the Tunisian farmer squatted to look at the empty hold where the day before, the Russian scientists and the Hungarian agent had removed the anthrax canister. He hurried back to the well to grab water to pour over the metal to cool it. If he got the metal out before whoever lost it showed up to claim it, he could sell it as scrap to a dealer in the market. A few extra coins would be welcome.

**"MR. PRESIDENT,"** SAID SECRETARY OF STATE BOB GIL-fort on the telephone. Bob nodded to Roger Maddock, the secretary of defense, sitting across from him alongside General Jeffrey Eaglefield, the chairman of the Joint Chiefs of Staff. "Sir, we have reached an agreement with him."

Bob nodded to the unheard comments of President Crawford on the other end. The three men sat in the Command Chambers of the secretary of defense, behind three-inch-thick steel walls and vacuum-sealed doors designed to protect those inside from electronic espionage or unauthorized observers.

"Yes, sir. He readily agreed to all our demands. I recommend, Mr. President, that you authorize the secretary of defense to implement Operation Tangle Bandit."

The faint voice of the president could be heard through the receiver, but as hard as Roger and the general tried, the words were too garbled to understand.

"Yes, sir, Mr. President." Bob handed the receiver to Roger. "He wants to talk with you."

Roger took the receiver, holding it slightly from his ear so General Eaglefield could listen.

"Roger, are the forces in place?"

"Yes, sir, Mr. President. The initial phrase of Operation Tangle Bandit started over three days ago. The forces are within one hundred miles of the objective, and according to General Stanhope, director of NSA, and Farbros Digby-Jones, director of CIA, they remain undetected."

"Roger, I don't want another Jimmy Carter Iran rescue fiasco."

"Decades ago, sir. Different military, different readiness focus. They're ready, and I have complete confidence in them doing the job."

"What does the chairman think? I haven't seen General Eaglefield today. When I saw him yesterday at our round table in the Oval Office, he echoed what you are telling me. Does he have the same confidence?"

General Eaglefield nodded and waved his finger in a circle, indicating he was ready to give the go-ahead signal.

"Mr. President, Korea is rapidly deescalating. The North Koreans are on the run. I have already detached two carrier battle groups to the Mediterranean. We don't need those forces in the Sea of Japan. We can now focus on resolving the North African crisis. I agree with Bob. Issue the order, and in twenty-four hours—"

"Roger, enough of our fine men and women have already died in North Africa and in Korea. I'm as concerned now as I was yesterday over this operation. I think it's very dangerous, and if any one item goes awry in its execution, then we will have a major catastrophe on our hands."

"Mr. President, that is why they train and train and train. Eventually, every military person has to go in harm's way. It's why we have a strong military; to go in harm's way, execute national policy, and have the best chance for survival and victory. Sir, now is the time. The forces are in place. The KC-135 Air Force tankers are already on station. It is either now or never, sir. With all due respect, sir, you need to make a decision," Roger said, his voice rising slightly, "and I recommend a 'Go.'"

Bob raised his finger and shook it slightly. Confronting Crawford could backfire. The president, for all his capacity for intellectual thought, never forgot a slight.

There was silence on the other end. After a few seconds, President Crawford replied softly, "Okay, Roger. I pray that everything you and the chairman proposed goes according to plan."

"Thank you, Mr. President. You won't be disappointed." As the seconds lengthened, waiting for a reply, Roger envisioned the president tapping his pencil on the desk at the other end, looking at Franco Donelli, his national security advisor.

"Mr. President?" Roger asked.

"Yes, I am still here, Roger. I hope you are right. Go ahead; execute Operation Tangle Bandit, and keep me up to date as it progresses. Tell me about the missiles launched by the Libyans. Have they been destroyed?"

Roger Maddock nodded at General Eaglefield, who slid his chair back, nodded to both men, and rapidly departed the secure compartment. By the time he stepped into the E Ring of the Pentagon, the general was running, his aide and bodyguard jogging alongside to keep up. The dim corridors seemed bright in comparison to the streetlights across the Potomac River that lit the near-vacant streets of the sleeping capital. Turning down the corridor leading to the National Military Command Center on the C Ring, General Eaglefield slowed to a fast walk. Ahead of him, the few military and civilians in the Pentagon at that time of night flattened themselves against the wall until he passed. Two uniformed Defense Protective Service officers saw him approaching and opened the wide, bulletproof glass door leading into the NMCC. The chairman nodded to their greetings as he hurried past the guard desk, through the small reception area, and into the main Joint Staff operations area.

**"CAPTAIN HOLMAN," COMMANDER STEVE CLOTH, THE** air operations officer for Task Force Sixty-seven said, drawing Dick's attention away from the long-range surface display in front of him.

"Yes, Steve."

"Sir, the Air Force B-52s have entered our operation area and are now under Sixth Fleet control. They have completed refueling and are ready for assignment."

Admiral Pete Devlin, commander of the U.S. Sixth Fleet, listening to the exchange asked, "Commander, have we downloaded the missile locations provided by the Italians?"

The location of the Libyan cruise missiles was important for his own force targeting effort.

"Sir, still in progress. Joint Task Force African Force operations officer reports the data is slightly incompatible with our own systems, so we are having to manually massage it. Shouldn't take too long." Steve Cloth looked at his watch. "Another ten to twenty minutes should do it."

The hatch to the Combat Information Center opened, and General Leutze Lewis, the commander of Joint Task Force African Force, entered. Dick was slightly surprised to see the three-star general in full uniform. Seemed to him, with the exception of the man's arrival over a month ago, that every time he saw the general, he was either in PT gear or getting in or out of it. Dick guessed if he was proud of his body, he wanted to show it off.

"Sir," Steve Cloth said softly to Dick Holman. "I have an Air Traffic Order"—He handed the message to Dick—"showing the presence of three Air Force KC-135s orbiting in three different geographical locations over the southern Algerian and Libyan desert. I have nothing to indicate they have air protection, and I have no idea why they are there."

Before Dick could answer, General Lewis entered the circle. "Looks as if your doctor was wrong, Pete. Seems the Libyans don't have to wait until tonight to fire those missiles."

"The USS *Hue City* has shot down the missile fired at Algiers, General. We are waiting on the report from the second, even as we speak."

"What is the holdup on taking out the other ten?"

"We are downloading the Italian targeting data now, General. Should be able to disseminate the target assignments within the next half hour."

Lewis crossed his arms. Dick noticed how the tall man's left eyebrow raised slightly. "Let's hope he doesn't fire any more, then, in the next half hour."

"Yes, sir. Let's hope and pray. The B-52s are on station with their air-launched cruise missiles. I intend to keep them to our northwest. Their Tomahawks have the range to reach anywhere in Libya from where they are orbiting now. No need to move them closer."

Commander Bailey, the Sixth Fleet CIC tactical action officer on duty, walked up. "General, Admiral, the targeting data is loaded, sirs."

"That took less time than I thought," Admiral Devlin said.

"Yes, sir. It was less of a problem than we thought."

The hatch slammed opened as Captain Paul Brooks burst into the space. Spotting the flag officers near the long-range display consoles, Paul hurried over to them. Behind him, through the hatch, appeared Captain Kurt Lederman.

"Paul, it makes me nervous when a cryptologic officer arrives out of breath and looking like you do," Admiral Pete Devlin said.

"General, Admiral, we have indications that the Libyans are in the process of launching the remainder of their missiles."

Kurt Lederman stepped into the growing circle of decision makers. "Paul is right, General, Admiral. We have minutes before those missiles leave their launch pads."

General Lewis's eyebrows bounced up and down several times before he grinned. "Then it seems to me, gentlemen, that we must launch our Tomahawks immediately."

"Yes, sir," Admiral Devlin replied. "But it will take some time to ensure that those missiles hit the right target. It would not be good to take out a bunch of civilians with them. Collateral damage—"

"Sir," Dick Holman added, interrupting before General Lewis had a chance to respond to Admiral Devlin. "Have you decided on our proposal for an air strike against the Libyan command post? We already have the aircraft airborne and ready for the order."

"No!" General Lewis shouted. "No, no, no. There is to be no cruise missile or air strike against the Libyan command post until I tell you." He looked at Pete Devlin. "You know why, Pete. I can't imagine why you want to continue trying to do this."

"General, we need to have a backup in event of failure."

"There won't be a failure."

"What is going on?" Dick asked. "Something is going on that you two know about." He looked at Kurt Lederman, who handed the general a folded note. Dick pointed at Kurt. "And it seems everyone knows but me."

Colonel Brad Storey attempted to read the note over the general's shoulder, but the general's superior height kept the

note secret. General Lewis read it, folded it, and handed it back
to the intelligence officer. "Okay, Dick. You can know now.
Pete, Operation Tangle Bandit is a go." He looked at Dick Holman. "Want to know why I haven't stopped you from putting
those fighters in the air for your command post attack?" Without waiting for Dick to answer, he continued. "It's because . . ."

**SERGEANT MAJOR JONATHAN ADAMS, CAREER SOLDIER**
and supervisor of the operations team at the United States Army
Land Information Warfare Command located deep within Fort
Belvoir, snapped a salute as Major General Gramps Morgan
came down the stairway. The sixty-one-year-old general
seemed to bounce off his heels as he moved down the broad set
of steps leading from the entrance to a small landing a couple
of feet above the operations floor. Master Sergeant Adams
straightened as Morgan approached, assuming a relaxed position of attention. Major General Morgan touched the sergeant
major on the shoulder and grinned at him. "Sergeant Major, I'm
glad to see you here, but weren't you here ten hours ago when
I left?"

"Yes, sir, General. A lot going on, sir. I felt this was where I
needed to be," Sergeant Major Adams replied.

Gramps Morgan winked at the man, the wrinkles along his
cheeks arching upward as he smiled. "You are right, Sergeant.
It is exactly times like these when our Army needs us old men,"
he said. Morgan scanned the room, his eyes taking in the two
rows of computers, their screens reflecting various colors in the
blue-lighted operations space. Morgan turned to the graying
sergeant major. "Shall we go, Sergeant Major, and give these
great, young soldiers the benefit of our age and experience?"
Without waiting for a reply, Morgan took the two remaining
steps to the operations floor and turned toward the center of the
room where the combat management consoles were installed.

Major General Morgan was the oldest flag officer still on active duty of all four military services. His spry steps, smile-
wrinkled face, and thin frame fooled those who first met him
with his beret on. They often mistook his age to be early fifties
when in fact next year he would reach the mandatory military
retirement age of sixty-two. When he removed his beret to reveal the thinning silver hair shining beneath, it was easy to re-

alize he was much older than fifty. Women loved to be around him. *They feel safe because they think of me like a grandfather.* He had grown accustomed to hearing the most intimate concerns of the wives at the most unexpected moments. Sometimes, Major General Gramps Morgan, career Army infantryman, thought that maybe in a previous life he had been a priest. If so, he hoped it was a warrior priest.

Flag officers usually retire after two or three years if they fail to advance to another star or the Army had no job openings for their pay grade and skill. This mandatory retirement opened opportunity for those following to move up. But Gramps Morgan was an Army icon. He was the Army answer to the Navy Rear Admiral Grace Hopper, who opened the door to computer programming. He was a founding father of the Army's information warfare effort. Major General Morgan graduated from the Industrial College of the Armed Forces in the class of 2000—Class of Y2K they called it—having studied information warfare as a sidebar to his ICAF studies. The Information Resource Management College, located in Washington, D.C., at Marshall Hall on Fort McNair, was home to some of the brightest thinkers the Department of Defense could find to teach what everyone liked to call a revolution in warfare. He graduated with honors and made colonel the same year.

His wife died of a heart attack after the two of them ran the Boston Marathon four years ago, and with no children or grandchildren to dote on, the aging warrior remained on active duty. His family was the army and its soldiers the children they never had. His two attempts to retire in the past four years had been turned down by the Army chief of staff, who personally invited Major General Morgan to the Pentagon so he could convince Gramps of his importance to the Army. After each of the two office calls, Morgan left the COS office and drove to his wife's grave at the edge of Fredericksburg, Virginia, where he discussed with her the prospects of remaining on active duty. With no concrete plans for retirement, he believed she agreed he still loved the Army, the uniform, the pomp and circumstance, and he would be bored with shuffleboard, canasta, and bingo—a personal joke between the two of them. Satisfied that she understood, he always drove back to the small government house on Fort Belvoir, called the COS, and agreed to remain for another two years. Last year, the new Army COS asked him to remain another two years. Whether the Army liked it or not, Major General Gramps Morgan had to go home next March when he turned sixty-two. It would take an act of Congress to extend him past this age, and Gramps had few friends in the hallowed halls of that great institution.

LIWC operations would have passed for a twin of the Libyan command post of Colonel Alqahiray. If Alqahiray and Morgan had miraculously exchanged places at that instant, it would have taken a few moments for each to realize he was not in his respective center. Gramps looked at the broad intelligence display that spanned the front of the room, much like a screen in a large theater. He was proud of what his soldiers had accomplished. Why use a multitude of screens for multiple displays, when one screen would do the job? You just programmed the data you wanted to see, and it appeared on the screen in whatever position you designated. By keying in the right program, the data were constantly updating, and certain keywords within the data could cause portions of the display to change color to highlight emerging and important events as they occurred. Across the broad expanse of the gigantic LED screen rode a virtual display of the east coast of the United States and the Mediterranean. Several small ship icons identified the location of Sixth Fleet ships and aircraft while different colors and shapes located friendly, allied, enemy, commercial, and unidentified air contacts. He knew clicking on any of the symbols on the control screen would bring a stream of data, giving in-depth identity. In Hawaii, a similar operations room ran the Korean War with LIWC providing a reach-back capability when they needed additional resources. It was hard to fight a computer war against an enemy that uses few to no computers to control their critical infrastructures such as electricity, water, transportation, and communications. Afghanistan had been a great example. A computer network attack initiated by the United States had never been authorized until now. He could retire gratefully now, knowing his LIWC had become a footnote in American military history.

The two rows of computers curved around the front of the room in such a fashion as to allow every operator visual access to the broad-screen display.

These young men and women at the Army's premier information warfare command possessed far superior technical expertise than he did. He had no illusions about their technical knowledge in comparison to his. His technological knowledge grew stale with each new development. Back in the late '90s, a man named Moore said information technology moved so fast that regardless of where it was at any given moment, within eighteen months, new technological developments made the current technology obsolete. The truth was, those developments were occurring so fast that six months was more realistic. Gramps Morgan believed he received more credit for the success of LIWC than he truly deserved.

"Status, Colonel?" Gramps Morgan asked the duty commander.

"Morning, sir. We still have access, General. They fired two missiles thirty minutes ago. Not sure exactly what is happening now." He pointed to two men and a woman who were moving from one console to the other, quickly scanning a screen, leaning down to whisper something to the soldier manning it, and then moving on. Several times, they shifted the small microphone of the cordless headsets they were wearing and whispered into it.

"The three Arabic linguists we got from NSA have been invaluable. Several more are on their way from Fort Meade. I called our contact at the National Security Agency and told him things were moving too fast for just three. They have asked the Naval Security Group Command at Fort Meade to provide us additional resources. The Navy linguists should be arriving shortly."

Morgan nodded. It was one thing to penetrate—hack into—another computer system, but if you could not read the language, it became an intellectual challenge—a time-consuming one—targeted against the ones and zeros that made up the program. They needed more than a computer programming attack; they needed to exploit the data the enemy operators were using, so they'd know what they were doing or planning.

The three linguists came to the end of the row as their hopscotch walk among the consoles, scanning each, brought them together. Their microphones shoved up alongside their ears, they put their heads close together and nodded in unison as they reached some unknown conclusion.

The spokesman of the three led the group as they crossed the floor to where Gramps stood with the colonel. The two men with her watched for a second before breaking apart and resuming their movement through the row of computers, observing and whispering their analysis to each other through the microphones.

"Colonel," she said as she walked around the edge of the console. "We think they are preparing to fire a whole bunch of missiles."

"How many?"

The NSA civilian shrugged her shoulders. "A whole bunch," she repeated, sounding slightly miffed that she had to repeat the answer again.

"Colonel, how soon can we assume control of the enemy's system?" Morgan asked. *"A whole bunch." Is that like a handful or a bushel? What is our military coming to?* He asked himself, knowing the NSA couldn't really be considered military. The story of the new NSA employee asking the gentleman in the elevator of the OPS One building what the four stars on the shoulder of his jacket meant flickered across his memory. This was just another example to Gramps Morgan of how the Department of Defense had changed over the past five decades. Some would say for the better, but they wouldn't be wearing a uniform.

The duty commander reached over the shoulders of the two Army captains manning the main control console and pushed the mouse so the arrow pointed to a red execute banner in the top right corner of the screen. "All we have to do, sir, is click on this. When we do, our system will go automatic, wipe out their displays, and transfer their control protocols to our position."

"Any way they can counteract our actions?"

He bit his lower lip. "I am sure there are ways, sir. Methods we may be unaware of but, even if they do, I doubt they can counteract our actions before Tangle Bandit is completed."

An NSA linguist, leaning over the shoulder of an operator in the first row, turned. "They are preparing to launch those missiles. We've got less than a minute, probably seconds, and they're gone!" he shouted.

"Colonel, I think we need to execute," Morgan said.

Another colonel standing in the shadows stepped forward. "General, I am Colonel McCormack, sir; judge advocate general's office. I have been assigned to—"

"General, the legal eagles haven't decided yet the legality of us actually doing this," the duty operations colonel interrupted. "The United States has never launched a computer network attack before, and whatever we do now establishes a precedent we will have to live with in the future."

"Yes, sir, General," McCormack continued. "I have to get permission from Lieutenant General Smitters before we can actually launch an information warfare attack. Until then, I can't give permission for you to activate the attack."

"Colonel, if we don't act now, innocent people are going to die."

"Yes, sir, General, that may happen, but I was given a direct order by the judge advocate general of the Army to not allow you to execute a computer attack until it has been cleared by him personally. Until then, sir, we cannot legally execute."

"You mean, Colonel, you lawyers are holding up this operation?"

"We don't mean to, General. I know even as we speak, my cohorts in the Pentagon are meeting to resolve the international laws surrounding this type of warfare."

"I think they have had years to resolve it, and they haven't. What makes you think they will now?"

The lawyer shrugged his shoulders. "I know they are working on it, sir."

Gramps Morgan stared down at the mouse, glancing up briefly at the screen where the arrow still rested on the execute banner. "All we have to do is click on this banner?"

"Yes, sir."

General Gramps Morgan leaned forward. "Let me move it, so we don't have an accident." He clicked the banner. "Oops . . . now, how did I do that?"

Gramps turned toward the JAG colonel. "Colonel McCormack, seems that I have accidentally launched the attack. My, my," he said, shaking his head. "What a shame. Why don't you go to my office down the hall and call Lieutenant General Smitters and tell him what happened. Sergeant Major Adams, have someone escort Colonel McCormack to my office, where he can remain until I am through here trying to stop this inadvertent action. Make sure he has plenty of coffee."

Colonel McCormack jerked forward and grabbed the mouse, sliding it around. The Army captain sitting at the console grabbed his wrist and pulled his hand away from the mouse. "Sir!"

Sergeant Major Jonathan Adams touched Colonel McCormack on the shoulder. "Colonel, if you would come with me, sir?"

The screen blanked out for a fraction of second, and series of ones and zeros began to scroll at unreadable speed across the face of the display.

"We have to stop it!"

Gramps shook his head. "Too late, Colonel."

Sergeant Major Adams motioned two military policemen over. "Escort Colonel McCormack to the general's office so he may use the phone.

General Morgan turned to the Army lawyer. "Colonel, you wait there until I send for you. We're going to be busy here trying to stop this accident."

"Sir, I do not for one moment believe that this was an accident."

General Morgan shrugged his shoulders. "And I do not believe innocent lives should be sacrificed for the sake of judicial expediency."

The duty operations officer and Major General Gramps Morgan watched the lawyer for a few moments until they were sure he was out of the operations room.

"Sorry, Colonel. Seems I have accidentally initiated the action."

The colonel grinned. "Yes, sir. Seems you have. Captain," he said to the officer in front of him. "Switch to phase II."

The colonel straightened and turned to the general. "Sir, it is a pleasure to fight with you."

The young soldier standing behind Sergeant Major Adams answered the telephone and nervously interrupted the general and colonel to announce that the chairman of the Joint Chiefs of Staff was on the other end, asking for General Morgan. Gramps knew what Jeff was going to tell him even before he took the receiver of the STE secure handset. A minute later when he hung up, he turned to the two men and told them their computer network attack timing was impeccable. He stepped away and slid into one of the twelve observer chairs above the room, leaving the colonel to run the show. He knew his limitations.

Satisfied that everything was going according to the plan, he shut his eyes and silently said a short prayer for the brave soldiers who were hurrying into harm's way: *May they survive with few casualties.* No one believed they would escape with no casualties.

*What is brown and black and looks good on lawyers? Dobermans.*

He smiled and shut his eyes. The game was afoot and out of his hands.

Sergeant Major Adams walked up beside the general, leaned down, and whispered, "Sir, you know the telephone doesn't work in that office."

Without opening his eyes, Gramps smiled and took a deep breath. What a great day to be alive.

# TWELVE

**DUNCAN RAISED HIS THIRD FINGER. THE DOOR JERKED**
open, snatching the doorknob out of Bud's hand. An Algerian
rebel stepped out, nearly tripping over Duncan. The rebel
shouted. Reacting instinctively, Duncan slit the man's throat,
changing the shout to a gurgle to silence. The dying Islamic fanatic grabbed his throat in a futile attempt to stop his life's
blood from flooding away. Duncan shoved him back into the
room.

Monkey jumped around Duncan and brought the barrel of
his heavy weapon up, catching one of the rebels under the chin.
The sound of the bone breaking punctuated the noise of the
SEALs scrambling to get inside the small room. Beau and Bud
followed Monkey, separating right and left. HJ dove up the center, pushing Monkey to the side, and jumping over the moaning
rebel who had dropped like a rock. Duncan pushed himself up
and rushed in after the four.

"Hell!" Beau shouted, jerking his knife from the scabbard as
he ran alongside Bud toward two rebels at the far end of the
room who were fumbling for their weapons. HJ rushed a wide-
eyed rebel standing in front of her, frozen as if paralyzed from
the sudden attack. The cup of her hand hit the man's chin,
knocking his head back. Simultaneously, her foot hooked

around his right ankle and jerked forward. The rebel's neck stretched involuntarily. The knife came easily into her hand and whipped through the neck of the Arab. She quickly shoved the dying man away.

A cut throat does not kill instantly. The arteries are severed, quickly flooding the throat with blood. It takes a couple of minutes for a person to die from such a mortal wound. The blood flows from the brain, soon killing this vital organ, while the blood filling the throat causes the victim to drown in his own blood. Some gain a few more minutes of life by leaning downward so the blood flows away, but eventually, one of three things kill someone with a properly cut throat. The victim becomes brain dead from lack of blood, drowns in his own blood, or bleeds to death. Whatever happens, the victim is no longer a threat. HJ was getting more practice than most in her first two months in the SEALs in this deadly technique.

A huge rat scurried from behind a counter one of the rebels fell against and dashed across the room to disappear behind the bed.

Beau and Bud were several feet away from the two at the far end of the room when one of them brought up an AK-47, aiming the Russian weapon directly at them. HJ drew back and hurled her bloodstained knife at the one with the AK-47. The knife buried itself in the man's chest, causing him to fall across the table in the center of the room. The AK-47 clattered harmlessly to the floor. Duncan was thankful the weapon, notorious for its feather trigger, failed to go off. Beau stabbed the remaining rebel in the stomach, jerking the knife up and to the side, slicing through vital organs. Blood gushed out of the wide wound, washing over his right hand and soaking the sleeve of his filthy cammie shirt. If the cut didn't kill the man, the filth from the sewers that covered Beau's glove and knife would.

The woman in the room was tied naked to a bed where the men had been torturing her. A host of medical tools nearby showed the instruments of torture. A fifth man standing over the woman dropped the scalpel and raised his hands. A neat circle of blood surrounded the nipple on the woman's left breast, where a scalpel had been pulled round and round it.

The American woman whimpered softly, her eyes glazed from shock as they darted between the Navy SEALs and the rebel standing in front of her.

Beau grabbed the rebel prisoner and shoved him to the floor. *Why?* Duncan asked himself.

HJ began to untie the woman, continuously whispering, "You're okay. We're United States Navy SEALs. You're okay, now."

"Go relieve Gibbons," Duncan said to Monkey. Gibbons was their nearest thing to a trained corpsman. He had had a little more than the basic medical training all SEALs received. Gibbons was a SEAL of many important skills ranging from radioman to personnel man to corpsman, with corpsman being the most important. Monkey dashed out the door and down the hallway to where Gibbons squatted, guarding the exit door.

A few seconds later, with the woman untied, Gibbons arrived and began dressing her wounds. "Boss, she'll live, but she needs a doctor."

Monkey and Bud tied the prisoner to one of the chairs, his arms strapped tightly behind him and each leg tied to one of the front legs of the chair. The man was scared. A dark stain spread across his trousers when Monkey slowly ran his finger along the sharp edge of his knife. "I think I should," he said to Bud, staring intently at the helpless rebel.

Duncan overhead him. "No, we don't do that stuff. Moral standards. International convention. The CNN factor. All that bullshit, Monkey."

"Yes, sir, Captain. I know that, but he don't."

The woman continued to whimper as HJ helped her put some clothes on. Cigarette burns traveled up and down her arms. HJ knew that regardless of how long or short the time the woman had been with her torturers, it would have seemed an eternity. Duncan had tuned out the crying, whispering conversation between HJ and the woman. He wanted to know where the hostages where. They had to be here someplace. Where else would this American woman have come from?

"Bud, you and Monkey search the other offices and make sure they're empty. See what you can find. HJ, see if you can calm the lady enough so she can tell us where the other hostages are."

HJ nodded and, in a soft, comforting voice, began questioning the woman, afraid to go too fast for fear of frightening her. She pushed the sweaty, dirty hair out of the woman's face and wiped it with a wet washcloth from a nearby sink. She wiped a few tears from her own eyes, keeping her back to Duncan and the others to hide the anger threatening to overwhelm her control. He saw the woman point toward the door and make a motion to the right as she talked softly with HJ.

Bud and Monkey eased out the door. Monkey leaned a few inches from the prisoner and ran the back of his knife along the man's throat as he walked out. Even from Duncan's position across the room, he saw the man's throat constrict and his eyes turn downward in an attempt to assure himself that his throat had not been cut.

HJ breathed deeply several times, bringing her anger under control. She knew what she had to do, and if an opportunity permitted, she would.

HJ patted the woman on the arm and walked to where Duncan stood near the door. "Captain, she says the others are here with her. She thinks this is a warehouse and that we are in an office at one end of the building. The large, open warehouse is where the hostages are being kept. They were all together when she was taken away. And they are guarded." She pointed to where Monkey squatted, guarding the far door leading from the hallway. "She said she came through that door."

"What happened here?"

"They were going to kill her and hang her body for the Marines to find. She was to be the second victim. According to her, the first American died from an apparent heart attack, and they mutilated his body in front of the hostages. Sort of an incentive to behave. They found out the Americans knew the hostage was dead before being cut up, so this time they were correcting their mistake."

"Then we arrived in the nick of time. I am going to shoot Bashir when we see him again. His promises of them not wanting to kill the hostages and just wanting us out of Algiers seems misplaced," Duncan said through clenched teeth. "God, this makes me angry!"

"What are we going to do with her?"

Duncan looked at the woman and shrugged his shoulders. "We can't take her with us, and we can't leave her here, because I'm not sure this is the way we will be going out. What do we have?" he asked and then continued, not expecting an answer. "About fifty hostages who have no idea we are this close to rescuing them." Three beeps came through his small earpiece.

"What the hell?" Then he remembered the urban warrior outfit the Marines gave him.

He pulled the small computer screen down in front of his left eye. "We'll have to take her with us. Tell her, and make sure she understands she's to follow our instructions to the letter and keep absolutely quiet while she's doing it."

The words, "We have contact with you," came across the screen. Duncan raised his left arm and typed back. "Good. Where are we?"

"We are working the location. What is your situation?"

He typed back. "In a warehouse somewhere within a few miles of where we entered. One hostage rescued. Others in main warehouse. On way to effect rescue. Would appreciate backup."

"We have you. You are in the old Algerian grain and storage warehouse six point five miles from where you entered. Estimate twenty minutes to on scene. Can you wait?"

"We will try, but we are going forward. If hostage rescue feasible, will execute." Six and a half miles! He was getting old.

"Bulldog sends well done."

"I want Bashir."

Several seconds passed before the screen lit up again. "Impossible. Has vanished."

"Roger, out," Duncan typed.

HJ came back. "She is shaken but young. She knows what to do."

"HJ, did they . . . ?"

She nodded. "They all did. They've had her down here all day, and looks like they got tired of her—like those temporary marriages Bashir told us about—and were getting on with their business." She looked at the prisoner, her eyes narrowing. She spat on the floor. "Ought to kill them all." Her voice trembled slightly.

"No, he surrendered. He's tied up and can't hurt anyone now."

"Boss, this is a war against terrorism. We can't fight it on normal terms. It's dirty, and we need to show them we can be as—"

"No. I don't want to hear another word. Just get her and let's get moving."

HJ's eyes narrowed, and her tight lips showed him she was fighting the temptation to argue. She turned away toward the victim.

HJ grabbed the woman under the arms and led her through the door. The woman staggered, moaning several times, causing HJ to realize how tight her grip was and to relax it. The woman walked with her legs far apart, each step gingerly taken, her face grimacing as she tried to stifle the moans.

Duncan nodded at HJ and put his finger to his lips.

HJ nodded, leaned down, and whispered to the woman, encouraging her to keep quiet. If the other rebels heard the noise, it wouldn't be long before they were discovered.

Beau and Monkey returned, blocking the doorway. "Other offices empty, Captain. Nothing in them except a bunch of papers written in Arabic."

Duncan nodded. "The Marines are on their way. We've got twenty minutes to get in position where we can protect the hostages until the Marines show up. The American hostage— What's her name, HJ?"

"Pauline King of Washington, D.C. She says the others are here in the main warehouse below these office spaces."

"Does she know how many guards?"

HJ stepped back and held a hurried conference with King. "She's not sure, Captain, but has counted as many as ten and as few as four."

"Okay, listen up, everyone. We plan for ten and hope for four. We want a quick resolution. Take out the guards, and take possession of the hostages. Then we go to ground and hold our position until the Marines arrive."

"We're not going to try to get out of here, Captain?"

Duncan shook his head. "Chief, I don't think we can take fifty hostages out safely. For all we know, there may be hundreds of Islamic fanatics out there who are just aching for a chance to kill more Americans." He tapped his helmet. "We'll be all right. I have comms with Colonel Stewart. The Marines are on their way. All we need to do is tuck the hostages safely inside a defensive perimeter and hunker down until they arrive."

HJ braced Pauline King against the wall. "Wait here. I'll be right back," she whispered. HJ glanced toward Duncan and the others and saw they were facing away. She quietly moved down the dim hallway.

Duncan moved out, he and Beau discussing quietly how they would split into two teams for the assault. Unnoticed, HJ opened the door and reentered the room where the prisoner was tied up, his mouth taped over. The rebel's eyes grew large as HJ unsheathed her knife. "My moral guidance changed a few weeks ago, asshole."

She placed the knife against the man's neck. He began to struggle against his bonds, pulling his head as far from the knife as possible. As she shoved the knife into the rebel's neck, a hand whipped around from behind her and jerked the knife back, pushing HJ away, causing the SEAL lieutenant to fall on the floor.

HJ rolled twice and came up in a crouch. Standing near the rebel was Chief Wilcox. "Sorry, ma'am. I thought you were going to execute a prisoner. My mistake," he said, wiping the blood on his trouser leg.

He reached forward and held his hand out to help HJ to her feet. She ignored the hand, standing to her taller height. Without a word, she glared at Chief Wilcox for several seconds. Then she cast a quick glance at the prisoner as if to say she'd be back. She turned to leave the room.

"Ma'am," Chief Wilcox said, causing HJ to stop and turn around. "Your knife, Lieutenant. You may need it." He held the knife by the blade. HJ took it, nodded, and shoved it into the scabbard.

Chief Wilcox looked at the rebel. A slight stream of blood ran down the man's throat, but he'd live. He grabbed the half-eaten loaf of bread off the table and reduced it to crumbs, covering the prisoner's lap. Smiling, the chief hoisted his carbine and followed the lieutenant out of the room, turning the light off and pulling the door shut behind him. Hungry rats have been known to gnaw through wood when eating. It wouldn't take them long to discover the bread.

"Where is HJ?" Duncan asked as they reached the end of the hall. The woman stood by herself, where a minute before Lieutenant Heather J. McDaniels had been beside her.

"Right here, Captain," HJ answered as she appeared from behind the woman.

"HJ, keep up. Gibbons, take point."

Gibbons nodded and moved to the front of the formation.

Duncan looked at McDonald and made a downward motion with his finger. The second class petty officer reached over and flipped off the hallway lights.

Beau squatted and slid the spy camera under the small space between the door and the floor. He twisted the cord so the camera gave a quick view and then, after several seconds, Beau pulled it back inside. He gave a quick nod to Gibbons. "Balcony, Gibbons. Exit to the left. Looks like open space five to six feet ahead."

McDonald pulled the door open. Gibbons stuck his head out, looked both ways, and crawled through the doorway. McDonald eased the door within a few inches of being closed. The dark-haired New Jersey native slid down the wall until he squatted on his haunches. He stuck his M-60 heavy machine gun through the door, ready to jump to the middle of the hallway if Gibbons shouted.

Gibbons crawled to the balcony edge and peered downward. The balcony overlooked the end of a crowded warehouse floor. Barrels, boxes, and crates created a haphazard maze of stored goods. Small chest-wide spaces marked unaligned passages between the materials and the far end where an array of bright lights pointed inward to light up the area. Loot, thought Gibbons, stolen by the rebels and stored here.

The faint light of dawn grew through windows that ran around the top of the huge warehouse, weaving a series of shadowy grays across the warehouse floor. Gibbons could see no light fixtures on the ceiling of the warehouse. Dangling from the rafters to about ten feet from the warehouse floor, evenly spaced, naked lightbulbs, most burned out, provided some light. Gibbons moved his eyes systematically, searching for rebel locations. Satisfied that he was unobserved, with no rebel presence apparent, he turned his attention to the group within the illuminated area at the far end of the warehouse. Western suits, ties, business dresses, women's slacks: the hostages. A few stood, walking gingerly among several who were lying down, as if they were ministering to the sick. Most sat braced against boxes with their heads on their arms or lying down with their arms across their eyes as if sleeping.

McDonald hissed from the doorway after a couple of minutes. Gibbons stuck his hand up, waved, and crawled backward until he was inside the corridor. McDonald shut the door.

"They're there, Captain, at the far end of the warehouse. Most of the place is dark. Didn't see any rebels. No overhead lights. Dawn is trickling through a bunch of windows that line the top of the warehouse. Once the sun is up, it will light the warehouse."

"How many guards?"

Gibbons shrugged. "I didn't see any. If they are there, then either they are watching from somewhere up here or mixed in with the hostages down there. Lots of boxes and crates between us and them. Could make us easy targets or make it easy for us to approach the hostages. Depends on when they finally discover we are here."

"Good job, Gibbons."

"Then it's an unfair fight," Beau said.

"Why's that?" Bud Helliwell asked, his eyebrows bunching to a V.

"Because in the world of the living, us SEALs are bigger assholes than they are," Beau said, pausing slightly before continuing. "And that is why we go on among the living while those we oppose do not."

"Beau," Duncan said. "You, Bud, and McDonald split to the right when we reach the bottom of the stairs. Me, HJ, Monkey, and Gibbons will go down the left side. Five minutes after we hit the main floor, we take the hostages back. Watch your brick for the red light to come on. Three blinks, it's a go; one blink, it's wait. Same back to me."

"Chief Wilcox," Duncan said, looking up at the chief, who stood while the others squatted. "You stay here with Miss King. You know the way out if something goes wrong. Get back into the sewers and find another manhole somewhere."

"Captain, beg your pardon, but how about someone else staying here? You'll need me down there."

"You're right, Chief. I do need you. You're our reserve backup and our cover if we have to retreat. We can't take the lady with us, and we can t leave her here by herself. If something goes wrong, we may have to exit the way we came: through the sewers. You're the backup."

Chief Wilcox nodded, raising one eyebrow in a questioning

slant. For a fraction of a second, his and HJ's eyes met before
HJ turned her attention back toward Duncan.

"I'll be here, Captain."

"Let's go. Gibbons, lead the way."

Two minutes later, the two SEAL teams were on the floor of
the warehouse. The boxes, crates, and barrels looked bigger
once they were among them. The twists and turns of the logistic maze caused them to lose sight of each other as they worked
their way toward the far end. Duncan expected any moment to
hear the sounds of gunfire. Nearly every stack rose above their
heads, every turn was a potential confrontation, and every nook
an ambush site.

"No white rabbit to follow," Beau whispered. He gestured
emphatically to the right to Bud and McDonald. Then, leading
the way, he moved quickly among the rows and rows of stacked
goods.

Six feet, and they were out of sight of Duncan, HJ, Gibbons,
and Monkey. Duncan pointed to the path ahead, and the four
started along it.

Duncan looked at his watch. Three minutes. Two more to
get into position. He darted forward as Gibbons disappeared
around the edge of another stack. HJ followed, her eyes con-
centrating on the area behind them, keeping an eye on Duncan
in front, while making sure that Monkey was able to keep sight
of her in front of him. It would be easy to get separated from
the others in this mess.

The hostages' lives would be in danger if the Marines attacked before Duncan and the SEALs secured them. Any moment Duncan expected to run smack into a rebel rounding the
edge of a box. He didn't know who would be more surprised.
Just as the paucity of light in the warehouse benefited them, it
also helped hide the rebels. They were here somewhere. You
don't go off and leave hostages unprotected, unless . . . Shit!
Unless the area is rigged to explode! You tell the hostages the
place is rigged to explode if they leave the area. They become
their own jailers, keeping the more erratic members from trying
to escape, fearing for their own lives.

Duncan dashed ahead and motioned for Gibbons to wait. He
hurried forward, leaned around the next corner, and checked
both ways. HJ joined them and squatted on her haunches with
them. Monkey came up. Duncan pulled his brick out and

pressed the transmit button once. When the red light came on once and went off, he pulled the radio close to his lips.

"Beau, watch for trip wires and explosive devices."

The red light blinked once in acknowledgment.

Gibbons, squatting a couple of feet away, waved emphatically.

Gibbons pointed to a space in front of him and ran his finger from left to right. He laid his carbine down, cupped his hands, and then spread them out fast while his lips mouthed the word *Boom*.

"We have a trip wire in front of us. Seems they love trip wires, Beau. Keep alert for anything else," Duncan whispered into the brick.

The red light blinked once, silently acknowledging the warning.

Five minutes later, Duncan and his team reached the edge of the warehouse floor. He motioned HJ and McDonald to the left and watched them disappear around a huge stack of crates. Gibbons he sent farther to the right. Duncan edged forward, coming to a stop when the sound of footsteps walking slowly across the concrete floor reached his ears.

He drew back into the shadows and pressed his body against a nearby crate. The footsteps stopped at the end of the passage. A rebel wearing a huge black turban stood there, legs spread, looking down the small space that provided a walkway between the goods. The light from the hostage area caused the man standing about eight feet from Duncan to appear as a huge, dark outline, but the weapon held in his right hand told Duncan all he needed to know. The man unslung the weapon and slowly started up the narrow passage. Two more steps, and the man would walk right into Duncan.

Duncan wanted to delay firing as long as possible. A perfect rescue would have been one where they took a defensive position around the hostages a few minutes before the Marines burst through, thereby reducing the duration of a firefight while better protecting the hostages. However, it looked as if that opportunity was going to be lost in a few seconds. He eased the barrel of the carbine to the left and up a few inches to line it up with the rebel moving cautiously toward him. His finger slipped into the trigger guard, while his thumb rested on the safety. The sound of the safety going off would alert the rebel, so Duncan prepared to flip the safety off a millisecond before he fired.

A second shadow entered behind the rebel. *Jesus,* thought Duncan. *They're all over the place.* The second person took two quick steps, reached up, and jerked the head of the rebel back. Duncan watched a knife slice through the man's neck, only a slight sound escaping. The second shadow shoved the dead rebel forward to where it fell at Duncan's feet.

"You all right, Captain?" Gibbons asked softly.

"Yeah," Duncan said, standing and stepping over the twitching body. "Good work."

Gibbons leaned down and wiped his knife on the dying man's back. "Two more guards to the right, Captain. Three on the far side. I have a trip wire on the left, and you have one to your right when you exit."

Duncan glanced to the right. It took a few seconds before he saw the end of the trip wire, stretching across the exit. Good job they had the young eyes of Gibbons. "Thanks, Gibbons."

Gibbons looked down at the Algerian rebel. "My pleasure, Captain."

Duncan hurried forward to the edge of the passage. A space of twenty yards separated them from the hostages. A series of small floor lights surrounding the Americans focused inward on them, blinding anyone inside to those patrolling the perimeter. It also kept Duncan from giving any kind of sign to the hostages to let them know they were there.

Duncan looked to the left and got a thumbs-up from Gibbons, who had moved down a couple of gaps to take position between a stack of barrels and a row of pallets. To his right, HJ and Monkey had their backs pressed against huge piles of what looked like paper. HJ nodded. Monkey jumped across the way to the other side, opposite HJ and out of sight of Duncan. For a moment, the light caught Monkey as he changed position.

Duncan pulled his brick and pressed three times on the Transmit button, waiting for the red light to blink in acknowledgement. Nothing came. He transmitted again and waited. He put his hand over his eyes to shield them from the bright lights in front to see if he could spot Beau and the other team from his position. The red light blinked once. He pressed three times again to be sure and received the waiting acknowledgement.

Now, it was up to him. Once he opened fire, the others would follow suit. But open fire against what?

They had seen only one guard, and Gibbons had quickly dispatched him. Other rebels were out there. Gibbons had seen them. If he went forward, he knew both sides were going to be surprised, and they were going to have to fight a lopsided battle against an enemy who had the advantage of knowing the terrain. If he didn't attack and the Marines arrived before they were in a defensive position, the risk of the rebels killing the hostages or blowing them up increased.

That further complicated his mission. It wasn't just enough to take possession of the hostages and wait until the Marines arrived; he had to move them from the area because of the explosives. They had to get in there fast and move them before the rebels could hit the explosives. Move them into this maze and find another position to defend until the Marines could secure the warehouse. And they would have to do that without hitting a trip wire and killing a bunch of them. Duncan figured he had less than three minutes to move the hostages. But to where? Anywhere but here. They would have to hit fast. The hostages might not even realize they were being rescued in those three minutes. His only hope was that the explosives were unmanned. If the switch was unmanned, he would have his three minutes before the rebels realized what was happening.

Duncan slid down to the floor and began to crawl forward. Maybe if he could alert the hostages, it would reduce the time factor. Gibbons was to his left, HJ and Monkey farther to the right, providing cover. As the moment of decision approached, the edge of confidence grew, and he found himself crawling faster. Duncan soon reached the edge of the lights. He rose to his haunches behind two of the three-foot-high security lights and glanced around him. Seeing no one, he hissed at one of the male hostages.

The man squatted on a piece of cardboard, his back pressed against a nearby box. A tie hung out of his back pocket where the hostage had shoved it. The former white shirt, now a dingy yellow, hung tattered and dirty from the man's emaciated body. The dark stain on the shoulder looked like blood. A scraggly beard had grown in the weeks of captivity, and even from nearly ten feet away, the smell of unwashed bodies mixed with the sewer scents Duncan brought with him.

The man's head rose, his nose twitching as he sniffed the air. Duncan hissed again. The male hostage shielded his eyes, trying to see past the lights toward the hissing noise. He knew better than to approach the edge of the area any closer.

"You," Duncan said.

The man blinked with surprise. "Me?" he said aloud, pointing to himself.

"Shhhh," Duncan warned.

Three other hostages nearby looked up at the man. "Be quiet," one of them said. "You want to draw attention to yourself?"

"But someone just hissed at me," he said, his voice breaking.

"Hiss will be the least of your worries if our captors hear you talking," another man whispered. "Keep quiet, or we're going to move away."

Duncan hissed again, drawing the attention of all four. "You, where are the other guards?"

The man began to cry, slapping his hands against the boxes as he rose to his feet. "They're here!" he shouted. "Listen, everyone, they're here!"

Two of the three male hostages near him jumped up and grabbed the shouting man. "Be quiet, you fool!"

*Too late,* thought Duncan. He jumped up and ran into the hostage area. From the other side, Beau, McDonald and Bud burst through the lights, like apparitions appearing out of the ether. At first, their appearance was greeted with silence, but as the hostages began to gather around them, the noise of their cries rose in tempo until the crowd surged forward, trying—needing to touch their rescuers. Duncan attempted to push them away.

Gibbons, HJ, and Monkey ran into the area from the other side.

"Gibbons, Bud!" shouted Duncan. "Kill those lights."

Monkey opened up with his M-60 on the lights. *Damn, not that way,* Duncan thought, still pushing hands away from him. Unplug them, he meant, but it was too late.

Sparks flew from a nearby generator, and the lights went out suddenly, causing everyone to lose their vision temporarily as eyes adjusted to the low light of breaking morning.

The hostages drew back at the sound of gunfire. Their wails

grew into a cacophony of fragments with "Thank God," "You're here," and "We never thought you would come" filling the air.

Duncan grabbed a box and stood on top of it. "Listen to me, people. We only have a few seconds. Follow that man," he said, pointing to Beau. "Beau, lead them out your way. This place is rigged with explosives. Follow the short man, and do exactly what they tell you. And be quiet."

Beau ran over to Duncan. "What's going on? I thought we were going to take defensive position here and wait for the Marines. You know the story—Fort Apache and they get to play calvary?"

"Beau, the place is rigged to explode. I don't know where the other guards are, but move fast, and get these hostages out of here before they return." Somewhere out there were six guards who had disappeared somewhere into the maze of the warehouse.

The sound of someone shouting Arabic came from above their position.

"Just thought I'd ask," Beau said, turning and running to the other side.

"Everyone, stay close and follow me. No talking—and do what we say when we say it! No questions allowed!"

"Who are you?" asked a young lady near Beau. Her hair was matted to the side of her face, and her lips were swollen from where someone had hit her.

"Ma'am, we're the United States Navy."

"Where are the others?"

"Ma'am, we are the others. No questions, please. Follow me," Beau said, stepping across the electrical cords that ran between the darkened lights.

Duncan gestured to HJ, Monkey, and Gibbons to follow.

"No, Captain, you go ahead," HJ said. "I'll bring up the rear."

"Wait a minute, ma'am," Gibbons said, raising his left hand. "That's my job."

"Wait a minute! That's my job. You've been point man the whole trip, and now you want to bring up the rear, just when it's getting dangerous?" Monkey asked. He turned his back to them and leveled his M-60. "Me and ol' reliable here will make sure they don't follow. You go with the Captain, Gibbons. You be de man with him. The lieutenant and I will bring up the rear. Now, expedite it out of here."

"I be de woman with him, Petty Officer," HJ said, running toward Duncan.

Four of the hostages who Gibbons had seen being treated from the balcony were draped across the shoulders of four of the other hostages. They passed Duncan in the middle of the crowd, treading their way to wherever Beau was leading them. Duncan had no idea where Beau was taking them, but knew the officer would find the right place to hole up and defend.

From a walkway above, the sound of irate Arabic being shouted traveled over the noise of running boots as Algerian rebels scurried into the warehouse. Unable to clearly see the floor of the warehouse, the Algerian rebels began to fire massive volleys into the area where the hostages had been. Pings reverberated and ricochets bounced as bullets hit all around Duncan. He did a quick survey to make sure all the hostages were out of the confined area before he jumped over the electric cords. He wished he had stepped over. A sharp pain shot through his right knee when he landed, causing him to trip and land on his knee. Gibbons grabbed Duncan under the arm and helped him up. Light was beginning to travel down the high walls of the warehouse as the sun began its day's travel across the hot Saharan sky. They still had about an hour before the shadows were chased from the warehouse.

"What the hell! Gibbons, let me go. If I want a Boy Scout, I'll ask for one."

"But . . . Sure thing, Captain," the second class said, releasing Duncan, shaking his head slightly, and grinning. A bullet hit the petty officer in the shoulder, spinning the SEAL around twice before he hit the floor.

Duncan grabbed Gibbons and pulled him up. Gibbons shook his head a couple of times and pulled away. Blood ran down his left arm. "I'm okay, Captain. Flesh wound," Gibbons said through clenched teeth.

"You all right. Can you make it?" Duncan asked, releasing the man.

Gibbons nodded and started off after the rescued hostages and other SEALs. Duncan watched him bounce off the side of a stack of palleted barrels. He wasn't all right, but Dunan hoped he could last until the Marines got here.

HJ and Monkey squatted on either side of the makeshift passage between two stacks of boxes. Gibbons disappeared between them. Duncan followed.

"Go ahead, Captain. We've got the rear," HJ said.

"Don't, HJ. Come on."

The three entered the maze, traveling only a few feet before an explosion behind them sent them flying off their feet. Shrapnel, pieces of boxes, crates, lamps, and other debris from the hostage area whirled outward like small bullets to maim, mutilate, and kill. The blast hurled HJ into Duncan, knocking the two of them down. Monkey landed on top of them. Deadly debris sailed over them, heading upward and outward. Duncan glanced ahead and saw no sign of the wounded Gibbons.

Monkey pulled himself up and rolled HJ over. Her eyes were shut and her head hung loosely to the right. Duncan's ears rang with the pressure from the blast. He could see Monkey's lips moving, but the words seemed garbled.

"Captain, you all right?"

Duncan touched the side of his head, slapping his ears a couple of times. He understood the question. His hearing was coming back. Duncan forced himself up, his back braced against the crate behind him. He nodded to the big SEAL. He opened and closed his mouth a couple of times feeling the air equalize behind his eardrums. Duncan whirled his carbine to the right as running footsteps caught his attention. A rebel appeared suddenly over Monkey, who was helping HJ to her feet. Duncan shot him. The carbine noise disappeared amid the heavy gunfire originating from the walkway above them.

Duncan surveyed the area behind Monkey and ahead where the tail end of the fleeing hostages and SEALs had disappeared. The area behind them where the hostages had been held was covered in a fine cloud of dust. The explosion had not been that huge, but it would have been sufficient to kill most of the hostages and the SEALs if they had remained in the area. The tangy, acrid smell of cordite stung his nostrils.

A moan escaped from HJ, her eyelids flickered, and then they opened. "What happened?" she asked, her voice slightly slurred.

"You got knocked out, ma'am," Monkey said, handing her carbine to her. He released Lieutenant McDaniels. She weaved a little but remained upright. Monkey reached over and picked up his M-60 with his free hand and shoved the stunned officer down the passageway. "That way, HJ," he said.

Shouts in Arabic rose again as the dust began to settle from the explosion.

"Captain, you all right?"

"I'm fine, Monkey," Duncan said, pushing himself away from the crates behind him. "HJ, how are you?" he asked the stunned SEAL as she moved down the path.

"I'm okay, Captain. Let's get out of here."

She sounded okay; she just didn't look it.

Monkey peeped around the corner, his eyes searching the darkness for movement. "You lead, Captain. I'll bring up the rear." Ahead, HJ had stopped. She was bent over a body. It was Gibbons. The blast must have caught the point SEAL.

Duncan picked up Gibbons's carbine and handed it to HJ and shouted for her to keep going. He grabbed Gibbons's arm. Monkey rushed up and grabbed the other one. The two lifted Gibbons a couple of feet off the ground and, with his feet dragging, hurried after HJ. Gibbons's boots dragged along the concrete floor.

"I've got him, Monkey. Guard our backs."

Monkey released Gibbons and, assured that Duncan had the man, he turned around and began to walk backward, the heavy M-60 held in his right hand, pointing back the way they had come. Duncan moved forward, dragging the unconscious Gibbons with him. HJ kept slightly ahead of the three men, watching the floor for trip wires, and ahead for more rebels. Gibbons moaned.

"That's it, Gibs," Monkey said. "Don't let the bastards get you down. What would yer mom say?"

Duncan tightened his grip.

"Is he all right, Captain?"

"He don't look all right, Monkey." Blood covered the entire right side of Gibbons's face.

"Naw, Captain. Gibbons is okay. He's moaning, and that's his way of bitching when he's working up a good anger. Those rebels ain't gonna like what they gonna see when old Gibs wakes up."

"You and Gibs close friends, Monkey?" Duncan asked. He stopped for a moment to shift his grip on the unconscious SEAL.

"You might say that, Captain. Grew up together in Newark; went to school together, except when I had to do the eighth grade twice; and even dated the same girls sometimes, though we tried not to date the same one at the same time. I'd say we're more like brothers than friends. Lord, I don't know what I would do if he died. God, his family would never forgive me."

"And I'm not gonna forgive you if you don't put me down, ya bastard," Gibbons mumbled, thinking Monkey was dragging him. "Give me a second to stand on my feet, and I'll walk."

Duncan released the wounded SEAL.

Gibbons stumbled, he was caught by Monkey, he pulled away, and then he shuffled forward a couple of steps before he started to fall again.

"Here, Gibbons," Duncan said. "Lean on me. We don't have far to go, but we need to catch up with the others."

"Duncan, where are you?" came Beau's voice from the brick radio strapped to his web belt.

Duncan pressed the Transmit button. Before he could talk, Monkey's M-60 blasted away. "Here they come, boss!"

"Beau, where are you?" Duncan shouted.

"Duncan, your machine gun is to our right. I have a defensive position against the wall, but we're trapped here until the Marines arrive. Come straight ahead. We'll be waiting."

More short blasts from the heavy M-60 rocked the confines of the warehouse as Monkey walked slowly backward. He glanced behind to see how much of a separation he had with Duncan, HJ, and Gibbons. The glance saved their lives. Out of the corner of his eye, he saw a grenade sail over the boxes toward them.

"Grenade!" he shouted, reached up with his left hand, caught the grenade in midair, and with a strong backhand toss sent it sailing back the way it came. "Hit the deck!" he hollered as he dove to the cement floor. Duncan and Gibbons were already there to meet him, their eyes tightly closed.

The grenade exploded in the air. Screams of pain mixed with Arabic expletives erupted from several yards away.

"I don't know what they were saying, but I doubt it was songs of praise," Monkey said.

"Let's go!" Duncan urged. "Run, Monkey. Gibbons, move your ass." Now was the time to beat feet, while the grenade slowed the rebel advance. "HJ!" he shouted. Where did she go?

"Here, boss!" she replied, standing ahead of them and motioning them forward.

The SEALs dashed between the warehouse supplies as fast as Gibbons's injuries allowed. HJ led the way, faster than Duncan thought prudent but slower than he wished they could go. Duncan realized that in this maze they could run right past Beau and the hostages and never know it. He also hoped that Gibbons's condition was more of a light concussion than any major life-threatening event. The shoulder wound was another factor, but he couldn't tell if the man was still bleeding.

Duncan rounded a crate and came to a three-way fork. HJ stood there. She looked at Duncan. "Which way, boss?"

Duncan pressed the brick. "Beau, where are you?"

"Duncan, I have not the slightest idea of where the hell I am. Where are you?"

"Shit, Beau. Shout or scream or do something!" Duncan released the Transmit button. Then came Beau's voice, breaking through the noise of the gunfire.

"Duncan, is this shouting loud enough? Do you think everyone can hear it?" Beau shouted.

The shout seemed to originate from the left.

Duncan pointed to the left passage. "Come on!"

An explosion ripped through the area behind them, the same place where Monkey had grabbed the grenade and lobbed it back. Thirty feet later, they stumbled into where Beau had positioned the SEALs surrounding the rescued hostages. The hostages were shoving crates and boxes forward, building a barrier to fight behind.

"Oh, there you are, Captain. We've been expecting you."

Bud ran up and helped HJ take Gibbons and guide the dazed petty officer to the back of the area, bracing him in a sitting position with his back against the warehouse wall. They handed the SEAL his carbine.

"Beau, what's the plan?"

"Duncan, you don't have one?" The two looked at each other and grinned. "Just like Pentagon duty."

"I am beginning to feel the fatigue, boss. Where are the Marines?"

As if hearing his question, their bricks erupted. "Duncan, this is Bulldog. Are you ready? We are in position. Tell me yours."

Duncan pulled his compass from his vest pocket and glanced at the reading. "Bulldog, we are against the northeast side of the warehouse. Directly against the bulkhead—the wall. We are under attack, and your presence would be greatly appreciated."

"Roger, stand by one. We will be entering—" the brick clicked off. Several seconds passed before the radio came back on. "From the north end. Time check, Duncan. I have ten after."

Duncan looked down at his watch. The crystal was shattered. "Beau, do the time check."

Beau looked at his watch and clicked his brick. "We have ten after."

"We'll be coming in hot, two minutes at my mark. Mark!"

Monkey and McDonald's M-60s erupted simultaneously as Algerian rebels burst from four different openings between the warehouse supplies. Algerian rebels ran along a balcony walkway along the other side of the warehouse; the familiar shouts of *"Allah akbar"* accompanying their approach. Fire from their automatic weapons rained down on the SEALs and hostages. Monkey raised his heavy machine gun and sent a wave of bullets along the metal balcony. Sharp chimes echoed as his bullets hit the steel railing and walkway from where the rebel sharpshooters were trying to get into position. Screams from the wounded and dying rebels followed. Duncan thought he saw a body fall, but it was hard to tell in the poorly lit spaces, even with daylight increasing as the sun rose.

The distance from the supplies to the haphazardly arranged perimeter where the hostages continued to shove supplies and material to build a makeshift wall gave them about twenty feet of open space, not enough to hold out against a concerted attack. Duncan looked at his watch, forgetting it was broken.

"Any moment now, Duncan!" Beau shouted.

"Now!" came the command from the brick.

Duncan gestured to Monkey and McDonald. "Quick, back behind the boxes!" he commanded as he and Beau jumped over the perimeter defense the hostages had built.

The sound of an explosion outside the warehouse and behind them drew their attention.

"We're inside, Duncan! Where the hell are you?"

Duncan grabbed his brick. "Bulldog, you're not inside the warehouse we're in. Did you use an explosion to get inside?"

"No, dammit, we're Marines. I used a goddamn tank! I don't want to run over your ass."

"You're behind us somewhere. Sounded like to our northeast."

"Hold out, Duncan. We're moving now. We're in the wrong warehouse. There's nothing here; just empty space."

Rebels poured out again from the four passageways leading toward the makeshift barrier as they mounted a new attack. Duncan whipped up his carbine and slipped the setting to automatic. He blasted away, firing toward the oncoming waves. Beau slid up beside him, raised his carbine and, with his back touching Duncan's, fired at those coming through the far side. The M-60s of Monkey and McDonald raised the decibel level within the warehouse. To Duncan's right, HJ stood, exposing herself to the rebels. She was screaming, tears running down her cheeks, but the noise of the firefight obliterated her words. Her carbine moved back and forth rapidly in large, sweeping motions, mowing the rebels down.

"We hear the fighting, Duncan! My recce squad has you located. Two minutes. Give me two minutes!" Bulldog transmitted, but the noise of the firefight drowned out the transmission, and no one heard it.

Three Algerian rebels jumped the boxes. Beau shot one. The other two whipped their weapons around toward him. McDonald's M-60 filled the two with bullets, causing them to jerk like puppets as they fell back across the boxes. An Algerian rebel dodged through the fighting, stopped, and drew back to throw a grenade. HJ shot him and then she dove to other side of the barrier. The grenade dropped from the lifeless hands to bounce off a nearby crate.

"Grenade!" shouted Bud as the device bounced a couple of more times before sliding off the crate and into the secured area.

"Get down!" he shouted just as the grenade exploded, sending him flying backward into the crowd of terrified hostages.

Several of the Americans pushed him upright. "Christ, I'm getting tired of this job," Bud mumbled before passing out.

Another grenade sailed over the heads of the SEALs to land in the middle of the hostages. A silver-haired lady who could have passed for a small-town librarian scooped it up and, with an underhand pitch, tossed it over the heads of the SEALs into one of the passageways from where the rebels were attacking. The grenade exploded, killing several rebels and stopping the attack from the center, but rebels continued to pour out of the left and right passages to be mowed down by the M-60s.

Monkey's was the first to run out of ammo. "That's it, Captain." He turned to discover Gibbons crawling toward him. "Get back, Gibs. This is no place for you."

"I'm out, too!" McDonald shouted, tossing his M-60 to the side and drawing his pistol.

"Screw you, Monkey. You always did want all the fun; ain't no way you're stopping me." He lifted his carbine and shot a rebel who appeared behind Monkey.

"Keep your eyes forward, Monkey. I'm coming."

Monkey pulled his knife and waited.

An almighty crash shook the building as the north end of the warehouse exploded. The rebel attack seemed to stop in mid-stride, with them looking toward the noise before fleeing back into the logistical warehouse maze that masked the floor. The primal *"Ooyah"* yells of United States Marines in full battle gear filled the warehouse as hundreds of them rushed through the opening. The warehouse supplies blocked the view of the Marines, but the fighting sounded intense as Marine riflemen fought hand to hand against Algerian rebels attempting to flee the combat. Devil Dogs were not for them.

Duncan turned to HJ and Beau. "Chief Wilcox," he said. "If the rebels try to escape through the tunnel, they'll overrun him."

Duncan grabbed his brick. "Chief, you hear me?"

"I not only hear you, sir, but I see you."

"They're coming your way, Chief. Get out of there."

"Already out of there, Captain. Look to your left, along the wall."

From a small, maybe two-foot-wide passage running along the side of the warehouse, Chief Wilcox and Pauline King strolled into the perimeter.

"Chief, how did you get here?"

"Elevator, Captain." He pointed to the southern end of the warehouse. "I watched everything from up there, and when I saw the firefight start, I knew we couldn't stay there long. I heard the Marines preparing to enter, and, knowing Marines, I knew they would do it in such a way they'd either piss them off or scare the shit out of them. It doesn't take a rocket scientist to figure out that if you had them trapped here and the Marines had them trapped there, there was a damn good chance I would prove only a small bump in the road when they decided to leave via the only other exit. I did as you ordered and made preparations for the two of us to leave via the sewer, but—Christ!—Captain, I've had it with being underground."

"Glad you made it, Chief."

"So when I heard the Marines were coming and saw the odds you faced over here on this side of the warehouse, I started looking around and discovered this old warehouse had a small elevator on the right side. You went down the stairs on the left side. So, Pauline and I, when it became obvious we might be having company, took the elevator, followed by a leisurely stroll along the side of the warehouse until we reached here. No rebels, no problems, no sewers."

The fighting began to taper off. The sound of military English began to fill the warehouse. They all listened as the fight moved across the warehouse, and they prepared to repel the Algerians if the Marines forced them this way.

"Ahoy, the SEALs!" came a shout from inside the warehouse.

"Over here!" Beau shouted back.

From the passages where only moments ago Algerian rebels had attempted to overrun the SEALs and hostages, United States Marines emerged. Leading them was Colonel Bulldog Stewart, the right sleeve on his cammies torn in several places and blood running down from a slight wound on his left arm.

Duncan stood, followed by the other SEALs.

Bulldog smiled and walked over to him as his Marines moved among the hostages. He shook Duncan's hand. "Congratulations, Captain James. Well done! Sorry we ran a little late."

Following the Marine riflemen came several United States Navy corpsmen who moved among the SEALs and hostages, assessing their condition and marking medical priorities for their removal. Duncan was thankful when he saw one of the corpsmen working on Gibbons. Another was holding up fingers in front of a conscious Bud, who was holding his head and trying to tell the corpsman how many fingers he saw. A third corpsman ran up to Colonel Stewart. "Colonel, let me see that wound."

Bulldog pulled his arm away. "It'll keep, Corpsman. You take care of the civilians."

"I think if you had been any later, Bulldog, this"—Duncan waved his hands across the perimeter—"would have been a different story."

"Captain," HJ said, sliding down to a sitting position on the cement floor, resting her back against a crate. "Think we can go home now?"

"Ah, Commander," Beau said, nudging her gently on the leg with his combat boot. "You'd think you didn't like this action adventure we've been on."

"Fine for you to say. You don't have all these nanorobots in you. You're not invincible."

They laughed, the adrenaline draining from their combat. "You know what else those nanorobots can do?"

Beau shook his head. "No. What?"

She leaned down and whispered in his ear. Duncan grinned as Beau's face turned a scarlet red.

"No way."

"Yes, *way*," she replied. "And I may ask them to do it again tonight."

"Captain, this woman is one sick cookie," Beau said, hooking his thumb at the laughing HJ.

"Duncan," Bulldog interrupted. "We need to load up and move out. We're pulling out ASAP from Algiers. The first group of Marines have already left for the Fleet."

Why were they moving so quickly to pull out of Algiers? Yesterday, when they entered the sewers, Bulldog said it would take at least a week to commence evacuating, unless some drastic event required them to step up the timetable.

"What's going on, Bulldog? I thought we'd be here another week at least."

"I'll tell you as we move, Duncan, but we have to move. But it's all good news, Shipmate."

Bulldog turned to the Marines around him. "Let's get these Americans loaded and out of here!" he shouted. Then he turned to the hostages, who were being led toward the gaping hole at the end of the warehouse. "Next stop, ladies and gentlemen, is the United States Sixth Fleet, waiting offshore for you."

An emotional cheer erupted from the civilians as they moved forward, following the young Marine riflemen. Many of the rescued hugged, touched, or wanted to touch the United States Marines and the Navy SEALs who had saved them from the terrorists and eventual death. The shock of their captivity would come crashing down around them later, after they arrived within the safety of the ships, sailors, and marines that made up the United States Sixth Fleet.

# THIRTEEN

⚓

**"CAPTAIN, TWENTY SECONDS TO IMPACT,"** THE TACTICAL
action officer said to Buc-Buc. The two radar returns on the
screen showed the two extended-range surface-to-air Standard
Missiles launched by the USS *Spruance* on a collision course
with the Libyan ballistic missile.

Buc-Buc detected a slight tremble in the TAO's voice. *Remain calm.* He flipped a switch on the arm of his chair, and the
scope picture appeared on the overhead screen. He leaned back.
*Ninety-degree approach,* he said to himself. *A crossing shot. A
hard one to hit.* The least mistake, the tiniest miscalculation in
trajectory, a gale gust of wind at the crucial moment, and the
ballistic missile would shoot past the *Spruance* missiles. Anything could happen and, if it did, there was little anyone could
do to stop that missile from hitting its target in Italy. He
couldn't fire a backup salvo because if the *Spruance* missiles
missed but exploded close enough, they could alter the flight
profile sufficiently to cause anything he threw up to miss also.
*Hue City* would have to wait, and waiting was something awfully hard for him to do. He realized he was drumming his fingers on the arm of the chair and stopped.

The Libyan cruise missile was slightly over one hundred
nautical miles north of Tripoli. On current course, the target

was either Sigonella, Sicily—the combined Italian/U.S. NATO airfield already bombed once by Libya—or Naples. Naples had not been bombed from the air since World War II. In his mind, he saw the morning bumper-to-bumper rush-hour traffic already pouring into the narrow and congested streets of this major Italian port. The deaths would be incalculable if this missile reached Naples.

"Our solution?" he asked. He lifted his hand and neatly rubbed his chin. Not only did he need to remain calm, but he had to appear calm. Display professionalism. Act as if he had done this numerous times. Practice what he had been preaching to his officers and crew for the past year of his command. A professional crew was a quiet, methodical, well-trained crew.

"Take us right up to the part where we press the firing button, Commander. I want to launch immediately if *Spruance* misses."

"We are prepared to fire three seconds after a miss, Captain."

"Good work, Commander."

The tactical action officer flipped his microphone over his mouth and began to review the launch process again for two more SAMs against the ballistic missile traveling slightly below the speed of sound. It was an almost impossible hit if the *Spruance* missiles missed. Especially, if they had to recalculate the trajectory because of a near miss.

"I have video merge on my scope," reported the air search operator over the net, his words reaching Buc-Buc through the headpiece.

He glanced up at the displays surrounding the CIC, returned to the air search one, and waited—crossed his fingers—for the video to disappear. If the radar video disappeared, it indicated the missile was destroyed.

"Video fading," added the air search operator.

Buc-Buc released his breath, unaware until now that he had been holding it. He knew that if the *Spruance* solution had failed, their attempt had little chance of successfully destroying the missile. They would have tried, but it would have been a Hail Mary shot.

One hundred twenty-seven nautical miles east of Surface Action Group Tango Foxtrot, the first *Spruance* extended-range Standard Missile exploded when its nose radar registered twenty meters from the Libyan missile that was passing from the south. The warhead did not need to hit the target to destroy it. It had a proximity warhead, designed to explode when its radar return reached certain intensity. The explosion of the extended-range surface-to-air Standard Missile hurled whirling pieces of metal like an expanding buzz saw that cut into and through the Libyan Al-Fatah III cruise missile. The resulting destruction at thirty-two thousand feet activated the aerosol warhead, releasing trillions of anthrax spores into the atmosphere. The roiling east-to-west summer wind at that altitude began to disperse the descending biological agent westward across the Mediterranean Sea and toward the operating area where the USS *Hue City* and USS *Spruance* sailed. Some of the spores traveled a faster route, riding the path created by falling pieces of metal headed for the seas beneath where the two missiles had destroyed each other.

**COLONEL ALQAHIRAY SLID DOWN FROM HIS CHAIR. "I** ordered those missiles fired! Why haven't they been?"

"Colonel, I am clicking and clicking, but nothing is happening!"

"Then move to another console!" he screamed, jerking the soldier by the collar out of his chair and shoving him aside. "Stupid!" he shouted to the soldier, who scrambled to his feet and hurried to the other side of the console array, away from the screaming Alqahiray.

Alqahiray ignored the frightened soldier, already turning to another operator. "Fire the missiles!" he ordered the man seated in front of him.

"Sir, I have tried. I cannot. The system is locked. When I click on the execute button, the screen scrolls up and around for a few seconds before stopping. Then it locks for a minute before I can shift the mouse arrow again."

"Am I surrounded by traitors and imbeciles? How can you tell them apart?" he screamed at Sergeant Adib.

Sergeant Adib drew his Beretta, his finger slipping onto the trigger as he held the weapon alongside his leg, pointing down.

"Colonel," Major Bahar said from behind the two men. "With your permission, we can bring the system down and reload it."

"How long will that take, Major Bahar?" Alqahiray asked, bringing his face within inches of the older officer.

Without moving his face or showing fear, the career Libyan soldier answered, "At least one hour, most likely two."

"I don't have two hours, you imbecile!"

"I am sorry, my Colonel, but it is the only suggestion I have. Hopefully, the reload will restore the computer program."

A thin thread of spittle ran out of the corner of the Libyan leader's mouth. "Two hours . . . two hours? I want it done in one hour, Bahar, and I am holding you responsible."

"Yes, sir. I have always been responsible."

"You won't be responsible for anything if this doesn't work!"

Sergeant Adib's finger twitched on the trigger, his angry eyes staring at Major Bahar's back.


**THE TEN UH-60 BLACKHAWK HELICOPTERS FLEW OVER** the desert at fifty feet, high enough to avoid sucking sand into the intakes and low enough to avoid radar detection. Each Blackhawk was capable of carrying up to twenty-two fully armed, combat-ready soldiers, but only eight carried troops and then only twelve in each one. One of the other two was a spare in the event they had to abandon a helicopter en route to the operation area. The light combat load of the eight prime choppers gave Colonel Robert "Dusty" A. Cooper the flexibility to double up in the remaining helicopters if they suffered combat or mechanical casualties. The second noncombat helicopter was outfitted as a flying medical clinic. Two doctors and four medical technicians filled the empty space in the rear of the Blackhawk with their medical equipment. Equipment Colonel Cooper hoped he wouldn't need it. Colonel Cooper, Army Ranger and career West Point officer, folded the diagram he had been studying since the helicopters completed air-to-air refueling an hour ago. He wanted no mishaps on this mission due to piss-poor planning. He glanced at his watch. The navigator riding behind the pilots in the cockpit tapped the pilot on the shoulder. Then he turned toward Dusty, smiled, and gave him a thumbs-up before holding up ten fingers. Ten minutes to objective. He checked his M-16 for the thousandth time and made sure the safety was on. His chopper would be one of the first into the hot landing zone. If the other elements in this operation did their job, they would do theirs.

**SERGEANT ADIB PULLED HIS GUN AND FOLLOWED COLONEL** Alqahiray to the operations station responsible for relaying his orders. Two hours had passed since Major Bahar ordered the reloading of the command post servers. The body of the most competent officer in the CP remained in a sitting position against the far wall. The trail of dried blood from the small bullet wound in the center of the forehead ran down the left cheek of the tilted head. The glazed, open eyes of Major Bahar stared sightlessly at nervous soldiers manning the computer consoles.

The Libyan captain jumped to his feet, and beads of sweat ran down the man's face when Alqahiray stopped behind him. The armpits of his shirt were soaked with spreading stains of sweat moving visibly across the front.

"I don't know, Colonel. The computers are still locked up. I keep restarting them, and they work well until I go into an operational program. Then they lock up. They operated better before we reloaded the programs. Colonel, we can't fire the other missiles from here. Our computers have been compromised. The Americans? The French? Maybe even the Italians? I don't know who, but we no longer have control of our systems."

Colonel Alqahiray took the cigarette in his right hand and grabbed the back of the captain's neck. He ground the lit cigarette into the forehead of the man. "You fool! It's not the computer!"

The man screamed from the pain. The smell of burning flesh whiffed around the three.

Colonel Alqahiray released the Libyan captain. The man fell back against the console, bouncing off it as he tripped and fell to the floor.

"You are part of Walid's plan against me. I am surrounded by traitors!"

Alqahiray reached behind him and jerked the gun out of Sergeant Adib's hand, leaned down, and before the captain could remove his hands from the cigarette burn, shot him through the hands and through the head. The back of the head blew off, scattering brain and blood over the operations behind the unfortunate victim.

The Libyan officer who was preparing to report the destruction of the second missile clamped his teeth together and moved slowly away from the group, the news of the missile kept confined inside him.

"You!" Alqahiray shouted, pointing to the officer. Movement near the steel doors caught his attention.

He raised the pistol and shot Major Ahsan Hammad Maloof, former electronic warfare officer and, until the bullet hit him, Alqahiray's aide. The bullet caught the fleeing officer in the small of his back, shattering the spine, which stopped the bullet from entering the abdomen. The scream of pain from the wounded man continued even as Maloof pulled himself toward the door. Across the room, frightened soldiers stood up, looking at each other. Panic erupted in the room. Like a herd of stampeding cattle, the remaining operators rushed the door, trampling Maloof as they fled the belowground operations room deep within the command post. The aide's screaming stopped abruptly. Alqahiray calmly fired into the crowd until the nine-shot pistol clicked empty. The bodies of the dead and wounded trapped the steel doors open.

Sergeant Adib stepped calmly into the light. "Colonel, it's over, sir. We need to go."

Alqahiray pointed the empty pistol at the one person who had stood by him loyally throughout these past few days. "Another Walid conspirator." He pulled the trigger several times, ignoring the clicking of the hammer against the empty cartridge.

Sergeant Adib reached forward, holding a fresh cartridge in his hands. "Here, my Colonel," he said.

Alqahiray jerked the cartridge from Adib's hand. The empty cartridge fell to the rubber-coated deck and bounced under the nearby computer console. Alqahiray shoved the full cartridge into the handle of the pistol. He pointed it at Sergeant Adib.

After a few seconds, Alqahiray lowered the pistol and glanced around the room. With the exception of himself and Adib, only the groans of several wounded identified others still alive in the operations room.

"Why, Sergeant Adib? This was a great enterprise. One that would have restored Arab greatness. It would have brought prosperity and power to our people. It would have showed

America that no matter what they do, the Muslim nation will rise and keep rising until we control the world."

The sound of gunfire from the corridor filled the room, but neither man turned toward it, even as the fight edged closer. Sergeant Adib stuck his hand out for the pistol. Colonel Alqahiray looked at the weapon in his hand briefly before handing it to the sergeant.

"Everything I did, I did for my people," Alqahiray said, knowing he was lying but trying to convince himself of his sincerity. Maybe he believed his own lies. "If not for the conspiracy and intrigues of those I trusted, today would have seen a great Islamic empire rise out of Jihad Wahid. *Jihad Wahid— Holy War One.* Only I could have accomplished it, but what happened, Sergeant Adib? The Chinese promised to provide us support but only gave us enough to start a war here so they could encourage their Korean ally to attack South Korea. We were fodder to hold the Americans captive in the Mediterranean while they absorbed the prosperous South Korea. The Americans should not be here. The Sixth Fleet should be gone. It should never have been in the Mediterranean." His head dropped as he reluctantly accepted the failure of his plan and the futility of continuing. "This is not an American sea; it is an Arab sea or even a European one; but not an American."

Shouts from outside and the firefight ongoing between whoever approached the operations room and remnants of Sergeant Adib's Special Forces grew louder.

Adib stepped away from Colonel Alqahiray and picked up an AK-47 propped against the railing of the observation platform. "Sir, I have to see what is going on," he said, moving toward the steel doors and the bodies blocking it.

"Give me your pistol, Sergeant. At least I will go down fighting as a soldier." Adib handed Alqahiray the Beretta just as the firefight reached the bodies at the steel door. *"Allah akbar,"* he said to the sergeant.

**"ADMIRAL," COMMANDER BAILEY INTERRUPTED. "ADMI-**
ral Sir Ledderman-Thompson sends his respects and requests permission for his battle group to join the United States Sixth Fleet."

"Where are they?"

"Northwest of our position about fifty nautical miles, closing at twenty knots."

"The admiral still on the HMS *Invincible*?" Admiral Devlin asked, referring to the aging British Harrier aircraft carrier.

"I presume so, sir. It was the call sign of the *Invincible* that reported."

Admiral Pete Devlin looked away briefly from the long-range displays. "Give the admiral my compliments and tell him we welcome the Royal Navy to the battle group. And then, Commander Bailey, create a two-carrier battle group layout to take us through the Strait of Sicily and into the central Mediterranean . . . if we have to go through."

"Yes, sir, Admiral. We are about three hours from the Strait."

Admiral Pete Devlin acknowledged the status report and urged Commander Bailey to incorporate the Royal Navy battle group into Sixth Fleet operations as soon as possible. The presence of the six British warships would double the size of the *Stennis* battle group.

"Yes, sir, Admiral. One other thing, Admiral, Captain Holman, the French are closing on Algiers. They are moving their carrier along with several French amphibious ships toward the Algerian capital."

Pete Devlin stroked his chin. "Have they told us their intentions?"

"Yes, sir. Admiral, you may not like this, and it could be a language misunderstanding . . . but they said they are replacing Sixth Fleet since we have left the area."

"We haven't left the area. We still have the *Nassau* Amphibious Task Force offshore!"

"And, the USS *Nassau* has about the same number of aircraft as the *Foch*."

"About the same age, too. They do use the Super Etendards."

"Enough," Devlin said. "We'll worry about the French later. They're the most arrogant ally a friend could want; sometimes I think they'd make better enemies."

"The British would agree with you," Dick Holman said.

Commander Bailey excused himself and hurried off to incorporate the Royal Navy into the Sixth Fleet battle group, putting the French actions in the back of his mind. The commander of the Amphibious Task Force would have to worry about them, and as long they didn't interfere with the withdrawal of American forces, which had started, then there should be no problems. The French-American relationship had always been one akin to sibling rivalry, with the French always jealously guarding actions that might suggest they were anything but completely independent. On the other hand, it never ceased to amaze the French why so few recognized their inherent right to lead.

"When will we know if Operation Tangle Bandit worked?" Dick Holman asked as he nodded to a sailor standing across from him and pointed to an area on the chart. Dick waited while the sailor pushed his sound-powered phone button, asking the person on the other end for the winds in the area where Dick Holman had pointed, the same area where the first Libyan missile was shot down.

Pete Devlin shrugged his shoulders and looked across the compartment to where General Lewis stood talking to Kurt Lederman. "Whenever the general tells us or when Kurt decides to slip us a tidbit of information. You'd think he'd remember that he is my intelligence officer, not Army General Leutze's, and when this is over with, he will become my intell officer again."

"Admiral, if you don't mind me asking, how long have you known about this operation?"

Dick Holman looked at the sailor with the sound-powered phone set while he waited for Admiral Devlin to respond. "Get me the winds for the area."

The sailor reached forward with his pencil and ruler and drew a small inch-long line with an arrowhead leading from the shootdown area along a course of two nine five. Along the line, he wrote the caption "10 knots-true."

Dick Holman nodded at the sailor, who stepped slightly back from the two men to where his body from the shoulders up disappeared into the shadows.

"A week, Dick. I would have told you, but it was compartmented. More compartmented than most other secret operations I have been involved in."

"Let's hope they all live."

"Admiral, Captain Holman," Commander Bailey said, approaching the two men. "The SEALs have recovered the hostages. Colonel Stewart has initiated the second phase of the operation. We should know something soon."

The assistant TAO approached the group. "Sirs, Task Force Tango Foxtrot reports destruction of second missile by *Spruance*." He leaned forward and made a small diamond on the chart. "Right here, according to the long-range display, Admiral."

General Lewis and Captain Kurt Lederman worked their way into the group. "Good. With both of those missiles out of the way, we need to take out the remainder. How long before we launch our attack, gentlemen, or am I the only one curious?" General Lewis asked.

"General, we need several more minutes to coordinate the launches. The B-52s have already turned toward their launch zones—"

"Well, I am glad the Air Force is doing something right."

"General, with all due respect," Admiral Devlin said irritably, "this is a joint operation, and we are working to make the launches coordinated and correct. If we hurry this, we run the risk of missing or even worse killing those who have nothing to do with this small war."

**TEN MINUTES HAD PASSED SINCE THE SECOND LIBYAN** ballistic missile had been destroyed. The whipping winds of altitude had dispersed the anthrax spores across a broad front of two hundred miles as they descended through the clouds into the lower atmosphere where the winds changed slightly to a more northwesterly heading. Below them, over one hundred merchant ships closed upon themselves as they approached the narrow Strait of Sicily between Tunisia and Sicily. Directly in the path of this invisible swath of deadly spores lay the USS *Hue City* and the USS *Spruance*, steaming in a large MODLOC as they waited for further instructions.

Directly below the missile flight path, parts of it fell, spreading deadly cargo in a ten-mile cone across the surface of the Mediterranean. The roll-on roll-off automobile carrier *Maru Caracas* steamed through the cone, unaware of the trillions of spores raining on the exposed decks of this huge ship destined for Livorno, Italy. The fifty-six Asian crewmen who manned the Japanese-owned merchant vessel breathed in the odorless spores as they sailed through the invisible biological rain. The ventilation system of the ship sucked the spores into the interior of the vessel and deep into the cargo holds, where new Nissans and Toyotas waited to be driven off the ship when they docked in twenty-four hours. These anthrax spores would find their way into the interiors of these new cars. By the time the ship docked in Livorno, most of the crewmen would begin to experience flulike symptoms. The captain would be confined to his bunk, each breath a fight. The first officer, assaulted by a raging fever, would dock the ship, slightly bumping the pier as three tugs attempted to steer the huge ship to its berth.

By the time the Italian public health service became aware of the problems on board the *Maru Caracas*, the efficient port services would have already offloaded the cars, driving them directly to a protected storage area fenced off near the customs facility. It would be ten hours after the deadly ship docked before health officials hurried to quarantine it, thinking they were fighting a variant of Asian flu.

Only when the crew members began to die, vital organs shutting down, drowning in their own blood, bringing gushes of dark blood out the mouth and nose, would be the first warning to the doctors that it was anthrax and not a virulent flu they were fighting.

By then, the cars had been loaded on trucks and were scattered throughout the Italian mainland, heading for central distribution points throughout Europe. One by one, dockworkers would come down sick and begin to die. The majority wore work clothes contaminated by the spores and transported them home. Members of many of their families joined the afflicted. Two weeks after the arrival of the *Maru Caracas*, the port of Livorno closed as authorities rushed to clean up the biological agent. Over four hundred civilians around the port died because of the deadly anthrax cargo delivered along with new Nissans and Toyotas.

Fast work by Interpol and the European Union quickly located most of the lorries transporting the infected cars, but not before 150 people, including drivers, were infected along the route of the huge trucks. Along the roads leading from Livorno, many of the spores blew off the vehicles and floated harmlessly to the ground, where the next wind lifted them, blowing the anthrax toward other warm bodies needed to let it grow and mature.

## THE *MARU CARACUS* ROUTE CARRIED HER NORTH OF the USS *Hue City* and USS *Spruance*.

Buc-Buc put the handset back in its holder after congratulating Louise Edwards on the success of the firing. He turned to the TAO, patted him on his back, and then keyed the bridge that he wanted to address the crew. He waited for the boatswain whistle to finish piping over the 1MC before he took the microphone.

"Men and women of *Hue City*, this is the captain speaking. Congratulations on a job well done. Task Force Tango Foxtrot—*Hue City* and *Spruance*—destroyed two ballistic missiles launched from Libya against our forces in Algiers and against either Sicily or Naples to our north. Your dedication to training and keeping this ship in its high state of readiness was directly responsible for that success. Now, we wait for further orders before we can do anything else other than watch for further launches. Any other hostile actions will be met with the complete firepower the USS *Hue City* has to offer. No threat passes our bow. Remember the *Gearing*!"

He clicked off for a moment to take a sip of water. He tweaked his nose as he pushed the Talk button again. "The bad news is that the missile the *Spruance* destroyed may contain the biological agent anthrax. We have fought this enemy before, and all of you know the precautions to take. The winds are flowing east to west toward our position. If there is a biological agent in that missile, then it will reach our area within the next two to three hours. I am ordering all topside watches belowdecks. I want no one topside or outside the skin of the ship. We are setting circle William to ensure all ventilation is secured and are doing everything we can do to protect ourselves. I want all of you who have never had anthrax shots to report to your supervisors so we can start antibiotics. Sailors, great job; now we protect ourselves and wait for further orders. I want everyone in the ship to check your chemical, biological warfare garb. I know they're hot, but better a little hot than taking a chance on breathing anthrax".

The TAO handed Buc-Buc a small note he had hastily scribbled. He read it and continued. "We have just received further orders to launch several Tomahawk missiles within the next few minutes at targets in Libya. Godspeed and His blessing to each one of you as we do our nation's work. I know each of you will do your jobs professionally and competently. Let's roll." He put the microphone down. Several hands clapped in CIC, and even as Buc-Buc, embarrassed, tried to stop it by raising his hands, it rose in tempo. This was not the quiet CIC he envisioned, but the accolade did wonders for his soul.

As quickly as it started, the applause died out and the crew turned to the new task at hand. Buc-Buc looked over the tasking message from CJTF African Force: "At 0800 Zulu, Surface Action Group Tango Foxtrot will commence launch of Tomahawk missiles against the following military targets within the Republic of Barbary and North Africa, formerly known as Libya. . . ." Below the short action order were six geographical coordinates with sequential designations and times for *Hue City* launches. He wondered about the geographical box outlined in the desert south of Tripoli with the warning that no missiles were to be targeted within those coordinates, but his curiosity only lasted seconds as he prepared the ship for action. Zero eight hundred Zulu was the action hour, the action minute. Zulu was the military language for Greenwich mean time, used throughout the United States military to provide one common measurement of time. The ship's clock read zero eight hundred local, one hour ahead of Zulu. They had sixty minutes until launch. The assigned platforms would launch their missiles at staggered intervals designed so the entire missile pack would hit at nearly the same time. Buc-Buc raised his eyebrows when he saw Air Force B-52s included in the operation order. He knew they were scheduled but figured it would take the Air Force another forty-eight hours for them to arrive on station. The B-52 launch box put them about one hundred miles northwest of the *Hue City* and *Spruance*.

"TAO, what is the status on those threat naval targets?" Buc-Buc asked, referring to the enemy warships detected earlier to the south of them.

"They have turned south, sir, and are leaving the area."

"Keep an eye on them, and let me know if they turn north again."

The decision whether to use Tomahawks with their longer

range or the new improved Harpoons with their shorter, inter-mediate range was usually left to his discretion, depending on the distance from the target. This time, the decision was made by Sixth Fleet, who really made up Joint Task Force African Force. The entire attack would be Tomahawks. Tomahawks, with their superior land terrain mapping capability and low flight altitude, reduced the chance of detection until it was too late. The superior targeting computer in its nose also reduced the chance of collateral damage, a Pentagon euphemism for killing civilians. Failing to respect the chance of collateral damage was a sign of a badly planned operation.

Buc-Buc turned to the TAO just as his command master chief handed him his CBW gear along with the bulky gas mask. His attempt to wave the master chief away met with ironclad resistance. Even as he discussed targeting events and maneu-vering requirements with the TAO, Buc-Buc struggled into the CBW gear. He knew he should have been one of the first to don this gear, instead of one of the last.

The command master chief whipped his own gear on before helping the captain. Just what he needed at sea, Buc-Buc thought with a twinge of amusement; here he was, command-ing officer of one of the mightiest warships in the world, hav-ing a mother figure help him dress. His attempt to delay cramming his face into the hot gas mask met with the same in-violate spirit. Two things a good commanding officer needed to be successful, other than himself or herself: an energetic exec-utive officer and a command master chief unafraid to tell him or her what most times he or she would rather never hear. The problem with master chiefs were they made up 1 percent of the entire enlisted force, and someone told them that. They were the best and, unfortunately, they knew that, too.

"TAO, tell *Spruance* to open up our separation to ten miles. I want them off our beam when we fire our missiles."

"Yes, sir, Captain. Starboard or port beam?"

"You decide, TAO. Just give us a separation so our missiles don't interfere with each other's when we launch." He handed the OPORDER—operational order—back to the TAO. "Ac-cording to this, we are doing simultaneous launches from both us and the *Spruance*. It wouldn't look pretty if we both launched six Tomahawks only to have them collide with each

other before they got a mile from us. Let's make sure we have
done everything we can to deconflict our launches."

"Sir, I would recommend a minimum eighteen-mile separation. That will reduce electromagnetic scatter between the nose
cone radars and should—"

"Okay, TAO. Make it so." *Eat your heart out, Jean-Luc
Picard.*

A couple of minutes later, the cruiser turned as *Hue City*
moved farther south, opening the distance between itself and
the USS *Spruance*. Buc-Buc glanced at the surface picture display as the surface operation clicked on the video of *Spruance*.
It showed their sister ship crossing behind the *Hue City*, heading southwest at twenty knots, opening the distance. East of
the ships, the clouds of anthrax spores continued their slow
descent, expanding along the long, tumbling front with the
Mediterranean winds.


**SERGEANT ADIB FIRED HIS AK-47 AT DESERT-CAMOUFLAGED**
soldiers who appeared in the doorway. Firepower from four automatic weapons arrayed against him tore through his body before he could fire a second burst in return.

Alqahiray stared at Adib. No expression registered on his
face. The intensity of the firepower kept the sergeant's body upright as the dead Adib bounced like a disjointed puppet along
the railing behind him, bullets ripping into and through him.
When the firing stopped, the body tumbled forward, landing
facedown on the rubber matting. Blood poured from multiple
wounds, spreading across the floor.

Sergeant Adib's Beretta rested in Alqahiray's right hand
along his leg. Soldier after soldier poured through the door. It
took a few moments before the Libyan leader realized the attackers were shouting in English. What were Walid's traitors
doing speaking English?

Several soldiers kneeled and pointed their automatic
weapons at the Libyan colonel who stood all alone in the command post operations room. He gripped his pistol tighter. Walid
was not going to take him prisoner again.

"Who are you?" he asked, in strongly accented English.

No one answered. Through the doorway stepped a tall,
barrel-chested man with an armed soldier on each side of him.

The helmet with the small microphone pushed upright alongside of it hid most of the man's face. From the walk and the guards with him, Alqahiray knew this was the man in charge.

"Who are you?" he demanded, directing his question to the tall soldier.

The soldier stopped inside the steel door, taking a couple of steps to the side so the light from the hallway wouldn't provide a better outline as a target. The man removed his helmet. Gray hair shaded the sides of the military haircut.

"Colonel," a soldier nearer Alqahiray said. "He has a gun, sir."

"Colonel Alqahiray, drop the weapon."

Alqahiray reached into his left shirt pocket and pulled out a cigarette, all the while keeping the pistol pointing downward along his right leg. He shook the cigarettes out, most falling on the floor before he managed to get one into his mouth. He dropped the remainder of the pack on the floor so he could pull his lighter out. Alqahiray lit the strong, Greek cigarette. The hand with the pistol remained motionless alongside his right pants leg.

"You can tell Walid, the traitor, that he will never succeed," he said, blowing a ring of smoke out as he finished his sentence.

"Sir, I am Colonel Robert Cooper, United States Army. Colonel, please drop the weapon."

Alqahiray lifted the cigarette back to his lips. He hated that his hand shook. *Americans here!* He let out a deep sigh. *So, even here, Americans could come with impunity. What arrogant bastards they are! What infidels! Don't they ever realize when they have lost?* He concentrated on stopping his hand from shaking, afraid they would mistake his anger for fear. He took another deep breath, drawing every bit through the lightly filtered cigarette. If he must die, then let it be remembered as a brave death. The smoke burned slightly.

"No, Colonel. You have no right to be here."

"Sir, you are under arrest as a war criminal. I ask that you drop the weapon. Our orders are to take you dead or alive. The decision rests with you, but we aren't going to stand here waiting for you to make up your mind. We have helicopters and other forces topside. There is no way to escape or to call in further forces. Surrender or . . ." Colonel Robert "Dusty" A.

Cooper, United States Army Ranger, said, leaving the end of the threat unspoken.

"Colonel, you Americans have to learn that the world is not yours. Do you think you can continue to pursue this war of terrorism forever?" he asked venomously. "Killing me is like cutting off the head of a snake that divides into more and more serpents. You can never stop us. One day, America will be destroyed. You know it, I know it, and the rest of the world knows it. You just refuse to admit it. From here, more serpents will grow."

"Colonel, I have no intention of taking you to America, if that is what worries you. You are being taken to Base Butler to stand trial before a military tribunal. At that time, you can use anything you want in your defense."

Alqahiray shook his head. "You fool, you fool. Do you really think I would submit myself? The Arab world? My country? To such a fair? No, I think we both know what I have to do. It is what a man of honor must do." Alqahiray brought the pistol up fast, pressed it against his head, and pulled the trigger. A bullet from an M-16 hit him in the shoulder at the same time. Several other American soldiers fired.

"Cease fire!" Colonel Cooper shouted. "Cease fire!"

"Damn!" the soldier nearest Alqahiray said, as brain parts and blood splattered the floor and consoles near him, some hitting his uniform and face.

"Damn it!" Colonel Cooper said, his lips pressed tightly.

The sergeant major of the operation walked up to Dusty Cooper. "Think it's true, sir? Killing him will grow more terror cells? What did he say? Something about cutting off the head only grows more and more serpents."

"Yeah, Sergeant Major. That may be true, but they're smaller serpents and a lot easier to kill."

He walked around the still-operating computer consoles to the body of the fanatic who had sent the entire North African coast descending into chaos. The man who started the events that threatened NATO and sent America into another Korean War was dead. He stuck his combat boot under the man's body and rolled it over. The eyes of the Libyan leader hid in the cavernous shadows of the sockets. Dusty could not tell whether they were open or not. He squatted beside the body to pull the pistol from the dead grip. He reached over and ripped the embossed name tag from the top of the right-side pocket. Dusty stood, looked around the room, then back down at the dead man below him.

"I guess honor is measured different ways, Colonel," he mumbled to the dead Alqahiray.

"Sergeant Major, cut his ear off so our bosses can confirm he's dead. Let's go home, boys. Between rescuing those Marines the other week and sneaking in the Libyan back door this week, it's time to go home. Captain," he said, motioning to a thin Ranger standing near the door. "Get topside and give headquarters a situation report. Sergeant, you and the other two military intelligence guys take what you need from here, but make it snappy. The longer we remain, the more likely the Libyans may get up the nerve to try to regain their command and control headquarters before we get out. When that happens, we'll have a chance to see those vintage MiG fighters we heard about."

**LIKE A BROAD WEATHER FRONT MOVING SLOWING ACROSS** the sea, the anthrax spores reached sea level. Some fell into the Mediterranean, floating on top of the salt water while most, whipped up and down by the east wind, continued moving west toward the operations area where the USS *Hue City* and USS *Spruance* maneuvered.

Buc-Buc leaned against the captain's chair in the Combat Information Center, the aroma of the fresh, steaming coffee whiffing around him from the cup the CIC supervisor handed him a couple of minutes ago.

"Combat, Engineering; is the captain there?" came the call from the 12MC box to the right of the chair.

Buc-Buc reached over and flipped the Talk lever. "Go ahead, CHENG," he said, using the familiar Navy acronym for chief engineer.

"Captain, Circle William set, and we are ready to commence saltwater wash down," CHENG reported, her North Carolina nasal twang drawing out the word *commence*.

Buc-Buc pushed the gas mask to the side. CIC looked as if it was manned by a bunch of clumsy aliens trying to operate human buttons, levers, and handles. The military CBW gear was not made for looks or to wear for a long period. *You could stop teenage pregnancy by making military CBC uniforms mandatory wear for high school.* The very thing that protected the wearer from exposure—its impenetrable nature—also created a risk of heat stroke. He might have jumped the gun on ordering the ship into the gear too early. Setting the ship material condition at Circle William shut down every ventilation shaft, every fan, every air conditioner with a purpose of providing fresh air. The only machinery noises were the small units designed to cool the hot electronics that were the heart of a warship.

"CHENG, commence saltwater wash down and keep it going until I tell you different."

"Aye, aye, sir."

"TAO," Buc-Buc said. "Order *Spruance* to commence saltwater wash down. What is her position, course, and speed?"

"Yes, sir," he said, grabbing the red phone from its rest. The TAO pressed the Push to Talk button and over the speaker the electronic tonal oscillations preceding the secure mode filled the immediate area.

The TAO reached over, rolled the mouse embedded in the metal console, and clicked on the *Spruance* video return. As he talked with *Spruance*, he reached over, touched Buc-Buc, and pointed to the overhead display. The information displayed alongside the *Spruance* video showed the destroyer southwest of the *Hue City* on a course of one two zero at twelve knots. Rather than disturb the TAO, Buc-Buc reached forward and clicked on the *Hue City* to reveal his own Aegis-class cruiser on a course of one two zero at twelve knots. He ran a distance line from the *Hue City* to the *Spruance*. They had a twenty-one-mile separation. Their targets were in eastern Libya, which explained the southeasterly course he had ordered.

He picked up the coffee mug and took a deep draught of the fresh brew. Nothing was finer than a fresh cup of Navy coffee made for no other reason than the person making it wanted to do so. Never order a mess specialist to make a cup of coffee if you were the only one wanting it. To do so invited all kinds of abuses to that cup and that coffee. Abuses Buc-Buc made sure he never thought about.

He put the half cup of coffee back beside his chair. Buc-Buc pushed in the bridge button on the 12MC and held the Talk lever down. "Bridge, Captain here; I may have put our crew into the masks too soon. You heard the CHENG. Circle William is set, and we are commencing saltwater wash down. We should be good. Go ahead and have those not on the bridge take their masks off, but be prepared to put them back on at a moment's notice."

"Aye, Captain."

The bridge activated the saltwater wash down. The wash down system had been designed to rid a ship of nuclear radiation expected to be present in a war-at-sea environment. Since the end of the Cold War, the threat of a nuclear explosion at sea during combat had ceased to exist, but the wash down system continued to be part of every ship design. Though designed for nuclear war, the Navy recognized the wash down system had other applications ranging from cosmetic—washing away dust, dirt, and grime prior to port visits—to practical, such as now. A nondescript civil servant at Naval Sea Systems Command made the right pencil mark on the right design process that kept this capability in the fleet. It was a capability no one questioned and few would have been able to articulate.

Internal pumps began to pull seawater into the ship and shove it through interconnecting pipes leading to a series of nozzles installed all along the superstructure of the USS *Hue City* and USS *Spruance*. A powerful umbrella of seawater enveloped the ships, washing down the exposed gray topside. The sea itself was cleaning the hulls and sweeping anything not tied down into the Mediterranean. The two ships looked as if they were miniature rain squalls sailing slowly across the surface of the sea.

"Captain, we are twenty minutes until launch. Missiles are prepped and ready to fire."

"Sequence?"

"*Spruance* has first two firing events; targets near Tobruk and Egyptian border. We have next four. Two at targets northeast of Benghazi, one near the coastal city of Darnah, and the last of this series at Al Bayda. Both Darnah and Al Bayda are located along the coast between Tobruk to the east and Benghazi to the west. Benghazi is a complicated shot, Captain. Danger of collateral damage, if we are reading these coordinates right."

"We have any intelligence to support these targets?"

"Sir, we only have Intelligence Specialist Smith, and he is in the Cryptologic Combat Support Center working with the Cryptology Technicians trying to resolve this one target."

Buc-Buc picked up the red telephone. His mission was to take out valid military targets. He had no intention of taking out innocent civilians if it could be avoided, but he knew those missiles had to be stopped or even more innocent civilians would die. He listened to the tonal resonance as the secure telephones between him and Sixth Fleet synchronized. He wanted assurance from his bosses about the Benghazi shot.

**PRESIDENT CRAWFORD THANKED BOB GILFORT, SECRE-**
tary of state; and Roger Maddock, secretary of defense; for joining him and Franco Donelli in the White House. On the speakerphone in front of the four men the chairman of the Joint Chiefs of Staff, General Jeff Eaglefield was speaking.

"And that's what we have so far, Mr. President, from Colonel Cooper. Alqahiray killed himself at the end of a successful raid. The Tangle Bandit raiding force is already airborne and heading southwest, away from the enemy command post. There are no signs of pursuit nor of enemy reaction."

Bob Gilfort leaned forward, resting his elbows on the table. "General, one problem we will have once the news leaks is the accusation that we assassinated Alqahiray. I doubt if any of the Arab countries will believe he killed himself."

There was a momentary pause before the speaker cackled to life. "Yes, sir, Mr. Secretary. I understand what you are saying, but in the fog and friction of war, that is what happened. We don't assassinate or murder. Besides, whatever they want to believe, they will, as long as they reach the same conclusion not to screw with us. Never again will America sit back and try to rationalize anti-American rhetoric. We will take it at its face value and respond accordingly."

The door opened and the director for Central Intelligence, Farbros Digby-Jones, nervously entered the room. The briefcase he carried was half opened, with ends of papers protruding in a disorganized way. The diminutive political appointee pushed his bifocals back on his nose as he mumbled apologies for being late.

President Crawford wished his wife was back at the White House. His trip to the Naval Medical Center at Bethesda yesterday encouraged him that she was improving. The world events in Korea and the Mediterranean had kept the press occupied and away from his wife's depression. The one mistake of his second administration was the appointment of this neophyte to the critical office of DCI, making him in charge of all the federal intelligence agencies in the land. Thankfully, the deputy at CIA was a professional who had moved up through the ranks and knew what the hell he was doing.

"Farbros, you're late again," Crawford said.

"Yes, sir, Mr. President," Farbros replied, his voice betraying his nervousness. "But—"

"No, buts, Farbros. What's the story?"

"He has agreed, sir, that we have accomplished our part of the bargain." Farbros grinned. "We have kept the line open on a secure satellite link between Langley and him throughout the night."

"Where is he?"

"Colonel Walid is at Benghazi, Mr. President. He controls the city and the forces within it, but until the news reaches the surrounding countryside, forces loyal to Alqahiray are still in control. We expect him to assume full command of Libya within the next two days, at which time he will recall Libyan forces from Tunisia and cut the military ties with the Algerian rebels."


"SPRUANCE'S MISSILES ARE AWAY, CAPTAIN. THREE minutes until we fire. Air-launched Tomahawks fired by B-52s and are inbound central Libya."

Buc-Buc eased back into his captain's chair. He pushed the buttons on the 12MC sound-powered phone system. "Bridge, engineering, this is the captain. Cut off the saltwater wash down system until we execute our firings. Then I want to bring it back on line, but wait for me to say so."

They both acknowledged the captain's order. On the bridge, the OOD nodded to the boatswain mate of the watch, who turned the switch off. The dozens of wipers on each of the bridge windows continued to work, quickly clearing the trailing water from the windows.

The bow of the *Hue City* cut into the invisible anthrax front as the saltwater wash ceased.

"One minute to launch," the TAO announced.

Anthrax spores settled onto the deck of the *Hue City*. Aboard the USS *Spruance*, twenty-one nautical miles to the south, the saltwater wash down had recommenced. As the anthrax reached the *Spruance*, the saltwater umbrella over the ship shoved, pushed, and moved the anthrax away from the aging destroyer. The *Spruance* moved through the anthrax cloud unknowingly and impervious to the threat.

"Let's put our masks back on until we restart the wash down," Buc-Buc said reluctantly.

The officer of the deck made the announcement on the 1MC.

The virulent spores began to cover the bow of the *Hue City*, moving quickly over the exposed signal bridge, across the topside amidships deck, down along the topside walkways that ran along the port and starboard sides of the ship. The cloud settled on the helicopter and the helicopter deck of the USS *Hue City* before moving on to cover the five-inch, sixty-two-gun mount near the stern of the cruiser.

Circle William kept the deadly spores from penetrating the skin of the ship, but outside the hatches of the *Hue City*, anthrax had coated the cruiser.

"Five, four, three, two, one," the TAO counted down. The roar of the missiles igniting filled the CIC spaces. Throughout the ship, the subsonic sound of the rocket engines could be heard.

The missiles rose out of the vertical launch cells located belowdecks on the bow of the ship. The doors covering the VLS blew aside to allow the Tomahawk land cruise missiles to exit. One after the other, the hot blast of the rocket engines sent the missiles skyward. Behind each missile, the hot air created by the blast sucked the air out of the cells. The cooler air rushing in to fill the vacuum brought anthrax spores from the deck and air with it, filling each cell with the deadly biological threat.

"Shut the missile tube doors, TAO."

One minute elapsed before the TAO turned to Buc-Buc and reported the VLS doors shut.

"Good. Bridge, this is the captain. Recommence saltwater wash down."

"The masks, Captain?"

"Give the wash down a few minutes, and then we'll take them off."

Belowdecks in the four empty missile cells, anthrax spores weaved and bopped in the disturbed air of the compartments.

**THE SECOND MISSILE FIRED BY THE USS *HUE CITY*** arched upward to an altitude of two thousand feet before descending to five hundred feet for its approach. Flying at subsonic speed, the missile straightened its course for the assigned target. In the nose cone, the computerized mapping system used internal radar returns to determine its location. It would be unable to determine exact location until it crossed the coastline in twenty minutes. At that time, the profile of the coast would be compared with a data bank developed from satellite imagery. The comparison technology would allow flight correction to where radar images matched the terrain-mapping data in its targeting profile.

The cruise missile crossed the coastline south of the port city, corrected the navigational error, descending to seventy-five feet for its approach, turning northeast toward the Libyan ballistic missile site. A ballistic missile powered up and waiting for the command to launch, a command that was being endlessly cycled by the information warriors of the United States Army Land Information Warfare Command at Fort Belvoir. A command that would never come because it was being held hostage within a computer system in the United States.

The Tomahawk matched the geographical profile of the city appearing in its scope and began to maneuver through and over the various man-made obstacles. On the ground, the roar of the rocket engines and appearance of the Tomahawk missile as it weaved through the streets between the huge buildings sent panic into the crowds. The civilians, running for cover, trampled those younger and older in their haste to seek shelter.

On the other side of Benghazi, the missile terrain mapping technology matched the land profile with its own programmed targeting data, climbed to two hundred feet, and dived on the missile complex in front of it. The American

Tomahawk hit within ten meters of the Libyan ballistic missile.

The resulting explosion sent pieces of both missiles high into the air to rain down over an area more than two square miles. The warhead of the Libyan ballistic missile tumbled intact upward, crossing the three hundred foot altitude, where its altimeter activated the biological device within it, telling the warhead that the Al-Fatah III missile was airborne, en route to its target. At four hundred feet, the warhead lost its momentum and began its fall to earth. The computer program of the altimeter recognized the descent and although it was designed to activate at five to six thousand feet while in descent, it activated and exploded at three hundred feet. The anthrax spores rocketed out in all directions. The rolling smoke from the missile explosions below it and the roaring fire of the burning fuel sent the spores upward into the clouds, where westerly winds blew the biological weapon west toward the port city of Benghazi.

At the naval base, Colonel Walid informed the person on the other end of the telephone that he could see the results of the American attack against Alqahiray's missile array northwest of the city. A huge column of black, roiling smoke marked where the Tomahawk missile had impacted. He laughed as he and the intelligence officer, Colonel Samir, watched the results of the attack. Switching from French to Arabic as he hung up the telephone, he congratulated both of them for their success in getting the Americans to do their dirty work. With Alqahiray out of the way, there was nothing to stop them from completing Allah's work in creating a true Islamic government dedicated to the people. A government stretching from the Atlantic to the Indian Ocean was gone for the time being, but eventually, they would make the original dream come true. Then they would return to their religious purpose of destroying America.

The French were already moving their ships into position off Algiers to replace the American Marines who were evacuating the city. Americans were funny people. You would think their naïveté would have worn off by now, but they still believed everything you told them. He knew Algeria was lost. The Spanish had already restored the former government of Morocco to power, having found some obscure Moroccan cousin to the king to assume power. Tunisia he might be able to salvage. It would depend on what the British and Italians did. The French had agreed to him having Tunisia and them resuming their influence over Algeria without his interference. The French were to be feared more than the Americans. This telephone call had confirmed that. His French contact left an implied threat about Walid trying to double-cross them, but Walid, confident in his ability to manipulate the French as he had the Americans, grinned. He had resumed power, and Alqahiray had been deposed.

Colonel Walid and Colonel Samir walked outside of the Navy Headquarters building and stood with Admiral Asif Abu Yimin.

"Admiral, I congratulate you, sir, on a job well done."

The admiral nodded. "And I, you, sir." He reached over to the tray on the small table on the veranda and poured himself another small glass of port. "Would the colonels enjoy a small drink in celebration?"

Walid turned his nose up at the alcohol. "Not for me, Admiral. I just want to stand here and watch the smoke of Alqahiray's last hurrah." He looked at the two men as Colonel Samir took an offered glass from the admiral. "My fellow warriors, we have truly won. Nothing can stop us now. We have the future to build a true, independent Islamic nation dedicated to our people, our heritage, and our faith."

He lifted a glass of water from the tray and, as the cloud of anthrax spores settled over them, the three men toasted each other. The first breaths inhaled the spores as they looked out over the port city. Throughout Benghazi, the inhabitants breathed the anthrax spores along with their new leaders. Everywhere along the streets and sidewalks, the spores landed, only to be picked up by shoes, breathed by the rats and vermin living beneath the streets, and landing in and on the cars hurrying out of the city. The anthrax spores were on the move, heading out of Benghazi to other parts of Libya and the world, for the spores landed on merchant ships, which were loading and off-loading merchandise in the port. Within the next few days, widespread flulike symptoms would send many in Benghazi scurrying to the hospitals and clinics for medicine. Merchant vessels would exit the port for destina-

tions ranging from Seville, Spain; to Japan; to Australia; and
to the United States.

The coughs would turn from dry to wet to bloody within
thirty-six hours of the onset of the flulike symptoms. A week
after Walid, Samir, and Abu Yimin drank their toast, 98 percent of Benghazi would be dead. Those living would be too
weak to take care of themselves and there would be no one
willing to enter the death city to help. But these three would
be in no condition to know all of that.

# FOURTEEN

⚓

**THESE THREE WEEKS HAD BEEN A WHIRLWIND SINCE THE** rescue of the hostages and the defeat of the North Koreans. So much had happened. Duncan touched the folded letter in his back pocket. The letter from his wife arrived ten days ago and went through the ultraviolet sanitation before being delivered to him. It was beginning to tear along the seams from being folded roughly and jammed into his back pocket. He refused to be separated from it for fear he'd lose it or some well-meaning mess specialist assigned to his stateroom would throw it away as trash. He had given the seven-page letter a lot of thought—nearly five full days—before arranging a ship-to-shore call to Reston, Virginia, where he had wakened her at two in the morning. He had been as nervous as a young boy waiting for the prom queen to answer his request for a date. They had talked for over an hour. He hoped he made the right decision in agreeing to try to patch things up. Marriages—especially military marriages—were never easy. They required a lot of work, and maybe he had been slack on his end, failing to recognize her goals, needs, and the hardship his career fostered on her. It would be an uphill battle to save their marriage, but she believed him leaving the Navy would remove a lot of the stress. A lot of harsh words and actions had burned a multitude of bridges between them since June, but he would try, and if they both really worked at it, then it might just survive what happened last week. He should call her with the news before some well-meaning friend would. *Lord, protect me from the do-gooders in the world.*

Duncan pulled the saucer forward across the linen table-cloth, careful not to spill the coffee the mess specialist had just topped off. He folded the *Stars and Stripes* newspaper, laid it on the left side of his coffee, and from the right side lifted the *International Herald Tribune.* The papers were downloaded daily from the satellite and printed on newspaper print to give the semblance of newsstand quality. The only difference was that your fingers did not turn black from reading downloaded versions.

This wardroom for flag officers was great for solitude and opportunity to arrange a person's plans for the day. He was glad he had the use of it. He glanced at his watch—zero seven-thirty hours. This was his second day of taking advantage of this little-used wardroom. He reached up and stroked his collar devices, running his fingers beneath to make sure the small clips were holding the rank insignia securely. It had been over seven years since he had last bought new rank devices for his collar or hat. He just kept recycling the metal things as his uniforms wore out.

Satisfied they weren't going to fall off, he opened the second newspaper. The USS *Hue City* was still making headlines as she journeyed across the Atlantic en route to Norfolk, Virginia. The USS *Spruance* accompanied the ship like a military escort alongside the coffin of a heroic war veteran. Sixteen sailors and officers had died on the *Hue City* from inhalation anthrax. Some, including Captain Horatio Jurgen McTeak, were laid up for over a week before finally recovering sufficiently to leave their cabins. Starting the antibiotics when they did saved most of them. It would be up to CDC and Bethesda National Naval Medical Center to figure out why those sixteen died.

Most, like Buc-Buc, suffered flulike symptoms that signaled inhalation anthrax. A few of the survivors even spewed blood from both ends. The one commonality between the inhalation anthrax survivors was that they had all had anthrax inoculations years ago. Those who had managed to keep their boosters up to date had been exposed, according to the blood test, but never came down with the deadly disease.

The anthrax had run its course on the *Hue City*. Those recovering refused to be evacuated, opting to remain on board with their fellow shipmates. Only a sailor could understand the reason behind that choice.

Duncan grinned at the memory of the photograph of Buc-Buc holding the Army doctor by the rubber protective shirt and shoving him out of his stateroom when the doctor tried to have him forcibly evacuated.

The Army chemical-biological warfare units flown out from Fort Bragg were still on board the cruiser with a smaller unit on the USS *Spruance*. Two days after the *Hue City* was exposed, the first sailor died. The medical team sent from USS *John Stennis* to assist during the epidemic suffered the same exposure. For five days, while the ship wallowed along, barely making way through the sea, these forty some odd officers and senior enlisted, who had been inoculated against anthrax and had also received their booster shots as required, had manned the *Hue City*. The Army team brought a computer chip called a Zebra chip, which they installed in the medical laboratory. Blood tests were analyzed using the chip, revealing immediately whether a subject had been exposed to anthrax. Throughout the United States Sixth Fleet, the chip was being installed hastily in every medical facility. Every crew member was being tested. A Navy message a few days ago notified the military forces deployed in South Korea to receive the same chip. Since the attack by Libya, America now worried that other rogue nations, such as North Korea, might follow the senseless act with their own. He doubted North Korea would do such a thing. Once again, they were safely corralled back across the border. For how long, he had no idea.

Duncan chuckled at the telephone interview with Master Chief Higgins of the *Hue City*. The newspapers loved him. They loved the senior chief, too, but the crusty master chief had a gift for saying the right things in the wrong way to shock the nation. Master Chief Higgins and Senior Chief Derby were heroes newspapers loved and the public admired. Together, the two men had fifty-eight years of combined Navy service. The two had taken charge of the bridge when the majority of the officers and chiefs lay helpless in their beds. The chief engineer, who was a thirty-year mustang, had had the anthrax vaccinations also. CHENG lived in the engine rooms during the same five days the two senior enlisted men manned the bridge. The master chief and senior chief took turns napping in the captain's chair. They bounced between the helm, the navigation plotting table, and the bridge wings as they and several junior sailors steered the ship. CHENG gave most of the orders from belowdecks, but it was these two sailors, enlisted surface warfare specialists with their silver pins, who drove the ship.

They only left the bridge to make head calls or dash to the mess decks to grab soup and sandwiches before dashing back up three decks to the bridge. Duncan knew the two were heroes. These two and the CHENG kept the USS *Hue City* moving until other members of the crew began to recover and help arrived. Duncan noticed a small tickler on the right side of the paper and quickly turned to page four. He laughed at an AP announcement that *Playgirl* intended to "profile the two lean, trim fighting machines who had saved the ghost ship USS *Hue City*. *Playboy* had obtained official photographs of the chief engineer from Navy Public Affairs, but had been curiously silent after receiving them." Two Navy official photographs of the two men stared back from the borders of the article. *That should make their wives happy,* thought Duncan. He touched the letter in his back pocket.

Reading on, the *Herald Tribune* quoted a chief of naval operations spokesman as saying forty-six crewmen had been unaffected by the anthrax. Duncan let a small grunt escape. No, that was inaccurate. Everyone on the ship had been affected some way or other by the anthrax. Those with the stronger immune system boosted by vaccinations over a decade old had just been affected less. Buc-Buc had the vaccination series, but it still took him nearly a week before he was well enough to make the twenty-foot trip from his at-sea cabin to the bridge.

By the fourth day of the epidemic, when members of the medical team began to show signs of anthrax exposure, Admiral Devlin had made the grim decision to refuse additional personnel access to the plague ship. The Quebec flag in its grim solid yellow brightness fluttered from the signal bridge of the USS *Hue City*, warning everyone of the presence of a great plague.

General Lewis knew exactly where to go for the experts to

save the *Hue City*. It took one telephone call for Fort Bragg to launch two CBW teams. Within three days, Army CBW teams flew into Sigonella. Duncan had heard negative comments on the general's leadership style, but this one episode convinced him the Army flag officer was a warfighting professional. He hoped he was right, because the general flew off the aircraft carrier yesterday, heading to new duties on the Joint Chiefs of Staff as the new J3 on the joint staff.

The CBW teams had done an outstanding job. Duncan had expected the teams to land on the aircraft carrier before flying to the two warships, but somewhere in the air between Sigonella and the *John Stennis*, the Army colonel in charge ordered the helicopters diverted in flight directly to the affected ships. General Lewis had been furious at first but had just as quickly realized the importance of time in combating the anthrax. There were the owllike noises of "Hooah" emanating from the three-star general's lips that drew perplexed expressions from the Navy personnel standing near the Army Ranger.

Thirty-six hours after the CBW teams landed on the *Hue City* and *Spruance*, the major portions of the ships were clean and pronounced sanitized. *Spruance* had been easy, but the *Hue City* was contaminated internally. The Army colonel had had the helicopter deck and stern deck cleaned first. From there, he established his command post within a known safe place for his men and women to take rest breaks out of their bulky, hot CBW uniforms. It was important in this hot climate and burning sun to watch for dehydration, and wearing those suits continuously could quickly cause his team to falter.

Daily, each member of the Army team had blood samples taken and analyzed by the Zebra chip. The colonel was taking no chances.

Reconstruction of the events concluded that when the saltwater wash down was stopped while *Hue City* fired Tomahawk missiles, it had allowed airborne anthrax spores to gain access to the interior of the ship. The *Spruance* avoided internal contamination. The Sixth Fleet meteorologist offered that the *Hue City* entered the anthrax area much like sailing into an invisible weather front. While it sailed through and fired its Tomahawks, anthrax rained on the ship. The USS *Spruance*, ten miles farther back and to the north of *Hue City*, fired first and had restarted its saltwater wash down before entering the biological front.

The umbrella of saltwater spray kept the deadly spores away from the inside of the warship and washed most of them away from the outside. The USS *Spruance*, though quarantined like the *Hue City*, suffered no casualties or sickness, but that did little to alleviate the days of fear that swept the destroyer. Every little cold symptom produced an avalanche of fear.

Duncan sipped his coffee. A mess specialist approached and laid a small china plate with a couple of small pastries on it.

"Thanks," Duncan said without looking up from the paper.

A lot of the American intelligentsia were trying to whip up a groundswell of public opinion to keep the ships from returning immediately to the continental United States. "Oh, no, we support our military, we love our military, and we only want the best for these men and women in the service, but let's wait a while to make sure they don't bring anthrax into the United States."

The bioterrorist attacks of 2001 were still fresh in the minds of everyone who suffered through it. But the majority of Americans wanted their heroes back, and to hell with the small chance of anthrax being spread from the ship. They had fought this bioterrorist threat once, and they would fight it again if they had to.

Europe was experiencing the same thing America did in 2001, with anthrax cases cropping up across the continent. Lab results had shown that the anthrax in those cases was undistinguishable from the anthrax found on *Hue City* and *Spruance*.

He bent the paper in half and laid it on the table and read a column with excerpts from the major newspapers in America as he ate. The *Virginia Pilot*, the *Washington Times*, the *Frederick News Post*, the *Newnan Times Herald*, the *Washington Post*, the *New York Times*, and the *Atlanta Journal* had thrown their weight behind the two ships returning to the States. Most of the other major papers had, also. Others wanted the cruiser and aging destroyer quarantined for several months until all doubt of anthrax contamination was removed. And still others suggested taking the crew off and sinking the ships in the middle of the Atlantic.

Scientists and medical specialists across the States, Europe, and within the military agreed there was no danger from the anthrax-infected ships. President Crawford in his weekly radio address had advised the nation that he had personally decided the ships would return to Norfolk, Virginia.

Flipping to the international section, Duncan saw where the Italians who fled Livorno were being allowed to return to their homes after the Italian government assured the city that the threat of anthrax in the harbor had been cleared. The merchant vessel, which had crashed into the pier upon arrival, was still quarantined with armed guards keeping the curious—few though they were—hundreds of yards from the ship. Along the coasts of the United States, several hundred merchant vessels floated at anchor after being denied entry into American ports because they had sailed through the Mediterranean. Duncan supposed that one could argue against American paranoia, calling it an overreaction. But since the home-grown right-wing religious terrorist who had initiated the anthrax bioterrorist attack in 2001 had been caught, there had not been one incident of another biological attack in the States. And that was the way the government and the people wanted to keep it.

The door opened to the flag wardroom, and Dick Holman entered. Duncan lifted his hand and waved. The oldies, but goodies radio station on the carrier played softly in the background; the Beatles were the feature of the day. Dick weaved his way past the other two tables to where Duncan sat.

"Looks as if we have the entire mess to ourselves, Duncan. Mind if I join you?"

"Not at all, Admiral," Duncan said. "Those silver stars look impressive on those khakis."

Holman reached up and touched the devices. "Thanks. It will take some getting used to, you know. Six months ago, I was on my way out because of my weigh-in, and now I have a single star on each collar, and I'm leading the *Stennis* battle group as we prepare to reopen the Suez Canal."

"The other carriers should be here soon."

Holman nodded. "Should be arriving in the Mediterranean sometime tomorrow morning. At least, they won't have to tow them through the Strait of Gibraltar like we did the *Stennis*."

Duncan motioned to the already moving mess specialist, who saw the new one-star admiral enter. Seconds later, another cup of coffee graced the table.

"How is our new vice admiral taking the fact that Sixth Fleet will grow from the small naval presence it had in July to a three-carrier Marine Task Force powerhouse by tomorrow? Not to mention the Royal Navy Amphibious Task Force that is scheduled to arrive by the end of the week."

"Devlin will do what he is ordered to, of course, but"—Holman smiled and raised a finger—"he'll bitch and moan about it all the way. Let me read the *Stars and Stripes* if you're done with it, Duncan?" Dick Holman asked, reaching across the table for the military newspaper.

Duncan handed the paper to Dick Holman, glancing over the top of it at the new stars. One-star admiral: something he never was and now never would be. There had been a lot of surprises two days ago when General Lewis and Admiral Devlin had announced the results of the promotion board that had been hastily convened in Washington last month.

"How about that?" Dick Holman asked, slapping the newspaper. "The President gave Warren Spangle's wife his Medal of Honor yesterday. If they don't name a ship after that hero, then the Navy has its head up its ass."

Duncan looked up. "Congratulations on your Silver Star, Admiral. What you did, taking this carrier battle group through a minefield, is something like Spangle's actions that will live on in Naval history."

Dick pointed at Duncan's left chest. "And the same congratulations on your Silver Star, sir," he said respectfully. "I think our Navy will have more heroes and history this year than anytime since World War II. Of course, those Purple Hearts you and your fellow SEALs received made me realize how much I prefer my line of duty to yours." Rear Admiral Lower Half Dick Holman slid his chair around sideways to the table and crossed his legs. The new one-star flag officer handed a small slip of paper with his breakfast order on it to the MS and crossed his legs.

"Did you notice the two Marines behind Spangle's wife?" Dick asked.

"I saw them. Don't know what they did, but according to the article, they both received Medals of Honor, also."

"The young man is twenty-six years old and was in charge of a Marine force that fought its way out of the southern Algerian desert with a bunch of American oil riggers. The other Marine is Gunny Sergeant Stapler, who refused to be wheeled into the White House for the ceremonies. He was shot up pretty badly and nearly died. Typical Marine, refuses to acknowledge his own mortality. Of course, I wouldn't want them any other way. According to the article, after the ceremony, he collapsed back onto his bed at Bethesda Medical Center and slept for sixteen hours."

"I remember reading about them. Quite a story when you stop and think about it. A small group of Marines, stranded in the desert, forced to take off across the sands with unarmed civilians, fighting off enemy forces and, as they are about to be overrun, the cavalry charge over the hill to save them. Somebody ought to make a movie out of that."

"This has been and is a challenging time to America's leadership in the world, Duncan. But, we will weather these trying times like we did in our first war of the twenty-first century. The men and women in the armed forces sacrifice so much for their country. A sacrifice our fellow citizens who have never experienced military life find hard to appreciate sometimes; though, I think, most recognize it. That's what tells me America's day in the sun is far from over."

Duncan lifted his cup, Dick did the same, and the two clicked the edges of the porcelain china together. "I'll drink to that."

The two men returned to their newspapers. The French were not reacting well to the political victory of the British last week. When America withdrew its NATO nomination of Admiral Walter Hastings as the new Allied Forces Southern Command and threw its weight and influence behind a Royal Navy nominee, the French had foamed at the diplomatic mouth. They even made veiled threats about the future of the European Union. The other members of NATO, seeing a quick exit to the impasse between the French and American nominees, confirmed the British admiral within twenty-four hours. The French blustered they would refuse to turn over command to the British admiral when he arrived. Despite the bluster, the actual change of command went off with only a mild diplomatic rebuff when the acting AFSouth, French General Jacques LeBlanc, refused to shake the British admiral's hand. At the end of the ceremony, the British admiral had surprised the French general by awarding him an Order of the Garter signed by King Charles. LeBlanc could hardly refuse, and the photograph of the two shaking hands with Admiral Walter Hastings, the new commander of the United States Naval Forces Europe, standing between them made world news—front page in most European newspapers.

An audible sigh escaped Duncan, drawing Admiral Holman's eyes briefly before he returned to the *Stars and Stripes*.

Duncan flipped the page. Page two had photographs of the dead in the streets of Benghazi. Italian troops patrolled the city in masks to filter out the smell. The anthrax threat was still real, according to the article, but only inside buildings yet to be cleaned. He had read the "Secret—No Foreign Dissemination Allowed" message yesterday about what happened. One of the *Hue City* Tomahawks had destroyed a Libyan Al-Fatah III missile as it was preparing to launch. The anthrax warhead destroyed in the attack had dispersed its deadly cargo into the air and rapidly covered Benghazi. Over one million Libyans had died of inhalation anthrax in and around Benghazi, nearly one-forth of the population. Without the intervention of the Italians in eastern Libya, more would have died in civil chaos. Italian forces had also occupied Tobruk and the border area with Egypt. The Islamic Republic of Barbary and North Africa had faded from its short political life. Only Egypt emerged unscathed in this attempt to unite the entire North African coast from the Atlantic to the Indian Ocean. Intelligence was still analyzing the enormous volumes of papers and computer data obtained from Libya. Al-Qaida had never died. Like a malevolent virus, it had just evolved, and the work was pointing more and more to the radical Islamic government of Egypt.

The same message also reported that the Libyan leadership responsible for the crisis in North Africa died in Benghazi, but not before ordering their troops to leave Tunisia. Tunisia routed the remaining Algerian forces a week ago, taking about one hundred miles of Algerian territory in the process. The most westernized nation on the North African littoral was already beginning to rebuild its country with the help of Britain and Italy.

The French had gotten some of what they wanted. They had replaced the American Marines in Algiers and were already negotiating with President Hawali Alneuf, who had reentered the country at Oran, once Spanish forces had joined up with the remaining loyal Algerian forces. The French could do little, other than appear magnanimous and return control of the capital back to the democratically elected President of free Algeria. The formal ceremony was scheduled to occur next week. If there was one thing the French knew, it was how to have a ceremony.

Great Britain was the surprise winner. A toothless lion the world called this island nation after World War II when, economically broke, it had little recourse but to withdraw as it rebuilt a shattered infrastructure. What many failed to recognize was that Britain capitalized on its skill in diplomacy, a skill unsurpassed by the rest of the world as it managed to maintain a role as a world leader through the remainder of the twentieth century. Now that very art of diplomacy had restored it as a major naval power and the leader of a free Europe. The special relationship between the United States and Britain had grown over the years. It was a strong bond, forged in mutual interests and history.

"Says here that President Crawford fired his National Security Advisor Franco Donelli," Dick Holman offered.

"Yeah, I read that. I thought he was the real power behind the throne."

"I think he pissed off the old man. I heard he was behind Admiral Cameron being relieved, court martialed, and forced to retire, and when the president figured out what happened, all fingers pointed to Mr. Donelli."

Duncan lifted his cup, motioned toward Dick with it before taking a sip, and replied, "Then being fired is the least that should have happened to him. What is Admiral Cameron doing now?"

Holman shrugged his shoulders. "Last I heard, he was taking some time off, but CNO has asked him to serve as an unofficial member of the Chief of Naval Operations Executive Advisory Board."

Duncan nodded in reply and then asked, "How is your former command master chief taking his promotion?"

Holman chuckled. "Not too well, I heard. He had not even sent in a package to the special promotion board, and they selected him for warrant officer three. I wasn't there when the new four-striper Tucson Conroy made the announcement, but I can imagine the cursing and swearing that erupted."

The MS returned with Admiral Holman's chipped beef on toast—fondly known as SOS by the Navy—and placed it in front of him. He lifted the silver-plated coffeepot to refill the cups. Duncan put his hand over his and shook his head.

"You going to miss being CO of the *Stennis*?"

"You going to miss being a captain in the SEALs?" Holman retorted, smiling, his eyes raising with the question.

Duncan laughed. "No, I think I can handle the situation."

"You're flying off tomorrow, right?"

"Yeah, Beau, who is still staring in the mirror at the silver commander's leaves, and HJ, who was released from medical yesterday, will also be going with me.

"What happened to her?"

"Those nanorobots that Bethesda put in her don't want to die. They keep reconstituting themselves. Looks as if our lone woman SEAL will have these little medical machines circulating through her body while those mad scientists from Bethesda keep watch to see what happens. She will be released from the SEALs upon our return. When we talked yesterday, she said the medical team expects the nanorobots to continue to decrease in number until they eventually fade away. But what they are not sure about is that the programming of those 'little shits' include a subroutine to build new 'little shits' if she is injured or gets sick."

"Little shits. Got a nice ring to it, Duncan."

"We'll fly off this afternoon to Gibraltar, where an aircraft is waiting to fly the three of us back to Washington."

The door opened to the flag mess. Newly promoted Commander Beau Pettigrew of the Pettigrews of Newnan, Georgia, stuck his head inside. Seeing Duncan, he smiled, motioned behind him, and entered. HJ McDaniels followed, her new lieutenant commander leaves shining on the collars of her khaki uniform.

"Admiral," Beau said as he approached.

Both Duncan and Holman answered, "Yes."

"Sorry, Admiral Holman, I meant Admiral James."

Duncan noticed the reflection of the two stars on his collar in the shiny water glass in front of him. They had skipped the one-star rank at the ceremony two days ago because of the orders received from the Bureau of Naval Personnel.

"Beau, how is my EA doing?" Duncan joked, remembering how speechless his sidekick had been when he told the blond-haired Romeo that his new orders were to be the executive aide to the new commander, Naval Special Warfare Command.

Beau blushed. "Sir, we need to get to the flight deck as soon as possible. The flight to Gibraltar has been moved up. We're leaving this morning."

"HJ, how are you doing?"

She straightened her arms by her sides, rolled her eyes back in her head, and bounced several times from one stiff leg to the other before stopping the theatrics to look at Duncan. "Okay, Admiral, just every now and then these little shits want to trade sides within my body," she said, grinning. Secretly, she was glad she was leaving the SEALs. She had proven her point about women in Naval special warfare, but the incident with the captured rebels haunted her. Chief Wilcox had never said anything about stopping her from cutting the prisoner's throat, and she had never thanked him for doing it. For the two of them, the incident never occurred.

The three laughed. Duncan noticed that faraway look he had seen several times since Algeria cross HJ's face for several seconds before she relaxed and joined the laughter. He wondered what went through her thoughts at those times.

"The truth is, Dick, *little shits* wasn't my term."

Duncan slid his chair back. He reached forward and shook hands with Dick Holman, who stood in deference to the senior officer. "Good luck, Dick. When we get back to the States, Beau and I will be visiting the Western Pacific Theater, and I will try to spin through the *Stennis*."

"But, boss," Beau said.

"I'll look forward to seeing you, Duncan. Good luck in your new job in Washington. You will need it with all the politics there. At least our success here and in Korea stopped Congress from considering reactivating the draft."

Duncan agreed. "Sometimes I think it wouldn't be a bad idea to have a draft, but I have to admit that we have a strong volunteer force, and if we can avoid returning to the draft, then we should."

"But—" Beau said.

"We'll discuss that over a beer or two once I get back to Norfolk," Dick Holman said.

"Boss—"

"No but bosses, Beau. You can go to London after the war."

A twinkle in his eye, Dick Holman stared at Beau. "London? I'm heading east, and you want to take time off to go to London?"

"Yes, sir," HJ added. "He fancies a small Irish pub there called the O'Conor Don and has this fantasy about adding his photograph to the hall of heroes leading up to the restaurant."

Duncan laughed. "It's more than that. He fancies leaning on the bar, slurping Guinness, and flirting with the waitresses that work there."

"In that case, Admiral, I will relieve him of that duty and go myself," HJ offered, bowing at the waist. "There is a redhead I fantasize about."

"Methinks Bethesda doth want you first," Duncan said, laughing. "See you around the waterfront, Dick. Good luck, and hope the war is over soon."

"And, you, Duncan?"

"Well, Dick, I think my wife and I are going back up to Frederick, Maryland. Spend some time antiquing at the Antique Station and just sitting in the shade outside of the Church Street Café, watching the tourists."

The two admirals shook hands. "Godspeed, my friend, and good luck."

"You, too, Dick."

Duncan stepped toward the door, stopped suddenly. Beau bumped into him. "Beau?"

"Yes, sir?"

"You're my EA, right?"

Beau sighed. "Yes, sir, I am."

Duncan handed him his briefcase. "According to the manual, you carry the briefcase." He reached up and touched the stars on his khaki collars. "I never saw Admiral Hodges carry his own briefcase."

"Well, I wouldn't want the admiral to strain his arms," Beau said, taking the briefcase and trying to balance it with his seabag.

"Beau, if you can't be kind, then at least have the decency to be as vague as hell."

Duncan winked at HJ. "I think I am going to really enjoy being an admiral."